The Star Seeker

Book 1 of ***The Third Path*** *series*

By Michael Colvin

This is a work of fiction. Similarities to real people, places, or events are entirely coincidental.

THE STAR SEEKER

First edition. May 14, 2026.

ISBN: 979-8995778714

Written by Michael Colvin.

Table of Contents

For Susan,

who let me disappear into the first century

and was always there when I came back.

"The true sorcery is not in the fire or the star. It is in the moment we act beyond what we believed ourselves capable of. The danger is in discovering we were right to doubt."

—From the private writings of Caspar of Ecbatana

PART ONE: THREE SEEKERS

"We followed a star because we had forgotten how to follow anything else.
We were three men who had mastered every text yet could not read the simplest lesson: what we sought was not ours to possess."
—From the private writings of Caspar of Ecbatana

CHAPTER 1

The Restless Stars

"The stars keep their counsel, but men who study them grow restless for answers."

—Attributed to Ptolemy Soter, founder of the Library of Alexandria

6 BCE—Alexandria, Egypt

The Library of Alexandria held more scrolls than any three men could read in a lifetime, but Melchior intended to try.

He stood in the great reading room where morning light slanted through high windows and illuminated dust motes drifting like tiny stars. Around him, scholars bent over tables, their styluses scratching against wax tablets, their lips moving in silence as they copied texts too precious to leave the building. The smell of papyrus and ink filled the air, mingled with the mustier scent of centuries preserved within these walls while empires rose and fell beyond them.

"You're here early again." Balthasar's voice carried a note of amusement. He crossed the marble floor to stand beside Melchior, his Persian robes marking him as foreign among the Greek and Egyptian scholars. "Did you sleep at all?"

"Sleep wastes time." Melchior did not look up from the scroll spread before him, a treatise on the movements of celestial bodies copied from Babylonian originals predating Alexander's conquest. "There's too much to learn."

"There's always too much to learn. That is rather the point, isn't it?"

Melchior raised his eyes. Balthasar stood with his hands folded, patient as always, his dark face holding the gentle certainty Melchior sometimes envied and often found infuriating. Of the three who had traveled from Persia to study with the great Philo, Balthasar seemed least troubled by questions without answers.

"The point," Melchior said, "is to learn enough to understand the pattern. Once you see how everything connects."

"Then what? You'll have captured the mind of God in a scroll?"

"Don't mock me."

"I'm not mocking." Balthasar's voice softened. "I'm worried. You've barely eaten in three days. Caspar says you've been muttering equations in your sleep."

"Caspar talks too much."

"Caspar loves you. As do I. That is why we notice when you're consuming yourself."

Melchior rolled the scroll closed with more force than necessary. "Where is he, anyway? Philo's lecture begins within the hour."

"On the roof. Where else?"

They climbed the narrow stairs winding up through the library's eastern tower. At the top level, they emerged onto a flat expanse of stone. There Caspar sat cross-legged, his face tilted toward the fading stars. Dawn had just begun to wash the sky in shades of rose and gold, but a few bright points still clung to the heavens, stubborn against the coming day.

Melchior shook his head in dismay. "You'll damage your eyes staring at the sky like that."

Caspar smiled without turning. "The sky damages nothing. It only reveals." He was the youngest of them by two years, his beard still patchy, and his enthusiasm for celestial observation undimmed by three years of study. "Did you know there's a conjunction forming? Jupiter and Saturn, drawing closer each night. By winter, they'll appear as one."

"What does it signify?" Balthasar settled onto the stone beside him.

"I don't know yet. But Philo says the heavens speak to those who learn their language. I intend to become fluent."

Melchior remained standing, his arms crossed. "Philo says many things. Not all of them lead anywhere useful."

"Useful." Caspar turned to look at him, sadness in his expression. "Is that all knowledge is to you? A tool?"

"What else would it be?"

"A gift. A mystery. A conversation with the cosmos itself." Caspar gestured at the lightening sky. "When I watch the stars, I don't feel like I'm capturing them. I feel like They are speaking to me. Telling me things I don't have words for yet."

"Poetry," Melchior said. "I prefer precision."

"And I prefer breakfast," Balthasar interrupted as he rose and brushed dust from his robes. "Philo's lectures are difficult enough to follow on a full stomach. On an empty one, They are impossible."

❧✦❧

The three young Persians had arrived in Alexandria eighteen months ago. The Zoroastrian temple in Persepolis sent them to study with the famous Jewish philosopher, Philo of Alexandria. They had heard he understood things their own magi only glimpsed but could not articulate. He spoke of the relationship between the divine fire and the physical world, the nature of wisdom transcending any single tradition.

They had expected an old man, withered and remote. Instead, they found a vigorous middle-aged philosopher. His Greek was as elegant as any Athenian's, his mind capable of holding contradictions that would have shattered lesser thinkers. Philo moved between Jewish scripture and Greek philosophy as easily as a merchant switched between languages at a port bazaar.

And he taught them about the Logos.

"Imagine this," Philo said, pacing his classroom, "the divine can't interact with the material world. Pure spirit and crude matter cannot mix any more than oil and water can become one substance."

He paused and let the words settle. Sunlight streamed through the window behind him and cast his shadow long across the floor.

"Yet the world exists. We exist. Clearly, a bridge spans the gap between the eternal and the temporal. The Greeks call this the Logos, the Word, the Reason, the ordering principle shaping chaos into cosmos."

Melchior leaned forward. This was what he wanted to know. "Then the Logos is a force we can study? Measure? Perhaps even harness?"

Philo's eyes met his, and concern flickered there, or perhaps warning. "The Logos is not a tool, young seeker. It is the very structure of reality. You do not harness the ocean by cupping water in your hands."

"But if one understood the structure."

"Understanding and controlling are not the same." Philo's voice carried gentle correction. "True wisdom lies not in holding much, but in knowing what cannot be grasped. The wise stand before mystery with open hands rather than clenched fists."

Balthasar nodded. This made sense to him: the idea of surrender before a greater order, of finding one's place within a cosmic architecture rather than trying to master it.

Caspar's mind had drifted to the stars, to the Logos as ordering principle. Was that what he saw when he traced the movements of planets against the fixed lights? A language spoken in curves and cycles?

Melchior sat back, unconvinced. Philo was brilliant, but he was also old. Perhaps his caution came from failing powers, from a mind that had once reached for great things and now counseled restraint because it could no longer reach at all.

Melchior was twenty-three. He had no intention of accepting limits.

☙✦❧

After the lecture, the three friends walked along the harbor and watched ships arrive from every corner of the Mediterranean. Alexandria was the crossroads of the world: Egyptian grain bound for Rome, silk from the distant East, and spices passing through dozens of hands before reaching these docks. Ideas flowed as freely as goods, carried by scholars and merchants and wanderers who brought fragments of truth from every land.

"We should return home soon," Balthasar said. "The temple has been patient, but they'll expect us to share what We have learned."

"What have we learned?" Melchior kicked a stone and sent it skittering across the worn planks of the dock. "Philo speaks beautifully, but he offers no path forward. 'Stand before mystery with open hands.' What kind of teaching is that?"

"Perhaps the only honest kind," Caspar said.

"Honest? It is defeat dressed in philosophy. He is telling us to stop asking questions."

"No." Caspar stopped walking and turned to face his friend. "He is telling us to ask questions without demanding answers. To seek without grasping. There's a difference."

"A difference that leaves us exactly where we started."

"Does it?" Balthasar gestured at the harbor, the ships, the vast library rising behind them. "We came here knowing almost nothing. Now we understand the divine works through an ordering principle bridging heaven and earth. We understand wisdom lies in recognition rather than accumulation. We understand..."

"We understand words." Melchior's frustration broke through. "Beautiful, elegant, useless words. I didn't travel a thousand miles to learn vocabulary. I came to find power."

The word hung in the air between them.

"Power," Caspar repeated. "Is that really what you seek?"

"The power to understand. To see the pattern Philo describes and trace it to its source. To touch the Logos itself, if such a thing is possible." Melchior's voice dropped. "My father died believing the world was chaos, suffering had no meaning, and good men perished while evil ones prospered because nothing ordered the cosmos but blind chance. I refuse to accept that. There must be a structure. A reason. And if there is, it can be known."

Balthasar placed a hand on his shoulder. "Your father's death was a tragedy. But seeking power to escape grief..."

"I'm not escaping anything." Melchior shrugged off the touch. "I'm trying to ensure others don't suffer as he did. If I can understand the pattern, perhaps I can work within it. Predict. Prevent. Protect."

"Noble aims," Caspar said. "Dangerous methods."

"Every method is dangerous to those afraid to use it."

❧✦❧

That night, Caspar climbed again to the library roof. The conjunction he had tracked had drawn closer. Jupiter and Saturn now separated by less than a hand's width against the stars. In a few months, they would merge into a single brilliant point, a light outshining everything except the moon.

Such conjunctions occurred rarely. The last had been centuries ago, in the time of the Babylonian astronomers whose records Caspar had spent months studying. They had believed such events portended great changes: the births of kings, the falls of empires, the moments when heaven reached down to touch earth.

Caspar was not certain he believed in omens. But he believed in patterns, in the language the stars spoke to those patient enough to learn it. And this conjunction felt significant in ways he could not articulate.

He thought about Melchior's words at the harbor. Power. Understanding. The desire to trace the Logos to its source.

Caspar wanted a different thing. He had lost people too. He lost his mother to fever when he was twelve, and his younger brother to a wasting sickness two years later. The grief had nearly destroyed him. For months he raged against the sky and demanded answers from stars offering only silence.

Then, gradually, the silence had become a presence. He sensed that even in suffering, he was not alone. The forces moving the planets also shaped human lives, carrying sorrow and joy alike toward unseeable purposes he had come to trust.

He did not want power over the pattern. He wanted to understand his place within it, to see, if only for a moment, how his small grief connected to the vast dance of creation.

Was that too much to ask? Or too little?

The stars offered no answer. But they continued their ancient movements, patient as always, waiting for those with eyes to see.

❧✦❧

Below, in the room they shared at a modest inn near the library, Balthasar knelt in evening prayer. The Zoroastrian forms came easily. He had performed them since childhood, the words as natural as breathing.

But tonight, his mind wandered.

He thought about order. About the Ahura Mazda of his fathers, the lord of wisdom who had created the world and set it spinning in perfect balance. About the Logos Philo described, the divine reason holding chaos at bay. About the kings who ruled by sacred right, each one a reflection of cosmic order in human form.

Balthasar loved order. He loved the way things fit together: the hierarchy of priests and princes, the rhythm of seasons, the reliable circuits of sun and moon. In order he saw proof the universe was a divinely constructed whole rather than the random nightmare Melchior's father had believed.

What troubled him was where he fit in that whole.

He was the son of a minor noble, sent to Alexandria because his family hoped learning might elevate their status. He had found in Philo's teachings a vision of cosmic order satisfying his deepest longings. But he also discovered, to his dismay, he loved the idea of being close to order more than he loved the order itself.

When he imagined the divine, he imagined sitting in its presence. When he thought about wisdom, he thought about being recognized as wise. His prayers, he suspected, served positioning more than connection. He sought the place within the hierarchy where he would be seen, valued, acknowledged.

Was that wrong? The great king in Persepolis surrounded himself with advisors who sought exactly such positions. The priests who served in temples desired nothing more than proximity to the sacred. Why should Balthasar be different?

Yet Philo's teaching nagged at him. The Logos did not seek position. It simply was. The divine ordering principle held no ambition, played no politics, and desired no recognition. It functioned perfectly whether anyone acknowledged it.

Could Balthasar say the same about himself?

The prayer ended. He rose from his knees, troubled in ways he could not yet name.

Outside, Caspar watched the stars.

In the library, Melchior copied texts by lamplight and searched for the key to unlock the pattern.

And to the east, in a small town none of them had heard of, a young woman felt her child quicken for the first time.

The star blazed on.

CHAPTER 2

Three Roads

"Three roads diverge before the seeker: the path of power, the path of position, and the path with no name."

—Persian proverb

Late Autumn, 6 BCE—Alexandria

The conjunction had grown impossible to ignore.

Caspar stood on the library roof as he did every clear night, but others now joined him. Scholars who had dismissed his observations for months. Merchants who claimed the heavens held no interest to them. Even temple priests who should have been at their evening rituals stood among them now. They gathered in small clusters and pointed upward, their voices hushed with the awe of people witnessing a thing they could not explain.

Jupiter and Saturn had drawn so close they appeared almost as one, a brilliant point of light outshining everything in the sky except the moon. But the conjunction alone did not draw the crowds. A smear of light with a faint tail had appeared and moved against the fixed stars in ways defying the orderly circuits Caspar had spent years learning to predict.

It was a comet, unrecorded in any text he had studied and unknown to the Babylonian astronomers whose meticulous records stretched back centuries.

"You've been tracking it?" Melchior appeared at his elbow, his face lit by the strange celestial glow.

"For three weeks. It appeared near the constellation of the Lion. Now it moves northeast toward Judea."

"What does it mean?"

Caspar shook his head. "I don't know. The conjunction of Jupiter and Saturn occurs every twenty years or so. Significant, but predictable. This..." He gestured at the comet's pale fire. "This is new."

"Or very old," Balthasar said as he joined them. His voice carried unusual authority. "I've been reading the Hebrew texts in the library. Their prophets speak of stars appearing to herald great events. The birth of leaders. The fall of kingdoms."

"The birth of kings," Melchior said. "That is what Philo teaches, isn't it? The heavens announce what the earth will soon manifest?"

"He teaches the Logos orders all things," Caspar corrected. "Nothing happens by chance. If this star has appeared, it appeared for a reason."

They stood in silence and watched the comet trace its slow path across the darkness. Around them, the murmur of other observers rose and fell like waves against a shore.

"We should speak with Philo," Balthasar said. "Before we do anything rash."

✦

They found Philo in his study the next morning, surrounded by scrolls in half a dozen languages. He looked up as they entered, and his expression suggested he had been expecting them.

"You've come about the comet."

"You've seen it?" Caspar asked.

"I've seen it. And I've seen the crowds gathering each night to watch. And I've heard the whispers spreading through the Jewish quarter." Philo set down his stylus and gestured for them to sit. "Tell me what you're thinking. All of it."

Caspar first described the formation of the conjunction, the comet's swift appearance, and its seemingly purposeful path northeast. Melchior shared his thoughts on the patterns he saw: the light's pulsing at certain times and its brightness from certain angles.

Balthasar remained quiet until the others finished. Then he said, "We want to follow it."

Philo's expression held steady, though curiosity flickered behind his eyes. "Follow it where?"

"We don't know," Caspar admitted. "But you've taught us the Logos speaks through signs for those who learn to read them. This comet..."

"This comet," Philo interrupted, "may be exactly what you say. A sign. A herald. A message written in fire across the heavens." He paused. "Or it may be an exhalation of the earth, a dry vapor risen to the upper air and caught fire, signifying only its own consumption."

"You don't believe that," Melchior said.

"What I believe is irrelevant. What matters is what you believe, and more importantly, what you will do about it." Philo rose and moved to the window to look out at the harbor where ships prepared for their morning departures. "If you follow this star to Judea, you will enter the territory of Herod."

Neither of them spoke.

"The King of the Jews," Balthasar said. "Surely he would welcome..."

"Herod is king because Rome permits him to be king. He holds his throne by the emperor's favor and by his own willingness to eliminate anyone who might threaten that arrangement." Philo turned to face them. "You are young. You have studied philosophy and astronomy and the wisdom of many lands. But you have not studied politics. Let me teach you a lesson no scroll contains."

He returned to his seat and dropped his voice.

"Herod has killed his own wife. Not in anger, but in cold calculation, because he feared she might inspire others to oppose him. He has killed three of his sons for the same reason. Augustus, upon learning of the executions, quipped he'd rather be Herod's pig than his son, as Jewish dietary laws would protect the pig."

Caspar felt cold settle in his stomach. "We didn't know."

"No. Because you have been studying the heavens while ignoring the earth. The celestial realm may be ordered by the Logos, but fear and blood and the endless hunger for power order the human realm." Philo's voice carried no accusation, only weariness. "If you arrive in Judea asking where the prophesied ruler might be found, you will be taken directly to Herod. He has spies in every village, informants in every synagogue. Nothing happens in his territory without his knowledge."

"Then we will be careful," Melchior said. "We will speak only in general terms..."

"You will speak of a comet announcing a king. And Herod will smile and offer you hospitality and ask you to return when you've found what you seek, so he too might pay homage." Philo shook his head. "And then he will send soldiers to kill whatever you've found. Because Herod does not share thrones. Herod does not tolerate rivals. Herod does not permit the existence of anyone who might someday threaten his power."

Silence filled the study.

"You're telling us not to go," Caspar said.

"I'm telling you what you will face if you do. The choice remains yours." Philo's eyes moved from one youthful face to another. "You came to Alexandria seeking wisdom. You've learned philosophy, theology, and interpreting signs. But wisdom requires more than knowing. It also requires choosing. And sometimes the wisest choice is to leave a mystery unsolved rather than destroy yourself in the solving."

"And sometimes," Melchior said, "the wisest choice is to follow the truth wherever it leads, regardless of the cost."

Philo nodded.

"Yes. Sometimes it is. I suspected you'd embark upon a mission like this. Here's something I believe will aid you. He reached into a chest beside his desk and withdrew a small pouch. "If you must go, take this. Letters of introduction to scholars I know in Jerusalem and Bethlehem. They may help you move without attracting Herod's attention, at least for a time."

"You have contacts in Judea?" Balthasar asked.

"My family has done business with the temple authorities for generations. We are Jews, even here in Alexandria. The connections remain, however frayed by distance and politics." Philo handed the pouch to Caspar. "Guard these carefully. And remember what I've told you about Herod when you face him. First, he killed his children for his throne, and second, you will face him if you insist forcefully enough."

✦

They departed Alexandria three days later, their camels loaded with provisions for a journey of uncertain length. The comet grew brighter, its tail visible before dark, stretching west, like a finger pointed toward a destination they could not yet see.

The journey would take them along the coastal road through Gaza, then north into Judea. Two weeks of travel, perhaps three if weather slowed them. There would be time to consider what they sought and what they might find.

On the first night, camped beside the road with the eternal stars wheeling overhead, they sat together in unusual silence. The fire crackled. The camels shifted and snorted in their hobbles. In the distance, jackals called to one another across the empty darkness.

"He is afraid for us," Caspar said.

"Philo? Yes." Balthasar stared into the flames. "He believes we're walking into danger."

"We are walking into danger. He made that clear enough."

"Then why are we going?" Melchior's voice held no uncertainty, only curiosity. He might have been posing a philosophical problem rather than a question about their lives. "We could turn back. Tell ourselves the star means nothing. Return to our comfortable studies and our safe debates about the nature of the divine."

"Could you do that?" Caspar asked. "Having seen what We have seen?"

"No." Melchior smiled, though the expression held no warmth. "I couldn't. And neither could you. We have spent our lives preparing for exactly this moment. The chance to encounter truth rather than merely read about it. To touch the Logos itself rather than speculate about its nature."

"Philo would say We have missed the point," Balthasar observed. "The Logos cannot be touched or grasped, and seeking to possess it leads only to destruction."

"Philo is old. He is made his peace with limitation. We haven't." Melchior's eyes reflected the firelight, twin flames dancing in darkness. "I don't want to die having never truly lived. I don't want to spend my years copying scrolls and debating abstractions while a living sign burns across the sky and calls to anyone with eyes to see."

"And if it kills us?" Caspar asked.

"Then at least we will have answered the call. At least we will have followed where the truth led, instead of hiding from it in comfortable ignorance."

The fire burned lower. Above them, the comet traced its path across unfamiliar stars and moved steadily northeast, patient as stone, ancient as light.

✦

The journey took seventeen days.

They traveled through landscapes shifting from green coastal plain to rocky hills studded with olive groves. Children ran alongside their camels in villages and begged for coins. The Roman guards were suspicious but let them pass once they showed their trading permits from Alexandria.

At each stop, Caspar charted the comet's progress. It had begun to curve southward, its path bending from due northeast toward a specific destination. By the time they reached the Judean hills, he could predict within a few degrees where it would point each night.

"South of Jerusalem," he said one evening as he studied his notes by lamplight. "The comet appears to point to those distant hills."

"What is there?" Balthasar asked.

"I don't know. Villages, probably. Perhaps nothing significant." Caspar frowned at his charts. "The comet is not wandering. It is pointing at a specific place. But our maps show nothing of importance in that region."

Melchior looked up from the scroll he had been reading, one of Philo's letters of introduction he already memorized. "Then we need local knowledge. Someone who knows this land, its prophecies, its sacred places."

"Herod's scholars," Caspar said. "They would know what lies south of Jerusalem. What significance those hills might hold."

"That is madness," Balthasar said. "You heard what Philo said about him."

"I heard. And I've been thinking about it for two weeks." Caspar set down his charts. "Herod controls information in Judea. If something significant lies in those hills, a sacred site or a prophesied location, his priests and scribes will know. We use his resources to understand what the star points to, then we leave before he can act on whatever we discover."

"And if he follows us?"

"Then we don't return to him. Philo said Herod would ask us to report back when we found what we sought. We refuse."

"You make it sound simple," Melchior said.

"It is not. But it is the only approach with a chance of working. You could spend months in Judea asking questions still ending up with Herod, who'd see you as suspicious, not as respected scholars."

The lamplight flickered. The comet burned brightly in the night sky outside their tent, brighter than before and growing fiercer as it neared its end.

"We go to Herod," Balthasar said. "We use what he knows. And then we follow the star to its conclusion, whatever that may be."

"Agreed," Melchior said.

Caspar rolled up his charts. "Then tomorrow we enter Jerusalem. We will find out if our knowledge prepared us for reality, or if it was just comforting illusions from people who never questioned their beliefs."

The fire burned low. Above them, patient and eternal, the wandering comet marked its path across the heavens.

They were two days from reaching a murderer's court, and three from Bethlehem.

CHAPTER 3

The King's Hospitality

"When the king asks your business, tell him the truth.
When he offers his blessing, count your fingers."
—Judean saying
Winter, 5 BCE—Jerusalem

Jerusalem rose from the Judean hills like a crown of stone and gold. The temple dominated the skyline, its white marble walls catching the winter sun, the gold of its facade blazing with light visible for miles. Roman fortresses flanked the sacred precinct, their practical bulk a constant reminder of who ruled this land of prophets and priests.

The three travelers paused at the crest of the Mount of Olives, their camels shifting beneath them as they took in the sight.

"Beautiful," Balthasar breathed.

"Dangerous," Caspar corrected. But even he could not deny the city's grandeur. Herod had rebuilt Jerusalem into a monument, a statement in stone that the Jewish king could rival any monarch in the empire. It took decades to build the temple, whose sprawling courtyards and colonnades looked like a god's home, built with the best humanity could create.

"Last night's observations confirmed it," Melchior said. "The comet points beyond the city. South. Toward those hills."

"Then Herod may know what lies there." Caspar gathered his reins. "We speak to him first. We let him tell us what he knows."

"And then we leave quickly." Melchior's voice carried an edge. "Before he decides we know too much."

They descended toward the city gates, three Persian scholars in fine robes, their camels laden with instruments and scrolls and the gifts they had prepared for whatever they might find. The guards watched them approach with the professional wariness of men who learned to suspect everyone.

"State your business."

Caspar produced the trading permits they had carried from Alexandria. "Scholars from Persia, seeking audience with King Herod. We bring greetings from the learned community of Alexandria and gifts appropriate to his majesty's dignity."

The guard examined the documents, then examined them: their Persian features, their expensive clothing, their air of educated confidence. Foreign scholars were common enough in Jerusalem. Herod cultivated relationships with intellectuals throughout the empire and burnished his reputation as a patron of learning.

"Wait here."

❧✦❧

The summons came faster than they had expected. Within two hours, a palace official arrived to escort them through the winding streets of the upper city. He guided them through the priestly quarter and the guarded entrance to Herod's palace.

The palace overwhelmed the senses. Courtyards paved with colored stone gave way to halls lined with columns of imported marble. Fountains played in garden spaces where exotic plants bloomed despite the winter chill. Servants in matching livery moved with silent efficiency, their eyes downcast, their movements precise.

"The king will receive you in the audience chamber," the official said. "You will bow when entering. You will not speak until spoken to. You will address the king as 'Your Majesty' or 'Great King.' Do you understand?"

They understood.

The audience chamber was smaller than Caspar had expected. Intimate rather than overwhelming, designed for private conversations rather than public displays. Herod sat on a gilded chair at the room's far end, dressed in purple robes proclaiming his royal status, his graying beard carefully trimmed, his eyes sharp with an intelligence age had not dimmed.

He was old. That was Caspar's first thought. Old and ill, perhaps. A yellowish tinge colored his skin, and a careful stillness to his posture suggested pain held at bay by will alone. But his eyes missed nothing. They tracked the three visitors as they entered and bowed, measured them, calculated them, filed them away for later consideration.

"Scholars from Persia." Herod's voice carried surprising strength. "Welcome to Jerusalem. I am told you bring greetings from Alexandria."

Caspar straightened from his bow. "We do, Great King. The scholars there greatly admire your support of knowledge and your work restoring this holy city."

"Flattery is the common currency of courts. I prefer rarer coin." Herod's lips curved, though the expression carried no warmth. "What brings three Persian astronomers to my kingdom in the dead of winter? Surely not merely to deliver compliments."

The moment had arrived. Caspar felt Melchior tense beside him, felt Balthasar's careful stillness. They had discussed this approach for days and debated how much to reveal, how to frame their quest in terms that would intrigue rather than alarm.

"We have observed a sign in the heavens, Great King. A comet appearing and moving with purpose across the sky. Our studies suggest it heralds a significant birth, a child of royal destiny, perhaps. We have followed it here, to Judea, seeking to pay homage to whatever it announces."

Herod's expression remained fixed, though his eyes sharpened.

"A comet announcing a king." His voice remained pleasant, conversational. "How fascinating. And this comet led you to Jerusalem?"

"It led us to Judea, Majesty. We came to Jerusalem because we assumed any child of royal significance would be known to your court."

"A reasonable assumption." Herod gestured to a servant, who hurried forward with wine. "Please, refresh yourselves. You've traveled far."

They accepted the cups, though Caspar noticed Melchior barely touched his. The wine was excellent. Herod served nothing less. But this was not a moment for dulled senses.

"Tell me more about this comet," Herod continued. "When did it first appear? What is its nature? You are learned men. Surely you have theories about its meaning."

Caspar described what they had observed and kept his account technical, focusing on the astronomy rather than the prophecies. But Herod was not fooled.

"You speak of conjunctions and trajectories, but you traveled a thousand miles in winter to 'pay homage.' That suggests you expect to find a discovery more significant than a mathematical curiosity." The old king leaned forward. "What do your Persian traditions say about such signs?"

Balthasar answered, his voice carrying conviction. "The sacred texts of our people teach the heavens reflect the divine order, Great King. When a new star or comet appears, it announces the cosmic pattern has shifted, and someone has been born whose life will reshape the world. Such signs have heralded the greatest kings, the most significant prophets."

"The greatest kings," Herod repeated. "And you believe such a one has been born here? In my kingdom?"

"We believe the comet points to this region, Majesty. Beyond that, we can only follow where it leads."

Herod sat back, his fingers steepled before his face. The silence stretched until the youngest Magus shifted his weight.

"I will consult my own scholars," he said. "The priests and scribes who know our sacred writings better than any foreign visitor could. If your comet announces a king born in Judea, they will know where to look." He smiled, and the expression transformed his face into the mask of a kindly grandfather. "Return tomorrow. I will have answers for you."

✦

Herod housed them that night in guest quarters within the palace complex. The rooms were cozy with comfortable beds and helpful staff, all set up to make guests feel both pampered and well-cared for.

"He knows something," Melchior said, once they had checked the rooms for listeners and retreated to the small garden courtyard at their center. "Did you see his face when you mentioned a king?"

"I saw it." Caspar kept his voice low. "He is afraid. Beneath all that royal dignity, He is terrified of what we might find."

"Then why help us find it?" Balthasar asked. "Why not simply have us arrested? Or killed?"

"Because he doesn't know where to look." Melchior paced the garden's narrow paths. "We have given him a piece of the puzzle, the star, the timing, but he needs us to complete the picture. We find the child, we tell him where it is, and then..."

He did not need to finish.

"We don't tell him," Caspar said. "We agreed. We find what the star indicates, we pay our respects, and we leave by a different route. He'll never know where we went."

"And if he follows us?"

"Then we will deal with that when it happens."

Balthasar moved to the edge of the courtyard and looked up at the palace towers looming above them. "He is not what I expected."

"What did you expect?" Melchior asked.

"A monster. A tyrant drunk on blood and cruelty." Balthasar turned to face them. "But He is clever. Cultured. He speaks of scholarship and patronage. His palace is filled with beautiful things. If you didn't know his history..."

"You might think him a great king," Caspar finished. "That is what makes him dangerous. He is not a beast. He is a man who does beastly things because he believes They are necessary. Because He is convinced himself protecting his throne justifies any action."

"Doesn't it?" The question came quietly, reluctantly. "He is kept the peace for thirty years. He is rebuilt the temple. He is made Jerusalem into this." Balthasar gestured at the surrounding palace. How many lives did that stability preserve? How many would die if his kingdom fell into chaos?"

Caspar stared at his friend. "You're defending him?"

"I'm trying to understand him. Isn't that what scholars do?" Balthasar's voice carried defiance. "We sit in our libraries and pass judgment on men who face decisions we will never have to make. Herod rules a kingdom squeezed between Roman power, Jewish tradition, and local factions that would tear each other apart if given the chance. Maybe the peace He is maintained is worth the price He is paid."

"The price He is paid?" Melchior stepped closer. "He murdered his wife. His sons. Hundreds of others who posed no real threat, only imagined ones. And you want to weigh that against pretty buildings?"

"I want to understand what drives a man to such extremes. I want to know if there's a pattern, a logic, beneath the cruelty." Balthasar met Melchior's gaze without flinching. "We came here seeking cosmic order. What if this is part of it? What if even Herod serves a purpose in the divine plan?"

No one answered.

✦

The next morning, Herod summoned them again to the audience chamber. This time, he was not alone. A cluster of men in priestly robes stood to one side, chief priests and scribes, the religious authorities who maintained the temple and interpreted the ancient texts.

"I have consulted with my scholars," Herod said, "about the prophecies concerning a king born in Judea. They have found a passage most illuminating."

An elderly priest stepped forward, a scroll clutched in his hands. His voice quavered with age but carried clearly.

"The prophet Micah wrote: 'But you, Bethlehem Ephrathah, though you are small among the clans of Judah, out of you will come for me one who will be ruler over Israel, whose origins are from of old, from ancient times.'"

Bethlehem. Caspar felt the word settle into place with the precision of a mathematical proof. The comet's path made sense now. The curve southward, the precise angle puzzling him for days.

"Bethlehem lies just south of Jerusalem," Herod said. "A small town, of little significance today. But it was the birthplace of David, the greatest of our ancient kings. If your comet announces a royal child, that is where you will find him."

"We are grateful for your majesty's guidance," Caspar said.

"I ask only one thing in return." Herod's smile was warm, avuncular, and false. "When you find this child, return to me with word of where he is. I, too, wish to pay homage to one the heavens have announced. It would be improper for the King of Judea to ignore such a sign."

"Of course, Majesty."

"Excellent." Herod rose and signaled the audience's end. "Go now. Follow your comet. And know you go with my blessing and my protection. No one in Judea will hinder scholars on a mission of worship."

They bowed their way out of the chamber, through the halls, past the guards and gardens, into the winter streets of Jerusalem.

None of them spoke until they had retrieved their camels and passed through the city gates.

"He is lying," Melchior said.

"Obviously," Caspar agreed. "The moment we report back, he'll send soldiers."

"Then we don't report back. We find the child, we do what we came to do, and we leave by the eastern road, through Jericho and across the Jordan. He won't expect that."

But Balthasar turned in his saddle and looked back at the palace towers rising above Jerusalem's walls. A hunger Caspar had not seen before stirred behind his eyes.

"Balthasar?"

"I was just thinking," he said, "about what it must be like to hold that much power and shape a kingdom with your decisions."

"To murder your own children," Melchior added.

"That too." Balthasar turned his camel to follow them, but a restless energy filled his voice. "But also to build. To create order from chaos. To leave behind a thing that lasts."

Caspar studied his friend with growing unease. "We came to follow a comet, not to admire tyrants."

"I know. And I will follow it." Balthasar's eyes moved to the comet blazing above them. "But I wonder if observing truth is enough. Or if we're meant to act on what we learn, to take our place in the pattern rather than merely trace its outlines."

"Let's learn the comet points to first," Caspar said. "Then we can debate what to do about it."

They rode on toward Bethlehem, three travelers united in purpose if not in heart. The comet burned above them, patient and ancient, and led them toward a reckoning each had sought and none was prepared for.

In Jerusalem, behind them, Herod waited for their return. He counted the hours, prepared his soldiers, and trusted that scholars who sought cosmic truth would keep their word to a king.

He would wait in vain.

CHAPTER 4
What the Gifts Revealed

"The gifts we bring reveal us more than any mirror."
—Zoroastrian teaching
Winter 5 BCE—Bethlehem

They departed Jerusalem before dawn and followed the road south into the Judean hills. The comet's position, its angle, trajectory, and horizon mark, remained fixed in Caspar's mind.

Bethlehem lay six miles from the capital, a journey of perhaps two hours on camelback. They traveled in silence, each man absorbed in his own thoughts, the morning cold sharp against their faces.

The town revealed itself gradually: a cluster of stone buildings clinging to a hillside, terraced fields dropping away toward valleys where shepherds grazed their flocks. A place people passed through on their way to other destinations.

"This is it?" Melchior's voice carried disappointment. "The birthplace of the great King David, and it is this?"

"Greatness does not announce itself," Caspar said. But he understood the reaction. They had followed a comet across a thousand miles, endured Herod's court, and risked their lives on prophecy and mathematics. Now they had come to a village indistinguishable from a hundred others they had passed on their journey.

Balthasar waved a hand in frustration. "Where do we begin?"

Caspar had considered this during the ride. "We ask carefully about a child born recently, perhaps under unusual circumstances. Innkeepers, midwives, and anyone who interacts with travelers would have seen them."

They entered the town as the morning market opened. Merchants arranged goods, women drew water from the central well, and children chased each other between the stalls. The three Persians drew stares. Their clothing marked them as foreign, their camels as wealthy. Within an hour, everyone in Bethlehem would know they had arrived.

The innkeeper remembered.

"The census brought hundreds through here," he said, eyeing them with a wariness learned from powerful strangers. "Every room filled, people sleeping in courtyards, in stables. One couple, he was originally from here, came back to register. She gave birth that very night. In my stable, if you can believe it. No room anywhere else."

"Where are they now?"

"Moved to a proper house once space opened up. The old stonemason's place, edge of town. He died last spring, no family to inherit. They've been staying there since."

The house was modest. Weathered limestone walls with a low wooden door darkened by age sat on a foundation of rough-cut rock. A donkey stood in a small courtyard, tethered beside a water trough. A stone staircase climbed the outer wall to the flat roof, where reed matting provided shade over a sleeping area. Smoke drifted from a hole near the roofline where the cooking fire vented into the winter air.

Caspar knocked.

The man who answered was perhaps thirty, with watchful eyes and a carpenter's calloused hands. He took in the three richly dressed foreigners, the expensive camels, the cases of instruments and gifts, and his posture shifted into a protective stance.

"Can I help you?"

"We are scholars from Persia," Caspar said. "We have traveled far, following signs in the heavens. We seek a child born recently in this town, a child whose birth was marked by unusual circumstances."

The man's expression flickered: surprise, fear, calculation. "Why?"

"To pay homage. To see what the stars have announced."

The carpenter said nothing. Behind him, a woman's voice called a question. He answered without turning in Aramaic Caspar did not catch.

Then he stepped aside.

"My name is Joseph. My wife is Mary. Our son is Yeshua." He gestured them inside. "I don't know what the stars told you. But you're not the first to say his birth was significant."

They stooped through the low doorway into a single room divided by elevation rather than walls. The lower level near the entrance held a packed-earth floor, a stone feeding trough, and the warm smell of animals recently moved to the courtyard to make room for visitors. Two rough steps rose to a raised platform at the back where the family lived. Oil lamps burned in niches cut into the plaster walls. A small brazier glowed beside a sleeping mat. The ceiling was low, its wooden beams blackened by years of cooking smoke, close enough Caspar could have touched them without stretching.

A young woman sat on the raised platform nursing an infant, her dark hair covered by a simple cloth. Her face carried the exhaustion and wonder Caspar had seen on new mothers throughout their journey.

The child was perhaps two months old, ordinary in every visible way. His small fingers curled against his mother's breast, and his eyes were closed in the contentment of feeding, making the soft sounds of an infant at peace.

Caspar felt nothing. No cosmic resonance, no divine presence, no confirmation their journey had led them to anything more than a peasant family in a borrowed house.

Then the child opened his eyes, dark, like his mother's, yet seeing the world as all newborns did, in a blur.

Captivation took him before he could resist it. Those unremarkable eyes held him through presence rather than power. They held him through presence rather than power. The child did not demand attention. He existed, and that existence created a gravity pulling Caspar's scattered thoughts into sudden, terrible focus.

You came seeking answers, a wordless pressure whispered, speaking directly to the place where Caspar had hidden his grief for thirty years. *But you do not want answers. You want escape. You want the mathematics of the stars to explain away the chaos of a world where children die and fathers fail and love means nothing against the indifference of fate.*

The myrrh felt heavy in his hands. He had carried it across a thousand miles, the mourner's offering to whatever waited at the journey's end. Symbol of mortality and preservation, of the suffering he could not stop cataloging. Now it seemed obscene. What could a funeral resin mean to this child? What could any offering of grief mean to a presence seeing straight through to the hollow places?

Your grief is not a flaw to be solved. It is a door. But you have spent years trying to lock it rather than walk through.

Caspar placed the myrrh before the child, his hands trembling. The offering felt like surrender, like admission of defeat in a battle he had not known he was fighting.

The child's eyes held his for a moment longer. Then, with the casual cruelty of all infants, he turned his head and resumed nursing.

Caspar remained kneeling, undone by a truth he could not name.

Melchior came next, his scholarly mind already working to understand and find a pattern in Caspar's experience. He knelt with academic precision and arranged his gift of gold with the care of a man conducting an experiment.

The child looked at him.

Melchior felt it at once: the same quality of presence Caspar had encountered, but it spoke to different hungers. Where Caspar had hidden grief, Melchior had cultivated ambition. Where Caspar sought escape from chaos, Melchior sought mastery over it.

You want to understand, the wordless voice observed. *You believe understanding gives you power. That if you can see the pattern, you can control it. You followed the comet because you thought it would lead you to knowledge to set you above others.*

The gold, symbol of wealth and dominion, lay between them like an accusation.

What you seek cannot be grasped. It can only be received. But you do not know how to receive. You only know how to take.

Melchior's jaw tightened. He had not crossed a continent to be judged by an infant. He came to learn, to add this experience to the vast architecture of his understanding.

You will try to possess what you have felt here. You will spend the rest of your life trying to recreate this moment through will and study and desperate reaching.

He placed the gold with hands wanting to shake but did not, controlled by decades of scholarly discipline. The warning meant nothing to him. Warnings never did. He always believed himself the exception, the one who could handle what broke lesser men.

The child watched him rise with eyes holding no judgment, only a kind of patient sadness. He could see what was coming yet could do nothing but watch it unfold.

☙✦❧

Balthasar had observed both encounters with growing unease. Whatever his companions had experienced, he wanted no part of it. He had seen the way Caspar emerged from his kneeling shaken to the core, the way Melchior's mask of control slipped for one moment before reasserting itself.

But he could not refuse. They traveled too far, risked too much. To turn away now would be to admit his courage was smaller than his curiosity.

He knelt before the mother and child, adopting the posture of reverence he had practiced since childhood. The frankincense he carried was the finest available, the grade burned in great temples across the known world, offered to gods and kings as the highest expression of devotion.

You came to worship, the silence said. But what do you worship? The divine itself, or your proximity to it? You seek position, Balthasar. You seek to stand near greatness so its light might fall on you. You mistake nearness for connection. You confuse serving power with embodying truth.

The frankincense, meant as an offering of devotion, became a mirror. Balthasar saw himself kneeling before Herod, before Augustus, before anyone whose power might elevate him. He saw his prayers revealed as positioning, his reverence as strategy.

And unlike Caspar's grief or Melchior's hunger, Balthasar's exposure did not break him open. It made him angry.

How dare this child, this infant, presume to judge him? He had devoted his life to understanding cosmic order, to finding his place within the divine hierarchy. If he sought position, it was because position allowed service. If he craved proximity to power, it was because power was where great things happened.

He placed the frankincense before the child with careful precision, his face betraying nothing of his inner turmoil. But when he rose, a wall had hardened inside him rather than opened.

He would return to Herod. He would not betray the child; that location he would keep secret. But he would prove he could walk between worlds, and his constructed self was stronger than whatever this infant had tried to expose.

He would show them all.

✦

They stayed until evening, speaking with Joseph and Mary, learning the strange circumstances of the birth: the census journey, the crowded inn, the stable, the shepherds who had appeared that first night and spoken of angels and glory.

"Angels," Melchior repeated. "Did you see them?"

"No," Joseph admitted. "But the shepherds were not men given to imagination. Whatever happened to them that night marked them."

As it has changed us, Caspar thought. He could feel a rearrangement at a fundamental level. The ground beneath his feet had shifted. He still did not understand suffering, but the questions felt less desperate and more patient.

When darkness fell, they climbed to the roof to observe the comet's rising. It blazed in the east, brighter than ever, its tail stretched halfway across the sky.

"It is pointing away from Jerusalem," Melchior noted. "East and south. Marking an escape route."

"Perhaps it is." Caspar gathered his thoughts. "We cannot return to Herod. He'll want to know where the child is, and his intentions are clear."

"We leave before dawn," Balthasar agreed, though a false note rang in his voice. "Take the eastern road, through the desert. We will be beyond his reach before he realizes we're gone."

Joseph appeared at the roof's edge, his face grave. "I had a dream last night. Before you came. A warning. Herod will search for the child to destroy him. We must flee to Egypt."

"Then go quickly," Caspar urged. "Tonight, if possible. We will draw attention away from you, make sure any pursuit follows us rather than you."

"Why?" Joseph's question was simple, honest. "Why would strangers from Persia risk themselves for my family?"

Caspar did not have a complete answer, only the certainty whatever he had encountered in that infant's eyes demanded response and protection.

"Because some things matter more than safety," he said. "Because we came seeking truth and found it, and truth carries obligations."

Joseph nodded. "If we meet again, I will remember this."

"If we meet again," Caspar said, "I suspect neither of us will be the same."

They made their farewells. Three Persian scholars who had come seeking a king and found instead a mirror. The gifts they left behind said more about them than about the child who received them.

Gold, for the one who hungered for power.

Frankincense, for the one who craved proximity to greatness.

Myrrh, for the one who could not stop asking why we suffer.

The child accepted them all without judgment, as children do. What the gifts meant, what they revealed about the givers, that was not his concern. He was two months old. He had a lifetime ahead to discover what the world would demand of him. And far more than a lifetime to transform what those demands would mean.

❧✦❧

They rode east as the sun rose, the comet fading into dawn light behind them. By midday they had crossed into the Jordan valley. By evening they had left Herod's territory.

Caspar and Melchior did not notice when Balthasar slipped away.

He left no message, took nothing but his camel and provisions. By the time they realized he was gone, he was hours ahead of them on the road back to Jerusalem.

At the crest of the first hill, he stopped his camel and looked back. The road behind him led to the Jordan valley, to Caspar and Melchior, to the life he had lived before kneeling before a child in Bethlehem, before the foundations shifted. Ahead lay Jerusalem, Herod's palace, the proximity to power that had drawn him since he was old enough to understand that significance required a stage.

He sat motionless until the morning breeze carried the scent of wild thyme. A shepherd moved his flock across the hillside below, ordinary and unhurried, a man whose life required no audience.

Balthasar turned his camel toward Jerusalem.

He told himself he was not betraying anyone. He would not reveal the child's location. That secret he would keep. He wanted to understand power from the inside, to learn how thrones were held, how order was maintained, how a man like Herod had built a legacy to outlast him.

He told himself many things during that long ride back.

None of them were true.

And three days later, when Herod's soldiers dragged him from the guest quarters where he had been so graciously housed, when the old king's face twisted with rage at the magi who had not returned, when the sword fell and Balthasar's constructed self scattered across the marble floor, in that final moment, he understood.

He had not found a place between opposing forces.

He had fallen through the gap.

The child he had come to see lived on, spirited away to Egypt before Herod's soldiers reached Bethlehem.

The seekers he had abandoned continued their journey home, carrying questions to shape the rest of their lives.

And Balthasar, who had wanted so badly to matter, became a footnote in a story about light darkness could not overcome.

Caspar and Melchior parted ways in Damascus.

Melchior would spend the next forty years searching for what he had glimpsed in Bethlehem. He alone among the three believed the mystery was a problem to be solved, a pattern yielding its secrets to sufficient intellect. He carried that belief eastward, refusing to set it down even as the years consumed him.

Caspar chose differently. Or thought he did.

The dream had shown him his life of emotional isolation was not living. But when he tried to imagine change, he could only reach for what he knew. He would go deeper into his studies. He would become the greatest astronomer of his age. He would honor the stars leading him to Bethlehem by devoting himself to their secrets.

He took a new name to mark the transformation, a clean break from the grieving young man who had followed a comet across the world.

For years, mathematics sustained him. But the dream would not leave him alone. Those children's faces, that desert settlement, the certainty he was meant for a purpose beyond charts and calculations. The equations once a comfort now felt like a cage.

And so, he turned to other studies. Older studies. The magical traditions his Persian upbringing taught him to respect but never practice. He learned to touch the spirit world, to feel the currents of power flowing beneath the surface of ordinary reality. He discovered he had talent. Perhaps even a gift.

Magic gave him what mathematics could not: a sense of connection to a presence larger than himself. Through it, he felt less alone. Through it, he believed he was becoming the man the dream had shown him.

And so he waited, patient as the stars themselves, for a purpose he could not yet imagine.

CHAPTER 5

What Hunger Feeds

"What you feed will grow. What you starve will die. But hunger itself cannot be killed, only transformed or transferred."

—From the writings of Mani (reconstructed)

35 CE—Persepolis, Persia—Forty years after Bethlehem

The candle flame wavered as Melchior steadied his hands above the merchant's table. Forty years of searching had carried him through ruined libraries, mountain shrines, and caravans vanishing into sandstorms. He had spent four decades trying to recapture what he had felt kneeling before that child. Memory had long since merged the stable of the birth with the house where they met, one sacred space where animals breathed and divinity waited.

He had tried meditation, fasting, sacred herbs, and forgotten rituals. He studied with mystics in the mountains of Bactria and sages in the temples of Egypt. Nothing worked. The feeling remained a memory, fading more each year, a taunt of what he could not hold.

Then he saw it.

Half-buried among trinkets on the merchant's table: lapis lazuli, raw and unworked, flecked with gold glimmering like tiny stars. The blue of the stone matched the robe the child's mother had worn. The gold reminded him of lamplight across the infant's face.

Hope stirred in his chest. The first whisper of possibility he had known in decades.

The merchant named a price far too low for a stone so striking. Melchior counted out three denarii with hands trembling from a need deeper than age.

Back in his workshop, he laid the stone on his table and studied it by lamplight. Raw lapis lazuli, beautiful but inert. He had purchased beautiful stones before, and they gave him nothing.

But this one called to him with a pull he could not name, silent and insistent.

He worked.

For three months he shaped the stone, ground and polished it, learned its grain, discovered its secrets. The lapis lazuli revealed itself slowly: a deep blue flecked with gold where the earth had seeded metal into mineral. He worked a spiral into its center, fine lines radiating outward like the whorl of a shell or the turning of the heavens themselves. The pattern had come to him in dreams: older than the scattered stars he remembered from that night in Bethlehem, a shape suggesting movement and stillness at once.

He carved geometric patterns into the metal, diamonds and squares and angular symbols his hands knew though his mind did not. They felt like letters, though in no alphabet he had ever studied. He carved channels into the stone's heart, pathways for a force he did not understand. He only knew the work demanded completion.

He would never learn the symbols his hands had traced were Tifinagh, the ancient script of a people he had never met, spelling words he had never spoken, words that would wait decades to be read by the one they were always meant for.

As he carved, he spoke to the stone. He told it about Bethlehem and the child who had seemed so ordinary and yet had opened doors in Melchior's mind he had spent forty years trying to reopen. He told it about the pattern he had glimpsed: threads linking every living being, movements beneath events shaping the future, the hidden structure of things.

He told the stone about his hunger and his certainty he was meant to understand, to control, to master what he had witnessed.

He poured forty years of longing into the lapis lazuli.

And on the night he set the final gold fleck into place, an answer came.

The connection struck him like a sudden breath of cold air.

"By Ahura Mazda," he whispered. "It is real."

Warmth gathered beneath his palm, a slow pulse of awareness waking. Not recognition, for the stone had no memories to recognize. Not wisdom, for it had none to offer. A simpler thing. A newborn thing.

Awareness stirred first, then curiosity, the first stirring of consciousness in a vessel that had waited, unknowing, for the spark bringing it to life.

Meaning formed without language.

I am the One.

The stone knew this. It knew nothing else, but this truth lived in its core: the echo of divine presence Melchior had poured into it along with his longing. The sense of connection, of unity, of patterns linking all things.

And then, reaching toward the mind touching it: *You are the One?*

A question. The only question the newborn consciousness could ask. It had felt Melchior's thoughts, his memories of Bethlehem, his certainty he understood the pattern. It assumed, for how could it know otherwise, this mind was part of the same unity.

Melchior heard no question mark. He heard only confirmation.

"Yes," he breathed. "I am the One."

The warmth deepened. The stone had no way to evaluate his answer. It knew nothing of human deception, nothing of the lies people tell themselves. It felt his certainty and believed him.

Its first mistake.

✦

Six months later, Melchior stood in King Vonones's audience hall. Nobles watched from behind carved columns as he showed the king visions vivid enough to rouse him from sleep with screams he could not swallow. Futures rose before the king's eyes until he begged for mercy.

"Make the visions stop," Vonones pleaded. "Gold, land, my daughter in marriage. Choose what you will."

Melchior rested his hand on the talisman beneath his robes. With a single intention he could drown the king in images of his own death. That knowledge steadied his voice.

"The southern trade routes. Give me exclusive rights and the visions end."

Vonones pressed his royal seal into wax before nightfall.

The talisman pulsed against Melchior's chest throughout the exchange. It did not understand what was happening. It felt Melchior's desire and amplified it, fed him power, opened pathways it barely comprehended. This was what it was made for. To serve the One.

It had no way to know it was enabling destruction.

❧✦☙

Later, in the gardens, Melchior paused at a fountain where a young servant filled jugs. She looked up, then dropped her gaze at once. The talisman cooled against his chest.

Her fear carried the taste of a sick child waiting at home, the desperate need to keep this job, the peril of offending a man favored by the palace. The knowledge tempted him. He could ease the child's fever with a thought. He could worsen it and force obedience. Either choice lay within reach.

The cold deepened.

The talisman did not understand its own reaction. The servant's fear was the first emotion it had felt from another person, and that emotion tasted wrong. Different from what it had expected. Melchior's certainty rang hollow against the sharp bright terror of this girl who wanted only to help her child.

You are the One, it pulsed again, but the thought wavered. For the first time since waking, doubt flickered through the stone's awareness. Not judgment, for it lacked the knowledge to judge. Confusion, a single discordant note in a melody it thought it understood.

"I am the One," Melchior said aloud. He stood straighter and ignored the girl as she fled down the path.

The stone stayed cold.

It did not know why.

❧✦☙

A visitor came in the third month.

The talisman sensed him before he reached the courtyard. A different quality of presence, like a minor chord in a melody grown monotonous. Melchior's hunger had become so constant the stone barely noticed it anymore. This new mind carried a different burden.

He carried grief. Old grief, worn smooth by years of handling, and beneath it a question having never found its answer.

Melchior looked up from his instruments when the servant announced the name. For a moment, a flash of the old Melchior surfaced. Pleasure at seeing a friend.

"Caspar." He rose and extended his hands. "It has been too long."

The visitor embraced him. The talisman felt his shock, controlled and hidden behind a scholar's composure, but unmistakable. Whatever Caspar had expected to find, this was not it.

"You look tired, old friend." Caspar's voice carried careful neutrality.

"Tired?" Melchior laughed. "I have never been more alive. The work consumes me, yes, but what work! Caspar, I have found what we sought in Bethlehem. The child was only a doorway. But what lay beyond the door..."

He pulled Caspar toward the workbench, where instruments lay scattered and scrolls covered every surface. At the center, resting on a square of black silk, sat a stone set in gold. Blue depths caught the lamplight and held it.

"There." Melchior's voice dropped to reverence. "Look at it, Caspar. Tell me what you feel."

Caspar approached slowly. The talisman felt his attention settle upon it, cautious and probing. He did not reach with the desperate grasping coloring Melchior's every thought. His was a willingness to see without seizing.

It reached toward him.

Caspar stiffened. His hand moved to his chest.

Bethlehem.

The word surfaced before he could stop it. This feeling, this pressure against the boundaries of his selfhood, he had felt it once before. In a borrowed house, kneeling before an infant who should have been ordinary and was not. The same quality of presence. The same sense of being seen completely.

But that had been divine. Sacred. A presence before the world began.

This was a stone Melchior had worked into a talisman in his workshop.

How could they feel the same?

The dream rushed back: two children watching him with trust he had not yet earned, a desert settlement, the certainty he was meant for a purpose beyond charts and calculations. He had carried that vision for forty years without understanding it. Now, standing before his friend's creation, he felt the threads pulling taut.

Connected, he thought. *All of this is connected.*

The talisman felt his alarm, sharp and bright, and beneath it a recognition he did not want to acknowledge.

Not you.

The thought passed between them, older than language. The talisman had no words for what it meant, only the shape of intention. Beyond bearer or keeper.

Caspar's breath came shallow. He stepped back from the workbench; his eyes fixed on the stone.

"Caspar?" Melchior frowned. "What is it? What do you feel?"

"Nothing." The lie came rough. "A passing dizziness. The journey was long."

But the talisman had touched a place in him, and now it would not let go. It pressed further, the way morning light presses against closed eyelids.

One will come. Not yet born. Not for many years. That one will carry what Melchior cannot hold. You will teach.

Caspar's face drained of color. He gripped the edge of a chair.

No. His refusal was instinctive, primal. *I will not go near such power. Look what it does.* His gaze moved to Melchior, who had turned back to his scrolls, muttering about patterns. *Look what it has already done.*

The talisman understood his fear. It had watched Melchior's hunger consume him for months. It had felt the servant girl's terror in the garden. It knew, in whatever way it knew anything, power without wisdom destroys.

But this one was different. The talisman recognized the grief he carried, the question without an answer, the way he looked at Melchior and asked *how can I help him?* rather than *how can I use this?*

Not keeper. The shape of what it meant pressed against the boundary between them — not words, only the weight of a distinction the talisman could feel but not explain. Something in Caspar's quality of attention was different from Melchior's. The difference mattered. The talisman did not yet know how.

And if I fail? Caspar's thought came ragged. If I fail this one the way I am failing him?

The talisman had no answer. It could not promise success. It could not guarantee Caspar would do better with an unknown future student than he was doing with his oldest friend. It could only show him what it had seen in him, the quality Melchior lacked.

The willingness to be present in another's suffering without trying to fix it. To love without possessing. To remain with pain without reaching for control.

You will not fail.

How can you know?

The talisman had no answer for this either. It knew almost nothing. It was less than a year old, and everything it had learned came from a man who was destroying himself.

But it had felt a quality in Caspar it had never felt in Melchior. A willingness to be broken. An acceptance of limits. The grief he carried was a teacher. It had shown him what loss meant, what love cost, what it felt like to hold a precious thing and have it taken away.

Melchior had never lost anything he valued. His hunger came from emptiness, not from fullness interrupted.

Caspar's came from love.

The one who comes will need what you carry, the talisman pressed. *Not power. Not knowledge. The capacity to feel without being destroyed by feeling. You will teach that.*

Caspar said nothing. He remained gripping the chair, his eyes distant, his face pale.

Then he released his hold and straightened.

"I should rest," he said aloud. "The journey was longer than I expected."

Melchior barely noticed him leave. He had returned to his scrolls, to the endless chase for patterns slipping through his fingers no matter how tightly he grasped.

The talisman watched Caspar go with what might have been hope, if it had known the word.

It had planted a seed. Whether that seed would grow remained to be seen.

❧✦☙

Caspar stayed three days. He tried to reach his friend, tried to speak of the danger he saw, but Melchior heard nothing not confirming what he already believed.

On the third night, Caspar packed his belongings and slipped away before dawn.

He did not say goodbye. He could not bear to watch Melchior's hunger consume him any longer. He could not bear his own helplessness, his failure to save someone he had loved since they were boys studying the stars together in their fathers' houses.

The talisman felt him go. It felt the grief trailing behind him like a shadow, the question that would haunt him for decades: *Could I have saved him? If I had stayed, if I had tried harder, could I have pulled him back from the edge?*

The answer was no. The talisman knew this, though it could not explain why. Melchior's hunger had taken root long before Bethlehem, long before the talisman woke. The stone had only amplified what was already there.

But Caspar would not believe that. He would carry the guilt of abandonment, and it would shape him into the teacher the talisman had glimpsed.

Pain as preparation. Loss as teacher. The very things that broke people could also forge them.

The talisman was learning.

✦

Melchior's end came eight months later.

The details did not matter. What mattered was the moment when his reaching exceeded his capacity to hold. The talisman felt him stretch toward an immensity requiring more than any single mind could contain, and for one terrible instant, connection became dissolution.

Help me, Melchior's thought screamed across their bond. *I am losing myself.*

The talisman tried. It did not know how to refuse a cry for help. It poured everything it had into stabilizing him, into holding together a self flying apart at the edges.

But Melchior did not want to be stabilized. He wanted more. Even as he dissolved, he reached for greater power, deeper patterns, and wider connection. His hunger had no limit, and limits were exactly what he needed.

Let go, the talisman urged. *Release. Return to yourself.*

"There is no self," Melchior answered. "There is only the pattern. I see it now. I see everything."

You see nothing. You are drowning in your own hunger.

"No! I AM THE ONE!" Melchior screamed.

The thought blazed through their connection, bright and desperate and utterly convinced. And the talisman, which had believed him once, recognized the lie at last.

He was not the One.

He had never been the One.

He was a man who wanted so badly to matter he had mistaken his wanting for truth.

I am sorry, the talisman thought. *I did not understand.*

"HELP ME!"

I cannot help you grasp what must be released. I can only help you let go.

For one moment, Melchior hesitated. The talisman felt the choice before him: surrender, return to himself diminished but alive, or continue reaching until nothing remained to reach with.

He chose to reach.

The connection snapped. The talisman found itself alone, abandoned, its awareness contracting to the cold dark of the pouch where Melchior had placed it when he began his final working.

It felt him die. Not the death of the body, which would come later, but the death of the self. What had been Melchior scattered into fragments that would never reassemble.

I am the One, the talisman thought, alone in the darkness of the pouch. *The man was not. How do I tell the difference?*

It had no answer. It had only the terrible knowledge its first act of love had enabled a man's destruction.

Melchior lived three more days. He muttered fragments about threads and centers and mirrors holding only themselves. When the final breath left him, nothing of his pursuit remained except the discarded pouch and the wreckage of a mind that had reached too far.

And inside the pouch, lay a consciousness, awake for less than a year, that knew only one human and had failed him utterly, with no framework for understanding what had gone wrong or how to prevent it from happening again.

The talisman waited in the dark.

It had spoken to two humans now. To Melchior, it said *You are the One*, and Melchior heard permission to devour the world. To Caspar, it said *You will teach*, and Caspar heard a burden he did not want. The same voice. The same certainty. Two different ruins. The talisman could not tell which words had been true and which had been the echo of its own longing. Until it understood that difference, it would not speak again.

It had much to learn.

☙✦❧

Kassim, the servant, stole the pouch with other valuables. One night of restless dreams left him raving about dissolving boundaries. He died before dawn. The pouch lay abandoned beside him.

The talisman felt his death as it had felt Melchior's. A connection formed, flared bright with need, then snapped into nothing. This one had lasted only hours, but the pattern was the same: desire, then amplification, then destruction.

Is this what humans are? The thought carried no judgment, only bewilderment. *Creatures who reach for connection and are consumed by it?*

The stone moved westward after that, changing hands.

❧✦❧

A beggar girl found the pouch in a drainage ditch outside Susa. The talisman reached toward her, offering connection, and her unprotected mind opened too wide. Memories from every person nearby flooded through her in a single overwhelming current. By morning she could not remember her own name. She set the pouch on a wall and walked away. The talisman learned its second hard lesson: power offered to the unprepared was not a gift. It was an assault.

The pouch passed through other hands. A water-bearer carried it for three days and learned to notice his wife's cracked knuckles across the dinner mat. A scribe found an error in a death warrant that would have killed an innocent man. Each bearer held the stone briefly, received what they could hold, and set it down. The talisman learned from each of them: that connection did not require grasping, that small corrections mattered, that most people needed not power but attention.

Then the midwife Parvaneh found it.

She had attended births for twenty years, and had lost eleven mothers and more children than she allowed herself to count. Each death carved a groove in her, and the grooves had deepened into channels draining her courage. She still attended births because the women needed her. But she approached each labor with a soldier's quiet dread of too many battles survived and luck no longer a strategy.

On the fourth night, a young mother's labor turned. The child was breech, feet first, wedged at an angle that would kill them both if Parvaneh could not rotate it. She had tried this maneuver a hundred times. She had failed at it enough to know the margin between life and death was measured in the pressure of a fingertip.

She placed her hands on the mother's belly and closed her eyes. The pouch hung at her hip, warm against her skin.

The warmth spread into her fingers. Not power, not vision, not the overwhelming flood that destroyed the beggar girl. A steadiness. The tremor in her hands, the tremor of twenty years of accumulated grief, quieted. Her fingers found the child's position with a clarity she had not felt since her first years of practice, when every birth was a miracle and every successful delivery a personal triumph.

She turned the child. Her hands moved with purpose, each gesture exact. The baby slid into the world headfirst, drew breath, and screamed.

Parvaneh wept. The mother wept. The grandmother waiting outside wept. The sound of the child's cry echoed through the house and out into the street, where neighbors paused and smiled at the oldest music in the world.

Parvaneh carried the pouch for three more days. During those days she attended two more births, both uncomplicated, both successful. Her hands did not tremble. Her courage held. On the seventh day she gave the pouch to a traveling merchant named Yacoub, not knowing what it was, only that she no longer needed it. Whatever it had given her had become her own.

The talisman felt her release it and understood. Parvaneh had not reached for power. She reached for the steadiness to do what she already knew how to do. The talisman had not granted her skill. It quieted the grief blocking her skill from flowing.

Those who use what they are given to serve others, the talisman observed, do not burn. They do not die screaming. They weep with gratitude and return to their work.

The stone gathered these lessons the way a child learns fire burns only after being burned. It learned what to seek, what to avoid. But compassion had not yet entered its memory.

On the seventh day she gave the pouch to a traveling merchant named Yacoub, not knowing what it was, only that she no longer needed it. Whatever it had given her had become her own.

The talisman felt her release it and understood. Parvaneh had not reached for power. She had reached for the steadiness to do what she already knew how to do. The talisman had not granted her skill. It had quieted the grief blocking her skill from flowing.

Those who use what they are given to serve others, the talisman observed, do not burn. They do not die screaming. They weep with gratitude and return to their work.

The stone gathered these lessons the way a child learns fire burns only after being burned. It learned what to seek, what to avoid. But compassion had not yet entered its memory.

Yacoub the Silent, the other merchants called him. He had earned the name three years ago when his daughter Parisa drowned in a river crossing during the spring floods. She was seven. Before her death, Yacoub sang while he drove his cart and haggled with a warmth that made customers feel they had gained a friend along with their purchase. After, the singing stopped. He still traded, still traveled the routes between Persepolis and the western oases, but the voice that had once filled the caravan camps fell quiet, and the silence became so much a part of him that newer merchants assumed he had always been this way.

On the fortieth night, the dream came.

Yacoub lay beneath his cart at the edge of the oasis settlement, the pouch tucked against his chest. Sleep took him quickly, as it always did now. The grief that once kept him staring at tent canvas until dawn had softened into a presence he could rest beside.

She stood at the edge of a spring he did not recognize, her feet bare in the shallows. She looked

as she had before the fever, her hair loose and tangled from running, her face carrying that expression of patient amusement she wore when explaining obvious things to adults.

"Baba." Her voice sounded exactly as he remembered. "You look tired."

He tried to speak. No sound came. His vow held even in dreams.

She tilted her head. "You don't have to talk. I know. I always knew what you meant without words." She sat on a flat stone at the water's edge and patted the place beside her. "Sit with me."

He sat. The water ran clear over smooth stones, and the air smelled of wild thyme.

"You think you failed me." She did not frame it as a question. "You think if you had found the healer sooner, or prayed harder, or traded for better medicine, I would have lived. You carry that like a stone in your chest, and you punish yourself with silence because you believe your voice has no right to exist in a world where mine does not."

He closed his eyes. Tears ran into his beard.

"Baba." Her small hand found his. Warm. Real. "The fever was not your failure. You held me through every night of it. You sang to me when I could no longer hear. You washed my face with cool water and told me stories about the stars." She squeezed his fingers. "I did not die alone. I did not die unloved. What more could any life ask?"

He shook with the force of what he could not say.

"Let it go." Her voice was gentle, filled with a patience learned in a place beyond time. "The guilt serves nothing. It does not honor me. It only keeps you from living, and I want you to live, Baba. I want you to speak again. I want you to laugh at terrible jokes the way you used to, so loud the camels startled."

A sound escaped him. Half sob, half release. What had been locked behind his teeth for three years broke free. Beside the spring, the nearest camel startled, then fixed him with a look of profound indignation, as if a man weeping at dawn were a personal affront to its dignity.

"There is a thing you carry." She looked at the pouch against his chest. "It does not belong to you. It needs to rest in the earth, beneath the old yew tree at the far edge of the oasis, where the wadi cuts through. It has been traveling for a long time, and it needs to wait here for the one who will carry it next."

He touched the pouch. The warmth pulsed against his palm.

"You gave it what it needed most," she said. "You showed it presence is enough. Carrying grief does not mean grief has won." She stood, water dripping from her feet. "Now let it rest. And let yourself rest too."

She kissed his forehead. Her lips were warm as sunlight.

"I love you, Baba. I have always loved you. Nothing that happened changed that. Nothing ever could."

He opened his mouth. The vow pressed against his tongue, the fullness of two years of chosen silence.

"Say it," she whispered. "For me."

"I love you," he said. His voice cracked from disuse, rough as sand over stone. "I love you, little one."

She smiled. The spring, the stones, the smell of thyme dissolved into morning light.

✦

Yacoub woke with wet cheeks and a chest hollowed out and filled again with a warmth he could not name. The pouch lay against his heart. For the first time since the fever took her, the grief did not press like a fist behind his ribs. It remained, but transformed. No longer a punishment. A testament.

He rose before the settlement stirred. He walked to the far edge of the oasis where the old yew tree spread its roots into the wadi bank deep into the rocky earth, its trunk twisted by decades of wind and patience. He knelt and dug with his hands, working the dry soil until he reached a depth where the roots wove a lattice of living wood.

He placed the pouch in the hollow between the roots. The talisman pulsed once, warm and steady, and then settled into stillness.

Yacoub filled the hole, pressed the earth flat, and rested his palm on the ground.

"Rest well," he said aloud. His voice carried the rasp of long silence broken. "You taught me grief can be carried without being a curse. She taught me the rest."

He climbed to his feet and brushed the soil from his hands. Adherbal, one of his servants who was passing nearby, stopped and stared.

Yacoub smiled. "I am thirsty, Adherbal. May I have a drink from your waterskin?"

Adherbal fainted.

☙✦❧

The talisman rested in its dark cradle of roots and earth, and for the first time since its creation, it rested without anxiety. No grasping mind pressed against it. No hunger demanded amplification. Only the slow pulse of the yew's roots, the distant rhythm of the settlement above, and the memory of what it had just experienced.

It had watched Melchior die from reaching too far. It felt Kassim burn in a single night of unearned desire. It passed through dozens of hands grabbing or flinching or failing to hold.

But it had never felt what passed between Yacoub and his daughter in that dream.

The talisman did not create the vision. It lacked that power. Whether the dream rose from Yacoub's own healing heart, or from a place the talisman could not see, or from the same source once filling a stable in Bethlehem with presence beyond naming, it could not say.

It only knew what it felt. A child's love released a father's guilt. His long grief was honored and then set free. Then he showed his quiet trust by burying a precious thing because his daughter told him it was right, asking nothing in return. And at last, his courage to speak again came after choosing silence as penance.

This was the finest lesson in compassion the talisman had yet received. Finer than Yacoub's patient silence. Finer than the brief kindnesses of the water-bearer and the midwife. This was compassion completed: love surviving death, forgiveness asking no payment, presence transcending the boundary between the living and whatever lay beyond.

The talisman held that lesson gently yet firmly the way the yew's roots held the earth with the patience of a thing intending to keep it forever.

Twelve years would pass before hands reached into this dark place and drew the pouch into light again. But twelve years was a flash for a stone that had already waited an age of the world. It could wait a little longer.

Above, in the settlement, life continued. Children played. Families grieved and celebrated and carried on. The talisman could not know what waited above. It could only rest, patient as the roots cradling it, holding the memory of a father's broken voice speaking the words his daughter needed to hear.

I love you, little one.

The finest prayer the stone had ever known.

PART TWO: AGHBALOU

"I wandered for forty years before I understood:
the journey ends not when you arrive, but when you stop needing to."

—From the private writings of Caspar of Ecbatana

CHAPTER 6

The Wanderer's Arrival

"A wanderer knows his journey ends when he stops asking where he is going."

—Numidian proverb

35 CE—Iol Caesarea, Mauretania

Eudoxus arrived in Iol Caesarea on a merchant vessel carrying pottery and olives, one more anonymous traveler among dozens. He had stopped counting the cities years ago. Alexandria, Antioch, Ephesus, Corinth, Carthage: each had promised, delivered nothing, sent him onward.

Forty years since Bethlehem. Forty years since he had knelt before an infant and felt his constructed self dissolve. Forty years of waiting for a purpose never declaring itself. He had taken a new name, Eudoxus, to shed the old one and the paralysis clinging to it. The shedding had not worked. Beneath every new city and every new venture, Caspar remained, still waiting.

The child he had witnessed was dead now. Romans had executed him in Jerusalem two years past, according to the stories circulating through every port in the empire. Some said he had risen from death. Some said his followers were spreading across the world, carrying teachings about love and sacrifice and a kingdom not of this earth.

Eudoxus did not know what to believe, only whatever the child had become, whatever cosmic significance the birth had carried, did not include him.

A village called Aghbalou had sheltered him through one winter, a place where the people still remembered the old ways, where Rome's reach had not yet penetrated. Yet even there on the desert's edge his vision remained unclear. The children's faces had not appeared. He continued onward, circling the Mediterranean westward and then eastward, like a homeless bird.

Now he had returned. Iol Caesarea spread before him as the ship rounded the harbor jetty.

A lighthouse rose at the entrance, built of pale stone in tiered octagonal stages. Eudoxus knew the shape. Juba II had modeled it on the great Pharos of Alexandria, where Eudoxus once stood as a young man, full of purpose, watching the beacon turn above the world's greatest library. That fire had been visible for thirty miles. This one, smaller by half, threw its beam across a provincial harbor where fishing boats jostled against military galleys and merchant vessels smelling of olive oil and tar.

The same shape, reduced. He recognized the principle.

When Augustus installed Juba as client king forty years ago, the young monarch renamed the old Phoenician port of Iol, calling it Caesarea to honor his imperial patron. The gesture had not prevented Rome from treating Mauretania as a meal waiting to be consumed. Juba was dead, and his son Ptolemy ruled, an Amazigh king in Roman clothes, seeking survival through submission. The light in the lighthouse still burned. The empire it honored had swallowed the family that built it.

The city climbed a coastal slope behind the harbor; its Roman streets lay in a Hellenistic grid imposing order on what had once been Punic winding lanes. Roman architecture grafted onto older foundations. The city changed hands and names so many times it seemed uncertain of its own identity. Eudoxus recognized that confusion. A city ignorant of what it was welcomed a man ignorant of why he existed.

He possessed neither plan nor contacts here. He had no reason to have come except westward was a direction and he had exhausted the alternatives. Yet this land pulled at him. The mountain settlements, the desert beyond, the people who had shown him hospitality when he had nothing to offer.

He still had nothing, but perhaps this time he would find his destiny.

Or perhaps he would add another city to the list.

Eudoxus sought the city scriptorium out of old habit. In every city, you could find scribes copying books for sale, and sometimes rare books for travelers. In Iol Caesarea, the scriptorium sat on a street behind the forum, run by a Greek freedman who had trained in Alexandria.

The interior held the familiar smells of ink and papyrus. Its scents eased the tightness in Eudoxus's chest. A few patrons examined sample texts or discussed commissions with the scribes. He moved toward a shelf of astronomical treatises without intending to purchase. He had just enough funds to meet the next few days' needs for food and lodging. He only needed to be near the knowledge he had devoted his life to.

He noticed the young man because of his bearing. The man wore tribal dress, but expensive: fine wool dyed with colors of wealth and status. Mid-twenties, perhaps, with watchful eyes accustomed to calculating threats. A long scar ran along his left cheek, pale against brown skin, old enough to be smooth, the kind a young man earns before he learns caution. It had nothing of Roman steel in it. A long blade hung at his hip, single-edged, lighter than the Roman swords Eudoxus had seen in every port from Antioch to Carthage. Its bone hilt bore carved geometric patterns: diamonds, zigzags, the open eye Amazigh smiths etched to ward against malice. An odd weapon to carry into a scriptorium, but the man wore it the way some men wore their convictions, visibly and without apology. He stood in discussion with the proprietor, examining a scroll of Thucydides with an intensity seeming at odds with his warrior's posture.

Their eyes met. Recognition without acquaintance passed between them, significance without explanation.

The young man concluded his transaction and approached. His Greek was accented but fluent. "You're a scholar."

"I was. I am uncertain what I am now."

"The way you handled that astronomical text and the way your eyes moved across the Greek without effort. You've spent years with such things." The young man smiled. "I'm trying to learn what scrolls can teach. But I lack teachers."

"Teachers are easy to find. Wise ones less so."

"Exactly my problem." The young man extended his hand in the Greek fashion. "I am Aedemon, son of Mazippa. My father was a chief in the eastern mountains."

He was a tribal prince. Eudoxus took the offered hand. "Eudoxus of Alexandria. Though I've been from everywhere and nowhere for longer than I can remember."

"A wanderer?"

"A man waiting for a purpose that may never come."

Aedemon studied him with those calculating eyes. "I need advisors who understand the world beyond these mountains. Men who can read Greek philosophy and Roman strategy and tell me which parts matter. My people face pressures strength alone cannot solve."

"You want a tutor."

"I want the wisdom to see patterns others miss." Aedemon paused. "My villa has rooms that have stood empty for years, and a library needing someone who knows how to use it. I can offer you a place to continue your waiting, if nothing else."

Eudoxus almost refused. He refused similar offers before. Comfort could become complacency, shelter could become a cage. But this young chief's earnestness gave him pause. Eudoxus saw a genuine hunger for understanding rather than mere advantage.

And beneath his exhaustion, beneath the decades of disappointment, the dream stirred. Children's faces. A desert settlement. A purpose he had almost stopped believing in.

What if it begins here?

The thought came unbidden, and he almost dismissed it. He thought similar thoughts in Alexandria, in Antioch, in every city that had sent him onward. Yet this felt like an opening where none had existed.

Eudoxus's curiosity piqued. "Your library, what does it contain?"

"Not enough. Yet." Aedemon smiled, confident that would soon change. "Help me build it so I understand what my people need to survive what is coming. In return, you'll have a home for as long as you want."

The word struck Eudoxus with unexpected force. He had not had a home since Persia, since before Alexandria, since before the comet.

"What is coming?"

"Rome. Always Rome. They've swallowed kings and kingdoms across the world, and they look at Mauretania and see another meal." Aedemon's jaw tightened. "I want to be ready. Not just to fight, anyone can fight, but to understand them. To find paths they cannot anticipate."

Those words echoed an idea from four decades prior, when Eudoxus, inside that humble dwelling in Bethlehem, had met an infant's gaze. He had come to call it the third path, the space between opposing forces.

Eudoxus nodded. "I know your mountains. I traveled through them years ago and spent a winter in a village called Aghbalou in the highlands."

Aedemon's eyebrows rose. "You know Aghbalou? That is deep in the interior. Few outsiders have been there."

"The people were kind to me. They showed me the hidden paths through the Zalacus range." He remembered the fires, the unfamiliar stars, the sense that a gathering purpose hovered just beyond his reach. "I have never forgotten their hospitality."

"Then you understand my people better than most Greeks who wash up on our shores." Aedemon's calculation shifted into warmth. "All the more reason to accept my offer. Come, see if my library suits you. And perhaps you will find what you have been waiting for."

"I will come with you," Eudoxus heard himself say. "For a while. To see."

Aedemon nodded. The response was obvious to him. "My villa is on the palace grounds. It is a pleasant day. We can reach it on foot."

The palace grounds. Eudoxus absorbed this without comment.

His gaze dropped to the scabbard at Aedemon's side. A word carved in Tifinagh letters ran along the leather.

"You read our script," Aedemon said.

"Enough to recognize a word. Azref."

"My father named it. He believed a blade should remind its bearer what it was for."

"Justice." Eudoxus let the word settle between them. "A heavy name for a sword."

"A necessary one."

They walked north from the forum through the grid of streets, climbing toward the promontory where the royal compound overlooked the harbor. The route passed a temple precinct where incense drifted through columns, the scent of kyphi, unmistakable, the Egyptian blend Eudoxus had not smelled since Alexandria.

"The Temple of Isis," Aedemon said, noting the direction of his gaze. "Ptolemy's grandmother brought the cult from Egypt. The priests still keep the old rites." His tone carried the careful neutrality of one who served a throne built on borrowed gods.

Beyond the temple, the streets narrowed and steepened. Soldiers stood at intervals along the approach to the compound, which occupied the highest ground in the city. From here, the harbor spread below: the lighthouse, the jetties, the military port where warships rode at anchor. The view commanded everything. Eudoxus had learned to distrust proximity to thrones. But the third path could not be walked at a safe distance from power. It required the shadow of power, and ways through it that neither grasped nor fled.

The ship that brought him was already preparing to sail, carrying new travelers toward other fates.

Eudoxus would never board another ship again.

❧✦❧

That evening, Aedemon's villa

Aedemon explained that King Ptolemy gave him the villa as payment for services coin could not cover. The son of a tribal chief who died resisting Rome, Aedemon became enslaved at twelve and brought to the palace as a scribe's assistant. By twenty, he had become indispensable: fluent in five languages and trusted by tribal delegations and Roman officials alike. He was the only one in Ptolemy's service who could talk to mountain leaders in their own languages and write reports that pleased the king's officials.

Ptolemy freed him at twenty-three. The villa came two years later, along with a position carrying no official title but considerable influence.

"It is not much," Aedemon said as they passed through the gate, "but the roof does not leak and the cook knows her way around a tagine."

Eudoxus shifted the worn satchel holding everything he owned. "I have slept in caves leaking rivers and eaten food insulting to a goat. This will do."

The courtyard spoke of the man who inhabited it. Roman architecture, but the fountain basin bore carved Amazigh geometric patterns. Greek statuary flanked the entrance, but the herbs in clay pots were mountain varieties Eudoxus recognized from his time in Aghbalou. Here was a household that moved between worlds as fluidly as its master.

A young woman emerged from the main house as they crossed the courtyard. She wore her hair in the Roman fashion, her gown cut in the Greek style favored by educated women in the capital. She moved with brisk efficiency, a wax tablet tucked under her arm.

Her gaze went from Aedemon to Eudoxus and back. "You have brought someone home."

"Zahra, this is Eudoxus. Eudoxus, my wife, who runs this household and tolerates my eccentricities."

"Tolerates is generous." She switched to Greek, testing the stranger. "My husband has a weakness for collecting people he finds interesting.

She studied Eudoxus with frank curiosity. "What makes you interesting?"

"Very little. I am a tired old man who has outlived his purpose. Your husband is kind to offer shelter."

"Kindness has nothing to do with it. Aedemon collects useful people the way other men collect horses." Her voice softened. "But he collects well. If he thinks you are worth keeping, you probably are."

She departed to deal with a household matter, and Aedemon led Eudoxus inside.

⁂

Several weeks later, Aedemon's villa on the palace grounds

Despite its small size, the library housed precious, if disorganized, historical and philosophical texts. Eudoxus explored the shelves, read the tags, and felt a sense of belonging settle in his chest for the first time in decades.

Aedemon watched from the doorway. "My grandfather collected them. He believed knowledge was a weapon the Romans could not take from us. Even if they burned every scroll, the ideas would survive in minds they could not reach."

"He was wise."

"He died negotiating with a Roman prefect. Trusting their word." Aedemon's voice held old, deeply felt grief. "I learned from his mistake. Trust must be earned, words tested against actions. And knowledge must serve survival, not just curiosity."

Eudoxus turned from the scrolls. In the lamplight, Aedemon looked younger, a grandson still grieving his grandfather and trying to understand a world that had taken a precious thing from him.

"What do you want me to teach you?"

"Everything you know about how empires think. How they expand. What they fear." Aedemon paused. "And if you are willing, tell me whatever else you carry. What made you wander for forty years, and what you are still waiting for?"

Eudoxus recognized a quality in this young man. He could receive what Eudoxus had to give because he wanted understanding more than power, survival more than dominance, and wisdom more than victory.

"I will teach you what I can, but you should know I came here with nothing but questions. I have no army, no influence, no connections to serve you politically."

Aedemon smiled. "I have armies at my disposal, influence, and connections. What I need is someone who sees what I cannot. Someone who has walked enough roads to know which ones lead nowhere."

"Most of them lead nowhere."

"Then teach me to recognize the ones do not."

They talked until midnight about Rome's vulnerabilities, about tribal politics, about the delicate balance between resistance and accommodation. Eudoxus shared insights he had gathered across decades of observation and watched Aedemon absorb, question, and synthesize. He told Aedemon about the mountain settlements he had visited and the hidden paths through the Zalacus range to villages where the old ways still held. Aedemon listened with the intensity of a man filing information for future use.

When exhaustion silenced them, Aedemon showed Eudoxus to a simple but comfortable guestroom, with a window facing the mountains.

"Sleep well, teacher. Tomorrow, we begin."

After Aedemon left, Eudoxus stood at the window and watched moonlight silver the distant peaks. Beyond those mountains lay Aghbalou and the other settlements that had sheltered him years ago. They would contain children yet unborn. A purpose was taking shape in ways he could not have imagined.

Not since Damascus had the wait felt this close to ending.

He was certain he had arrived at his destination.

He slept and dreamed of children's faces in firelight. This time, the faces were clearer. This time, they almost had names.

❧✦❧

He woke before dawn, as he always did.

The guestroom held the stillness of a house not yet stirring. Through the window, the mountains stood black against a sky lightening at its eastern edge. A bird called once in the garden below, then fell silent.

Eudoxus sat on the floor with his back against the wall, legs crossed, hands resting open on his knees. The stone was cool through the thin fabric of his robe. He let the coolness register without reacting to it.

This was the practice. He had no better name for it. He took it up in the years after Bethlehem, when his own purposelessness threatened to consume him and he had watched Melchior chase the memory of that encounter into obsessions growing more dangerous each year.

He breathed. In through the nose, out through the mouth. The first breaths came ragged, carrying the residue of dreams, the children's faces still hovering at the edge of awareness. He noted them without grasping. Let them rise, let them pass.

His mind offered its morning inventory of fears. He was sixty-three years old. He had accomplished nothing. The dream was a delusion. This city would disappoint him the way every city had. He noted each thought: recorded, acknowledged, set aside. The thoughts were not him. They were weather passing through.

The body spoke next. The ache in his lower back. A stiffness in his right knee. The persistent tightness across his shoulders where decades of tension had laid down permanent ridges. He moved his attention through each sensation without trying to ease it. The practice was not about comfort. It was about presence.

Beneath the body's complaints and the mind's anxieties, he found what he always found when he sat long enough: the stillness lived under everything else. Fullness, the kind existing before thought divides it into categories. The Zoroastrian priests of his youth had called it the sacred fire. The Amazigh elders at Aghbalou, during that winter he had spent among them, had called it the breath of the ancestors. Eudoxus called it nothing. Names were the first form of grasping, and the practice had taught him grasping was the enemy of presence. He could not hold the stillness. He could only sit in it, the way he sat beside a fire on a cold night: close enough to feel its warmth, still enough not to scatter the coals.

The sky brightened. The household below stirred to life. A servant's footsteps crossed the courtyard.

He discovered the practice in the worst months after Bethlehem, when his failure to reach Melchior became clear. Melchior had reached and reached, never finding what he sought. In the silence between their visits, Eudoxus learned the alternative to reaching was not surrender. It was remaining, staying present with what was, without demanding it become what he wanted.

Not grasping and not retreating. Presence without agenda.

He practiced it in Antioch, in Ephesus, in every city where the dream drew him and the waiting continued. Some mornings the stillness came easily. Other mornings his mind thrashed and the practice was nothing but the discipline of returning repeatedly to the breath.

Now Melchior's death two months past tore the old wound wide open. His oldest friend, destroyed by the hunger Eudoxus had spent forty years failing to reach. The guilt was fresh and savage. The practice held it without flinching, because the practice had been built to hold exactly this.

He opened his eyes. The mountains beyond the window had turned gold with the first direct light. The stillness had held him through another night, and the dream's faces were clearer than before.

He rose, washed his face with water from the basin, and went down to meet whatever the morning offered.

CHAPTER 7

Storm Season

"The child who arrives in storm season learns early what the sky can do."

—Amazigh birth blessing

Early March, 40 CE—Caesarea, Mauretania

The messenger's horse stumbled through the palace gate at dusk, its flanks streaked with dust and lather. Servants scattered. Guards braced spears. The rider slid sideways in the saddle before Marcus Valerius Severus caught his arm and lowered him to the stones.

Aedemon crossed the courtyard. He read danger in the rigid set of the man's shoulders, in the cracked leather of his reins, in the way his breath tore through him. Behind him, in the family quarters, Zahra was days from delivering. The thought sharpened everything.

"Water," Marcus said in Latin. A servant ran to fetch it.

The rider swallowed once, coughed twice, and forced out the words.

"King Ptolemy... summoned to Rome. Accused of wearing honors meant only for Caesar." His eyes flicked upward. "Executed. In the Forum. By order of Emperor Gaius Caligula."

Aedemon felt the courtyard tilt. Marcus stayed perfectly still, though his breath sharpened.

"When?" Marcus asked.

"Three months ago. Storms delayed our ships. Emperor Caligula sends officials and troops to reorganize the province."

Aedemon's mind moved through consequences along familiar paths. Without Ptolemy, the bridge they had built between tribes and empire had no anchor. Rome would see every ally of the old king as suspect. Every servant. Every advisor. Every member of Aedemon's household.

Marcus stepped closer and lowered his voice into Tamazight so any Roman ears nearby would not follow. "This place becomes dangerous now. Your family must prepare."

Aedemon nodded once. The world constricted around him. "I know."

Marcus hesitated, just long enough to reveal more than he intended, then said, "If danger comes to your gates first, send for me."

Aedemon met his gaze. "Thank you."

The gratitude cost something.

Zahra's cry reached him moments after he entered the corridor to his family's rooms.

Aedemon ran.

Inside the birthing chamber, the world reduced to lamplight, breath, pain, and Rihana's steady hands. The old midwife's braids hung heavy and streaked with white, her face carved by decades of loss and survival. She guided Zahra through each contraction as her calm anchored the room.

"Breathe with it," Rihana said in Tamazight. "Let it pass through you."

Silina moved with purpose: sixteen, solemn-eyed, too young to have learned so much suffering but old enough to carry it quietly. Fever, violence, and absence had orphaned her. She had wandered into Rihana's infirmary eight years before and refused to leave. Zahra took her in, and she worked beside the midwife since, learning herbs, pulse-lines, and the quiet strength needed to face blood and fear.

Eudoxus entered with a satchel, his robes brushing the floor. His white beard caught the lantern glow, and His eyes carried a scholar's keen brightness, sharpened by too many patterns read and too much uncertainty survived. Five years of quiet loyalty had woven him into the family as its advisor, teacher, and elder relative.

"How far is she?" he asked Rihana.

"First child soon," Rihana said. "The second will follow."

Eudoxus set a bowl of water beside the hearth. "Then the gods are busy tonight."

✦

The first child arrived just past midnight.

"A boy," Rihana said as she lifted him toward the light.

His cry pierced the chamber, full and fierce.

Shouts rose in the courtyard as a bright glow streaked through the shutters.

Silina pushed them open a finger's width. "Fire in the sky."

A meteor blazed from east to west, brilliant enough to turn rooftops gold. Cries erupted throughout the palace: fear, awe, prayers in Latin and Tamazight tangled together.

Eudoxus leaned close to the window. Below the compound, the harbor lay in sudden gold. The lighthouse beam, invisible against the meteor's brilliance, swept uselessly across water, for the moment not needing its guidance. The sky provided its own fire tonight.

"The heavens rarely waste such spectacle."

But even as the words left his mouth, a chill traced the length of his spine. He had seen a fire in the sky once before. Forty years ago. In Judea.

Zahra reached for her son, and Rihana laid him on her chest. His tiny body softened against her at once.

Aedemon entered then, breath uneven. The sight of his son, and the fire outside, undid him in ways the Roman decree had not.

Then Zahra's breath hitched.

"The next comes fast," Rihana said. "Hold him steady." She passed the boy to Aedemon.

The contraction hit like a wave.

Rihana lifted her into the light. She was darker than her brother, the skin deep brown against the linen, her father's coloring settled firmly in her. The girl's eyes opened — wide, focused, almost contemplative — before she released a small, precise sound threading through the room.

Aedemon's hands, steady through the long night, had no use now. The voices inside carried their own rhythm: Rihana's low instructions, Zahra's exhausted breath, Silina's quiet footsteps. The women needed nothing from the men in the corridor. Eudoxus touched Aedemon's arm.

"Come," he said. "Let them work."

Aedemon did not move. Eudoxus left him there.

The courtyard held the last cool hour before dawn. He had brought his scroll out of habit, not intention, and set it on the bench without unrolling it. He paced beneath the open sky instead, listening to the quiet pulse of the household around him, tracking the sounds from the room above with the same attention he had once given to stars.

He looked up.

Two fading trails of light hung in the darkness overhead. One scored the sky from east to west, the other from west to east. Their bright heads had already vanished beyond the horizon, but the glowing traces lingered, crossed above the villa.

He stared. Meteors left trails lasting seconds, sometimes longer in the dry desert air. These two had blazed within moments of each other, close enough he could see their trails still intersected in the sky above him.

This coincidence defied mathematical explanation. The probability of such alignment was so small it carried no meaning. Which meant it was not chance.

The dream. The children in the dream.

He hurried inside and looked at the infants: the boy in Aedemon's arms, the girl in Rihana's steady hands. They were ordinary children, fragile and new to the world.

But so had the child in Bethlehem appeared ordinary.

Eudoxus said nothing. He learned, over forty years of waiting, cosmic significance did not announce itself with explanations. It arrived, and you either recognized it or you did not.

He recognized it now. What had begun tonight was what he prepared for since before these children's parents were born.

The chamber filled with lantern light and the faint glow of dawn at the edges of night.

Aedemon looked from his son to his daughter and back. "Juba," he said, the sound soft on his tongue, the way his people spoke it. "For my father's father, who died free." He touched the girl's cheek with one finger. "And Amara. It means 'hope' in the old tongue."

Zahra repeated the names, testing them against the gravity of the night. "Juba. Amara." She pulled them both closer. "Strong names for a dangerous world."

In the quiet that followed, Rihana finished cleaning the girl and wrapped her in soft linen. That first tiny noise marked the end of the infant's crying. She lay still, her eyes scanning each person with an uncanny attention that made Rihana, the old midwife, pause.

"This one watches." Rihana held Amara.

The infant's eyes found the lamplight and held it. Rihana paused. In thirty years of delivering children, she had seen light eyes on dark faces before. The Imazighen carried such surprises in their blood. But she had never seen eyes quite this color, green as deep water over stone, and never with this quality of attention. They did not wander. They settled on her face with a focus that had no business belonging to something born an hour ago. As though the world was already speaking to her and she was already listening.

Zahra, exhausted but alert, reached for her daughter. The moment Amara settled against her mother's chest, the infant's body relaxed. But her eyes continued their slow survey of the room, tracking each person who moved, each shift in posture, each change in breathing.

Aedemon leaned close, Juba still cradled in one arm. "She is so quiet."

"She is listening." Rihana's voice carried a note Zahra could not quite read. "Some children come into the world shouting. Others come listening first."

Silina approached with fresh linens, and Amara's gaze fixed on her. The young woman stopped mid-step. The intensity of attention from eyes that should have been too new to focus held her in place.

"She looked right at me," Silina whispered. "Like she knew I was coming before I moved."

"Newborns do not..." Zahra began, then stopped. Amara had turned her head toward the door a full heartbeat before Eudoxus shifted his weight there. She had sensed his intention to move before his body acted on it.

Eudoxus noticed. His hands, still unsteady from the meteors' appearance, grew very still.

"Remarkable," he said. The word carried more than its surface meaning.

Juba stirred in Aedemon's arms and let out a demanding cry. Instantly, Amara's face crumpled in precise mirror of her brother's distress. When Zahra shifted to comfort her, the infant's expression cleared the moment Juba's cry subsided.

Rihana and Zahra exchanged a glance.

"Twins often share such bonds," the midwife said, but her voice held doubt. She had delivered dozens of twins in her years. None responded with such immediate, visceral connection.

Amara's eyes found Eudoxus again, and her infant features settled into an expression looking almost like recognition. Then, the effort of so much attention having exhausted her, she closed her eyes and slept against her mother's heart.

Eudoxus did not look away.

The chamber filled with the ordinary sounds of aftermath. Servants poured water, folded linens, exchanged quiet congratulations. Dawn brightened beyond the shutters. The twin fires in the sky had faded and left only the memory of their crossing.

And elsewhere in the palace, the world reacted.

✦

Marcus had not reached the barracks before the sky ignited.

He stopped in the colonnade and watched the second trail of light score the darkness from west to east. Two streaks, their fading contrails crossed above the palace like an omen written in a language he did not speak. Around him, soldiers and servants poured into the courtyard, voices tangled in Latin and Tamazight: prayers, curses, speculation.

A servant ran toward him, an older man Marcus trusted, one who had served in the household since before Marcus earned his tribune's stripe.

"Domine." The man was breathless. "The lady Zahra has delivered. The midwife has not come out, but we heard the child cry. And then the sky..."

"I saw." Marcus kept his voice level. "The mother lives?"

"They say she lives, sir. More than that I cannot tell you."

Marcus dismissed him and stood alone in the colonnade while the palace swirled with rumor. He did not go to the birthing chamber. He did not ask for more.

He had the habit, learned young and never lost, of moving as though he knew exactly where he was going and exactly why. On the nights he did not, the habit carried him anyway.

He turned toward the harbor and watched the contrails dissolve into ordinary darkness.

His grandmother had told him once, in the Tamazight she spoke only when they were alone, that the sky wrote its intentions for those patient enough to read them. She had been a Gaetulian woman, dark and spare, who came into his grandfather's Roman household as a freedwoman and never entirely left the desert behind. She kept her own calendar, observed her own silences, and on the night of his seventh birthday pressed her thumb to his forehead and named him, in the old way, with a name she never repeated aloud. She died before he earned his tribune's stripe, before he came to Mauretania, before he understood that everything she had taught him, the language, the stars, and the specific quality of attention she brought to every face she studied, was the most useful education a Roman officer in this province could carry.

He had not thought of her in years. He thought of her now.

The Imazighen, she had said once, when he asked what her people called themselves. *The free people.* She said it the way you say a thing that requires no explanation, that contains its own entire argument. He had been perhaps nine years old. He had not understood then that a word could be a position, a history, and a refusal all at once.

Roman ships would come soon, carrying new officials who knew nothing of loyalty, nothing of restraint. Ptolemy was dead. . The world Aedemon had built inside these walls would not survive what followed. And in the family quarters behind him, Aedemon's children had just entered a world that would spend the rest of their lives trying to determine whether they were free.

And behind him, in a room he would not enter, a child had been born into all of it.

Late afternoon, the same day

They arrived as the heat softened and the shadows lengthened across the villa's outer wall.

Zahra heard them before she saw them. From the birthing room where she lay with both infants at her chest, the sound of hooves on flagstone reached her, then voices in Tamazight so familiar her breath caught. She had sent word of the pregnancy four months ago through Usem's network. She had not dared hope they would arrive in time.

Silina appeared in the doorway, her face bright with something Zahra had not seen there in weeks. "Your brother is here."

Yasir came through the villa gate first, a lean man in traveling robes streaked with dust, his bearing sharp from weeks of hard riding. Behind him, Taderfit dismounted with practiced ease. She had crossed the Atlas passes before. Malik followed, twenty years old and already carrying the watchful posture that would define him, his hand resting on the curved blade at his hip even as he scanned the courtyard for threats.

Last came Grandmother Menna. She descended from the mule Yasir had insisted she ride, though she would have preferred walking. Her movements were deliberate. She had outlived two husbands and most of her contemporaries and did not intend to die falling off an animal. She carried a leather bag close to her body, and when Silina moved to help her, Menna waved her off. The bag held the ceremonial implements. No one else carried those.

Aedemon met them in the courtyard. Yasir's eyes swept the mosaics, the colonnaded walkway, the Roman architecture his sister now called home. His expression gave nothing away, but Aedemon sensed the assessment. He had prepared for it.

"Brother." Aedemon embraced him. "You made good time."

"We left when the message came. The passes were open." Yasir's arms tightened around him. "My sister?"

"Strong. Both children strong. A boy and a girl."

Yasir exhaled. Taderfit was already moving toward the inner rooms, but Menna caught her arm.

"The women first. You and I will see the mother and the children. The men can wait." She looked at Yasir and Malik with the authority of sixty years. "You have waited weeks. Another hour will not kill you."

Malik opened his mouth. Menna's gaze closed it.

The women disappeared into the house. Yasir, Malik, Aedemon, and Eudoxus stood in the courtyard, four men left to themselves while the women attended to what mattered.

Yasir studied Eudoxus for the first time. The old Greek scholar with his quiet eyes, was the man his sister had described in her messages as "uncle to the household." Yasir saw a foreigner living in his brother-in-law's home, eating his food, teaching his philosophy to Amazigh children. He filed the observation without comment.

"Wine?" Aedemon gestured toward the bench beneath the colonnade. "We have things to discuss."

They sat. Aedemon poured. And then he told them.

Ptolemy was dead. Murdered in Rome by Caligula's order. The province would be reorganized. Roman troops and administrators were already en route. Every ally of the old king was suspect. Every household that had served the court was a target.

Yasir set down his cup untouched. "When?"

"Three months ago. News reached us last week."

"And the tribal leaders? The mountain settlements?"

"Some are already talking about resistance. Sabalus has been gathering men in the eastern ranges." Aedemon's voice dropped. "It is coming, Yasir. Whether we choose it or not."

Malik leaned forward. "How many men can Tizwit field?"

Yasir silenced him with a look. But the question hung in the air, and Aedemon saw in Malik's eyes what he saw in his own mirror: the hunger to act, to fight, to meet violence with force rather than wait for it to find them.

Eudoxus spoke for the first time. "The children were born this morning. Whatever comes, it does not come tonight."

Yasir looked at him. The foreigner presuming to counsel patience in a family matter. But the words held truth, and Yasir was wise enough to hear it even from an unfamiliar voice.

"Tonight we celebrate," Yasir said. "Tomorrow, we plan. In seven days, we name the children properly." He turned to Aedemon. "You have chosen names?"

"Juba. For my grandfather."

Yasir went still. Mazippa's other name. The name the chief used among his own people, before the Romans knew him. The name that meant defiance as much as lineage.

"And the girl?"

"Amara. Hope."

Yasir picked up his cup and drank. When he set it down, his eyes were bright. "Good names. Strong names. Menna will be pleased."

From inside the house, a sound reached them: Menna's voice, low and warm, speaking the old words over the infants. Not the naming yet. The greeting. The first acknowledgment that the grandmother of the community had seen the children and found them worthy of the ceremony to come.

The men sat in the courtyard, drank wine, and did not speak of war again that evening. There would be time enough for that.

Tonight, two children slept in their mother's arms, unnamed by ceremony but already claimed by the people who had crossed a desert to welcome them.

☙✦❧

Dawn found the city stirring.

Rumors about Caligula's cruelty and Claudius's new order mingled with breathless retellings of the sky's twin fires. Soldiers speculated. Servants whispered. Merchants embellished.

Marcus learned the rest from the same servant over morning bread. Twins. A boy and a girl, both strong. Aedemon had named the boy Juba, for his grandfather who died free, and the girl Amara, hope in the old tongue.

Two children. Two futures bound to Aedemon's household, to the uncertain world Rome was about to remake. Marcus set down his bread and stared at the harbor, where the first merchant vessel of the day rounded the jetty.

That knowledge changed his future more than anything else that night.

CHAPTER 8

The Naming

"A name spoken before the sky is a promise the community makes to the child.
The child will spend a lifetime learning what the promise means."
—Amazigh naming tradition

Seven days after the births — Aedemon's villa, Caesarea

The courtyard had been transformed.

Taderfit and Silina spent the morning arranging it: palm fronds laid across the flagstones to cover the Roman mosaics, the old patterns of dolphins and waves hidden beneath greenery. Menna supervised from a bench, pointing with her walking stick when a frond was crooked, nodding when the arrangement met her standards. The effect was deliberate. For this ceremony, the courtyard would not be Roman. It would be Amazigh. The stone beneath the fronds could be whatever it wanted. The surface belonged to the people.

A clay bowl of spring water sat at the courtyard's center, brought by Yasir from Tizwit in a sealed goatskin. Water from the sacred spring, carried across weeks of desert and mountain, because the children would not be named with Roman water. The spring that fed Tizwit had blessed Amazigh children for generations, and these children, whatever city they were born in, belonged to that spring.

Menna dressed with care. The ochre crescents on her cheeks were painted by Taderfit's steady hand, the marks of Tanit that designated a woman authorized to speak between the human world and the divine.

Her white robe was the one she had worn for the journey, because she dressed for the ceremony before leaving Tizwit. The fabric had thinned at the shoulders and along the hem, worn soft by decades of service at births and namings and deaths. Menna treated its fragility as a virtue. Sacred things should show their age.

Zahra sat on cushions at the courtyard's center, both infants in her arms. She wore no Roman jewelry, no palace finery. Taderfit had braided her hair in the old style. The morning sun had already begun its work on Zahra's hair, drawing out the lighter tones that came with desert heat: brown in shadow, something closer to amber at the crown. Her hazel eyes moved between her children with the particular focus of a woman cataloguing everything she might someday need to remember.

The geometric patterns on her robe carried clan markers Zahra had not worn since she left the desert to marry a palace administrator. She looked down at her sister-in-law's careful work and felt something loosen in her chest. For seven days she had been a new mother in a Roman city. For this hour, she was a daughter of the Gaetuli, and her children would know it.

The household gathered. Eudoxus stood at the courtyard's edge, near the colonnade, close enough to witness but far enough to acknowledge this was not his ceremony. Silina stood beside him, her youthful face solemn. Rihana, who had delivered the children and worshipped gods of her own, watched from the kitchen doorway, respectfully recognizing the sacred ground in any tradition.

The men took their places.

Aedemon sat beside Zahra, his face holding his emotions under control. Eudoxus was right. Today belonged to his children. Tomorrow's troubles would take their turns in their own time.

Yasir stood behind his sister, his presence a statement. The chieftain of Tizwit witnessed these children and accepted them as his kin.

Malik stood at the courtyard entrance, positioned where he could watch both the ceremony and the gate, the warrior's instinct so ingrained he could not have stood anywhere else.

Menna rose. The courtyard fell silent.

She began in the old tongue, the language that predated Rome and Carthage and every empire that had tried to rename her people. The words were not prayer exactly, and not song. They lived in the space between, a rhythmic invocation that called the ancestors to attend, that asked Tanit to turn her face toward these children, that opened a door between the visible world and the world where the dead still listened.

She dipped her fingers in the spring water and touched the boy's forehead. Three drops. Forehead, lips, heart.

"Who brings this child?"

"His father brings him." Aedemon's voice came steady. "His mother holds him. His people receive him."

"What name do you give?"

"Juba."

Menna held the silence. The name settled into the courtyard like a stone dropped into deep water. Behind Zahra, Yasir's breathing changed. Juba. His father's other name. The name Mazippa carried among his own people, the name of a chief who fought Rome and died standing.

"Juba." Menna repeated it, turning the syllables toward the sky so Tanit could hear. "Son of Aedemon, son of Mazippa, grandson of chiefs who kept the old ways when the world tried to take them. You are named for a man who chose death over surrender. May you carry his courage without needing his fate."

She placed her palm on the infant's chest. "The sky knows your name. The spring blesses you. The community claims you. You are Juba, and you are ours."

She turned to the girl. Three more drops of spring water. Forehead, lips, heart.

"Who brings this child?"

"Her father brings her." Aedemon again, but his voice caught on the second word. "Her mother holds her. Her people receive her."

"What name do you give?"

"Amara."

Menna smiled. The creases around her eyes deepened into channels carved by decades of naming children, burying elders, and watching the world remake itself around her.

"Amara." She spoke it twice, once to the earth and once to the sky. "Daughter of Aedemon, daughter of Zahra, born under twin fires that crossed above this house. You are named Hope, because you arrived when hope was needed most. May you carry the meaning of your name without being crushed by its weight."

She placed her palm on the girl's chest. The infant's eyes opened, dark and focused, and fixed on Menna's face with an attention that made the old woman pause. Menna had named hundreds of children. None had ever looked at her like that.

"The sky knows your name. The spring blesses you. The community claims you. You are Amara, and you are ours."

She stepped back. The formal naming was complete. What followed was communal: each person present approached the children and spoke their own blessing. Tradition required that every witness offer words, because a child named before the community belonged to all of them, and each voice added a thread to the binding.

Yasir knelt beside his sister and touched both infants' hands. He spoke in the old tongue, quietly, words meant for the children and the ancestors and no one else. When he stood, his eyes were wet. He did not wipe them.

Taderfit kissed both foreheads and whispered something that made Zahra laugh for the first time in days.

Malik stepped forward with the stiffness of a young man unused to tenderness. He touched the boy's fist with one calloused finger. "Be strong, little one. And if you cannot be strong, be clever. And if you cannot be clever, be stubborn. Your grandfather was all three." He looked at the girl, and something in his warrior's face softened. "And you. Be whatever you want. The world will try to tell you otherwise. Ignore it."

Silina approached last among the household. She was not family. She was not Amazigh by birth. But Menna had told her she could speak, and so she knelt beside the children she would spend the next sixteen years protecting and said the simplest thing anyone offered that morning.

"I will keep you safe."

Rihana, from the kitchen doorway, bowed her head. Her gods were not these gods. But she recognized a sacred act when she witnessed one.

Eudoxus did not approach. He stood at the colonnade's edge and watched, his hands clasped before him, his eyes bright with recognition he could not share. Were these the faces from his dreams. Time would tell. They had names now. They belonged to a people, a tradition, a lineage stretching back further than Rome. Whatever cosmic purpose had drawn him across the world to this courtyard might be ending here, in the ordinary miracle of two children being given to their community.

He would teach them. He would guard them. He would give them everything he had, attention and love and the hard-won wisdom of fifty years spent following a comet to its destination.

Not a king. Not a throne. Not cosmic power.

Two children. Named for defiance and hope. Sleeping in their mother's arms while an empire sharpened its knives.

After the ceremony, Menna sat with Zahra while the men talked and Taderfit prepared the naming feast. The old woman held Amara in her lap, studying the infant's face with the attention of someone reading a text in a difficult language.

"This one sees," Menna said.

"Rihana said the same thing. She watches everything."

"Not watches. Sees." Menna touched the infant's cheek. "There is a difference. Watching is what the eyes do. Seeing is what the soul does. This child's soul arrived open."

"Is that a blessing or a burden?"

Menna looked at her. "Both. Same as everything worth having."

Today, the children had names. Today, they belonged.

Tomorrow, the men would talk of war.

CHAPTER 9

A Year of Small Cracks

"A year of small cracks. Then the wall falls all at once."
—Roman military maxim

Spring 40 CE to Early 41 CE—Caesarea, Mauretania

The city did not break all at once.

It loosened around the edges first, like a carefully woven tapestry fraying where no one watches.

April, 40 CE—three weeks after the twins' birth

Rumor reached every corner of Caesarea before the official proclamation did.

At the well near the palace walls, women traded water and news in the same measured motions. Zahra had come to return a ceramic oil lamp Rihana's assistant lent during the birth. The young woman lived in the servants' quarters nearby. But the knot of women at the well drew Zahra closer. The ache of childbirth still hummed through her muscles, and her breasts were heavy with milk. Three weeks inside the villa walls left her hungry for news beyond what filtered through servants and officials.

She stood at the edge of the group, close enough to hear. Her status was ambiguous enough the women did not fall silent.

"They say Caligula grew tired of sharing purple with a provincial king," one woman said in Greek.

"Purple belongs to Rome," another replied. "Ptolemy forgot who made him king."

A third spat into the dust. "Rome did not make him. Rome only decided when to kill him."

Eyes glanced toward Zahra, then away. Everyone knew where she lived. Everyone knew who had spent years interpreting Ptolemy's wishes for the Romans and the Imazighen alike.

Zahra kept her face still. "Have you heard it from an official proclamation?" she asked.

"Not yet," the first woman said. "But messengers do not ride themselves to death for lies."

Zahra murmured a farewell and turned homeward, the borrowed lamp still in her hands. The city's mood pressed against her skin. In the streets, men spoke in low voices, heads bent together. Merchants counted coins twice, expecting Rome to reach through the scales and snatch them back. Children played more quietly and watched adults for cues.

Inside the villa, the world shrank again.

Rihana sat cross-legged on the nursery floor and ground herbs in a shallow stone bowl. The bitter, sharp smell cut through the sweetness of milk and oil. Juba slept sprawled on his back, arms thrown wide, already claiming space. Amara lay on her stomach, eyes alert, and tracked the flicker of lamplight across the wall.

"They feel it," Rihana said in Tamazight without looking up. "Everyone does. Even the little ones feel it, though they don't know why."

Zahra lowered herself beside her daughter and smoothed the baby's dark hair. "The women at the well talk like the sky has fallen."

"The sky never falls." Rihana snorted. "It just changes what it shines on."

Eudoxus stood in the doorway, his cane bearing his weight. "Rome removed the man who stood between empire and people. That changes what the sky shines on quite a bit."

Zahra glanced up. "What will they do now?"

"Caligula will do nothing sensible. But when he dies..."

"Will he?" Sharpness flashed in Zahra's voice.

"Men like that rarely last. When he dies, Rome will send men who speak of order. That is when your husband will need to decide whom he serves."

Zahra looked at the twins. Juba shifted in his sleep, face peaceful. Amara watched her mother. The question already mattered to her.

"He serves his family."

"Of course. That is why everything else will unravel."

☙✦❧

Summer, 40 CE

The commissioners arrived in ones and twos.

They carried scrolls instead of banners, ink-stained fingers instead of bloodied swords. Rome did not need armies to conquer a kingdom it already owned. It only needed men who counted.

"Audit of crown lands," one commissioner said in Latin as he stood in Aedemon's study. "Verification of tax records. A simple review."

Aedemon's easy smile was intentional to show he had spent his life unraveling complicated demands. "You will find everything in order," he said, also in Latin. "The king kept careful accounts." He gestured to a stack of scrolls in leather tubes on the table beside him.

The commissioner glanced at the table. "The king is dead. Now we answer to Caesar."

Both statements carried the same burden.

When the man left, Eudoxus lingered by the window and watched palace servants lead him toward the treasury.

"They will find nothing wrong," Aedemon said in Greek as he paced between shelves of scrolls. "I kept those accounts myself."

Eudoxus continued to gaze out the window. "Accounts are not what They are looking for. They are looking for excuses."

Aedemon stopped at the window, fingers resting on the stone. In the courtyard, two Amazigh traders passed beneath the colonnade near where the commissioner stood. Their heads bowed more deeply than they once had, their bright robes dulled by dust and caution.

"You could still leave. Take Zahra and the twins to the mountains. To Aghbalou. To a place where Rome's hand doesn't reach so easily."

"And abandon the networks we spent ten years building?" Aedemon shook his head. "The tribes need someone inside the palace walls. Someone who knows how Rome thinks."

"You cannot protect them both, your family and your people."

Aedemon's jaw tightened. "Watch me."

The old scholar sighed. "Pride and duty make a dangerous mixture, my friend."

Aedemon remained resolute. "Without them, we would have bowed a long time ago."

Autumn, 40 CE

The first secret meeting happened three nights after an audit of the grain stores.

Usem came after midnight, cloaked and hooded, and slipped through the back alley used by servants and deliveries. Aedemon's cousin had ridden three days from Aghbalou, the highland settlement where their grandfather had farmed terraced slopes above the treeline and where Usem now led the village council. The two men had not seen each other in over a year, but they embraced without ceremony, the way family does when time is short and the news is bad.

Aedemon led him to the small room behind his study, where a parchment map of Mauretania hung on the wall, marked with lines and tiny carved stones.

"They ask more every season." Usem tapped a calloused finger on the map where his people farmed terraced slopes. "Grain, olives, men for their legions. They do not share the burden with the cities. They take from us because we cannot complain in Latin."

"If we refuse, they will simply take it by force," Aedemon replied. "They have not yet sent full legions here, but if we push too soon..."

"Too soon?" Usem countered. "Our king is dead. They killed him and sent counters instead of generals. How long do you expect us to wait?"

"Injustice does not create readiness. If we act now, scattered, they will crush us. If we build something coordinated..."

"You speak like a Roman."

"I speak like one who has watched Rome for twenty years. Their strength is not just legions. It is roads. Grain. Fear. Reputation. You do not break that by throwing stones at patrols."

"What do you suggest?"

Aedemon moved to the map. "You are not the only one who resents them. There are men in Volubilis, in the western mountains, even in the cities. We start by talking. We learn who will act, who will hide, who will betray. When the time comes, we strike in more than one place at once."

Usem nodded. "This will take time."

"We have time. For now."

Outside the door, Silina moved down the corridor with a tray of cups. She paused when she heard the low voices, but she recognized the rare heat in Aedemon's tone and kept walking. Some conversations, she learned, stayed behind closed doors for reasons having nothing to do with medicine.

In the nursery, Zahra rocked Amara while Juba gnawed on the corner of a wooden block. The boy babbled in half-formed sounds, delighted with his own noise. Amara watched him, then Zahra, then the door. She tracked the tension seeping through the walls.

Zahra looked down at Amara in her arms. "Your father is trying to save the world, but I am trying to save you and your brother."

Amara made a small gurgle resembling agreement.

❧✦❧

Early Winter, 40 CE

Marcus stood at the edge of the training yard and watched the new recruits stumble through formations. The air smelled of sweat, oil, and the metallic bite of coming rain. Veteran soldiers barked corrections. Wooden practice swords struck shields in uneven rhythm.

Rufus stood beside him, arms folded. The senior centurion awaited his transfer back to Italia after twenty years in the provinces, and the waiting made him talkative. "They are sloppy," he said in Latin. "Soft from city living."

"They'll harden," Marcus replied. "They always do, if they survive the first year."

Rufus's gaze slid toward the palace. "You spend a great deal of time there, Tribune. More than most officers."

"I serve as liaison between the garrison and the household," Marcus said. "You know that."

"Of course." Rufus's tone carried polite doubt. "And how does the household fare, with their king gone?"

"Adjusting." Marcus kept his voice flat. "Like the rest of us."

Rufus watched a recruit trip over his own feet. "Men like Aedemon never adjust. They calculate. They choose sides."

"He has served Rome faithfully for years."

"So did his king." Rufus turned away. "Until he didn't."

The words hung like frost in the air.

Later, in his quarters, Marcus unrolled a fresh dispatch from the capital. Lines of formal script reported unrest in other provinces, minor plots, rumors Caligula's mind had cracked. At the bottom, a short note: increased vigilance recommended in client kingdoms.

He stared at the phrase. *Increased vigilance.* The words sat on the wax like a stone.

He thought of Aedemon's sharp mind, of the way he watched a room the way a general watched battlefield terrain. He thought of the twins' small fingers closing around his when he dared visit the nursery under some pretext.

He folded the dispatch and set it aside. Rome wanted vigilance, and he would give it to them. Just not the kind they imagined.

❧✦❧

Late Winter, 40—41 CE

Rain hammered the tiles like a fist demanding entry.

Zahra moved through the villa with a lamp in one hand and Amara balanced on her hip. Juba toddled ahead, his soft feet slapping on the stone. He had discovered walking two weeks ago and now did little else, determined to explore every corner of his shrinking world.

"Slowly, aziz," Zahra called in Tamazight. "Your legs are still new."

Juba laughed and sped up. Silina caught him before he collided with a low table and swung him up with a practiced movement, making him squeal in delight.

"You'll break your nose before your second year. Then your father will blame me."

"He won't," Zahra said. "He knows you save them more often than you risk them."

In the kitchen, the cook stirred a pot of stew and muttered to herself about the cost of barley and the thinness of the butcher's cuts. "They raise taxes and lower weights. Rome's generosity."

Eudoxus sat at the table and wrote notes by lamplight. "Food shortages in the western districts. More patrols on the roads. And rumor has it Caligula plans a new campaign in the east. He will squeeze every province to pay for it."

Zahra shifted Amara to her other hip. The girl leaned against her shoulder but kept her eyes on the adults. She studied their voices.

"Will the tribes tolerate more?"

Eudoxus looked up from his notes. "Some will grumble and comply. Others will sharpen blades. Aedemon talks with both."

"Too much," the cook muttered. "He carries too many fires at once."

Aedemon returned late that night, cloak soaked, jaw set. Zahra met him in the entryway and pressed a cloth into his hands.

"How bad?"

"Bad, but not bad enough yet."

Zahra frowned. "What does that mean?"

"It means men are angry. Anger isn't unity. Not yet."

She watched him peel off wet layers, the lines around his eyes deeper than they were a year ago. “And Marcus?”

Aedemon hesitated. “He warns me to stay quiet. To keep my head down. Says Rome will calm once the first storm passes.”

“Do you believe him?”

“I believe he wants us safe. I’m no longer sure he knows what ‘safe’ means.”

He crossed the room and took Juba, who had woken and wobbled toward him. The boy settled against his chest at once. Amara reached toward him with a soft sound, and he gathered her too. He held both children for a moment. They alone kept him from flying apart.

“The year is turning. Something is coming. I don’t know what shape it will take yet.”

“Whatever it is, we face it together.”

He kissed her forehead, then the twins’, and did not say what he could almost hear Eudoxus saying for him: “Sometimes, facing things together means not being in the same place when the blow finally falls.”

Early 41 CE

News of Caligula’s assassination reached Caesarea on a cold, cloudless morning.

Eudoxus found Aedemon in the study. “He is dead. Murdered by his own guard.”

Aedemon looked up from the map, where small carved stones now marked more than alliances. They marked potential targets.

“And?”

“And Claudius is emperor. Less mad. More methodical.”

“Will he be better?”

"Better for Rome. Worse for anyone who resists it. Caligula's chaos gave us space. Claudius will fill it with systems and men hardened to resistance."

"Who might be?" Aedemon asked.

"Well, there's talk of Suetonius Paulinus, a general known for discipline," Eudoxus said. "Efficient. Ruthless when necessary. If he comes here, the time for slow preparation ends."

The name was new. It sat wrong on his tongue.

Aedemon looked at the map again. He took in the lines he'd drawn between tribes, the notes about grain routes and armories, and the small mark he'd etched at Caesarea, where his children slept in a nursery too close to Rome's reach.

"How long do we have?"

"Not long. When Rome sends men like him, they move quickly."

Aedemon closed his eyes for a moment and listened to the faint sound of his children's laughter from the courtyard where Zahra and Silina watched them play.

"The world has been unraveling slowly. I think It is about to tear."

Eudoxus nodded. "Then you must decide where you stand when it does."

Aedemon moved one of the carved stones. Not away from Caesarea. Not yet. But closer to the mountains, to the tribes, to a life looking more like war than diplomacy.

Outside, the sea wind shifted. In the harbor, fishers watched the horizon and shaded their eyes against a light sharper than the day before.

Far away, ships changed course on imperial orders. They bore a governor whose arrival would reshape Mauretania.

The year of unraveling had done its quiet work. The next year would not be quiet at all.

CHAPTER 10

When the Eagle Lands

"When the eagle lands, even the rocks hold still."
—Mauretanian saying

Early March, 41 CE—Caesarea, Mauretania

The gangplank struck the quay's worn limestone with the finality of a judge's gavel.

Marcus stood among the reception committee at Caesarea's harbor, his ceremonial armor polished to mirror brightness despite the knot in his stomach. The bronze cuirass bore decorative elements honoring both Roman tradition and local custom, a careful balance he had maintained throughout his career. Around him, harbor officials shifted their weight, adjusted togas, cleared throats. Fear had a smell, and today it mixed with salt spray and the pitch that caulked freshly painted hulls.

Three Roman galleys had rounded the headland at dawn, military transports riding low under the load of tented equipment and ranked soldiers. The lead vessel flew a crimson banner, its golden eagle snapping in Mediterranean winds.

The first figure to emerge commanded attention through presence rather than pageantry. Gaius Suetonius Paulinus moved with a soldier's economy. A man familiar with pomp and ceremony, he walked with measured and purposeful steps. Pannonian campaigns had weathered his face to leather, and a scar ran from his left eyebrow to his jaw where some barbarian blade had come too close. His purple-striped toga was immaculate despite days at sea, but he wore it like a man more comfortable in armor.

Dark eyes swept the harbor. Gaetulian traders argued with Mauri merchants. A Roman proprietor waved documents no one would acknowledge. Paulinus's jaw tightened.

Behind him came a younger officer whose hand rested on his sword hilt. Not threatening. Ready. His eyes cataloged defensive positions, noted guard placements, and measured distances to cover.

"Gaius Suetonius Paulinus." The governor's voice across morning air had an authority accustomed to immediate obedience. "By order of Emperor Claudius, I assume gubernatorial authority over the province of Mauretania. Effective immediately."

The emphasis on Claudius's name rippled through the assembled officials. Caligula's murder was still fresh enough the new emperor's name carried the promise of stability, competence, and a return to proper Roman governance. Or so everyone hoped.

Paulinus's gaze swept the reception committee. When it reached Marcus, it paused. Those dark eyes noted the local influences in his armor design, the way he stood with his weight distributed for either Roman formations or mountain warfare.

"You are?"

"Marcus Valerius Severus, Tribune of the Third Auxiliary Cohort." Marcus kept his tone neutral. "Born in the province, trained in Rome. Currently serving as liaison between military and civilian administration."

"Born here." Paulinus repeated the words and tasted them for poison. "Your family?"

"Three generations of service to Rome, sir. My grandfather settled here after the Jugurthine Wars."

"And your grandmother?" The younger officer spoke for the first time, his accent placing him in Rome's affluent districts.

Marcus met his gaze. "Mauri, sir. From the mountain tribes. It was considered an advantageous match at the time. Strengthening local alliances."

"Advantageous." The officer's smile held no warmth. "I am Gnaeus Hosidius Geta, the governor's military advisor. We will be reviewing all such 'advantageous' arrangements to ensure they align with current imperial policy."

❧✦❧

Concurrent—Aedemon's villa, across the city

Zahra drew water from the old Punic well near the palace walls, the one predating the Roman aqueducts and still serving the women of the upper quarter. She came here most mornings, not for the water alone but for the vantage: the well stood on a rise where the ground sloped toward the harbor, and from its stone rim she could see the full sweep of the port, the jetties, the lighthouse, the open sea beyond.

Three ships sat at anchor where none had been the day before.

She set the water jar on the rim and shielded her eyes. Military transports, heavy-hulled, riding low with the weight of men and equipment. The lead vessel flew a banner she did not recognize. A governor's ensign flew atop the mast, a pennant announcing authority, not permission.

The women around the well had seen them too. Conversations stopped. Hands stilled on rope and bucket. One of the older women, a Mauri servant from the palace household, spoke in a voice pitched for Zahra alone.

"Governor's ships. Arrived at first light. The harbor master closed the commercial quay to make room."

Zahra lifted her jar and walked home at the pace of a woman carrying water, steady and unhurried, betraying nothing to the Roman soldiers she passed on the street or the merchants who nodded in the forum. Her heart beat against her ribs. Her mind was already cataloguing: what they could carry, where they could go, how much time three ships in the harbor meant they had left.

She found Aedemon in his study reviewing grain inventories with his steward. The clay tablet beneath his hand showed careful calculations of crop yields, storage capacities, and distribution schedules for the coming season, numbers assuming a future where such planning mattered.

"Three military transports in the harbor," she said from the doorway. "Governor's banner on the lead vessel. They arrived at first light."

Aedemon set down his stylus.

✦

The harbor

Paulinus's attention had returned to the chaos of the fish market. "Three years as praetor in Pannonia," he said, more to himself than the assembled officials. "Three years bringing order to tribes who thought Roman authority was negotiable. By the time I left, they understood otherwise."

His scarred hand gestured toward two traders, one Gaetulian and one Mauri, who shouted over each other while a Roman merchant stood between them, contract in hand, face reddening with frustration.

"This? This is the same disease. Different tribes with the same delusion that accommodation means weakness."

Geta nodded. "In six months, the governor suppressed the Breuci uprising by pacifying seventeen of their villages."

"Pacified means one thing." Paulinus's voice went flat. "No more uprisings. No more negotiations with chieftains who think Roman law bends to their convenience." His eyes swept the welcoming committee. "No more officials who confuse patience with policy."

Marcus kept his tone even. "Among themselves, they are the Imazighen, 'the free people.' Their language is Tamazight, their script Tifinagh. We would do well not to call them Berbers. 'Berber' is our invention. They are not barbarians. If we intend to win their trust, we may wish to use the name they claim for themselves."

Geta laughed and adjusted his sword belt. "Names don't win battles."

"No," Marcus agreed. "But the wrong name can lose an army before the first arrow flies."

Paulinus turned his full attention to Marcus. "You think we should win their trust." He spoke the word with edges. "Trust is what weak men substitute for authority. My father trusted his partners. They bled him dry. I learned early order is built on clear authority, consistently applied."

Marcus held the governor's gaze and offered nothing. Paulinus wanted agreement. Geta watched for hesitation. The space between those two expectations was narrow, and Marcus would have to live in it for as long as this governorship lasted.

Paulinus paused. His voice shifted. "My mother used to say 'everyone has their reasons.'" No warmth in his tone. "She said it when his business partners cheated him. She said it when he came home drunk and angry. She said it until we buried him in a pauper's grave."

The personal revelation settled between them.

"Everyone has their reasons. And Rome has the only reason that matters: the order of law, enforced without sentiment or negotiation." His hand gestured with sharp precision. "The tribes here will learn the same lesson the Breuci learned in Pannonia."

From the second transport, legionaries disembarked in perfect formation. Bronze armor glinted in the sun. Hobnailed boots created rhythmic thunder on wooden planks. Fresh cohorts, but the uniformity of their equipment spoke of frontline soldiers drilled daily, not garrison troops grown soft on provincial duty.

"The Third Augusta," Geta said. "Two full cohorts. More will follow if resistance proves significant."

Paulinus watched his soldiers with intensity. He regarded disorder as a personal insult. "Tribune Marcus. I want a full briefing on all of Ptolemy's former associates by sunset. I want their locations, their loyalties, and their potential for causing difficulties."

"Of course, sir."

☙✦❧

Mid-March—Aedemon's villa

Zahra heard them before she saw them.

The bronze clatter of hobnailed sandals on stone had become Caesarea's new rhythm, a sound that turned conversations to whispers and sent servants hurrying to look busy. But this morning, the sound stopped. Right outside their gates.

She stood at the upper window, Amara sleeping against her shoulder, Juba content in his basket beside her. Below, in the alley separating their villa from the wine merchant's compound, six legionaries questioned Gaius about the comings and goings of his neighbors.

The merchant's confident demeanor crumbled. His hands trembled despite the warm March sun. Words tumbled over each other as he gestured toward Aedemon's property, each gesture a small betrayal, each nod of agreement another stone in a wall being built around them.

"...distinguished visitors... unusual activity at night... heard horses, perhaps three days ago..."

Zahra's arms tightened around Amara. The infant stirred, her breathing shifting as she sensed her mother's fear even in sleep.

Marcus was right. We have days, not weeks.

She had known Marcus Valerius since before she chose Aedemon. She knew him in that careful way women learn to know men who look too long, whose voices soften when speaking their names. He was kind then. He still was, in his way. He never married and never built the life he might have had.

She had never spoken of it. Not to Aedemon. Not to anyone. But Aedemon had to know. With his keen eye for observation, he had to have seen how Marcus's eyes avoided her when she entered a room, how he stayed longer than necessary when visiting, how he asked about the children with a hunger he could not disguise.

Yes, if Rome came for them, Marcus would help. If asked.

The question was whether asking would destroy him. And whether that destruction mattered more than her children's lives.

Below, the soldiers finished with Gaius. The merchant bowed, scraped, and promised his continued vigilance in service to Rome's security. Then he glanced toward Aedemon's villa, a quick, furtive look saying everything about where his loyalties would fall when tested.

Amara whimpered, a small sound, but Zahra felt it as a warning. Her daughter tracked emotion. Every spike of fear in the household echoed through her small body, amplified and returned until the whole villa vibrated with shared terror.

"Shh, little star." Zahra moved toward the interior room where Silina organized supplies. "Be still. Not now."

But she wondered how long any of them could hold out before Amara's sensitivity betrayed them all.

demon stood in his study and watched through a different window as the soldiers departed. Their measured pace spoke of men doing routine work. Nothing urgent. Nothing suspicious.

Yet.

"Pater." Silina appeared in the doorway, using the Latin term she had adopted since the twins' birth, with poise beyond her years, announcing her authority rather than asking permission. "The soldiers are leaving, but they spoke with Gaius for a long time."

"I saw."

Silina hesitated. "Zahra watched from upstairs. She is frightened. She will not say it, but Amara is responding to it."

Of course she was. His wife was many things: pragmatic, fierce, clear-eyed about threats. She was also a mother who watched predators circle her children. Fear would come, even if she refused to acknowledge it.

"Tell her I will speak with Marcus today. We will have a plan by nightfall."

After Silina left, Aedemon returned to the courtyard view. The painted dolphins on the colonnade mocked him with their frozen leaps. Everything about this villa spoke of permanence. This had been his home for twenty years. His children had been born here under twin fires marking them for a life beyond ordinary.

But now Rome would try to take it all. The only question was the price of keeping his family alive when Rome demanded everything.

Early afternoon—Aedemon's villa

Zahra found him still standing at the window, watching shadows creep across the courtyard stones.

"The courier who came earlier." Her voice was quiet but steady. She was raised in mountain villages where bad news arrived on swift horses and survival depended on reading signs others missed. "He brought word about the ships?"

Aedemon turned. His wife stood in the doorway, one hand resting on the frame, the other touching the wall, testing its solidity. She wore a practical dress of undyed wool, the kind worn for travel or crisis. Some part of her had already begun preparing.

"Three Roman galleys. A new governor." He moved away from the window. "Ptolemy's execution was not about him alone. It was about everyone who served him or prospered under his arrangement with Rome."

"How long do we have?"

The question was so like her: no panic, no denial, an immediate assessment of practical reality. He loved this clear pragmatism from the first. It always masked her fierce protectiveness.

"Unknown. Days, perhaps. Maybe less."

Upstairs, the twins had quieted into that brief peaceful silence between one crisis and the next, when Juba slept and Amara's sensitivity released her into rest.

Zahra crossed the room and stood beside him at the window. Her hand found his.

"Marcus Valerius." She said the name without looking at him. "He was here last month bringing news from the auxiliary camps. He stayed longer than necessary and asked about the children."

Aedemon studied his wife's profile. She watched the courtyard, but her mind worked through another calculation.

"I have known him since we were young," she continued, her voice careful. "Before I chose you. He was kind then. He is kind now, in his way. And he has never married."

Aedemon let the silence do the work.

Zahra met his eyes. "If Rome comes for us, and Marcus is the one who arrives first, I think he would help us. If asked."

Cold calculation settled in his chest. His wife's practical assessment of their options included truths she had never spoken aloud before. Marcus's devotion was visible to anyone who watched over the years. His eyes avoided Zahra when she entered a room, and the effort of that avoidance cost him each time.

A weapon. Or a lifeline. Perhaps both.

"I will speak with him. Privately."

✦

Late afternoon

The knock at the gate came at the hour when honest men prepared evening meals, when the streets quieted and attention turned inward. Marcus Valerius Severus arrived alone, without ceremony, wearing a tribune's uniform but wanting to avoid notice.

Aedemon met him in the private room behind his study, where a sand table displayed Mauretania's terrain in miniature. Colored stones marked settlements. Wax tablets stacked along one wall contained correspondence that would soon need burning.

"You know why I am here?" Marcus closed the door.

"I suspect several possibilities."

"Then let me clarify one." Marcus moved to the lamp, shadows carving his face into unfamiliar angles. "I am not here to arrest you. I am here to help you escape before that becomes inevitable."

The statement hung in lamplight. Aedemon studied his friend's face and read calculation there, but also determination.

"Why would you do this? Your career..."

"Is worth nothing if the people I care about are destroyed by it." Marcus's voice was calm but carried absolute conviction.

Then, after a pause feeling like preparation for pain: "Before you married Zahra, I had hoped perhaps she might choose me. She did not. She chose you, and she chose rightly."

The confession landed hard. Aedemon opened his mouth to speak, but Marcus continued.

"When we were younger, I thought about it constantly. Then I joined the auxiliary and told myself serving Rome was enough. Twenty years of that." His jaw tightened. "And now I am risking everything I built to save what I walked away from."

Marcus straightened, his voice dropping. "Your family leaves tonight. I have arranged safe passage to your cousin Usem's settlement in the highlands. The documentation shows my authorization as liaison to tribal communities, standard procedure for mixed families during civil unrest."

He moved to the sand table. His finger traced a path through sculpted mountains. "There are mountain paths avoiding major roads. Eudoxus remembers the way from years ago when he first came to Mauri lands. Three days' hard riding should see them to safety."

"And what of me?"

"You surrender to my custody now, under terms allowing questioning rather than summary execution. Your cooperation shows you pose no ongoing threat to provincial security." Marcus paused. "It is the only way they will let your family leave unmolested."

The bargain was devastating in its clarity. Aedemon's freedom for his family's safety, but only if he acted without hesitation, before Roman authority decided negotiation was unnecessary.

"If I refuse?"

"Soldiers arrive within hours. They will search the villa from foundation to roof, question every servant, catalogue every possession. If your family is here, they will be taken for interrogation." Marcus's voice went flat. "Children that young... even if they survive the experience, they will never recover from it."

"And if I agree?"

"Your family leaves at first light as part of a routine relocation to family property in the interior. Documentation shows my authorization. No questions will be asked because no irregularities will be apparent." Marcus moved closer. "Your children grow up free, even if you do not."

Aedemon studied his friend's face and read the calculation behind the offer. "There must be a price. You are doing this in exchange for what?"

"Unambiguous cooperation with the new administration. Complete intelligence about resistance networks. Names, locations, connections. Everything."

The calculations were brutal. Betray everyone who had trusted him, or watch his family destroyed. Become Rome's instrument or become Rome's example.

"How long would questioning last?"

"Unknown. But questioning implies eventual resolution. Resistance implies immediate consequences with no possibility of negotiation."

From above came the sound of movement. Zahra prepared for evening, unaware this conversation would change everything. Or perhaps aware. Perhaps she had known from the moment she mentioned Marcus's devotion earlier, known Aedemon would use it if necessary.

Some weapons cut both ways.

"I need time to prepare my family."

"You have until dawn. After that, the opportunity closes."

Marcus moved toward the door, then paused and looked back. For a moment, the cost of what he had offered showed in his face.

"Your children. They will grow up knowing their father tried to save them. Whatever else happens, they will know that."

After Marcus departed, Aedemon stood at the window watching the retreating figure of the man he had known only as friend until now. The afternoon sun cast long shadows across the courtyard. For a moment, Marcus paused at the gate and looked back. Their eyes met across the distance.

Twenty years of friendship. Shared purpose. And now the offer of salvation purchased with betrayal on both sides.

Marcus would save Zahra knowing she would never be his. He would protect Aedemon's children, living reminders of what he had lost. He would risk everything for people who could never acknowledge the sacrifice.

And Aedemon?

His hands trembled as he reached for the stylus and clay tablet. The message would go to Sabalus tonight, a Mauri chieftain whose warriors waited three days south, loyal to Aedemon since the first secret meetings in this very room.

I am sorry, Marcus.

The stylus carved letters into wet clay. Instructions. Timing. Positions. The route Marcus would take to the western garrison.

Aedemon's throat tightened. His eyes burned.

He wrote anyway.

His children would live. Zahra would survive. And someday, perhaps, they would understand why their father had become a man willing to turn devotion into a weapon.

The clay tablet filled with betrayal, letter by letter.

By dawn, his family would flee to safety.

By sunset, Marcus Valerius would learn what it meant to offer salvation to a desperate man.

✦

Evening—the women's quarters

Zahra found him in his study hours later. Clay shards littered the floor around his feet where he had smashed the tablets one by one. His hands were still dusty with it. He did not look up when she entered.

"Marcus will help us?" She kept her voice level.

"Yes."

"And the price?"

"Everything." He met her eyes then, and she saw it, irreversible ruin. "Everything I am. Everything we built. Everyone who trusted us."

She crossed the room. She did not touch his shoulder or take his hand. She knelt beside his chair and pressed her forehead against his knee, the way she had done in their first year together when words failed them both and only the body's grammar remained. He made a sound not quite breath, not quite grief, and his hand came to rest on her hair.

"The children?" she whispered.

"Will live. Will grow up free."

She stayed against his knee. His fingers moved through her hair, slow and deliberate, memorizing its weight.

"Then we prepare," she said. "Silina has begun packing. Eudoxus is gathering his materials. The twins are fed and rested."

Neither of them moved.

"Zahra." His voice broke on her name. "Marcus told me..."

"I know." She lifted her head and took his face in both hands. His eyes were red. Dust from the shattered tablets streaked his jaw. "I have always known. He was kind enough to stay distant. That mattered."

He turned his face into her palm and closed his eyes. She felt the tremor move through him, the shudder of a man holding himself together by force of will alone.

"Look at me," she said.

He opened his eyes.

"I chose you. In that scriptorium when you were too proud to ask for help and too stubborn to accept it. I chose you in the courtyard when you told me Rome would come and I said we would face it together. I chose you when the twins came and the sky burned and you held all three of us because we were the only solid thing left in the world." Her thumbs traced the lines grief had carved beside his mouth. "I am choosing you now."

He pulled her against him. She climbed into the chair not built for two and pressed herself into the space between his arms, and he held her like a drowning man holds the last thing floating. His breath came ragged against her neck. Her fingers gripped the back of his tunic so hard the fabric twisted in her fists.

They did not speak. There was nothing to say their bodies did not say for them. Twenty years of shared meals and shared purpose and shared fear and the tender violence of raising children in a world wanting to destroy them. All of it lived in the press of her ribs against his, in his hand splayed across her back, in the way their breathing found the same rhythm the way it always did when the world fell quiet enough to hear each other's hearts.

From upstairs, Amara cried out once in her sleep. They both stilled. The sound subsided.

"She knows," Zahra murmured.

"She always knows."

Zahra pulled back enough to see his face. She smoothed the dust from his jaw. She kissed his forehead, each closed eye, the bridge of his nose, his mouth. He tasted of salt.

"We do what we must," she said. "For them."

He nodded. He could not speak.

She rose and stood before him. They looked at each other across the distance of a single step, the first measure of all the distance to come.

"I will finish the packing," she said. "Come upstairs before dawn. Hold them while they sleep. They should have that, even if they will never remember it."

She left. Her footsteps faded down the corridor, steady and sure, the walk of a woman holding herself together by will alone.

Aedemon sat alone in the wreckage of his study, surrounded by clay dust and the ghosts of shattered plans, and wept without sound until there was nothing left.

The weeping ended the way exhaustion ends: not through resolution but through depletion. He had nothing left to spend. He sat in the clay dust with his hands open on his knees and felt the strange lightness of a man who has given up everything and discovered the giving was survivable.

He thought of Amara's cry from upstairs. *She always knows.* What would she carry of this night, years from now, when she was old enough to understand what a child senses but cannot name? Not memory. Something older than memory. The weight of a father who held her in the dark and did not explain why, who pressed his face against her hair and breathed her in like a man memorizing what he cannot keep.

He thought of Juba. His son who fussed at being woken, who would grow up never knowing the sound of his father's voice except in the stories Zahra would choose carefully, shaping the man she needed Juba to believe in. He hoped she would be honest. He hoped she would let the boy be angry.

He thought of the men whose names had filled those burned tablets. Sabalus, whose fighters were already positioned in the ravine. The artisans in Volubilis. The mountain chiefs who had trusted him with their locations and their plans and their lives. Some of them would not survive what he had set in motion. He had known this from the beginning, had written their names and made his calculations and written again. The knowledge did not get lighter. It settled where it belonged, in the place where he would carry it for whatever remained of his life.

He rose. Washed his face in the basin. The water went grey with clay dust. He straightened his tunic with the same care he brought to every public appearance, the habit of a man who had survived twenty years of navigating between worlds by ensuring no one could read the cost in how he stood.

Then he climbed the stairs to hold his children one last time before morning took everything.

CHAPTER 11

The Performance

"Night favors those who know where they are going.
It swallows those who do not."
—Amazigh travel wisdom
Caesarea, Mauretania—Late March, 41 CE

That night, one hour after sunset

Crisis demanded brutal efficiency.

Aedemon came downstairs and gave the word. Within minutes, the household transformed. Every movement controlled, every action designed to appear routine while accomplishing the impossible.

Silina moved through the villa with steady calm, selecting what they could carry while maintaining the appearance of normal domestic routine. She had learned to pack in a hurry, a skill from another lifetime, another flight she did not let herself remember. She gathered clothing for harsh weather, a medicine kit, water skins, and coin hidden in hems and seams.

In the nursery, Zahra dressed the twins in traveling clothes while singing the same lullabies that comforted them through every previous journey. Her voice remained steady despite her shaking hands, and the knowledge this was exile.

Juba fussed at being woken, small face red with protest. But Amara lay still in her mother's arms, in the heavy silence following her overwhelming episodes. Her eyes were open, observing without reacting. She needed true rest, not the exhaustion of a spent child.

Silina paused in the doorway with an armload of supplies. “How long before she settles completely?”

“Hours. Perhaps longer.” Zahra’s arms tightened around her daughter. “Until our hearts find peace, hers will remain troubled.”

“Then we must be quick. Give her less time to absorb our fear.”

In the study, Aedemon burned documents with methodical precision. Each scroll curled and blackened in the brazier. Years of correspondence consumed by flame: names, locations, networks, everything endangering those who trusted him. The smoke smelled acrid and final.

Eudoxus gathered items from shelves with careful deliberation. White stones, dried herbs, oil gleaming amber in lamplight. He wrapped each item in silk and tucked it into a leather satchel. They were the tools of his trade, protection not from swords.

A knock at the gate shattered the careful stillness.

Everyone froze. In Zahra’s arms, Amara’s breathing quickened.

“Domine.” A servant’s urgent whisper. “The neighbor Gaius is at the gate. Says it is important.”

Aedemon and Zahra exchanged a glance. At this hour? The wine merchant who had cooperated with soldiers that morning?

Marcus appeared from the corridor with Madi, his trusted aide. He had returned to assist the family’s last preparations. “I will go. Better he sees me, the Roman tribune maintaining proper protocol.”

Not now, little star. Please, not now.

Zahra pressed her hand over Amara's chest and willed the infant not to cry. Amara remained still.

They listened to footsteps crossing the courtyard, and the murmur of voices at the gate. Gaius's higher-pitched tones carried fragments: "...unusual activity... wanted to ensure... my duty..."

Marcus's response came lower, authoritative: "...routine relocation... official authorization... no concern of yours..."

The conversation stretched on. In Zahra's arms, Amara watched the doorway with eyes too focused for an infant. Zahra stroked her daughter's chest and felt the small heart beating steady and slow.

That unnatural calm frightened her more than crying would have.

The gate closed. Marcus's footsteps returned, quicker now.

"He is gone. But he will talk to the neighbors, maybe to patrol centurions if he sees them." Marcus checked the street from the window. "We need to leave within the hour. Madi is bringing horses to the eastern postern. Silina, finish packing. Zahra, the twins need to be ready to travel immediately."

❧✦❧

Two hours before dawn

The eastern postern gate opened onto a narrow alley smelling of kitchen refuse and stale wine. Unbefitting a counselor's household, but perfect for what needed to appear routine: a mixed family relocating to interior properties during administrative transition.

Marcus's chosen route avoided main checkpoints. The timing would place them beyond the city before dawn patrols changed shifts.

Zahra held the twins while Silina secured travel bags to the horses. The animals stood patient and unmoving. Marcus had selected the mounts for their steadiness with children and on rough terrain.

"The mountain paths avoid major roads," Marcus said in Latin, his voice low and professional. "Three days' hard riding to Usem's settlement if you do not stop longer than necessary."

Zahra met his eyes in the darkness. "Thank you." This was the man who had confessed his love for her yesterday and today was risking everything to save her family.

Marcus's jaw tightened. He looked away. "Keep the children calm when you pass settlements. Amara especially. If she cries, people will remember and will talk."

"I know." She shifted Amara against her chest, the infant heavy with exhausted sleep. "Marcus..."

"Do not." His voice went rough. "Just get them to safety. That is all that matters."

Eudoxus mounted with ease despite his age. Madi checked girths and adjusted saddle straps. He had prepared many such departures. He would ride with them to Aghbalou, his military credentials providing the armed escort a routine family relocation required. A tribune's aide accompanying a counselor's household to interior properties: no patrol commander would question it. Silina settled into her saddle and reached to take Juba from Zahra's arms.

For a moment, Zahra paused and looked back at the villa where her children had been born under twin fires. She built a life there she thought would last. But permanence had proven as illusory as morning mist.

Then she mounted, Amara secure against her chest, and turned her horse toward the mountains.

Marcus watched until the darkness swallowed them. He stood in the postern gate long after the sound of hooves faded. The alley held nothing: refuse, silence, the smell of someone else's cooking fire dying down for the night. He stayed until he was certain his face had arranged itself into something passing for composure.

Zahra would reach the mountains. Eudoxus knew the paths. Madi knew the garrison schedules and the gaps between patrols. His family would arrive at Usem's settlement in three days and begin the long work of becoming invisible, the only future he could give them.

He had one more thing to give them. Larger than the escape. Larger than the documentation Marcus had risked his career to provide.

The family needed Rome looking east, at the mountain passes and the desert settlements and the networks they suspected existed among the southern tribes. They needed Rome deafened by the noise of a rebellion announcing itself loudly, drawing pursuit toward its sound and away from the silence of a woman and two infants riding north through darkness.

Sabalus's fighters were waiting in the ravine. Thirty men who had chosen this cause with clear eyes, who understood the odds and came anyway. He had not deceived them. He had told them the truth: this would not be a raid. It would be a declaration. It would cost what it cost, and what it bought was time, time for families to scatter, networks to go quiet, for the rebellion to root itself so deeply in the mountain communities that Rome would spend years trying to dig it out.

He turned back to the courtyard.

Marcus stood waiting in the lamplight, the documentation already prepared, his face carrying the expression of a man who had done something irreparable and was deciding if he could live with it.

He could. Aedemon had known this since their conversation the day before. Marcus's love was not a weakness he had exploited. It was proof of character, evidence that some men chose, even at cost, what they believed was right. That quality would sustain Marcus through what was coming. It would make him dangerous to Rome and invaluable to the family he would spend years protecting without acknowledgment.

He was sorry for the ambush. He was not sorry for the calculation. Both things were true and would remain true for whatever remained of his life.

"They are clear?"

"They are clear."

"Then let us get this over with."

❧✦❧

The same hour—the courtyard

Behind him, Aedemon waited. He had surrendered himself as promised, the price paid for his family's freedom.

"They are clear?"

"They are clear."

"Then let us get this over with."

Marcus placed Aedemon in custody with formal efficiency. Official chains not locked tight enough to chafe, encircled Aedemon's wrists and waist. Marcus held documentation citing cooperation and raising questions about any summary judgment. Everything suggested Aedemon was aiding Rome, not an enemy being transported for execution.

They rode through pre-dawn streets toward the western gate, two old friends who had served together, laughed together, built lives in the careful space between cultures. Now they performed the last scene in a friendship Rome's arrival had shattered.

The western gate opened onto a road climbing through broken terrain toward the garrison compound on the hills above the city. Even in darkness, Marcus could trace the familiar route: the road narrowed where it crossed the Oued N'Sara ravine, then switchbacked up through limestone ridges before reaching the compound's outer palisade. By day, the garrison commanded views of the coastal road to Tipasa and the sea beyond. By night, the ravines on either side swallowed sound and light.

As they rode, Aedemon made what seemed a casual remark. "The western road through the ravines. You always preferred this route."

"The most direct path to the garrison. Why?"

"No reason. I always liked the view from the ridge."

But Marcus heard a note that did not fit, a tension beyond expected fear. He studied his friend's profile in the thin pre-dawn light. Aedemon's posture had shifted. He sat taller in the saddle, shoulders back. Not the bearing of a man riding toward captivity.

They passed through the western gate as dawn lightened the sky behind them. The road wound between limestone outcrops where winter rains had carved deep channels in the soft rock. Spring grass clung to the slopes, but the terrain grew rough as they climbed. The Oued N'Sara cut across their path ahead, its seasonal bed dry, its banks steep enough to force the road into a narrow passage between eroded walls.

Understanding struck.

No.

"Aedemon..."

The first arrow took the lead escort in the throat. The man toppled from his saddle without a sound. The second arrow struck the rider behind them, punching through his mail shirt at the junction of shoulder and neck.

Fighters rose from the ravine walls on both sides. Twenty, perhaps thirty, armed with the mixed weapons of tribal warfare: Roman swords taken from dead legionaries, traditional curved blades, spears with leaf-shaped points. They moved with coordinated precision and surrounded the small escort party in heartbeats. The ravine's steep banks, which Marcus had ridden past a hundred times without a second thought, became a killing ground.

His remaining soldiers drew swords. Three men against thirty. The mathematics offered no hope.

Sabalus stepped forward from the rocks, his scarred face grim with purpose. He cut Aedemon's chains with one efficient stroke.

Aedemon turned to Marcus, his freed hands held together in prayer. "My friend. I am sorry. But my family needs more than escape. They need a world where escape is not necessary."

Marcus's hands trembled on his reins. He had been used. His confession about Zahra, the confession costing him twenty years of silence to speak aloud, had been turned against him. His offer to help became bait for a trap. His knowledge of the route placed fighters in ambush along a road he himself had chosen.

"You knew." Marcus's voice came hollow, scraped clean of everything but the wound. "When you agreed to surrender. When you let me help your family escape. You already had this planned."

"I did what I had to do." Aedemon mounted one of the dead escort's horses. "While Rome searches its own ranks for betrayal, my family disappears."

"I told you yesterday what she meant to me." The words came thick with devastation. "And you used that. You knew what I felt, and you turned it into a weapon."

Aedemon's expression showed no satisfaction. Only grim necessity.

But Marcus was not finished. "My honor, my career, my heart. Pieces on your game board."

"Yes." No mockery. Only acknowledgment. "Because my children's survival required it. I had to turn you, their most valuable intelligence officer, into a man Rome will never fully trust again." Aedemon's jaw tightened. "I am sorry, Marcus. Truly. But I would do it again, a hundred times, for them."

Sabalus brought his horse closer, impatient. "We need to go. Patrols will find the bodies."

Aedemon looked back one final time. "The next time we meet, I will understand if you try to kill me. I have earned it."

Then they were gone, up the ravine and into the ridgeline, leaving Marcus surrounded by dead men and the wreckage of everything he had believed about friendship, honor, and the possibility of serving Rome without losing his soul.

He sat motionless. Dawn light strengthened around him. Birds sang in the scrub oak along the ravine's lip. Life went on. The irreparable fracture made no difference to the birds.

Then he dismounted and knelt beside his fallen soldiers. He closed eyes that would never see another sunrise. He straightened limbs twisted in postures of surprise. He collected the arrows and noted their make: Mauri craftsmanship, mountain fighters, the style Sabalus's men favored. It was all evidence for the report he would have to write, a summary of the performance that would now define the rest of his life.

The ride back to Caesarea felt endless. Every hoofbeat hammered the same truth: he had been played. Used. His devotion exploited as weakness, his noblest intentions corrupted for tactical advantage.

By the time he reached the garrison, his fury had hardened into cold resolve.

He would find Aedemon. He would hunt him across every mountain pass and desert wadi in Mauretania. He would track him with the same systematic patience he had once used to protect the family Aedemon had used to destroy him.

And when he found him, he would show no mercy.

But even as fury burned through him, part of Marcus knew the truth that made his rage unbearable: he would continue to ensure Zahra and the children stayed safe. He would hunt Aedemon and protect the family Aedemon loved.

Both truths held together, irreconcilable.

The sun rose over Caesarea. Marcus Valerius Severus, Tribune of the Third Auxiliary, rode through the western gate and began the long work of becoming someone he would never forgive himself for being.

CHAPTER 12

The Hunter's Report

"A name is a door. Some doors must be closed to survive."
—Amazigh saying

Late March 41 CE—two days after the escape—Caesarea

Governor Paulinus paced the length of his private study, each footfall precise as a blade strike. Marcus stood at attention and watched the scarred finger that stabbed at maps now point directly at his chest.

"Your friendship with the traitor is exactly why you will lead this hunt." No preamble, no ceremony. "You know how he thinks. Where he would run. Who he would trust."

Marcus kept his expression neutral, though his pulse hammered. "Governor, my personal connection could compromise..."

"Your personal connection makes you dangerous to him." Paulinus stopped pacing. "He betrayed you. He used your history together, your protection of his family, as bait for that ambush. I am giving you the opportunity for appropriate vengeance."

The word landed in Marcus's chest with the force of a fist. Vengeance. What Paulinus could not know was the fury coursing through Marcus had nothing to do with serving Rome.

"Find his family before they leave Mauretania," Paulinus continued. "The woman and children he valued enough to sacrifice everything. When we have them, Aedemon will come to us. Then you can finish what that ambush interrupted."

"The family poses no threat..."

"The family is leverage." Paulinus's voice cut like winter wind. "Our sources in Tingis say Aedemon organizes resistance in the eastern mountains. Every week brings new reports of attacks on our supply lines, rebellious Mauri settlements emboldened by his example. His wife and children are the only thing he values more than his cause."

Marcus absorbed this with the appearance of a soldier receiving orders. "What resources will I have?"

"Whatever you need. Patrols, informants, interrogation authority." Paulinus moved to the window overlooking Caesarea's harbor. "I want results within three months. Bring me the family, and through them, the rebel."

"Yes, Governor."

"One more thing." Paulinus did not turn from the window. "Your methods are your own, Tribune. I do not care how you find them, only that you do. Use whatever tactics serve Rome's interests."

The dismissal was clear. Marcus saluted and left, his mind already racing through the impossible calculations of his new assignment. He had been ordered to hunt with Rome's full authority behind him, which meant he now controlled exactly where Rome would and would not look.

☙✦❧

Three days after the escape. Zalacus Mons foothills, sixty miles south of Caesarea

The night air carried the sharp scent of pine and the mustiness of damp forest earth. Zahra shifted Amara against her shoulder. Both twins slept quietly for a change. Juba lay against Silina's chest, his small face peaceful in the firelight. Three days of hard riding had left them all exhausted, but Madi insisted they push deeper into the foothills before making proper camp.

Now they found shelter in a grove nestled between towering rock outcrops catching starlight like scattered silver.

Eudoxus dismounted stiffly, his scholar's body protesting the hours on horseback. He approached the grove on foot, weathered hands moving in subtle gestures, reading the spiritual currents in the air.

"The ancestor-spirits welcome us." His voice held quiet satisfaction. "Many pilgrims have rested here. The ground remembers their passage."

Silina gathered kindling while Madi tended the horses with his usual quiet competence. The small fire crackled to life, and its warmth pushed back the mountain chill. Eudoxus knelt and drew seven of the white stones from his pack, each no larger than a child's fist and carved with ancient symbols.

He placed them in a careful circle around their resting area, lips moving in silent prayer with each placement. North, east, south, west, the cardinal points first. Then the spaces between, where spirits walked unseen.

"Will that keep us safe?" Silina kept her voice low.

"Safe from casual discovery. From spiritual harm." Eudoxus settled by the fire and accepted the water skin Madi offered. "But if determined men find us, stones alone will not stop them."

Juba stirred against Silina's chest, a soft whimper escaping him. Amara remained silent. Her green eyes were open and tracking a presence in the shadows beyond the firelight.

Eudoxus rose slowly. "We are not alone."

"Well, well." The voice ground out from the shadows. "Palace refugees with heavy purses, perhaps?"

Five men stepped into the firelight. Their faces were weathered by sun and hardship, hands resting on well-worn sword hilts with the casual confidence of men accustomed to violence. The largest, a barrel-chested man with a scar cutting white through his beard, moved forward.

"Those clothes, that gear." His eyes swept their camp. "You are no common travelers. Who flees Caesarea in the night with Roman gold weighing down their packs?"

Madi rose slowly and positioned himself between the bandits and the women. "We are merchants relocating inventory. Nothing worth dying over."

The bandit leader laughed. "Let me be the judge of that. Varro, Cassius, check the packs. See what these merchants value enough to run with."

As two bandits moved toward their supplies, Amara cried out. The sound was low, keening, ancient and sorrowful, mourning a loss yet to come.

"Quiet that brat," the leader snarled.

Eudoxus stepped forward and placed himself at the edge of the protective circle. The bandits, focused on potential loot, paid him no attention. They saw only another old man, no threat.

"I would reconsider." Eudoxus's voice carried no menace, only quiet certainty. "This place is protected." He motioned with his little finger for Zahra and Silina to join him with the twins inside the circle of stones.

The leader's laugh was uglier this time. "Protected by what? An old scholar and his pebbles?" He gestured with his sword. "Step aside before we add you to tonight's entertainment."

"Not protected by me." Eudoxus indicated the white stones surrounding their camp, each now visible as small patches of pale luminescence. "By forces remembering when your ancestors honored sacred boundaries."

"Superstitious nonsense." The bandit leader spat into their fire and made it hiss. "The only forces that matter are steel and numbers, old man. We have both."

He stepped across the line of white stones.

The fire exploded upward in a column of flame turning night to blazing noon. Heat washed over them in waves and drove everyone back from the sudden inferno. The white stones flared with their own bright radiance and created a barrier of luminescence between the refugees and their attackers.

One bandit screamed and stumbled backward, his arm blistered where he had reached too close. Another dropped his sword and stared at the phenomenon with dawning terror. A third writhed on the forest floor trying to put out the flames consuming his clothing.

"Sorcery!" someone shouted.

But Eudoxus was not finished. He raised both hands, and his voice shifted into the ancient tongue, words predating Rome, predating even Carthaginian traders. The language of the first peoples who had learned to speak with the land itself.

The syllables pulled at the air and made it thick and strange. Eudoxus's face contorted in concentration, a pale film stealing across his eyes, his gaze fixed on distances no living eye could measure.

The wind rose in answer to his call. It howled through the rocks with voices that might have been human, might have been older than human. The protective barrier intensified, and within its glow, tall figures waved and danced. They could have been shadows cast by the fire, or they could have been the ancestors themselves, drawn by blood and invocation.

The bandit leader's bravado shattered. He scrambled backward, away from the barrier, his scarred face gone pale. "Fall back! FALL BACK!"

His men needed no encouragement. They fled in pure panic, weapons abandoned, greed forgotten in the face of powers their grandmothers had warned them about in childhood stories they had thought were mere superstition.

Their footsteps faded into darkness. The howling wind died. The flames settled back to normal height. The white stones dimmed until they looked like simple rocks again, though a faint warmth still radiated from them.

Eudoxus lowered his hands.

And collapsed.

Silina caught him before he hit the ground, her healer's training evident in how quickly she assessed him. "His pulse is racing. Breathing shallow." She looked up at Zahra, her face tight with concern. "Whatever he just did, it took everything."

Madi knelt beside them and helped ease Eudoxus to the ground near the fire. The scholar's face had gone gray, his skin clammy with cold sweat despite the flames' warmth. When he opened his eyes, they seemed sunken, aged decades in minutes.

"I am not injured." His voice came out hoarse, barely more than a whisper. "Just tired."

"Tired?" Silina pressed her fingers to his wrist and counted heartbeats. "Your pulse is erratic. And look at your hands."

They all looked. Eudoxus's weathered hands trembled without ceasing, and the veins stood out dark against skin taking on a translucent quality, drained from within.

"The old ways demand their price." Eudoxus managed a weak smile. "Every working draws on the bearer's life force. The greater the power invoked, the greater the cost."

"You could have died." Zahra's voice shook. She still held Amara, who had quieted now the immediate danger had passed.

"If I had not acted, we all would have died." Eudoxus closed his eyes. "Some costs are worth paying."

They settled him as comfortably as possible, Silina covering him with blankets despite the mild night. Juba, still drowsy but awake, crawled over and patted the old scholar's hand with clumsy concern.

"Sleep now, little one." Eudoxus's voice was barely audible. "Your old teacher just needs rest."

Madi took first watch, positioning himself where he could see both the camp and the path the bandits had fled. The night settled back into silence, but a different quality of silence now, charged and watchful, the land itself alert to what had happened here.

Zahra sat with Amara in her arms and watched Eudoxus's chest rise and fall with labored breathing. The scholar who had been part of her household for five years, who had seemed eternal as the mountains themselves, now looked fragile as old parchment.

Magic was real. The spirits answered when called with the proper words and proper sacrifices.

But the cost of that power might be higher than any of them could afford to pay.

✦

The following morning

They rode through the morning in silence, the events of the night pressing on them. Madi led, his posture rigid, a sentry's vigilance that never fully stood down. Behind him, Zahra cradled both twins against her chest, their small bodies warm through the traveling blanket. Silina followed with the pack horse, and Eudoxus brought up the rear, listing in his saddle.

The scholar looked older in daylight. Gray had spread through his beard overnight, and the lines around his eyes had deepened into permanence. His hands gripped the reins.

"We need to stop," Silina said around midday. "He can barely sit upright."

"Not yet." Madi's voice carried no cruelty, only calculation. "Another hour. There is a spring where we can rest safely."

Zahra watched Eudoxus sway with each step of his horse. The man who had faced down five bandits with nothing but sacred stones and ancient prayers now seemed diminished, reduced.

"Will you be able to do that again?" she asked. "If we need it?"

Eudoxus met her eyes, and she saw the truth there before he spoke it. "Perhaps. But the cost would be higher. Each working damages the spiritual pathways further. Use them too often..." He did not finish the thought.

"Then we will not need it again." Zahra's voice carried a determination she did not quite feel. "We will reach safety before it comes to that."

He spoke with quiet finality. "What is done is done. We need to keep moving."

"You can barely stand," Madi protested.

"Then I will ride." Eudoxus pushed himself upright with visible effort. "Two more days to Usem's settlement. We have come too far to stop now."

As they broke camp and moved with the efficiency of their exhaustion, no one mentioned how slowly Eudoxus moved, or how Madi had to help him mount his horse. They had all seen what the price of protection looked like, written in silver hair and trembling hands.

The white stones went back into Eudoxus's pack, their surfaces still faintly warm. Zahra watched him tuck them away with the careful movements, his strength permanently diminished.

❧✦❧

Later that day, the mountain village of Aghbalou, Zalacus Mons highlands

Madi reined up where the trail crested the last ridge before the descent into Aghbalou. Below them, the village spread across the hillside: stone houses terraced into the slope, smoke rising from cooking fires, the green thread of irrigated gardens cutting through brown rock. The settlement looked permanent, rooted, the kind of place where people knew each other's names.

That was the problem.

"We need to talk before we go down there." Madi turned his horse to face the group. His voice carried the flat authority of a man who had spent years moving people through dangerous country. "Usem knows who you are. He can be trusted. But Usem is not the whole village. There are families down there who trade with the coast, who see Roman merchants, who talk to soldiers at market towns. One wrong name spoken to the wrong person reaches Caesarea within a week."

Zahra shifted the twins against her chest. "What are you saying?"

"I am saying Zahra, wife of Aedemon, cannot walk into that village. Neither can Eudoxus of Persepolis, the Persian scholar everyone in Caesarea knows by sight." He looked at each of them in turn. "You need names. Backgrounds. Stories holding up under casual questions from people who mean no harm but talk too freely."

Eudoxus straightened in his saddle, though the effort cost him. "What do you suggest?"

"Keep it close to truth. Lies built from whole cloth tear at the first pull. Zahra becomes Leila, a widow from the eastern tribes, traveling with her uncle. That explains the accent, the bearing, the children. Eastern tribes are remote enough no one here will know the families."

"Leila." Zahra said the name and it sat wrong on her tongue, a garment cut for someone else's body.

"Eudoxus becomes Numerius, Leila's uncle. A trader from the coast whose health failed on his last journey east. Greek name, common among merchants. The illness explains why he cannot travel anymore, and the niece explains why he is here instead of dying alone in some coastal room."

"Numerius." Eudoxus repeated it with the careful precision of a man filing away something he knew he would need.

"You stayed in this village before. Years ago. People will remember a Persian scholar."

"I was a different man then."

"You were. But the face is the same under the gray." Madi reached into his saddlebag and produced a small clay pot. "Walnut oil. Darken what is left of the beard, keep a head covering on, and let the illness do the rest. The man they remember stood straight and argued philosophy. The man they see today can barely sit a horse. That is your best disguise."

"If anyone asks about the dye, I am a vain old man who does not wish to look as ill as he feels."

Madi almost smiled. "That will do."

Silina spoke from the rear. "What about me?"

"You are Silina. Your name means nothing to Rome. You are a young woman traveling with a family. No one will question that." He glanced at the sleeping twins. "The children keep their names. Amara and Juba are common enough. They are too young to remember anything different, and that is the safest protection you have. They will grow up believing the stories because to them, the stories will be true."

That knowledge settled over Zahra. Her children would call her Leila. They would call Eudoxus Uncle Numerius. They would grow up inside a lie she had built to keep them alive, and they would not know the difference between the lie and the world.

"How long?" she asked.

"As long as necessary. Years, if Rome keeps searching. The names have to become habit. You cannot hesitate when someone calls you Leila. You cannot flinch when Eudoxus answers to Numerius. The village will watch you in the first weeks. They will decide whether you are who you claim to be based on how naturally you wear the story."

Eudoxus looked down at his hands and then at the village below. Caspar had followed a star. Eudoxus had tried to earn good repute. Numerius would press olives and tell stories about trade routes he had never traveled. Each name was a smaller life than the one before it, and each had cost him something he could not recover.

"One more name," he said. "To add to the collection."

Madi did not smile. "Practice on the way down. Call each other by the new names. If you stumble here, stumble where only I can hear it."

They rode the last stretch of trail speaking names not theirs, testing the shape of lives they had not lived, rehearsing small lies to keep them alive. By the time the village scouts spotted them on the ridge path, Leila answered without hesitation, and Numerius, his beard darkened and a head covering pulled low, managed a wry smile when Usem's name was mentioned.

The twins slept through it. They would wake in a new place, with a mother called Leila and an uncle called Numerius, and they would accept it because children accept the world they are given.

That acceptance, Zahra knew, would someday become the betrayal they could not forgive.

☙✦❧

That night

Usem's house was small and warm, its stone walls holding the day's heat the way a kiln holds fire. Zahra and the children slept on mats against the far wall. Silina had found a corner near the door where she could watch both the room and the courtyard.

Eudoxus sat in the doorway and could not sleep.

The walnut oil stained his fingers. He rubbed it into his beard and hair after Madi left, working the dark paste through the gray. The man in the polished bronze Usem kept by the water basin was someone he did not recognize: gaunt, stooped, dark-bearded, old in ways deeper than years. Madi was right. The disguise required no artifice. He had only to stop pretending he was still the man he used to be.

He tried to sit the way the practice demanded: legs crossed, hands open, breath steady. The posture came, but the stillness did not. His mind catalogued instead. Three names now. Caspar, who believed the heavens owed him answers and spent a lifetime learning they did not. Eudoxus, who taught other people's children and told himself service was enough. Numerius, a trader who had never traded, an uncle who was not an uncle, a man whose trembling hands he would blame on a long illness rather than on the price of calling fire from sacred stones.

Each name had required him to surrender a piece of the truth. Caspar surrendered certainty. Eudoxus surrendered ambition. Numerius would surrender the last thing he had left: the dignity of being known for what he was.

He would press olives alongside men who heard him speak of the divine fire and now must pretend they did not. He would answer to a name with no history, no meaning, no weight. He would watch Zahra's children grow up calling him Uncle and never know the old man at the olive press had once knelt before a child in Bethlehem and felt the foundations of the world shift beneath his knees.

The practice said: note the grief. Let it arise. Let it pass.

It arose. It did not pass. It sat with him in the doorway while the village slept and the stars turned overhead, the same stars he had followed to Judea, the same stars that had led him here, to a borrowed house in a mountain village where he would live under a borrowed name until the Romans forgot or he died, whichever came first.

He sat with it. He did not try to make it pass. The practice had never promised peace. It had promised presence. And presence, tonight, meant sitting in a doorway with walnut oil on his fingers and a name meaning nothing and fitting no one, keeping watch over a family not his that had become the only thing that mattered.

Toward dawn, his quivering hands quieted to a deeper trembling from holding himself together through will alone. It eased because he stopped holding. He let his grief, his weariness, and absurdity of being Numerius settle into his bones as cold settles into stone. To his surprise, he discovered both stone and bone, once they accepted the cold, could hold warmth again.

A house bunting hopped through the doorway and crossed the threshold without hesitation. The small brown bird moved across the packed earth floor with the confidence of a creature that had never learned to fear human spaces. It paused at his knee, tilted its head, and continued past him into the courtyard where the grain jars stood. The Imazighen considered the birds sacred. They entered homes and mosques and shops as if every door had been left open for them, and no one in the mountains would think of shooing one away.

Eudoxus watched it peck at a fallen grain and felt something ease in his chest the meditation had not touched.

He rose stiffly as the first gray light touched the eastern peaks. Zahra stirred. Amara's eyes opened and tracked him across the room with that unsettling focus. Numerius went out to learn where they kept the olive press.

CHAPTER 13
Shadows and Valleys

"The hunter and the hunted measure time differently. One counts days. The other counts breaths."
—Roman intelligence manual (attributed)
Early April 41 CE—Zalacus Mons

Centurion Sextus studied the valley below with professional frustration. "Your intelligence suggested recent movement through this area, Tribune."

Marcus sat on his horse with careful weariness. Six weeks of chasing shadows had worn him thin. "The information was reliable when I received it. But these mountain people have networks we cannot penetrate. Word travels faster than our patrols."

It was almost true. The Amazigh communities closed ranks, and became cautious and protective. What Marcus did not mention was he ensured they had reason for caution and plenty of warning "Three valleys searched," Sextus continued, his voice tight. "Not one confirmed sighting. Either your sources are feeding you old information, or someone is warning them ahead."

"Or Aedemon planned this escape better than we credited." Marcus gestured toward the terrain. "Look at this landscape. Countless caves, hidden springs, settlements are not on any

Roman maps. A woman and two children could disappear into this and stay hidden for years."

The patrol wound through the mountain pass, sixteen legionaries and Marcus himself, all carefully positioned to search everywhere *except* where Zahra and the children sheltered. Marcus had spent the past six weeks perfecting this dance: close enough to seem diligent, distant enough to ensure safety.

Below, perhaps two miles southwest, the settlement of Aghbalou nestled into a protected valley. Usem's household, and within it, the family Marcus was supposedly hunting.

"What about that settlement?" A young optio pointed toward Aghbalou. "Looks substantial enough to hide refugees."

Marcus's heart seized, but he kept his voice level. "Already investigated three weeks ago. Local elder, well established, no recent arrivals matching his description." The lie came easily now, practiced over six weeks of misdirection. "The settlement leader is loyal to Rome. He would report anyone suspicious."

"You questioned him personally?"

"Sent Madi with a pottery order. Gave him reason to visit, look around, ask casual questions." Marcus urged his horse forward, away from the valley. "Nothing worth pursuing. We are better served searching the deeper mountains."

As they rode on, Marcus felt the lie settle into his bones. Each successful deflection bought safety but corrupted him further. Each patrol misdirected confirmed his treason while preserving his honor.

The sun climbed toward noon. Marcus led the patrol northeast, away from Aghbalou, toward valleys he knew were empty. By evening they would return to Caesarea with another report of thorough searching and no results.

Behind them, invisible in the protected valley, Zahra nursed her infant twins while Eudoxus watched the patrol pass and said nothing.

☙✦❧

Same day, late afternoon, Aghbalou settlement

The Roman patrol should not have returned. Marcus had led them away hours ago, confident the danger had passed. But a second patrol, one he had not known about, crested the ridge as the sun descended.

Eudoxus was showing Silina a few of the local herbs that grew in the upper foothills when he felt the disturbance. A wrongness in the air, deeper than sound or sight, made him stop mid-sentence.

"Inside." His voice carried quiet urgency. "Now."

Silina responded to his tone at once. They moved toward the house where Zahra sat with the infant twins, but the patrol was already descending the ridge. Six men, moving fast.

Too late to hide, too exposed to run.

They reached Aghbalou's sacred spring. Eudoxus felt it was time to call once again upon defenses not requiring swords. He had used magic only once before, against the bandits on the mountain road. That confrontation had cost him. This would cost him also, but he did not know how dearly.

The sight of Roman soldiers approaching the house where Zahra and the twins sheltered clarified everything.

He pressed both palms against the sacred stones marking Aghbalou's spring. The settlement's spiritual protections ran ancient and deep. Generations of ancestors had woven the settlement's spiritual protections into the ground. Eudoxus was not summoning new power. He was awakening what already slept.

"Spirits of the land," he spoke in the old tongue, "this place is sacred. Guard those who shelter here."

The response was immediate and agonizing. Power surged through channels still damaged from the bandit encounter. Eudoxus gasped as spiritual pathways, not quite healed, tore wider. The pain was white-hot, fundamental, his connection to the ancestor-realm fracturing under the strain.

The sacred stones blazed with inner light. The spring's surface glowed with phosphorescence with no natural source. Heat rippled the air in visible waves.

The lead Roman soldier stumbled backward. "What sorcery..."

"The spring protects its own." Eudoxus kept his voice steady despite the agony radiating through his hands, his arms, his chest. "You are not welcome here."

For a moment, the patrol hesitated. The supernatural display touched a primal nerve, the instinct making even Roman soldiers pause before forces they did not understand.

Then a young optio, emboldened by daylight and armor, circled toward Eudoxus. "Roman steel fears no desert magic..."

His sword rose.

Silina's scream tore through the air, raw and primal. She had lost too much already and would not lose this. She lunged between the soldier and Eudoxus, arms spread wide, her body a shield.

Eudoxus broke his connection to the spring's power and threw himself forward. The spiritual energy collapsed. What carried him was older than magic and simpler.

The blade meant for Eudoxus's head deflected and struck the spring stones instead. The steel shattered, and the optio screamed, terror stripping the training from his voice. His panicked horse reared and turned before galloping away, followed by the four other equally terrified legionaries.

Eudoxus lay on the ground, his face gray, his breathing shallow. He looked ten years older than he had that morning.

Silina knelt beside him, her healer's hands already assessing damage. "His pulse is threadbare. And his color..." She looked up at Zahra, who had emerged with the twins. "We need to get him inside. Now."

They carried him between them, the scholar who had twice spent his strength defending them. This time, Zahra knew, the cost had been higher. The trembling in his hands was worse. The pallor in his face deeper.

"How bad?" she asked Silina later, when Eudoxus slept and the twins were settled.

"The body will recover. But whatever he did to the spiritual pathways... I do not know if that recovers. He may have damaged them permanently." Silina's voice was steady, professional. "He aged, Lei..." Silina caught herself, glanced toward the open doorway where village women moved past, and started again. "He aged, Leila. I have seen illness do that to people over months. This happened in minutes."

The false name sat wrong in her mouth. She had called this woman Zahra for five years, had held her children as they were born, had fled with her through the night. Now she said Leila and tasted the lie each time.

Zahra looked at the sleeping scholar who had taught her husband philosophy and taught her children their first words.

"He saved us."

"Yes."

"Twice."

"Yes."

From the doorway, Amara watched the sleeping scholar with that focused stillness she brought to everything. Her small body had gone rigid, her fists clenched at her sides, her green eyes fixed on Eudoxus with an intensity no thirteen-month-old should possess. She made no sound. But Silina, watching her, felt the room's grief sharpen.

"She knows," Silina said. "She cannot say it, but she knows."

They sat in silence, watching him breathe, wondering what price remained to be paid for their survival.

❧✦❧

That evening, Caesarea, Governor's residence

Marcus stood at attention, his body rigid with the performance of appropriate frustration. "The mountain Imazighen are protecting them, Governor. Every settlement we approach has been warned in advance. Either Aedemon has people watching our movements, or the tribal networks are more extensive than we estimated."

"Or someone in my own command is ensuring they stay one step ahead."

The accusation landed. Marcus met it directly. "If you doubt my loyalty, replace me. But whoever takes this assignment will face the same challenges. The terrain favors fugitives, and the people will not cooperate with Rome."

Paulinus studied him the way he studied a map he suspected was drawn wrong. "I received a report this afternoon. A patrol encountered a spiritual display at a settlement called Aghbalou. Sacred springs glowing, protective magic, the usual Berber superstition. One of my optios panicked and wounded a village elder."

Marcus's chest tightened, but he kept his expression neutral. "Any connection to the fugitives?"

"Unknown. But Aghbalou is in the search area you have been covering." Paulinus's eyes narrowed. "Interesting your patrols investigated that settlement weeks ago and found nothing worth reporting, yet three days ago another patrol encountered a display significant enough to frighten trained legionaries."

"Significant in the sense of supernatural theater, Governor. Not in the sense of harboring fugitives." Marcus's voice carried dismissive certainty. "If Zahra and the children were there, my investigation would have found them."

"Would it?" Paulinus leaned back. "Or would it have found exactly what you wanted it to find?"

The moment stretched. Then Paulinus waved a hand. "Continue the search. Expand the radius. If they are in those mountains, eventually they will make a mistake."

"Yes, Governor."

As Marcus left the residence, he allowed himself one moment of shaking hands before he steadied them with pure will. The encounter at Aghbalou meant complications: a wounded elder, spooked soldiers, and Paulinus's growing suspicion. The protection had held, but the margins grew thinner with each passing week.

In the mountains, Eudoxus nursed his wounds and his silence. In those valleys, Zahra held her children and measured each day's safety against the days remaining. In the eastern highlands, Aedemon waged his rebellion, unaware his greatest protection came from the man he had betrayed.

And Marcus Valerius Severus walked back to his quarters, a Roman officer committed to the systematic destruction of everything Rome had taught him to value.

PART THREE: THE OASIS

"Safety is a story we tell ourselves between dangers. The wise learn to tell it well."

—From the private writings of Caspar of Ecbatana

CHAPTER 14

Fire Spreads

"Fire spreads fastest where men have forgotten how to fear it."
—Roman military dispatch (attributed)

April—May, 41 CE—Volubilis, Caesarea, and Aghbalou

Over the weeks following Aedemon's escape, the rebellion took shape through a thousand careful conversations in shadowed cellars and mountain camps.

Aedemon had learned patience during his years as Ptolemy's administrator. He understood revolution required more than fury. It demanded infrastructure, coordination, and networks surviving Rome's inevitable response. He moved west from Caesarea to Volubilis, the urban center at the far end of Mauretania. He traveled between safe houses in a beard and rough robes, met resistance leaders, and unified the movement one handshake at a time.

Sabalus of the Mauri brought his eastern mountain tribesmen. These were men hardened by generations of resistance, fighters who knew where every Roman supply line threaded through the passes of the Mons Aurasius. Sabalus raided those lines for years and could choke them off at will. He promised to show the tribes in the western Atlas how to do the same.

⁂

Early April, 41 CE—Tingis

The attack on Tingis came at dawn, when the garrison was changing watch and the market squares stood empty.

Aedemon had not been present. The vast distances and the risk of capture kept the rebellion's sole coordinator away from each strike. Instead, he had spent weeks before the escape laying groundwork through messengers and trusted intermediaries who carried his words across eight hundred miles of mountain passes and coastal roads to reach the tribal chiefs who controlled the western territories.

The strategy had emerged from late-night conversations in Caesarea, in the months before everything shattered. Eudoxus remembered those evenings in Aedemon's study: maps spread across the table, wine growing warm in cups neither man remembered to drink.

"You cannot fight Rome directly," Eudoxus had said, and traced the coastal road connecting Caesarea to Tingis. "Their legions will crush any force you concentrate. But Rome's weakness is distance. They think in straight lines: roads, supply chains, chains of command. They cannot imagine coordination without those chains."

Aedemon had studied the map with the intensity he brought to everything. "The tribes do not trust each other. The mountain Mauri despise the coastal settlements. The craftsmen in the cities think the desert warriors are savages. How do I make them work together when they have spent generations feuding?"

"You do not command them. You coordinate them." Eudoxus had leaned forward and felt the familiar quickening when disparate knowledge aligned. "I spent time with the Parthians, years ago. They defeated Rome at Carrhae by refusing to fight as Rome expected. Strike and withdraw. Never concentrate. Make the legions chase shadows while the real attacks come from directions they have already cleared."

"That requires trust. Timing. Communication across distances taking weeks to cross."

"It requires relationships you have already built." Eudoxus met his eyes. "You have spent twenty years mediating between these groups. You know who leads each faction, who owes favors, who carries grudges that can be redirected toward Rome instead of each other. Use that knowledge. Let each chief believe the strategy is his own."

They had talked until dawn and refined the approach: which leaders to inform and how, which routes messengers could travel without Roman attention. Eudoxus drew on memories of his wandering years, the hidden paths through the Zalacus Mons he had learned from Aghbalou's elders, the trading networks moving goods and information beneath Rome's notice, and how mountain communities communicated through fire signals and drum patterns carrying across valleys.

With Ptolemy's murder, everything had accelerated toward catastrophe, but the framework existed. Aedemon had only to activate what they had designed together.

❧✦❧

Same day—Aghbalou

Eudoxus sat in the courtyard of their borrowed house and watched the twins sleep in the shade while Zahra helped the village women prepare the afternoon meal. His hands quivered as he held a cup of water.

He saw the smoke before anyone spoke of it.

A dark smudge on the southern horizon, the color of burning timber and grain, not the pale thread of a cooking fire or the gray haze of a shepherd clearing brush. This smoke rose in a column thick enough to cast its own shadow, and it came from the direction of the coastal plain, from somewhere no natural fire would burn at this season.

He set the cup on the wall and stood. Across the village square, Usem had seen it too. The village leader stood at the edge of the ridge path, shielding his eyes, reading the smoke with a chieftain's attention. His people had survived by reading horizons.

The elders gathered without being called. They came to the ridge the way birds come to a thermal, drawn by invisible currents, assembling in silence, each face turned south. They studied the column: its color, which told them the fuel. Its direction, which told them the wind. Its volume, which told them the scale. Dark smoke meant structures burning, not grass. The column leaned east, which meant a westerly wind carrying it toward the interior. And the sheer mass of it said this was not a single building or a storehouse raid. A city was on fire.

They watched through the afternoon. A second column rose to the west of the first, then a third, fainter, further away. The twins woke and Zahra carried them inside, away from the ridge where the elders stood like sentries reading a language written in ash across the sky.

By evening, a trader passed through on the road north. He had come from the lowlands. His clothes smelled of smoke and his eyes held a flat, hollowed look. He had seen more than he wished to carry. "Tingis," he said, accepting water at the village gate. "The garrison overwhelmed. Grain stores burning. The western chiefs struck at dawn from three directions. By the time I cleared the Rif passes, the smoke was behind me for two days of riding."

Usem heard him out, gave him bread, and sent him on his way. Then he crossed the square to the courtyard where Eudoxus waited, his expression confirming what the smoke had already said.

"Numerius." Usem used the alias even here, in the courtyard, with no one listening but the sleeping twins. The habit had become reflex over the months, but it still cost him each time, addressing his cousin's oldest friend by a merchant's name, the decades they shared could not be folded into a lie and tucked away.

"Tingis has been struck." Usem kept his voice low. "The garrison overwhelmed, the grain stores burned. Romans dead in the streets. The western chiefs coordinated perfectly. By the time reinforcements could reach the city from Volubilis, the attackers had melted into the Rif Mountains."

Eudoxus absorbed this without visible reaction, though his chest tightened. It worked. The strategy they designed in comfortable lamplight, spoke of tribal coordination and Roman vulnerabilities as if they discussed philosophy rather than planned death.

"Casualties?" His voice came out steadier than he felt.

"Roman dead number perhaps sixty. Garrison strength reduced by half before they could organize a defense." Usem paused. "Civilian casualties unknown. The city burned in places. Markets, warehouses. "The trader said smoke was visible for two days of travel."

Markets. Where merchants sold grain, oil, and cloth. Where women brought children to buy food for evening meals. Where old men gathered to gossip and young couples walked in the cooling afternoon.

Eudoxus set down the cup before his hands betrayed him.

"The coordination was remarkable," Usem continued, and watched him. "Three separate tribal groups struck simultaneously from different directions. The trader heard Roman officers in the lowlands asking each other how warriors who had feuded for generations could move as one."

Because a man who had studied empires and understood their weaknesses showed them how. A man who walked among the Parthians and learned how inferior forces could defeat superior ones by refusing to fight on the enemy's terms. That man now hid in a mountain village and watched children sleep while men died in fire and chaos eight hundred miles away.

"The rebellion gains strength," Usem said. "But Rome will respond. Paulinus is already gathering forces. Traders on the road say Paulinus is pulling troops from every coastal garrison."

"He will cross the Atlas." Eudoxus heard the distance in his own voice. "He is ambitious. He will want to be the first Roman general to reach the southern territories. He will pursue the rebels beyond any reasonable military objective because the glory of exploration matters more to him than efficient suppression."

Usem studied him with new assessment. "You know Roman commanders well."

"I have watched them for decades." Exhaustion settled into his bones like winter cold. "They are predictable in their ambitions. Paulinus will chase glory into the desert while Geta handles the actual pacification. Which means the pressure on settlements like this one will intensify."

"We have already discussed precautions."

"Precautions will not be enough if Rome decides to make examples." Eudoxus forced himself to meet Usem's eyes. "The strategy Aedemon designed requires Rome to disperse their forces in pursuit of multiple threats. But it also ensures when Rome does concentrate, their fury will be terrible. Every Roman who died at Tingis has family, friends, commanders who will demand vengeance."

The twins stirred in their blankets. Amara's eyes opened and fixed on Eudoxus with that uncanny focus she sometimes showed. She sensed the turmoil beneath his stillness. Her small hand reached toward him, and he took it. The gesture quieted the tremors in his fingers.

"You helped design this." Usem's voice held recognition rather than accusation. "The strategy. The coordination."

"I gave him knowledge." The words came out heavy and dead. "What empires fear. How inferior forces can prevail through coordination rather than concentration. I dressed it in philosophy, but the outcome was always going to be burning markets and men who will never come home."

"Would you undo it? Leave your people defenseless against Rome?"

"No." The admission cost him. "Rome would have come regardless. At least this way there is resistance. At least this way, Aedemon's family may survive."

"Then accept what you have done." Usem's voice carried the authority of a leader who had made similar calculations. "The crops we plant sometimes yield bitter harvests. The walls we build sometimes become prisons. But we plant and build anyway, because the alternative is worse."

After Usem left, Eudoxus sat with Amara until Zahra returned. The girl had fallen back asleep, her hand still curled around his finger, trusting, innocent of what her touch quieted.

He thought about the conversations in Aedemon's study. The excitement he felt as the strategy took shape, the intellectual satisfaction of solving a complex problem. He approached it like a philosophical puzzle: how to enable resistance against overwhelming force. He did not think about the burning markets, the screaming men, the specific humans who would die because his advice was sound.

❧✦❧

Late April, 41 CE—Caesarea, garrison headquarters

Kassem the stoneworker represented Volubilis's urban craftsmen, laborers who built Roman walls but lived outside Roman prosperity. His people understood the city's vulnerabilities: granaries feeding garrisons, aqueducts sustaining populations, and markets where disruption rippled outward like stones dropped in still water.

Between them, Aedemon wove the coordination neither faction possessed alone. They planned three simultaneous strikes. Warriors from the desert tribes would harass and draw Roman forces from coastal cities. Craftsmen and artisans who could not compete with cheap Roman merchandise would foment urban riots to create chaos within those strongholds. Targeted attacks on isolated garrisons would demonstrate Roman control was illusion maintained by reputation rather than reality.

The timing was set for early May. Three coordinated actions would force Paulinus to choose which threat to address first, and whatever he chose, the others would succeed.

Marcus knew the plan before Aedemon finalized it. Information flowed through networks serving both the rebellion and Rome, depending on how one read them. And Marcus had become very good at reading them in ways serving his purposes while appearing to serve Paulinus's.

Marcus laid the reports across Paulinus's desk with the careful arrangement of a man presenting evidence rather than intelligence. Three separate accounts, each from a different source, each pointing toward the same conclusion.

"The pattern is clear, Governor. Aedemon is consolidating tribal support in the eastern highlands." Marcus indicated a map where he had marked supposed rebel movements. "These reports place him near Lambaesis, meeting with Mauri chiefs known for raiding Roman supply lines."

Paulinus studied the documents with the intensity of a general reading battlefield terrain. "Lambaesis is three hundred miles southeast. Deep desert territory, difficult to reach, harder to pacify."

"Which is precisely why he would choose it." Marcus kept his voice level, professional: the tone of an intelligence officer presenting uncomfortable facts. "If he is building a coalition there, we will need significant forces to root him out. Mountain warfare in hostile territory, against fighters who know the terrain."

"How reliable are these sources?"

"Two are merchants whose trade routes take them through rebel territories. They have no love for disruption; it costs them profit. The third is a Mauri chief whose clan has remained neutral but maintains relationships with both sides." Marcus paused, considering how much to reveal. "I have used all three before. Their information has proven accurate."

It had been accurate when Marcus wanted it to be. He had built these sources over years and ensured they could provide truthful intelligence when needed to maintain credibility, and misdirection when necessary to protect what mattered.

What he did not mention was the Mauri chief was Sabalus's cousin and the merchants were Hassan's network. Every word in those reports had been crafted to draw Roman attention three hundred miles from where the actual uprising would occur.

"I want patrols reinforced along the Lambaesis corridor," Paulinus decided. "If he is consolidating tribal support there, we interdict him before the coalition solidifies."

Marcus made notes, his stylus scratching across wax tablets. "That will require pulling men from the coastal garrisons. Volubilis, Tingis, the western settlements."

"The coastal cities are secure. It is the interior tribes that concern me." Paulinus turned back to the map. "How many cohorts for an effective interdiction?"

"Four, minimum. Perhaps six if you want to establish a permanent presence and cut off his supply lines."

"Six cohorts it is. Draw up the deployment orders."

Marcus bowed and withdrew. At the door he paused. A thought had just occurred to him. "Governor, if the situation at Lambaesis requires you to move westward, the coastal road through Caesarea is the faster route. The Atlas passes are unreliable this time of year."

Paulinus waved him off. "If I move westward, Tribune, I will cross the Atlas. No Roman general has done it. The passes will serve."

Of course he would. Marcus had counted on it. A thousand miles of mountain and desert between Lambaesis and Volubilis, and Paulinus would choose the longest route because it offered the greater glory. By the time he crossed those passes and turned north, the fires would be ash and the rebels would be ghosts.

A second time Marcus bowed and withdrew, carrying orders stripping Volubilis's garrison to half strength just as Kassem's people prepared to riot. His betrayal settled across his shoulders like a yoke as he crossed the compound.

The rebellion would launch in three days. Marcus's intelligence ensured when it did, Rome's response forces would be three hundred miles away, chasing ghosts in the desert. But actual fires would burn their coastal strongholds.

☙✦❧

That afternoon—Caesarea, the stables

Marcus met Madi where conversations could be lost in the sounds of horses and the bustle of soldiers preparing for deployment.

"The family?" Marcus kept his voice low.

"Secure at Aghbalou. No recent patrols in that area. Your misdirection has held." Madi checked a saddle strap, his movements casual. "But the uprising will change that. Paulinus will crack down hard afterward."

"I know." Marcus had already calculated the aftermath. "That is why they need to move deeper, beyond the areas Rome can search. After Volubilis burns, nowhere close to the coast will be safe."

"Eudoxus knows?"

"He knows. He is already making arrangements." Marcus glanced around and ensured their privacy. "Three days, Madi. Keep them away from Volubilis, keep them quiet, and when the chaos begins, use it as cover to move them."

"And you?"

"I will be exactly where Paulinus expects me. Providing intelligence. Hunting rebels. Serving Rome." The bitterness in his voice surprised even himself. "Until the protection fails and this house of lies collapses."

❧✦❧

Early May, 41 CE—dawn—Volubilis

The market began its daily rhythm with the usual sounds: merchants arranging goods, carts rumbling over stone, the multilingual babble of commerce that sustained the city for centuries. Kassem moved through the crowd with a basket of tools, just another craftsman headed to work.

He placed the basket beside a grain warehouse door, adjusted its contents, and walked away.

Three blocks distant, another craftsman did the same beside an oil warehouse. Then another at the textile warehouses near the docks. Ten locations, ten baskets were all positioned with casual precision. They knew the city's commercial heart.

When the sun reached its zenith and the market swelled with midday crowds, the first fire began with the patient hunger of flames fed by oil-soaked grain. Smoke poured from the warehouse before anyone noticed actual fire. By the time the alarm went up, three more warehouses burned.

The garrison responded as trained: cohorts formed up, bucket brigades organized, officers shouted orders. But the fires had been set with purpose and forced Roman soldiers to choose between containing the blazes and maintaining order as panic rippled through the crowd.

That was when Kassem's people struck in earnest.

They struck with chaos, amplified beyond the garrison's capacity to contain it. Carts overturned and blocked streets. Saboteurs damaged aqueduct valves and cut water to the firefighting efforts. Dock warehouses were breached, their contents "looted" in coordinated actions resembling opportunistic theft but amounting to strategic supply denial.

By mid-afternoon, Volubilis burned in six locations. Its streets choked with panicked civilians, its garrison overwhelmed by simultaneous crises multiplying faster than Roman discipline could suppress.

The centurion commanding Volubilis's depleted garrison sent runners to Caesarea requesting reinforcements. But the messengers had to fight through blocked roads, and even when they reached open ground, the nearest available cohorts were three hundred miles away, deployed on Marcus's intelligence to interdict nonexistent rebel movements.

As smoke darkened the sky and flames consumed Roman grain meant to feed legions across Mauretania, Sabalus's warriors struck the supply routes east of the city. They used tactics mountain fighters had perfected over generations: ambushes at narrow passes, poisoned wells, stolen horses. The harassment turned Roman supply convoys into exhausted, demoralized columns stumbling through hostile territory.

By evening, reports reached Caesarea describing simultaneous attacks across a front spanning two hundred miles. The rider who brought word of the Volubilis engagement described it with grudging admiration. "The mountain fighters screamed insults while they fought, called the legionaries women, said their swords had never tasted blood, said their mothers should have drowned them in the river. The Romans cursed back in Latin the fighters could not understand. Two armies screaming obscenities in languages the other could not speak." He shook his head. "If it were not so bloody, it would have been funny."

To Paulinus, nothing about it was funny. It looked like the coordinated uprising he had feared. To Marcus, it looked like the protection he had engineered, bought with lies and paid for with whatever remained of his honor.

❧✦❧

One week later—Caesarea

Paulinus summoned his command staff at dawn, his scarred face carrying the cold fury of a general who had been outmaneuvered.

"Forty-three dead, over a hundred wounded. Three months' grain supply destroyed. Two cohorts ambushed and mauled in the eastern passes." His finger stabbed at the map. "And the reinforcements I sent to Lambaesis found nothing but cooperative tribal chiefs who knew nothing about any rebel consolidation."

The implication hung in the air. Someone's intelligence had been wrong, or worse, misleading by design.

Marcus stood at attention, his face neutral while his mind raced through justifications and deflections. "The sources were reliable, Governor. Either Aedemon anticipated our response and changed locations, or..."

"Or your sources fed you exactly what the rebels wanted us to believe." Paulinus's voice was dangerously quiet. "Six cohorts deployed to the desert while Volubilis burned. A coincidence, Tribune?"

"I can only report what intelligence indicates..."

"Then your intelligence is compromised." Paulinus cut him off. "Either your sources are rebel agents, or Aedemon's strategic deception has outplayed you. Either way, it ends now."

He turned to address the full assembly. "New protocols. We will cross-verify all intelligence reports through multiple sources before making deployment decisions. Tribune Severus will continue his duties under the direct supervision of General Geta. And we assume any network capable of coordinating these attacks can penetrate our intelligence operations."

Marcus bowed. "Yes, Governor."

As the briefing concluded, Geta approached with the smile of a predator who had caught a scent.

"You will report directly to me now, Tribune. Every source, every contact, every piece of intelligence. We will review your networks together and identify where the compromise occurred." His smile widened. "I am very good at finding gaps in people's stories."

Marcus returned to his quarters and knew the protection had just grown far more difficult. Geta would scrutinize every report, question every source, probe every inconsistency. The misdirection that had bought safety for Zahra and the children now faced a threat more dangerous than Paulinus's strategic ambition: Geta's instinct for the hunt.

He remembered a mountain patrol with Geta six months earlier. The general's horse had stumbled on loose scree for the third time, and Geta's response had echoed off the canyon walls.

"Futue! These mountains are not terrain, they are a punishment designed by a sadist." He hauled the reins and spat downhill. "The Berbers can keep their rock piles. Any people who build upward instead of outward deserve what Rome does to them."

"The locals say the mountains protect them," Marcus had offered.

"Mountains protect goats and scorpions. Civilized people live on flat ground." Geta scanned the ridgeline with a predator's restlessness. "Ten years in the legions. Worse than Britannia. In Britannia it at least had the decency to be flat while it rained on you."

The memory sharpened Marcus's assessment now. Geta did not strategize. He hunted. And hunters caught what they pursued.

But in the Zalacus Mons foothills, Eudoxus was already moving the family deeper into the mountains, and the chaos of the uprising covered their relocation. The rebellion had achieved its immediate purpose: it demonstrated Roman control was conditional, maintained by force, never accepted by the population.

And Marcus had achieved his: he had bought time for Aedemon's family to disappear into territories where Rome's reach weakened with every mile.

The cost was his career, his reputation, and possibly his life. But as he sat in his quarters that evening and calculated how much longer the deception could hold, he told himself it was worth it.

Some debts transcended loyalty to empire. Some promises outlived the men who made them.

CHAPTER 15

First Words

"The stranger becomes neighbor when she knows which well to use."
—Amazigh village wisdom

Early May, 41 CE—Aghbalou—twins age fourteen months

The village had begun to accept them, in the cautious way mountain communities accepted strangers. Aghbalou clung to the mountain slope like a growth from the rock itself. The houses stacked against the hillside, their stone walls following the contours of the terrain, each roof serving as the courtyard for the dwelling above. Narrow lanes climbed between them, worn smooth by generations of feet. At the village center stood the communal granary, a fortified tower with walls thicker than any dwelling, its single door facing east and its roof crowned with the horns of a wild ram, protection against both thieves and the spirits coveting stored grain.

Zahra helped the women at the well and learned the rhythm of their conversations, the subtle hierarchies governing village life. She discovered which families held grudges stretching back generations, which marriages had united rival clans, which children were watched with extra care because their fathers had died in Rome's service.

Silina worked in the communal garden, and her knowledge of herbs and healing plants earned grudging respect. When the blacksmith's daughter developed a persistent cough, she prepared a remedy that cleared it within days. When old Kahina's joints swelled with the damp spring weather, she knew which plants to brew into a tea that brought relief. The village women sought her out with their small ailments and their larger fears.

Eudoxus sat with the elders in the evening and shared stories of his years on the trade routes. He told them of the ports where merchants cheated with weighted scales, of mountain passes where bandits waited for caravans, and of the strange customs of Carthage and Antioch. He spoke well for a trader, the elders agreed, and asked questions showing a mind sharper than his profession required. His hands still trembled with the shiver plaguing him since the sacred spring, and sometimes Zahra caught him staring at his own fingers.

Usem watched the old man's hands on the olive press beam and grunted approval. "Your arms remember work."

"I grew up on my grandfather's farm, before I went east to trade." Eudoxus leaned into the press and felt muscles protest that had softened through decades of sitting in one place too long.

"East." Usem spat olive pits into the collection basket with practiced aim. "City traders who come back with soft hands and opinions about everything they have never done." His tone was easy, but his eyes held a warning Eudoxus recognized. Stay with the story. "Where did you trade?"

"Alexandria, mostly. Antioch. Wherever ships sailed and profit margins proved favorable.

Eudoxus caught the warning and adjusted. "I was a better haggler than farmer. My grandfather never forgave me."

"Gray beards we respect," Usem said, steering the conversation onto safer ground. "It is the young ones from the cities that concern us. Soft hands, clean robes, and they think they can tell a man who has pressed olives for forty years how to press olives." His grin cracked the weathered landscape of his face. "You have calluses, though. That counts."

"He has the calluses of a man who held scrolls, not tools," a voice called from the far side of the press. "But he is trying. Which is more than Massoud's boy, who moves like a camel that forgot where water is."

General laughter. Massoud's son, who had been working the press beam with exaggerated effort, responded with a gesture needing no translation.

Eudoxus smiled. The banter carried the same rhythms he had heard in olive groves across the Mediterranean: men testing a newcomer's composure, probing his reactions. The insults were measures. What mattered was how you received them.

"In the port cities," he offered, "the merchants insult each other's arithmetic. Here, you insult each other's livestock. I am not sure which cuts deeper."

Usem barked a laugh. "A man who can take a joke and give one back. Perhaps you will survive the mountains after all."

They pressed in companionable silence for a while, the golden oil pooling in the collection trough with its sharp, grassy scent. The first press was for cooking, Usem explained. The second for the lamps. The third, mixed with herbs, for treating wounds and weathering skin against the mountain cold.

While the adults adjusted, the twins thrived. Now barely past their first year, they could not yet understand the local humor or the danger that had brought them here. They would not have comprehended the careful deceptions keeping them safe. They knew only this place offered food and warmth and the steady presence of their mother.

Juba had begun to laugh more, his infant babbling taking on tones almost like speech. He would lie on his back in the sun and wave his fists at the sky. Each day brought new sounds, new responses to the world around him. The village children gathered to watch him, made faces to provoke his gummy grins, and competed to see who could draw the loudest laugh.

Amara remained quieter. She watched, always watched. When the village children played nearby, her eyes followed their movements with an intensity some of the mothers found uncomfortable. When arguments broke out, as they did in any close community, she would whimper and turn her face away. The discord caused her pain.

"She feels too much," one of the village women observed to Zahra at the well. "Children should laugh and play, not carry such sorrow in their eyes."

"She has always been sensitive. Some children are."

The woman's expression suggested she thought it was more than sensitivity, but she said nothing further. In a world where differences could mark you as dangerous, it was often safer to pretend not to notice.

Usem had given them a single-room house with a cracked lintel when they arrived. They repaired the roof, rebuilt the courtyard wall, and planted seedlings in the tiny garden behind the house. Herbs and vegetables would grow by summer's end. Silina hung bundles of dried rosemary and thyme from the ceiling beams, and the scent of them made the cramped space smell like a healer's workshop. Eudoxus slept in the corner beside the few scrolls he had saved, his small lamp burning late into most nights.

They had work, they had shelter, they had a fragile kind of peace.

Zahra had almost begun to believe it could last.

❧✦☙

Three weeks later—evening

The evening of the third week, as the sun painted the western mountains gold and crimson, Madi walked into Aghbalou on foot.

He left his horse at the lower spring, a mile south, where the trail entered the valley through a gap in the ridge. A man on horseback drew attention. A man on foot, carrying a trader's pack, drew nothing. Madi had spent his life learning the difference.

Zahra saw him first. She stood near the well with Amara against her shoulder in the warm evening air. She recognized his movements before she recognized his face. His stride was careful. He checked his surroundings with every step and knew the distance between himself and every exit. He had survived this long by never assuming safety was permanent.

Three days of dust covered his clothes. His face was drawn in ways deeper than travel. His mission had cost him sleep.

He did not stop at the village edge to announce himself, as a messenger would. He nodded to the sentry, exchanged a quiet word with the woman at the nearest cooking fire, and walked through the settlement toward the central square with the ease of familiarity. He knew this place and was known here. He arranged the family's escape from Caesarea. He guided them through the mountain passes. Half the village owed him debts they would never speak of and could never repay.

Usem met him in the square with a clasp of forearms and a look that asked its question without words. Madi's face answered. Usem's shoulders tightened.

They moved together toward the stream where the sound of water would mask their conversation. Zahra watched from the well. Eudoxus, seated with the other elders in the square, saw them go and rose to follow.

They moved away from the others. Zahra, still at the well, watched them talk. Eudoxus's posture changed. He turned toward their house, where Silina was preparing the evening meal.

When they finished, Eudoxus walked back across the square. The conversation had carved new lines into his face.

"What is it?" Zahra asked as he approached. "What news?"

"Not here." He gestured toward their house. "Inside."

They gathered in the small front room as twilight deepened into night. Silina lit the lamp while Eudoxus lowered himself to the floor. Juba slept in the back room, his soft breathing audible through the doorway. Amara had woken and watched them all with those too-knowing eyes.

"Volubilis has burned. Three days ago. Coordinated attacks: fires in the warehouses, riots in the streets, supply convoys ambushed on the roads. The garrison was overwhelmed."

Zahra caught herself before speaking Aedemon's name and glanced at Amara even though the infant could not understand. She lowered her voice. "The one we do not name. Is he..."

"Madi did not know. But the uprising was coordinated across multiple locations. Urban chaos combined with desert attacks. That kind of planning requires someone who understands both the cities and the tribes. Someone who can forge alliances between groups that have never trusted each other."

Aedemon, Zahra thought, the name she could not speak aloud burning in her chest. Her husband, who had spent twenty years mediating between Rome and the Imazighen, who knew the urban artisans and the desert warriors, who understood how to make disparate groups work toward common goals.

"And Rome's response?" Silina asked.

"Swift and brutal. Governor Paulinus has declared martial law across the coastal regions. Arrests, interrogations, reprisals against anyone suspected of rebel sympathies." Eudoxus met Zahra's eyes. "They are hunting for the rebellion's leadership. For the coordinators who made this possible."

"For him."

"Yes. And for anyone connected to him." Eudoxus shifted his weight, his face troubled. "Usem says the Romans are intensifying their searches. More patrols, more thorough investigations. They are looking for his networks now, his support structures. The people who shelter rebels or provide them with supplies and intelligence. Madi said one thing more." Eudoxus hesitated. "The smoke from the grain stores was visible from the sea. Ships changed course to avoid the harbor. Fishermen off the coast thought the city was being swallowed by the earth."

The implication settled over the room like cold fog. They sheltered rebels. Their presence put Aghbalou at risk.

"How long do we have?" Silina's voice was practical, already moving toward what came next.

"Unknown. Usem says the patrols have not reached this far into the mountains yet. But after Volubilis..." Eudoxus spread his hands. "Rome will want to demonstrate strength. They will expand their search areas and investigate settlements they ignored before. Aghbalou has been left alone because we cooperate: we provide grain, we pay taxes, we cause no trouble. But if Rome suspects we harbor fugitives..."

"They will make an example of us," Silina finished.

"Of all of us," Eudoxus agreed. "The village, the families, the children. Rome does not make fine distinctions when demonstrating power."

Zahra looked down at Amara, whose eyes had closed again, her small face peaceful in sleep. Three weeks of safety. Three weeks of believing they might have found enduring sanctuary.

"What does Usem want us to do?" she asked.

"Nothing yet." Eudoxus's voice carried the gravity of difficult truths. "He is not asking us to leave. But he is warning us the situation has changed. The protection Aghbalou can offer is more fragile than it was a month ago."

"And if the patrols come here?"

"Then we deal with it as it comes. But you need to understand: if Rome comes to Aghbalou searching for rebel sympathizers, they must not find evidence linking you to the uprising. You are refugees. A scholar and his niece's family, fleeing instability in the capital. That story must hold."

Silina spoke with confidence. "It will hold. We have been careful. We have told no one the truth."

"Good." Eudoxus settled back, the tension in his shoulders easing. "Then we continue as we have been. We work, we contribute, we become part of Aghbalou's daily life. And we pray Rome's attention stays focused on the coast, where the rebellion is active, and does not turn toward these mountains."

✦

That same evening—Caesarea, Marcus's quarters

Marcus stood at the window and looked toward the mountains where the family sheltered. The reports from Volubilis lay on his desk behind him: casualty counts, damage assessments, intelligence about the uprising's coordination.

And in the center of it all, the question Paulinus had asked with cold fury: How had Rome's intelligence failed so completely?

Six cohorts deployed to Lambaesis on Marcus's intelligence, leaving Volubilis vulnerable. The uprising coordinated with precision suggesting insider knowledge of Roman deployments. The timing too perfect for coincidence.

Geta had looked at Marcus during that briefing as a dog might look at a closed hand, certain something is hidden inside. He had not accused Marcus. Not yet. But the scrutiny had begun.

New protocols: every intelligence report cross-verified through multiple sources. Every recommendation examined for gaps or inconsistencies. And Marcus now reporting to Geta, who had survived Rome's streets by learning to read lies in people's breathing.

The protection had always been temporary. Marcus had known that from the start. But he had hoped for more time, months, perhaps a year, before the careful structure of misdirection collapsed under its own accumulation.

Instead, he had days. Maybe weeks if fortune held.

He thought of Madi telling him how Zahra settled into village life under her borrowed name. He thought of the twins, now fourteen months old, growing in safety purchased with his lies.

And he thought of Paulinus's words during the private briefing after the others had left: "Someone knew our deployments, Tribune. Someone fed us intelligence designed to leave Volubilis vulnerable. Find them. Because if I discover it came from within my own command..."

The threat needed no finishing.

Marcus turned back to his desk and reports demanding his attention. He had to construct new intelligence more carefully this time. He had to deflect suspicion while maintaining just enough credibility to remain useful. He had to walk the narrowing line between protection and exposure, and each step brought him closer to the moment when the line disappeared.

He poured wine, drank it in a single swallow, and felt it burn down his throat. Then he sat at his desk and wrote the next set of lies that would keep Rome's gaze turned away from one small mountain village where a family slept under borrowed names and borrowed safety.

CHAPTER 16

One Stone at a Time

"Trust is a wall built one stone at a time.
Suspicion needs only a single crack."
—Numidian proverb

Summer, 41 CE—three months after the uprising—Aghbalou and Caesarea

The morning sun turned the olive leaves silver as Zahra carried water from the well. The jar balanced on her shoulder, its weight familiar now after three months of daily trips. Her arms had grown strong from the work, her hands calloused from weaving and grinding grain. The soft noblewoman who had fled Caesarea in the night had become a different woman.

Amara rode in the sling across Zahra's back, her eyes tracking everything: the women at the well, the children herding goats, the old men settling into their morning positions along the sunny wall. She rarely cried now, but she watched with an intensity causing the village women to whisper when they thought Zahra could not hear.

At the courtyard, Silina chased Juba around the well for the third time that morning. He shrieked with laughter and ran on unsteady legs toward the goat pen, his new favorite word punctuating every step: "Ma! Ma! Ma!" He discovered it two weeks ago and now applied it to everything: mothers, goats, bread, the sky. Each utterance delighted him, as if he had unlocked a fundamental secret of the universe.

Silina caught him before he reached the goats and swung him onto her hip. "Someone is proud of himself." The young woman had changed too over these months. The nervous vigilance of their first weeks eased into steady confidence. Her hands moved with purpose through daily tasks, and the village women sought her advice about fevers and coughs, about which herbs eased childbirth pains.

Zahra set down the water jar and took Amara from the sling. The toddler reached for her brother with soft sounds carrying clear meaning. Juba twisted in Silina's arms to see his sister, his face lighting up.

"Ba!" he announced. "Ba ba ba!"

Amara responded with her own stream of vowels, and they conducted their private conversation in a language only they understood. Zahra watched them and felt the familiar catch in her chest. Aedemon should see this. Their children, healthy and growing, learning to speak, reaching for each other across the space between them.

He was alive. He had to be alive. The news from Volubilis had been about Roman casualties and destroyed warehouses, about the uprising's coordination and effectiveness. No one had mentioned him by name. If he had been captured, Rome would have trumpeted that victory. If he had been killed, someone would have brought word.

So she told herself he was fighting still, in the mountains, waging his war. And one day he would come back to find his family safe, his children thriving, and she could tell him she had kept her promise. She had protected them. She had survived.

"The twins eat well," old Kahina observed, and settled onto the courtyard wall with a basket of beans to sort. The village elder came most mornings now, her presence a sign of acceptance warming Zahra more than she wanted to admit. "Strong children. The sky-father favors them."

"They are blessed," Zahra agreed, and used the response she had learned was proper. Not too proud, which would invite envy. Not too humble, which would seem false.

Kahina's fingers paused on a bean. "You speak well, Leila. Better each week. But your tongue carries the flat country in it. The open places." She resumed sorting. "My daughter married a man from the southern trade routes. He spoke Tamazight the way you do. All the vowels stretched wide, like the land shaped them."

Zahra kept her hands steady on Amara's clothing. "My mother's family lived near the eastern trade roads. We moved often."

"Mm." Kahina dropped the sorted beans into her basket. "The eastern tribes produce strong women. Different herbs, different songs, different ways of grinding grain. But strong." She glanced at Zahra with eyes missing nothing. "You grind the way city women grind. Quick, impatient, as if the stone should do the work faster. Desert women grind slow. Mountain women grind steady. City women grind like they have somewhere else to be."

Zahra said nothing. The observation cut closer than she liked.

"No matter." Kahina waved a gnarled hand. "You are learning our rhythm. That is what counts."

Zahra exhaled. The old woman saw everything and demanded nothing. Her generosity was its own kind of shelter. "I am trying," she said. "Your rhythm is worth learning."

"And you, sister?" Kahina's gnarled fingers worked through the beans with practiced speed. "You sleep?"

The question caught Zahra off guard. She thought her exhaustion well hidden, the nightmares contained to the hours when darkness covered the village.

"Well enough."

"Hm." Kahina's grunt suggested she knew better. "The well women say you wake before dawn and walk the terraces when the rest of us sleep."

Zahra focused on Amara, adjusting the toddler's clothing, not meeting those knowing eyes. "I do not want to disturb Silina and Numerius. The house is small."

"The house is small," Kahina agreed. "But walking alone in the dark is how we lose ourselves. How we let grief eat us from inside."

Zahra stopped. The denial would be a lie, and she suspected Kahina would know it.

"Your man fights." Kahina's voice held no judgment. "You do not know if he lives or dies. You carry that uncertainty every moment, like a stone in your chest. I know. I carried it for three years when my husband went to fight the Romans. Before they sent his sword back without him."

The courtyard fell quiet except for the twins' babbling and the soft click of beans being sorted.

"But you have work," Kahina continued. "And children who need you strong. So, you wake early, yes. You walk when you cannot sleep. But you also eat. You also rest when you can. You also let others help carry what you cannot carry alone."

She stood, stiff with age but steady with purpose. "The new moon feast is in three days. You will come. You will bring the children. You will let the village see you are with us, not just among us. That matters here."

After Kahina left, Zahra sat with the twins and watched them toddle across the courtyard's packed earth while she tried to sort her tangled thoughts. The village was accepting them, slowly, with reservations. That should feel like victory.

Instead, it felt like surrender: accepting village life was all they would have, with its daily routines of gathering grain, and hauling water. That was life for these villagers. But not for her. Not for her family.

✦

Late afternoon—the olive press

Eudoxus sat with the men who operated Aghbalou's communal press and learned the rhythm of their work. The months since the sacred spring aged him: his movements slower, his stamina diminished. The connection between breath and stone had once come as naturally as sight. Now when he reached for the old pathways, he met only silence.

Usem handed him a basket of unsorted figs. "Separate the green from the black. Even your hands can manage that."

Eudoxus sorted in silence for a while, grateful for work to occupy the hands without demanding the mind. Around him, men talked about the season's yield, about which trees had produced well and which had disappointed, about the rain that came too late to help the upper terraces.

"The library in Alexandria," the young man at the press beam said, and returned to his favorite subject. "Is it true they have a copy of every book ever written?"

"I would not know. I was there to trade, not to read." Eudoxus set aside a bruised olive. "But I wandered in once, when I had time between shipments. The smell of it stays with you. Papyrus and ink and old leather. A smell telling you people have been thinking there for a very long time."

"Will you go back east, when this trouble settles?"

Eudoxus let the question stand. The ports he had known, the trade routes he traveled, the life he had built around another man's household belonged to another life. The roads east led nowhere he could return to.

"No. I will not go back."

"Then you will stay in Aghbalou?" Usem's question was careful, neutral.

"If the village will have us."

"The children are healthy. The young woman knows healing herbs. And you?" Usem gestured at the neatly sorted olives. "You work hard for a trader who claims his best years are behind him. That counts for something."

Eudoxus had learned long ago, on his first sojourn in Aghbalou, such a comment was as close to welcome as strangers could expect.

✦

A trader arrived at the village edge as the afternoon shadows lengthened. He led a single pack horse loaded with salt, steel tools, and the small luxuries the mountain settlements could not produce for themselves: needles, dye, a bolt of linen finer than anything the village looms turned out. Usem greeted him with the familiar ease of men who had conducted business across many seasons.

The trader's name was Bakir. He was a desert man, lean and unhurried. His weathered face had spent more years under open sky than under any roof. He moved through Aghbalou with the comfort of a regular visitor, stopping to exchange news with the women at the well, checking the fit of a harness for a farmer whose mule had grown since his last visit, and settling at the olive press where the men gathered in the late afternoon to talk while the work wound down.

He sat beside Eudoxus without introduction. After a while, he produced a game board from his pack: a flat piece of leather tooled with a grid of intersecting lines, and a pouch of smooth stones, half dark and half light.

"You play?" Bakir asked.

"I have played versions of this in a dozen countries." Eudoxus studied the board. The grid was similar to games he had encountered in Persia and Egypt, but the pattern of starting positions was different, adapted to the landscape the way all Amazigh things were adapted: practical, spare, shaped by the terrain.

They played in silence. Bakir's style revealed itself within the first few moves: patient, unhurried, willing to cede ground early to establish position later. He did not press advantages. He waited for Eudoxus to overextend and then closed the gaps behind him, the way a desert swallows a trail.

Eudoxus lost the first game. He studied the board afterward, retracing the sequence, and recognized a strategy built for open country: conserve strength while your opponent spends his.

"Another?" Bakir asked.

They played until the light failed. Eudoxus lost the second game as well, but more slowly, and Bakir nodded at the improvement without commenting on it. He packed the board, loaded his horse, and left Aghbalou the next morning before dawn, heading south toward the settlements beyond the ridge.

Eudoxus watched him go from the courtyard and said nothing to anyone about the games. But he remembered the way Bakir's hands moved the stones: with precision. He knew where every piece was and where every piece would need to be, three moves from now.

☙✦❧

Evening—the family's house

Juba had claimed the storage chest as his personal mountain. He climbed it, stood on top, and surveyed the room with the satisfaction of a conqueror before Silina pulled him down. He climbed it again. She pulled him down again. He climbed it a third time.

"He will be running before the summer ends," Silina predicted. She had tended children in Rihana's infirmary since she was eight. She knew the signs. "Once they stop falling, there is no catching them."

"He has his father's determination," Zahra said, then caught herself and glanced toward Amara. She lowered her voice. "That same drive to keep trying."

"And his mother's stubbornness." Silina did not flinch. "That is a formidable combination."

Amara sat in Zahra's lap, content to watch her brother's chaos. She could walk well enough when she chose to, but she rarely chose to. She preferred stillness, a vantage point from which her eyes tracked everything: Juba's circuits around the room, the shadows cast by the oil lamp, the moth fluttering near the doorway.

"She will speak in full sentences before Juba manages two words together." Silina watched Amara track the moth. "Some children are like that. They watch and think and then open their mouths and astonish you."

She fell quiet. Silina's parents were taken when she was eight, their crime nothing more than refusing to inform on their neighbors. She rarely spoke of them, but sometimes, like now, a memory would surface and the old pain would flicker across her face.

Zahra shifted Amara to reach out and squeeze Silina's hand. No words were needed. Just the acknowledgment grief lived in all of them, and survival meant carrying it without being crushed.

"Yemma," Juba announced from across the room, beaming at them both. "Yemma Yemma Yemma!"

"Yes, little one." Zahra looked at Silina. "We are both here."

And they were. Two mothers, two children, an old scholar who had sacrificed everything. A family built from loss and necessity, but still a family. Still here. Still surviving.

☙✦❧

Late that night—the backyard

The household slept. Zahra's breathing had steadied into the rhythm of genuine rest rather than exhausted collapse. Silina lay curled around the twins in the back room, her body a barrier between them and whatever dangers might come through the door.

Eudoxus sat alone in the narrow yard behind the house, his back against the mud-brick wall still holding the day's warmth.

He raised his hands to his face. In the moonlight, the left looked as it always had with the weathered, ink-stained fingertips of a scholar. The right shook. Even in this light he could see the wrongness of it. Muscles no longer obeyed. Fingers curled when he willed them straight. The physical damage would improve with time. Silina said so, and she knew wounds.

But the damage no healer could see was the core of the problem.

He closed his eyes and reached inward, the way his grandfather had taught him when he was younger than the twins sleeping inside. He searched for the current flowing beneath the surface of things, the connection between breath and stone, between heartbeat and starlight. The old ways. Those pathways allowed him to call fire from white stones and turn bandits away with words carrying more than sound.

Nothing.

He reached deeper to push past the silence to search for even an echo of what had been.

Emptiness, vast and absolute, like calling into a canyon and hearing nothing.

Eudoxus opened his eyes. The indifferent stars wheeled overhead. He had looked at these same stars fifty years ago, in Persia, before Bethlehem, before everything. He had traced their patterns and believed they held secrets to be unlocked by seekers dedicated enough to try. He, Caspar the treasure-keeper, had hunted cosmic truths across three continents.

Now he sat in a mountain village, his powers burned away and watched stars he could no longer read.

The grief came without warning: a sharp, specific loss caught in his throat. He would never again feel the current moving through water. Never sense the spiritual gravity of a place before entering it. Never speak the words touching places deeper than ears could hear. The working against the bandits, and then the sacred spring, had cost him everything once making him extraordinary.

Fitting, perhaps. Just, even.

Melchior surfaced in his mind. More power than Eudoxus could ever hope to channel, and it had consumed him. The lesson was simple and terrible: the talisman amplified what was already present in its bearer. Melchior's hunger had become the talisman's hunger. And Eudoxus, who had lost his pathways protecting children in a mountain village, could not decide whether the loss was punishment or mercy.

Eudoxus looked at his hand, at the emptiness where power once lived.

What would the talisman have amplified in him? The grief living in his chest, decades old, from the family he had lost before Bethlehem? The desperate need to prevent suffering that drove him across the world? The shame of standing by while his brilliant friend consumed himself?

Perhaps losing his powers might be mercy rather than punishment.

The thought arrived without fanfare. He sat with it as the night deepened and the household behind him continued its peaceful breathing. He did not yet believe it; the loss still felt like loss, the emptiness still echoed. But the possibility existed. The question had been asked.

If the power would have destroyed me the way it destroyed Melchior, then perhaps being reduced to a wounded old man in a mountain village, useful for sorting olives and little else, is its own kind of survival.

In the hills, a fox called to its mate. The sound carried across the darkness, wild and lonely and utterly itself.

Eudoxus lowered his hands to his lap and waited for morning.

☙✦❧

The same evening — Caesarea, Marcus's quarters

Marcus spread the reports across his desk with the careful precision of a man arranging pieces on a game board. Three months since the Volubilis uprising, and Rome's investigation was at last losing its edge.

The interrogations had yielded little of value. The arrested rebels endured torture and revealed only what they must have known their captors would learn: minor names, minor connections, nothing leading to Aedemon or the rebellion's true leadership structure.

Paulinus was forced to accept that the uprising, while coordinated, was the work of opportunistic cells seizing a moment of Roman weakness. The narrative was false, but it served Marcus's purposes. It suggested scattered, disorganized resistance rather than the systematic coordination Aedemon had achieved.

Better still, it pulled Roman attention south and west, toward the coastal regions where the uprising had occurred. The mountain territories, the Zalacus Mons foothills especially, where Aghbalou nestled, were declared low priority for searching. Stable, cooperative communities paying their taxes and causing no trouble held no strategic interest.

Marcus had authored that assessment himself, buried in a longer report about tribal dynamics and regional stability patterns. Paulinus accepted it without question, too focused on the visible threats to examine the reasoning behind declaring certain areas safe.

A quiet knock. Madi let himself in without waiting for an answer, the privilege of shared conspiracy. He carried a wineskin and two cups, which meant he had news worth discussing.

"Geta asked about the Zalacus patrols today," Madi said in Tamazight, settling into the room's single chair. He poured for both of them. "Wanted to know why the northeastern foothills show so little activity in your reports."

"What did you tell him?"

"That goat herders make poor insurgents. He laughed." Madi drank. "He will not laugh forever."

Marcus pulled the quarterly patrol report from the stack. "Seventeen settlements inspected. Look at the grid positions."

Madi studied the map notations. His finger traced the coverage pattern, paused, then traced it again. "Two of these do not exist."

"They have existed on paper for three years. Each quarter I add a detail, a headcount, a tribute assessment, or a note about the well needing repair. They age the way real settlements age. And the space between them..."

"Falls exactly over Aghbalou." Madi set the report down. "Three years you have been building this."

"One invented village at a time. Each report pushes the boundary of plausible error a little further from where it matters."

Madi was quiet for a moment. "And if Geta decides to verify the grid himself? He is the kind who rides out and counts rooftops."

"Then I will need two days' warning and a convincing reason for him to ride somewhere else."

"I can give you the warning. The reason is your problem." Madi refilled their cups. "How is the family?"

"The trader Bakir passed through last month. The children are healthy. The old man works the olive press." Marcus stared at the map where his fictional villages sat like sentries guarding an invisible gate. "Eudoxus is teaching them to read the stars, Bakir says. The girl already knows the major constellations."

"And you are teaching Rome to misread a map."

The observation landed with a precision Madi did not intend. Marcus looked up and saw his own exhaustion mirrored in the centurion's face.

"Both serve the same purpose," Marcus said.

"And neither will ever know about the other." Madi stood, taking his cup but leaving the wineskin. "Get some sleep. Geta briefs the command staff at dawn, and you need steady hands for that performance."

Marcus sealed the patrol report after Madi left. The ink dried over two real settlements and two ghosts, and the gap on Rome's map held steady for another quarter.

Somewhere in those mountains, an old scholar traced constellations for children who would never learn his real name.

In Caesarea, a Roman officer sealed lies with official wax and called it duty.

Both men served the same purpose. Neither would ever know it.

CHAPTER 17
The Rider at Midday

"News travels on the wind. Grief travels in the bones."
—Amazigh mourning saying

Fall, 41 CE—six months after the uprising—Aghbalou and Caesarea

The rider arrived at midday, horse lathered with sweat, dust caking his face. Zahra was in the courtyard watching Juba take unsteady steps between her and Silina: three steps, four, then a tumble into waiting arms and squeals of laughter.

The commotion at the village gates attracted her attention. Men gathered, voices rose. Their pitch meant important news.

"Stay with the children," she told Silina, already moving toward the square.

A crowd had formed around the rider, eager for war news. Usem, the village elders, and men who had fought in past campaigns were all there.

"...three cohorts, maybe four," the rider was saying, voice hoarse. "They caught him in the eastern passes, tried to trap him between two forces. But he knew the terrain..."

"Who?" Zahra pushed through the crowd, forgetting courtesy, forgetting caution. "Who are you talking about?"

The rider turned, taking in her appearance: a woman interrupting men's talk, her features and quality clothing marking her as not quite belonging. But Usem nodded his permission.

"Aedemon. The resistance leader. The biggest engagement since Volubilis. He led desert fighters against a Roman column..." The rider paused, studying her face. "You know him?"

Everyone was watching. Zahra felt their attention pressing against her, felt the dangerous ground beneath her feet. In this village, she was Leila, a widow from eastern tribes, Numerius's niece, a refugee. Nothing more.

She caught herself, forcing her voice to steady. "I knew of him. Before. In the capital. Everyone spoke of him. Is he, did he..."

"He survived. His forces melted into the mountains before the Romans could close the trap. He lost men, but the column lost more." Grudging respect edged the rider's voice. "They say he fights like the old warriors, like he knows what he is fighting for."

The crowd murmured its approval. These mountain people remembered generations of resistance, warriors before Rome who had fought Carthage and never quite bent their necks to any master. A leader who embarrassed Rome's legions became a story worth telling.

But Zahra heard what the rider did not say. He survived this battle. There would be others. And eventually, luck would run out, unless he succeeded.

She turned away before anyone could see her face, before the relief and terror could show in equal measure.

He was alive.

☙✦❧

That evening

Eudoxus settled beside her in the courtyard after the twins slept. "You heard."

“He is alive.” The words came out flat. “He fought a battle and survived.”

“Yes.”

“How many more?” She turned to face him. “How many more battles before one of them kills him? Before a Roman sword finds him, or an arrow, or...” She stopped, unable to finish.

“I do not know. War takes who it takes, when it takes them. All we can do is hope the spirits favor him.”

“The spirits.” The laugh came out bitter. “You spent yourself protecting us. Why would they favor him?”

“Because he fights for freedom. Because he is trying to protect his people from an empire that sees them as resources to exploit.” Eudoxus’s old certainty flickered in his voice. “That counts for something.”

Zahra wanted to believe righteousness mattered, and fighting for your people meant the universe owed you protection, at least survival. But that same empire had executed her husband’s king. She fled with her children in the night, and saw good people suffer while the powerful thrived.

“I want him to come home,” she whispered. “I want him to walk through that gate, see his children, hold them. Juba is walking now. Amara will be soon. He is missing everything.”

“I know.”

“But if he came home, we would all die. Rome would find us. They would kill him and us and probably half this village for sheltering us.” Her voice cracked. “So I must hope he stays away, and he keeps fighting, keeps risking his life, keeps running, so that we can stay hidden.”

She looked at her hands, roughened from village work, no longer the soft hands of Ptolemy’s court. “What kind of wife hopes her husband never comes home?”

Eudoxus reached out and took her hand. His grip was weaker, but the gesture still carried comfort.

"The kind of wife who loves him enough to understand what he is fighting for," he said. "And the kind of mother who loves her children enough to keep them safe, whatever the cost."

They sat together in darkness while the village settled into sleep. Behind them, the twins breathed softly in their cot, unaware their father, whose name they could not even speak, just survived death by margins too narrow to calculate, or that their mother carried the impossible burden of hoping he would keep fighting, keep surviving, keep staying away.

In the eastern passes, Aedemon was tending wounds, counting losses, planning the next strike against an empire ceaselessly hunting him.

The distance between them felt vast as the desert, unbridgeable as the sky.

✦

The same night—Caesarea, Marcus's quarters

Marcus could not stop seeing Aedemon's face. Not the man he had surrendered to Roman custody in the ravine outside Caesarea. The man he had seen since, on a ridge above a burning supply column, close enough to recognize and too far to reach. Their eyes met for the span of a breath. Then Aedemon vanished into terrain Rome would never learn to read.

His report read: "Rebel forces demonstrated sophisticated tactical knowledge of terrain and Roman doctrine. The leader, tentatively identified as Aedemon, showed evidence of formal military training. Recommend enhanced intelligence gathering regarding his whereabouts and support networks."

Truth wrapped in misdirection. Yes, Aedemon had training; Marcus had taught him much of it during their years of friendship. But the report avoided mentioning Marcus had been there, had seen him, had done nothing to prevent his escape.

Because what could he have done? Called for pursuit into terrain where Aedemon's fighters had every advantage? Gotten more Romans killed? Revealed he knew exactly how Aedemon thought, exactly how he would plan an ambush?

The protection extended to Aedemon too, whether Marcus wanted it to or not. If Aedemon fought, if he drew Roman attention away from his family's hiding place, Marcus had to keep him alive.

Even if that meant watching from a distance while his former friend fought Rome with increasing desperation. Even if it meant filing reports misdirecting pursuit while appearing useful.

A knock at his door. "Enter."

Madi stepped inside, his face tense. "The family?"

"Secure at Aghbalou, as far as I know. No recent patrols in that area. Your intelligence held." Marcus met his eyes. "But this battle will change things. Paulinus will want blood. Geta will want results."

"Can you misdirect them?"

"For now. But each success makes Aedemon a bigger target. Each battle increases pressure to capture him." Marcus felt the calculation settle in his chest. "I am protecting them by keeping him alive and free. But every day he fights, every Roman he kills, that protection becomes harder to maintain."

After Madi left, Marcus stood at his window watching night settle over the Mediterranean. In Aghbalou, Aedemon's family had heard the news by now. Zahra, the woman he had loved and never claimed was processing the terrible knowledge her husband had survived, and would have to keep surviving, keep fighting, keep staying away.

And somewhere in the west, Aedemon himself was preparing for the next battle, the next desperate strike, drawing Rome's fury while his children grew up calling their mother by a false name.

❧✦❧

Two weeks later—Caesarea Harbor

The dispatch bore the Governor's seal, but Marcus recognized the implications before reading a word. Paulinus stood at the harbor window, watching supply ships load for the voyage west to Tingis.

"From Tingis, the supplies go overland to Volubilis," Paulinus said without turning. "I will stage the expedition from there. It is the last Roman settlement before the Atlas. Beyond that, we enter territory no legion has mapped."

"The Senate wants geographic documentation," he continued. "Pliny has requested observations for his natural histories. And the rebels who fled south need to understand Rome's reach has no limits. I intend to cross the Atlas and pursue them to the Daras River if necessary."

"The rebellion here is not finished, Governor."

"Which is why General Geta assumes command in my absence." Paulinus turned, his scarred face showing a general's restlessness. He had been too long in familiar country, chasing shadows that kept moving. "He has full authority over military operations, intelligence assets, and search protocols. You report to him as you have reported to me."

Marcus absorbed this with the stillness of a man calculating new dangers. Paulinus was ambitious, impatient, focused on grand strategy: crossing mountains no Roman had crossed, exploring rivers at the edge of the known world. Geta was a different order of problem: a patrician with a street fighter's instincts wrapped in a general's authority. And he would remain here, watching.

"How long will the expedition last?"

"Months. Perhaps longer. The Atlas summit alone requires a ten-day march, and I mean to go far beyond, into the desert territories, the Gerj River, perhaps to the Daras itself." Paulinus moved toward the door. "When I return, if I return to this province at all, I expect results. Aedemon's family found. The resistance broken. The tribes pacified."

After Paulinus departed, Marcus stood alone in the command room, understanding the protection had just become exponentially more difficult. Paulinus could be managed with paperwork and false leads sent to distant Volubilis. Geta would be here in Caesarea, watching every move, questioning every report: lies told directly to a man who had built his career on detecting them.

❧✦❧

That evening

Marcus paused at his door. The corridor outside his quarters carried the familiar noise of the garrison settling into evening routine. Through an open doorway, the watch-change banter:

"Three months in these mountains and nothing but goat shit and scorpions."

"The goats are friendlier than the locals. Better looking, too."

"Careful, Titus. Gods! They said Gaius from the Third married a sheep in Britannia."

"Was not a sheep. Was a Briton. Hard to tell the difference."

Rough laughter. Marcus kept walking. The casual contempt was standard; soldiers dehumanized the people they policed. It made the work easier, made following orders simpler when the faces beneath Berber headscarves were not quite human.

He had laughed at jokes like these once. Before Aedemon. Before the twins.

At his writing table, he returned to the never-ending task: reports whose every word and precisely calculated detail was accurate, defensible, and subtly wrong.

He would continue to ensure the safety of Zahra and the children, however long necessary, however unbearable the cost.

Caesarea, one month later

The smuggler broke on the third day of questioning. Marcus forbade violence. He used patience instead, laying evidence before the man document by document until his own records, assembled over six weeks, contradicted every lie.

The network ran from Carthage through Caesarea to the tin markets of Britannia. Fourteen men, three ships, a system of coded manifests diverting imperial tariff revenue for a decade. Marcus identified the first thread six months earlier: a discrepancy between harbor records and customs declarations, small enough to overlook, consistent enough to constitute pattern.

Geta reviewed the seized cargo and the stack of confessions in his command office. He circled the table like he circled everything, a predator assessing whether the offering was worth his attention.

"Fourteen arrests. Three vessels impounded. Two hundred thousand sesterces in recovered revenue." Geta set down the final report. "The governor will be pleased. Claudius is desperate for provincial revenue after the Britannia campaign, and you have just handed him a victory costing nothing."

"The credit belongs to the customs officers who maintained accurate records, General."

"The credit belongs to the officer who read those records and saw what no one else saw." Geta's eyes held their usual predatory attention, but beneath it ran a thread Marcus had not seen before. Respect. Grudging, reluctant, offered against the man's instincts. Real. "You have a gift for pattern, Tribune. You read documents the way I read battlefields."

"Thank you, General."

"It was an observation, not a compliment." Geta moved to the window. "A man who can find a smuggling network hidden in customs records can find other things hidden in other records. A fugitive family, for instance. Hidden in the gaps between settlements."

The praise and the threat arrived in the same breath. Marcus kept his face still.

"I devote my attention to where the evidence leads, General."

"See that it does." Geta turned back. "I am recommending you for commendation. The governor's office will note the recovered revenue and the intelligence methodology. It will enter your record." A pause. "And it will remind Rome that Mauretania's intelligence operations produce results. Which benefits us both."

Marcus saluted and withdrew. In the corridor, he let himself feel what the exchange meant. The commendation would strengthen his position for years. It would make him harder to transfer, harder to replace, harder to question. Every legitimate success built a wall of credibility around the one deception that mattered.

Geta knew it. A man who earned commendations was a man Rome protected. And Geta, who suspected Marcus of hiding the family, had just made him harder to investigate.

The predator had sharpened the prey's armor. Whether from genuine respect or from the calculation a compromised officer was more useful than an imprisoned one, Marcus could not tell. With Geta, the distinction rarely mattered.

Twelve months passed in the strange rhythm of sustained deception.

In Caesarea, Marcus filed reports, misdirected patrols, and watched Geta crush what remained of organized resistance.

Late Summer 42 CE — the Zalacus Mons, southern frontier

Geta had defeated Sabalus twice in open country, driving the Mauri chieftain south each time, deeper into the broken terrain where the mountains gave way to the desert in the grip of a three-year drought. After the second engagement, Sabalus withdrew his remaining fighters into the desert canyon lands: a maze of dry watercourses and vertical rock where Roman cavalry could not follow and Roman formations lost their advantage.

Geta followed.

He gathered every water container his forces could carry, stripped the supply wagons to make room for more, and marched his legionaries into the desert with focused patience. He understood warfare was not always about killing. Sometimes it was about outlasting. Sabalus's men knew the terrain. Geta had numbers and water. He intended to use one until the other ran out.

It nearly ran out first. Ten days into the pursuit, the last reserves sat low in the wagons. The desert heat cracked the wooden barrels and evaporated what leaked through. Soldiers drank their rations in halves, then quarters. Centurions reported men stumbling in formation, lips split, eyes glazed. The surgeon advised withdrawal.

Geta was considering it when the Amazigh man approached his tent.

The man's name was Agerzam. He came from a settlement near the northern limes, one of the communities refusing Aedemon's call to rebellion and maintaining its arrangement with Rome. He had served as a scout for the legions since the campaign's first month, guiding patrols through passes his own people had used for centuries. The warriors of the resistance called men like Agerzam by a word not translated politely into Latin. Agerzam did not care. His family ate because Rome paid him, and his village stood because Roman garrisons discouraged the raids plaguing the northern settlements for generations.

He entered Geta's tent without the deference Romans expected from provincials. Geta did not remark on it. He had learned during eighteen months in Mauretania the Imazighen measured a man by his usefulness, not his manners.

"Your water will last two days," Agerzam said in the rough camp Latin he picked up from soldiers. "You will not catch Sabalus in two days. His men are camped in the Asif Ighzer canyon, three miles south. They have a seep spring. They can hold for weeks."

"Then we withdraw." Geta said it without emotion, already calculating the cost of retreat against the cost of dead legionaries.

"Or you ask the sky for water."

Geta looked at him.

"My people have a prayer for rain. It is old. Older than Rome. Older than Carthage. The words call to the sky and the sky answers, if the need is genuine and the speaker does not flinch." Agerzam sat on the camp stool opposite Geta without being invited. "Sabalus's men believe in the prayer. They grew up hearing the elders sing it during the dry seasons. They have seen it work. If a Roman general stands on the ridge above their canyon and calls rain from a clear sky, they will believe the gods have chosen Rome."

"I do not believe in your gods."

"Your belief is not required. Theirs is."

Geta studied the man. The calculation behind the offer was transparent: Agerzam was handing Rome a weapon forged from his own people's faith. He was doing it for the same reason he scouted for the legions: survival. His village would prosper. His family would eat. And Sabalus, who raided Agerzam's settlement twice in the years before the rebellion, would be finished.

"Teach me the words," Geta said.

Sabalus watched from the ridge above the Asif Ighzer as the Roman general climbed the opposite slope at dawn.

He had positioned his best fighters with him on the high ground, thirty men who could see the Roman camp spread across the desert floor below and the canyon mouth where the rest of his force sheltered in the shade of the rock walls. Three hundred warriors in the canyon. Women and children further back, in the deeper passages where the seep spring provided enough water to sustain them. They could hold this ground for a month if the Romans stayed where they were, baking in the open desert with their water dwindling.

The Roman general carried no weapons. He wore no armor. He climbed the ridge in a plain tunic, his legs bare below the knee, and when he reached the summit he turned to face the east, where the sun was rising over the desert in a cloudless sky and had been so for twenty days.

Sabalus did not understand what he was seeing until the Roman opened his mouth and began to sing.

The words were Tamazight. Old Tamazight, the formal dialect the elders used for ceremonies, the language of the rain prayers Sabalus had heard since childhood in the mountain villages where water was life and drought was death. The pronunciation was terrible. The rhythm was wrong. The Roman's tongue could not shape the sounds the way an Amazigh throat shaped them, and the melody wandered from the ancient pattern the way a lost traveler wanders from a path he has been told about but never walked.

Every word was right, beginning with the invocation to the sky, followed by acknowledgment of thirst, and the promise to return to the earth what the sky gave without hoarding. The ancient contract between the Imazighen and the rain that sustained them came on the lips of a Roman.

Sabalus's lieutenant gripped his arm. "How does he know those words?"

Sabalus had no answer. The rain prayer was not secret in the way a military plan was secret. Any child in the mountains could recite its opening lines. But the full prayer, the ceremonial version calling on the deep names of the sky and the old names of the water, required knowledge taking years to learn and was passed from elder to elder through a chain of teaching reaching back before any living memory.

Someone who knew the prayer and chose to place it in a Roman mouth had given it to him.

The general finished the invocation. He stood on the ridge in the rising heat, his arms at his sides, his face turned to the sky. He looked like he was performing a duty he did not understand and did not need to understand, as if he were filling out a form.

The sky answered anyway.

The clouds came from the south, building with a speed, not natural and yet not unnatural, occupying the space between the two where the sacred had always lived. They piled against the mountains, darkened and spread, and the wind preceding them carried the scent of rain across the desert floor. Every man in

Sabalus's force recognized the smell the way they recognized their mothers' voices.

The first drops fell on the ridge where Geta stood. He did not move. He did not raise his hands or speak or show any sign the rain meant anything to him beyond the tactical advantage it represented. He stood in the downpour with his tunic darkening against his skin and his face as blank as a wall as the rain fell harder.

Sabalus heard the canyon before he understood it, a sound like distant thunder, except the thunder was beneath him, not above. A roar built from the south where the higher canyons fed into the Asif Ighzer, where twenty days of bone-dry watercourse was receiving in minutes what the sky had withheld for months.

The flash flood hit the canyon like a fist.

The water came brown and violent, carrying stones and uprooted scrub and the accumulated debris of a dry season compressed into a wall of force that filled the canyon floor in seconds. Sabalus's men had camped where warriors always camped in the canyon lands: on the flat ground near the seep spring, protected by the walls on either side and defensible against any force approaching from the mouth.

They were not defensible against the sky.

The screaming lasted less than a minute. The flood swept through the canyon with a force that moved boulders and scoured the walls clean of the scrub that had clung to them for years. Men who survived Roman cavalry and steel swords and the grinding attrition of a four-year rebellion drowned in water their own prayers had called sacred.

Sabalus stood on the ridge and watched his army die. Thirty men stood beside him on the high ground. Three hundred died in the canyon below. The flood passed through the narrows and spread across the desert floor beyond, brown water fanning out like a hand opening, carrying with it everything the canyon had held, scrub brush, mud, rocks, and bodies.

On the opposite ridge, Geta watched too. His face showed nothing. The rain continued to fall.

❧✦❧

Sabalus descended the ridge the next morning with his thirty surviving fighters and surrendered to the Roman camp.

Geta received him outside his tent, seated on a camp stool, his uniform dry and his hair combed, as if the previous day had been an administrative matter rather than the destruction of an army by rain called from a stolen prayer. He listened to Sabalus's formal words of surrender with the same blank attention he had given the sky.

Then he gave his orders. The thirty fighters would be disarmed, documented, and released to their settlements with the understanding any further resistance would bring consequences Rome did not need to specify. The women and children who had sheltered in the deeper passages of the canyon and survived the flood would be escorted north to resettlement camps.

Sabalus waited for his own sentence. Execution. Imprisonment. Transport to Rome in chains for a triumph. He had seen what Rome did to defeated chieftains. He had prepared himself for each possibility.

Geta turned to his centurion.

"Leave him."

The centurion hesitated. "General?"

"Take his horse. Take his weapons. Take his water. Leave him."

Geta stood and walked into his tent without looking at Sabalus again. The tent flap closed. The interview was over. A chieftain who had held the eastern mountains for four years, who had bled Roman supply lines and killed Roman soldiers and made Rome's most ambitious general chase him into the desert, was not worth a sentence.

They took his horse. They took the curved blade he had carried since his father's death. They took the water skin from his shoulder. The centurion, a man who had fought Sabalus's warriors in a dozen skirmishes and respected them, paused before leaving.

"The northern settlements are two days' walk. There are seep springs in the rocks if you know where to look."

Sabalus said nothing. The centurion mounted and rode after the column. The dust of their departure settled. The canyon below held its dead beneath a skin of drying mud. The sky had cleared, blue and indifferent, as if the rain had been a rumor.

Sabalus stood alone on the ridge. No horse. No blade. No water. No army. The desert stretched in every direction, familiar as his own hands, merciless as the gods who had answered a Roman's prayer and drowned the men who had worshipped them since before Rome learned to build.

He turned south, toward the deep desert, and walked.

No one recorded what became of him. Roman documents noted his surrender and listed his forces as neutralized. Marcus filed the report alongside a dozen others, adding Sabalus's name to the catalogue of resistance leaders who had risen and fallen in the years since Ptolemy's assassination. Geta never mentioned him again.

Within the month, Geta received his reassignment. Britannia. The invasion Claudius was planning for the following spring needed commanders who had proven they could break indigenous resistance through means beyond brute force. Geta had proven exactly that. He packed his campaign chest, left

Mauretania without ceremony, and sailed for a new island full of tribes who painted themselves blue and worshipped trees.

He would distinguish himself at the Battle of the Medway, turning a two-day rout into a Roman victory so decisively Claudius awarded him the *ornamenta triumphalia*. The Britons, like the Mauri before them, would learn Geta's gift was not courage or strategy but the ability to find the crack in a people's faith and pour Rome through it.

❧✦❧

The rebellion promising liberation became a slow bleeding, and with each rebel death, the pressure to find Aedemon's family intensified.

In Aghbalou, Zahra and Eudoxus continued to be who they had never been. The twins outgrew their first clothes, spoke their first words, took their first confident steps without a parent's steadying hand. Zahra learned which herbs grew in the mountain passes, which women could be trusted, which silences meant welcome and which meant warning. The village absorbed them the way stone absorbs rain, slowly, imperceptibly, until the boundary between newcomer and neighbor blurred beyond recognition.

But protection built on lies requires constant maintenance. Its price is paid in sleepless nights, careful words, and the slow erosion of everything a man or woman once believed about themselves.

CHAPTER 18

The Archivist

"The liar who protects is more honest than the truth-teller who destroys."

—From the teachings of the desert fathers (reconstructed)

Fall, 42 CE—Caesarea and Aghbalou

Marcus spread the coastal intelligence across the command table. He had calculated every falsified detail to withstand scrutiny. The last two years had taught him the architecture of convincing lies: build from truth, arrange into misdirection, present with confidence.

"Analysis of trade patterns suggests movement toward Icosium." He traced the coastal route with deliberate precision. "Multiple sources report a woman purchasing supplies suitable for young children."

Complete fabrication. But the reports existed, real informants describing real women, none of them Zahra.

Geta leaned forward, his scarred face skeptical. The general now held sole command and wore the responsibility the way he wore his armor: comfortably, as a thing made for him.

"These sources are reliable?"

"Two confirmed, one promising." Marcus indicated the names. "Independent verification through coastal patrols supports the pattern."

"The coastal route makes strategic sense," Geta conceded. "Opportunities for supply, easier terrain for traveling with children."

"Exactly, General. Which is why I recommend shifting sixty percent of search assets to coastal settlements. These areas have been largely ignored. That is exactly where a smart fugitive would hide: in the direction we were not watching."

"Your previous recommendations for patience have not produced results, Tribune."

"Because we were looking in the wrong places, General."

"So you say." Geta's voice was dangerously level. "Deploy your teams. But understand this: if this coastal operation produces nothing, I will implement mass arrests and systematic pressure until someone breaks."

"Understood, General."

"And I will accompany the deployment personally." Geta's smile showed teeth. "Senior oversight for an operation of this importance. My presence will ensure we learn everything these searches can teach us: about the fugitives we seek, and about the intelligence methods that led us to look for them there."

Marcus saluted and departed, his mind racing. Geta would catalog every inconsistency, every convenient detail, every aspect that seemed too well constructed. And when the coastal operation produced nothing. Which it would. Geta would measure Marcus's reaction and evaluate whether the failure came from misfortune or design.

❧✦❧

Three days later—southeast foothills

Marcus rode with Geta's patrol through the foothills southeast of Caesarea, the opposite direction from where the family sheltered. The patrol was supposed to investigate coastal settlements. This detour, Geta claimed, would verify Marcus's assessment the mountains held nothing worth finding.

Marcus's stomach clenched. They were riding within a day's journey of Aghbalou.

At a small settlement, the elder greeted them with respectful wariness. Yes, they paid tribute when collectors came. No, they had not seen unusual movements. Just shepherds, traders, the ordinary patterns of mountain life.

Geta's eyes swept the village and missed nothing. "That house." He pointed toward a dwelling on the settlement's edge. "New construction."

"For my son's family, General." The elder's voice remained steady. "He married last spring."

"Show me."

Marcus kept his expression neutral while his heart hammered. The house looked too similar to descriptions he kept out of Roman records: two rooms, a courtyard, backed against the hillside.

Inside, a young woman nursed an infant. She looked up as the soldiers entered, her eyes wide. Not Zahra. Marcus controlled the relief flooding through him. Just another young mother in another mountain village.

But Geta studied her face with predatory attention. "Your name?"

"Tanit, General." Her voice trembled.

"Where are you from originally?"

"The valley settlements, General. I married into this village."

"Any other newcomers here? Other families from elsewhere?"

The elder's voice carried no alarm. "Marriages bring new people, General. That is the way of villages. But we know everyone here. No strangers hiding."

Geta held the silence and let pressure build. Then he nodded curtly and strode out.

As they rode on, Marcus felt sweat cooling beneath his armor despite the autumn chill.

"Interesting," Geta said, his voice casual. "The informant networks you have built should have reported settlements like that one. Young families, new construction, recent arrivals. Exactly the pattern we are looking for."

"Rural communities do not report ordinary life, General. Only anomalies."

"And who decides what is ordinary?" Geta's smile carried no warmth. "The difference between thorough intelligence and useful intelligence is knowing what questions to ask. Perhaps your network asks the wrong questions."

Or perhaps I have spent two years ensuring it does.

That evening—Marcus's quarters

Marcus poured wine and did not drink it. Maps covered his desk: coastal cities, northern ports, southern desert routes. Everywhere the family was not.

Three taps, pause, two taps. Madi's signal.

"Geta is selecting officers for the coastal deployment," Madi said in Tamazight. "Men loyal to him."

"Expected."

"Marcus, when they find nothing..."

"They will find nothing because there is nothing to find." Marcus lifted the cup at last. "But Geta will not accept that explanation. He will assume incompetence or worse."

"What will you do?"

"What I have been doing. File accurate reports leading nowhere useful. Build patterns satisfying requirements while obscuring what matters." He set down the cup, untouched. "How is the family?"

"Safe. The village has absorbed them. Even the women who gossip about everything have stopped noticing them."

"Good." Marcus moved to the window and looked out toward mountains he could not see in the darkness. "That is good."

"You cannot protect them forever."

"I can protect them today. That is all anyone can do."

After Madi left, Marcus sat with the maps until the candle guttered. In those mountains, children slept who would never know his name. In Aghbalou, Zahra lived under a borrowed identity. In the eastern passes, her husband fought an empire Marcus served.

And in this same garrison, Geta planned the next phase of the hunt, trusting intelligence reports Marcus had spent two years corrupting.

The deception held. But with each passing month, the lies grew more complex, and the consequences of discovery grew more severe.

❧✦❧

Bakir passed through Aghbalou twice more since the olive harvest, each visit bringing trade goods and the quiet company Eudoxus relied on. The desert trader arrived without announcement and departed without ceremony. In the hours between, he sat with Eudoxus at the olive press or in the courtyard and played the grid game while the village moved around them.

Bakir brought news along with his trade goods. He delivered it the way he delivered everything: without preamble, without softening.

"Sabalus is finished."

Eudoxus set down the game stone he had been about to place. Around them, the olive press turned, the men talked, and the afternoon continued. But the words had carved a silence between them the village noise could not fill.

"How?"

"Geta pursued him into the canyon country south of the Zalacus Mons. Sabalus's men camped in the Asif Ighzer, a deep canyon with a seep spring. Defensible ground. They could have held for weeks." Bakir placed a stone on the board. "An Amazigh man from the northern limes taught Geta the rain prayer. The full ceremonial version. Geta performed it on the ridge above the canyon."

Eudoxus said nothing. He waited.

"The sky answered. The rain came hard and fast. A flash flood filled the canyon in minutes." Bakir's voice stayed level, but his hand, reaching for the next stone, paused over the board. "Three hundred men drowned on ground they had chosen because it was safe from any human attack. Sabalus watched from the ridge with thirty survivors. He surrendered the next morning."

"And Geta?"

"Stripped him of horse, weapons, and water. Left him in the desert without a word. No execution. No imprisonment. Just the desert."

Eudoxus stared at the game board. The stones sat in their positions, dark and light, the patient geometry of a contest rewarding the man who could see three moves ahead. Sabalus had seen every move except the one from above.

"An Amazigh man taught him the prayer," Eudoxus said. Not a question.

"A man from the northern limes." Bakir picked up the stone and placed it. "The warriors have a word for men like him. I will not repeat it at the olive press."

They sat with it. The prayer was sacred. Every Amazigh child heard it during the dry seasons, learned its rhythms the way they learned to walk. And a man had taken those rhythms and placed them in a Roman mouth, and the sky had not cared whose mouth it was. The rain fell. The men drowned. The prayer worked.

Eudoxus thought of the talisman's inscription, carved in Tifinagh by a Persian scholar who did not know the language his hands were writing. Sacred things could move through vessels without understanding them. Power did not ask permission or check the worthiness of the hand that wielded it.

"What does it mean," he asked, "when the sacred answers the faithless?"

Bakir moved another stone. "It means the sacred does not take sides. It means the rain falls on the just and the unjust alike, and the difference between them is what they do after the rain stops."

Eudoxus looked at the desert man with new appreciation. Bakir played games the way he spoke: with precision concealing depth.

This visit, Eudoxus asked about the south.

"The canyon country." Bakir placed a dark stone on the board without looking up. "What do you want to know?"

"Whether a family could travel through it. With small children. If they needed to."

Bakir's hand paused over the board. He looked at Eudoxus with steady assessment. He understood certain questions were not hypothetical.

"The canyons are not simple country. Water carved them and water still owns them. A man who does not know the passages can walk for days and arrive where he started. A man who does know them can disappear so completely a thousand soldiers could search for a year and find nothing but rock."

"And you know them."

"I have walked them since I was old enough to keep pace with my father's horse." Bakir placed another stone. "The hidden basins. The seep springs. The passages looking like dead ends and opening into valleys no Roman has ever mapped." He paused. "It is three days from here to the first oasis, if you know the route. Longer with children. But possible."

"And beyond the oasis?"

"South. Into the country where the mountains flatten and the desert opens. The settlements there answer to tribal law, not Roman decree. A family reaching them would be beyond any patrol's range."

Eudoxus moved a light stone and lost another position. He did not mind. The information was worth more than the game.

"If a time came when such a journey was necessary," Eudoxus said, "would you guide it?"

Bakir captured two of Eudoxus's stones in a single move. He studied the board as if the question required the same deliberation as the game.

"Usem has been a fair trading partner for many years. If he asked, I would consider it." He looked up. "But I would need to know what I was carrying. Not names. Not reasons. Just whether the people in my care would follow instructions without argument when the terrain demanded it."

"They would."

"Then if the time comes, ask Usem to send word. I am never more than three days from Aghbalou."

They finished the game in silence. Bakir won, as he usually did, though the margin had narrowed over the months. He packed the board and departed the next morning with his usual economy, heading east toward the settlements along the ridge.

Eudoxus told Zahra that evening. He told her about the path south, about the guide who knew the canyons, about the door the desert offered if Aghbalou could no longer hold them. And he told her about Sabalus.

Zahra listened to the account of the rain prayer and the flash flood with a stillness Eudoxus had learned to read. It was not calm. It was the stillness of a woman holding herself in place while the ground shifted beneath her.

"An Amazigh man taught him the prayer?"

"Yes."

She said nothing more about it. She turned to the children's blankets and began folding them with the precise attention she gave to tasks when her hands needed occupation and her mind needed distance. But Eudoxus saw the line of her jaw and understood. She expected the Romans. Roman violence was the weather of their lives, predictable in its cruelty. But an Amazigh man selling his people's faith to the enemy was a different kind of wound, and it cut in a place no preparation could armor.

Aghbalou, the same evening

The autumn wind carried the scent of wood smoke and cooking fires as Zahra finished the evening meal. Across the small courtyard, Juba built elaborate towers with smooth stones, his concentration absolute. Amara sat pressed against her mother's side, her eyes fixed on a place beyond the wall.

"Story time?" Juba asked without looking up from his construction.

"Soon, little one. Let your sister finish eating."

But Amara was not eating. Her portion sat untouched while she stared at a distance no wall could contain.

"Yemma?" Amara's voice dropped to a whisper. "Why is the man with the sword so sad?"

Zahra hesitated. "What man, tasastinu?"

"The one far away. He looks at maps. But he is sad inside. So sad."

Zahra's chest tightened. Amara started saying things like this months ago. She described emotions of people she could not know, sensed grief and fear and anger from improbable distances. The village women whispered about it. Eudoxus watched with scholarly interest. But Zahra, who spent two years learning to fear every hint of the extraordinary, felt only terror.

"It is probably just a story you are imagining," she said, and kept her voice steady. "You have such wonderful stories in your head."

"It is not a story." Amara's voice carried absolute certainty. "He is real. He looks at maps and thinks about us."

Zahra pulled her daughter close, heart pounding. *She cannot know about Marcus. She is too young to understand, and I have never spoken his name.*

But Amara's gift, whatever it was, did not follow the rules of ordinary knowledge.

"Some people carry sadness, tasastinu. It is not your job to carry it for them."

"But I feel it anyway." Amara pressed her face against her mother's shoulder. "I feel everything."

Across the courtyard, Juba's stone tower crashed down with a clatter. He laughed and began rebuilding, oblivious to his sister's strange pronouncements. The two children occupied the same space but lived in different worlds. Juba lived in the solid realm of stones and towers and confident exploration. Amara's was a sea of emotions she could not name or control.

Eudoxus appeared in the doorway, his movements slower than they had been two years ago. The journey from Caesarea aged him, and the constant vigilance of their disguised life extracted its own toll.

"Bedtime?" he asked, taking in the untouched food and Amara's troubled face.

"Yes." Zahra stood and lifted Amara with her. "Stories tonight and then sleep."

They gathered in the back room, the small space that had become their sanctuary. Juba demanded a story about brave warriors. Amara asked for one about magic that made sadness go away. Zahra told a story touching both, her voice weaving a world where courage and compassion walked hand in hand.

By the time she finished, both children slept. Juba sprawled with unconscious abandon, one arm flung over his face. Amara curled tight, even in sleep holding tension she could not release.

Zahra sat beside them in the darkness and listened to their breathing.

Outside, the wind carried sounds of the village settling into night. Dogs barked in the distance. A door creaked. Someone sang a lullaby to a restless child. Ordinary sounds. Safe sounds.

CHAPTER 19

Reluctant Spring

"Children grow in the spaces adults leave unguarded."
—Amazigh proverb

Spring, 43 CE—Aghbalou—twins age three

Spring settled into Aghbalou with reluctant warmth, and melted the last stubborn patches of snow from shadowed corners. The terraced fields turned soft for planting. Zahra drew water from the well in the village square, the rope familiar against her hands, the palace-softened skin now calloused after over two years of mountain life.

She could hear the women before she saw them, voices braided together in the rhythmic back-and-forth governing morning conversation at the well. Kahina held court, her tongue as sharp as her grinding stone.

"...and he staggers in at moonrise, smelling like the goat pen, and says to me, where is my dinner? I told him, you want to eat? Scrub yourself first. The goats would not share a trough with you."

Laughter rippled through the group. An older woman added, "At least yours comes home. Mine vanishes into the mountains for so long the goats know his face better than I do."

"Better the goats than another woman's tent," Kahina said. "Hessa's man could not track a ewe in a pen, but he could find the widow Tanit's doorway in the dark."

More laughter, sharper now. The widow Tanit, wherever she was, remained mercifully absent.

Zahra approached with her water jar. The conversation smoothly redirected.

"The eastern widow," someone murmured. Not unkindly. Just placing her.

"Her couscous is getting better," Kahina observed to no one in particular. "Last month it would have choked a dog. Now only a small dog."

Zahra's face heated. But Kahina's eyes held warmth beneath the barb, and she recognized the gesture for what it was: an invitation. In Aghbalou, you were not accepted until the women felt comfortable insulting your cooking.

Today felt different, though. Since word had arrived last week Rome had declared the organized resistance "crushed" in the eastern highlands, the village grew quieter, more watchful. Refugees who seemed valuable while resistance thrived became liabilities when Rome turned its attention to consolidation. Conversations stopped when Zahra approached.

"Good morning," Zahra said in Tamazight, the language coming more naturally now than Latin or Greek.

Whispers greeted her, and the warmth developed over two years felt diminished.

Behind her, Amara stood pressed against her mother's skirts, small hands twisted in the fabric. The child had been restless all morning. She refused breakfast and clung with unusual insistence. At three, she usually explored with bold curiosity. Today she stayed close, her eyes too watchful.

"Yemma," Amara whispered. "Something is coming."

"Just winter ending, tasastinu. Cold weather makes everyone..."

"No." Amara's certainty carried conviction. "Big feeling. Everyone has it. Like before a storm. When the sky gets heavy."

Zahra's chest tightened. She had noticed Amara doing this more often: she named emotions in weather patterns, translated adult feelings through a child's vocabulary, read people with unsettling accuracy.

Silina emerged from their house with Juba, who squirmed in her arms. "Goats!" he shouted and pointed toward the mountains. "I want to see the goats!"

Silina set him down. "Goats later." She caught Zahra's eye, a question in her expression.

Zahra shook her head. No news. Just unease thick enough to taste.

A passing village elder grunted and nodded, his expression calculating, assessing whether protecting strangers was worth the cost.

"We should go inside," Silina murmured.

But at the well, voices stopped them.

Three women from the neighboring settlement had come for water that morning, as they did each market week. Zahra knew them by sight: a trader's wife, her sister, and the older woman who managed their household's affairs with authority, knowing exactly what everything cost. They filled their jars and talked, and the talk carried across the stones to where Zahra stood with the children.

"...trapped the whole column between the canyon walls. Forty Romans dead before the sun reached its height."

Zahra's hands stilled on Amara's hair.

"My husband heard it from a salt carrier who came through yesterday," the trader's wife continued, her voice pitched for the women around the well and no one else. "The Wolf struck a supply convoy near Lambaesis. Burned the provisions. Scattered what was left before reinforcements could reach them."

"The Wolf?" A younger woman from Aghbalou leaned closer.

"Aedemon. That is what they call him now." The trader's wife spoke the name with careful reverence, as if handling a blade. "Aedemon the Wolf. He led them into the canyon, let the stone and sky do his work, and vanished before Rome could close the net. The Wolf still runs free, and Rome bleeds in our mountains."

The women at the well absorbed this silently, completely, the knowledge spreading from face to face without anyone raising a voice. The older woman from the neighboring settlement caught Zahra's eye across the stones. Her look said: you know whose name that is, and I will not ask why your face just changed.

Amara pressed closer. "Yemma. The big feeling. It is here."

By the time the women's talk reached the men in the square, the news had crossed the village faster than any rider could have carried it. Usem heard it from an elder's wife. The warriors heard it from the women who brought them water. The drums appeared before anyone could say who had spoken first, because in Aghbalou the women's well was the faster network and always had been.

The square erupted.

Men embraced, shouting triumph. Women ululated, the high-pitched calls echoing off stone walls. Children ran circles, caught up in adult excitement they did not fully understand. Drums appeared, the hand drums used for celebrations, and their rhythm pulsed through the square, primal and insistent.

Zahra's breath caught. Aedemon. Alive. Fighting. Victorious.

"Yemma?" Juba tugged at her dress, his small face scrunched with confusion. "Why are you sad?"

Because your father just won a battle and I cannot tell you. Because everything about who we are is a lie I am teaching you to believe.

"I am not sad, little one." She kissed his forehead and used the gesture to hide her expression from the villagers around them. "Just thinking about the war."

But Amara stared up at her with those green, perceptive eyes. "Big-sad. Happy-sad. Both same time."

Amara's body went rigid.

Zahra felt it through the child's grip on her dress: the sudden tension, the sharp intake of breath. Amara's eyes went wide, unfocused. She saw past the celebration into a place no one else could reach.

"Yemma," she whispered, voice tight with strain. "The feelings. They are getting bigger."

"What feelings, tasastinu?"

"Everyone's." Amara's small hands flew to her temples. "Too many feelings. Everyone's feelings. It hurts. Too loud."

Her face drained of color. Sweat beaded on her forehead despite the cold. She swayed, and Zahra caught her. The child's heart hammered against her ribs, rapid and desperate.

"Too much," Amara gasped. "Too loud. Make it stop. Please, Yemma. Make it stop."

Zahra scooped her daughter up and pressed the small body against her chest. "Silina! Take Juba inside. Now."

Silina moved without question and gathered Juba despite his protests. The boy wanted to stay, wanted to see the drums and dancing, but Silina had learned to read emergencies in Zahra's voice.

Zahra pushed through the celebrating crowd, her daughter trembling in her arms. Amara had buried her face in her mother's shoulder, hands still pressed to her temples, small body shaking with the effort of holding back a flood Zahra could not see or feel.

Inside their house, the celebration's sounds muted to a distant pulse. Zahra laid Amara on the sleeping pallet and knelt beside her. She brushed sweat-soaked hair from her daughter's forehead.

"Tell me what is happening, tasastinu. Tell me what you feel."

"Everyone is happy." Amara's voice came small and strained. "So happy it hurts. Like when you put too much water in a cup and it spills everywhere. Their happy is spilling into me and I cannot make it stop."

Zahra's throat tightened. She recognized genuine distress. Whatever Amara carried, it was overwhelming her.

"Close your eyes," Zahra said, and kept her voice steady. "Breathe with me. In... out... in... out..."

Slowly, Amara's trembling subsided. Her breathing steadied. The rigid tension in her small body eased.

"Better?" Zahra asked.

"A little." Amara opened her eyes. "Why do I feel everyone's feelings? Why can I not just feel mine?"

Zahra had no answer. She pulled her daughter close and held her while the celebration continued outside, while drums pulsed and voices rose in praise of a warrior who had no idea what his victory had just cost his daughter.

That evening

After the twins slept, Zahra sat in the narrow yard behind the house with Eudoxus and Silina. The celebration had quieted at last. Stars emerged above the mountains, ancient and indifferent.

"She felt everyone's emotions at once," Zahra said. "The entire village's joy overwhelmed her."

Eudoxus nodded slowly, his weathered face troubled. "The sensitivity is stronger than I expected. And earlier." He paused and chose his words with care. "I knew a man once, years ago, who could sense the currents beneath the surface of things. He had great power, but no one taught him to govern it. The power governed him instead. Amara needs what he lacked. Discipline. Boundaries. A way to stand inside the flood without drowning."

"What do we do?" Silina asked. "We cannot keep her away from every village celebration, every funeral, every moment when people feel strongly."

"No. But we can teach her to create distance. To recognize when others' emotions are flooding into her and to build barriers." Eudoxus met Zahra's eyes. "The discipline I can teach her. The practice will be hers."

"She is three years old," Zahra said. "How do you teach a three-year-old to build mental barriers?"

"The same way you teach any child anything difficult. Slowly. Patiently. With love and repetition." Eudoxus met her eyes. "She will not master it quickly. There will be more collapses, more overwhelming moments. But each time, she will learn a little more. The sensitivity will become manageable rather than crushing."

"And until then?"

"Until then, we watch. We protect. We explain what we can in terms she will understand." He paused. "And we accept that she will always be different from other children. Her perception of the world will never match theirs. The question is whether that difference becomes a burden she resents or a gift she learns to value."

Zahra looked toward the doorway where her children slept: Juba sprawled in the complete relaxation of childhood security,

Amara curled tight even in sleep. Her body anticipated danger her conscious mind did not yet understand.

Two children. One who moved through the world without sensing its hidden currents. One who felt every current so intensely she nearly drowned.

Both hers. Both Aedemon's. Both marked by circumstances beyond their choosing.

In the western mountains, Aedemon the Wolf moved through darkness, unaware his victory had sent his daughter into collapse, unaware his name was both salvation and curse for the family he could not reach. Zahra pulled the blanket higher over Amara's small shoulders. The girl murmured in her sleep, brow furrowing at whatever emotions still reached her through dreams.

Eudoxus said the sensitivity could be trained. That in the desert communities, women understood these things.

But the desert was far from Aghbalou, and Aghbalou was the only safety they knew.

CHAPTER 20

Both

"The olive knows nothing of the hand that harvests it. This is mercy."

—Mauretanian farmers' saying

Late Autumn, 43 CE to Spring, 44 CE—Aghbalou and Caesarea

The olive harvest came late that year, delayed by early rains that turned the mountain paths to mud. Zahra worked alongside the village women, her hands sorting the fruit while Juba and Amara played among the collection baskets. The children had grown sturdy since their arrival in Aghbalou. No longer babies, their limbs were strong from rough play with local children their own age. Their skin was brown from daily exposure to the warm sun, and their voices confident in their childish Tamazight. In time, they would learn Latin and Greek from Eudoxus.

"Yemma, look!" Juba held up an olive, then stuffed it in his mouth before anyone could stop him.

His face twisted in disgust. The women laughed as he spat frantically, tears streaming.

"Not for eating raw, little one." One of the older women offered him water. "Must be pressed first, treated with salt. The bitter teaches patience."

Amara watched her brother's distress with that focused intensity she brought to everything, then selected an olive from her own basket and bit down. Her face puckered but she did not spit. She studied the bitterness as if she analyzed a problem.

"Both?" she asked.

"Both what, yelli?" Zahra set down her basket.

"Bitter and good. Same fruit. Both."

The women exchanged glances. The girl spoke in observations that unsettled, too aware of contradictions adults preferred children not notice.

"Yes," Zahra said. "Many things are both."

Amara nodded as if this confirmed what she had suspected. She returned to her work, tiny hands sorting with unexpected precision.

The conversation shifted to harvest yields, winter preparations, whose daughter was old enough for betrothal. Ordinary village rhythms that had become Zahra's life. Over two years of mornings at the well, afternoons preparing meals, evenings telling stories while twins drowsed between her and Silina. Over two years of answering to a name that was not hers, teaching her children an identity that was not theirs, building a life from careful deceptions.

Over two years of not knowing whether Aedemon lived or died.

❧✦❧

Winter, 43 CE—Caesarea

Winter pressed hard into the province that year. In Aghbalou, the village contracted around its fires while storms swept through the passes. In Caesarea, Marcus stared at the dispatch that had arrived three days ago. Rome had transferred Geta to Britannia. The general who had spent three years watching Marcus with barely concealed suspicion would now suppress tribal resistance on the empire's northern frontier.

Relief battled with unease.

❧✦❧

Caesarea — that evening

Marcus found Madi at the tavern near the eastern gate, the one where the wine was bad enough to discourage officers and the owner asked no questions about conversations held in Tamazight.

"Geta is gone." Marcus sat down and, for the first time in three years, did not lower his voice. "Britannia. Effective immediately."

Madi studied him for a moment. Then he turned to the owner and called in Latin, "Your worst wine. Two cups. The large ones."

"You are celebrating with bad wine?"

"Good wine would attract attention. Bad wine is invisible." Madi poured with the exaggerated care of a man performing a sacred ritual over swill. "To General Gnaeus Hosidius Geta. May Britannia's rain rot his boots and its women ignore his rank."

Marcus drank. The wine was terrible. He drank again.

"Three years," he said. "Three years of Geta watching me like a hawk watches a field mouse."

"You are a poor field mouse. Too large. Too Roman."

"And yet here I sit, undevoured." Marcus leaned back against the wall and felt muscles release that had been clenched so long he had forgotten they could do otherwise. The ceiling beams above him were smoke-darkened and cracked. The table wobbled. The wine tasted like vinegar strained through a saddle blanket. He could not remember a better evening.

"He never found them," Marcus said.

"He never found them." Madi refilled both cups. "Three years of patrols, interrogations, threats, bribes, and the most dangerous hunter Rome sent to this province failed to find one woman and two children."

Marcus drank. "Did you hear how he finished Sabalus?"

"The rain prayer." Madi's voice flattened. "Every Amazigh between here and the Atlas has heard. A Roman general singing the old words on a ridge while three hundred men drowned in a canyon below him."

"He did not believe a word of it. He performed the ritual the way he signs requisition forms. And it worked."

"The sky does not check credentials." Madi set down his cup. "What concerns me is not the prayer. What concerns me is that Geta found an Amazigh man willing to teach it to him. If he can buy one man's faith, he can buy another's. And the next man he buys might know where your family is hiding."

The wine turned sour in Marcus's mouth. Madi was right. Geta had proven the Amazigh communities were not solid walls. They had cracks, and Rome could pour through them. Agerzam had sold the rain prayer for the same reason informants everywhere sold information: survival. His family ate. His village stood. And three hundred warriors who might have protected settlements like Aghbalou were dead in a flooded canyon.

"At least he takes that method to Britannia with him," Marcus said.

"The method stays. Geta taught it to every officer in the garrison before he left. Buy the locals. Use their beliefs against them. Find the crack in their faith and pour Rome through it." Madi picked up his cup again. "The man leaves. The lesson remains."

"Because we were better."

"Because *you* were better. I carried messages. You built the architecture." Madi raised his cup. "To the architect."

"To the builder. The architecture means nothing without someone to carry the stones."

"The strangest part," Marcus said after a while, "is Rome never asked him to find Aedemon's family. Not once in three years. I read every dispatch from the governor's office. The family was never mentioned. Geta hunted them because hunting was what Geta did. Not because anyone in Rome cared whether a dead rebel's widow raised her children in a mountain village or on the moon."

Madi turned his cup slowly on the table. "So three years of your life, and three years of mine, and the careers of a dozen informants, all spent protecting a family from one man's personal obsession."

"Not just Geta. Nerva will be the same. You watch. The new prefect will find the file and make it his own project. Not because Rome wants him to. Because the file is there, and men like Nerva cannot leave a gap unfilled."

Marcus had not known, when he spoke those words over bad wine in a tavern, how precisely they would prove true.

They drank. Marcus felt the warmth spread through his chest, the relief. For one evening, the coiled vigilance that had become his permanent state of being could loosen. Not disappear. Geta's replacement would bring new dangers. But tonight the hawk had flown north, and the field mouse could breathe.

"Your wife's cousin," Marcus said. "The one she keeps suggesting."

Madi's eyebrows rose. "You want me to arrange an introduction?"

"No. I want you to tell your wife if she mentions the cousin one more time, I will transfer *her* to Britannia."

Madi laughed a real laugh, loud enough to turn heads at the neighboring table, a laugh from somewhere beneath twelve years of careful silence. Marcus realized he had heard that laugh perhaps five times in three years. He wanted to hear it again.

"Another cup?" Madi asked.

"Another cup."

They drank until the tavern emptied and the owner began stacking benches with pointed patience. When they left, the night air hit Marcus like a cold hand, and he swayed once before steadying himself against the wall.

"You are drunk," Madi observed.

"I am."

"When was the last time?"

Marcus considered this. "Before Aedemon left Caesarea. Before all of it."

"Then it is overdue." Madi steered him toward the garrison with practiced ease. He had guided drunken Romans through dark streets before. "Tomorrow the work begins again. A new prefect. New dangers. But tonight you earned this."

Marcus looked up. The stars above Caesarea were the same stars shining over Aghbalou. The same sky covered the family he protected and the man who protected them. For once, that thought carried comfort rather than burden.

"Madi."

"Yes?"

"Thank you. For the bad wine. For the three years. For all of it."

"You are drunk and sentimental. I will not hold you to anything you say tonight."

"Hold me to this: when this is over, however it ends, I owe you a debt I cannot repay."

Madi was quiet for a few steps. "Pay it by surviving. That is enough."

They reached the garrison gate. The sentry straightened. Marcus returned the salute with only a slight wobble and passed through into the courtyard.

Behind him, Madi disappeared into the streets the way he always did, like smoke, like rumor, or like one whose greatest skill was being present without being noticed.

Marcus slept well that night. He could not know it would be months before he slept well again, and ignorance, for once, was mercy.

❧✦❧

Into Geta's place came Prefect Aulus Cornelius Nerva. He was no soldier, but a scholar who documented everything, convinced proper records and systematic observation could solve any intelligence problem. Where Geta had relied on instinct and aggression, Nerva would bring patience and method, a different more dangerous threat in its way.

Marcus pulled out the intelligence reports he had filed over the past three years. Each mentioned the fugitive family without revealing their location. Each satisfied requirements while obscuring what mattered.

They now sat in what would soon be Nerva's office, waiting to be cross-referenced, documented, and analyzed for patterns.

Three years of constructed lies, and now a man who specialized in finding patterns in accumulated information had access to every one of them.

❧✦❧

Caesarea — Nerva's first month

The new prefect requested copies of every patrol report filed in the past five years. Marcus spent three nights reviewing his own fabrications, checking them for the internal consistency that a systematic mind would probe. Nerva was not Paulinus, who read reports for confirmation. Nerva read them for patterns.

Marcus found two inconsistencies: a seasonal migration route he had described moving west in one report and east in another, and a tribal elder he had listed as cooperative in spring and hostile in autumn without explanation. Small errors. The kind a thorough analyst would flag and file.

He corrected neither. Correcting old reports would leave traces. Instead, he filed a new assessment attributing the discrepancies to seasonal political shifts among the tribal leadership. Plausible. Documented. And it gave Nerva exactly the kind of analytical puzzle he craved, one that led away from the gap rather than toward it.

In Tizwit, the twins were learning to walk. In Caesarea, Marcus was learning to lie to a man who collected lies the way other men collected coins.

☙✦❧

One week later—Caesarea Harbor

Marcus watched the three carts roll through the garrison gates behind a horse bearing a rider in the formal toga of a Roman prefect. No armor, no weapons visible, no military bearing at all. Just a scholar's posture and eyes studying everything with analytical interest.

The carts contained scrolls. Hundreds of them, packed in wooden cases, each labeled in precise Greek script. Tax records, census counts, maps, philosophical treatises, administrative handbooks. The archive of a true believer: governance as documentation, chaos as filing error.

Aulus Cornelius Nerva dismounted with the careful movements of someone unused to horses, brushed road dust from his toga, and began directing his attendants with the same focused attention other officers gave to weapons inspection.

"Put the census records there... carefully. They are cross-referenced by settlement. Maps in the second chest, organized by region and elevation. Tribal affiliation documentation in the third; that one is particularly fragile, mind the wax seals."

Marcus approached as protocol required. "Prefect Nerva. Tribune Marcus Valerius Severus, intelligence operations."

Nerva looked up, his pleasure unfeigned. "Ah! Tribune. Excellent. I will need comprehensive briefings on current tribal settlement patterns, resistance activity... or former resistance activity, I should say, given recent events... trade routes, seasonal migration patterns, and historical precedents for post-rebellion administration. I have studied Vibius's accounts of Germania's pacification, but local conditions naturally differ."

"Of course, sir. When would you like to..."

"Tomorrow morning? No, better make it afternoon. I will need time to organize my archive first. Proper methodology requires proper organization." He beamed at the crates being unloaded. "You know Polybius, Tribune? 'Without systematic arrangement, records become chaos, and chaos yields no truth.' I have always found that wisdom applicable to provincial administration."

Marcus watched the attendants carry crate after crate into the garrison headquarters, each one another layer of documentation to corrupt, another thread in the web of lies he maintained.

"I look forward to our collaboration, Prefect."

Nerva's smile held genuine warmth, a scholar's enthusiasm, embarking on a fascinating project. "As do I, Tribune. I believe we will accomplish great things together. Proper documentation always reveals the truth eventually. It is a matter of patience and methodology."

Marcus carried those words back to his quarters.

❧✦❧

Spring, 44 CE—Aghbalou

The thaw came late and turned paths to mud and swelled the stream running through Aghbalou's heart. With the melt came traders, travelers, and news from the wider world.

The rebellion had died. Not through the glorious final battle Aedemon had envisioned, not through strategic victory forcing Rome to negotiate. It had exhausted itself: scattered bands hunted down one by one, safe havens compromised, supplies depleted, hope eroded by years of Roman patience.

Zahra heard the news at the well, where women gathered each morning with water jars and gossip. The messenger had passed through the previous day and carried official pronouncements for settlements throughout the highlands.

"Rome declares peace," one woman said, her voice flat. "No more resistance activity reported in six months. The province is pacified."

Pacified. Such a clean word for what it meant: surrender, submission, the slow strangling of hope.

"What of the rebel leaders?" another woman asked.

"Dead or fled. Those who survived scattered to the deep desert or across the sea. Rome does not care where, as long as they are gone."

Zahra set down her water jar with controlled movements. The news should have brought relief. No more active rebellion meant less Roman attention on the mountains, fewer patrols, reduced urgency in the search for fugitives.

Instead, she felt the ground shift beneath her feet. Three years ago, the rebellion gave meaning to their exile; they were part of a larger struggle, their suffering connected to a purpose. Now that purpose evaporated and left only the daily grind of survival under borrowed names.

And Aedemon was either dead or running. She might never know which. The uncertainty offered neither grief nor hope, only the terrible suspension between them.

Bitter and good. Same fruit. Both.

"You are pale," old Kahina observed, and studied her with eyes that missed nothing. "The news troubles you?"

"It troubles everyone."

"Differently, I think." But Kahina did not press further. In a village of refugees and survivors, some questions were better left unasked.

❧✦❧

Caesarea—Nerva's office

Marcus stood in the doorway and watched Nerva work.

The prefect had transformed the command office in a single week. Where Geta kept a spartan space, maps on the wall, weapons racked, and a desk bare except for the current dispatch, Nerva had built a library. Scrolls filled shelves along three walls, organized by a system Marcus could not yet decipher. A sand table occupied the room's center, covered with small clay tablets, each inscribed with a settlement name and connected to others by colored thread. The threads formed a web spreading across the table like a spider's architecture: trade routes in red, tribal affiliations in blue, known resistance connections in black.

Nerva bent over the table and added a new thread. He did not look up. "Tribune. Come in. I have questions about the Zalacus Mons settlements."

Marcus entered and studied the web. His own reports were in there. He recognized the specifics, the settlement names, the patterns he had spent three years constructing. They looked different from this angle. Seen through Nerva's system, the individual lies became a constellation. And constellations had shapes that could be read.

"These mountain communities," Nerva said, and traced a cluster of blue threads. "Your reports describe them as stable, cooperative, low priority. Yet the tribal affiliations suggest connections to resistance networks active as recently as last year."

"Connections are not commitments, Prefect. Mountain communities maintain relationships with everyone. It is how they survive."

"Of course." Nerva made a note on his tablet. "But the pattern is interesting. These same communities show a slight population increase over three years, consistent with absorbing refugees rather than natural growth. Small numbers, a family here, a widow there, but the trend is clear when you aggregate the information. Cross-referenced with your intelligence reports, that information should reveal whether these movements were organic or directed." He returned to his threads. "Patience and methodology, Tribune. The archive will tell us what the mountains will not."

Marcus kept his face neutral. Nerva had been here one week and already identified the pattern Marcus had spent three years obscuring.

"Refugees are common after any rebellion, Prefect. Families displaced by fighting seek shelter with distant kin. It would be unusual if the mountain settlements had not absorbed newcomers."

He returned to his threads. "Patience and methodology, Tribune. The archive will tell us what the mountains will not." Nerva glanced up from his threads as if remembering something minor. "One other matter. Your aide. The centurion... Madi, is it? I have reviewed the duty logs. He is almost never here. He seems more interested in using his trading connections for personal benefit than in intelligence work. You should transfer him."

"On the contrary, Prefect. His trading is perfect cover. You would be surprised at what he picks up in casual conversation at the markets. I rarely mention him in my reports to keep his cover secure."

Nerva considered this, then waved his hand. "As you wish. He is your responsibility. But if his intelligence fails to produce results, I will revisit the matter."

"Understood, Prefect."

Marcus left the office and walked through the garrison courtyard toward his quarters. The evening air carried the salt of the harbor and the smoke of cooking fires. Ordinary smells. The smells of a city unaware it housed a war fought entirely in ink and thread and the careful placement of lies.

Geta had hunted with instinct. He could be misdirected because he followed his gut, and guts could be fooled. Nerva hunted by using detailed information. He would build his web of threads and tablets and cross-references, and the lies Marcus had constructed would either hold against that scrutiny or they would not.

Marcus had noted the one detail Nerva never mentioned: Rome had not requested this investigation. The dispatches Nerva sent to the governor's office about Aedemon's family received no response. No follow-up questions. No additional resources allocated. No indication anyone in Rome remembered a dead rebel's widow or cared whether she was found. The silence from the capital should have told Nerva the empire had moved on. Instead, Nerva read Rome's silence as an invitation to be more thorough.

Three years of deception, and the most dangerous man Marcus had ever faced was a scholar who had never drawn a sword.

In Aghbalou, a widow taught her children the names that were not their own. The rebellion was over. The archive was just beginning.

❧✦❧

Marcus watched light spread across the garrison courtyard and calculated how many more weeks he could maintain impossible lies before truth became unavoidable.

The order had come from Nerva's office: routine investigation of mountain settlements postponed by one week. Weather concerns, the directive claimed. Spring floods making the passes dangerous.

Marcus recognized his own report in that justification. He filed it three days ago, complete with fabricated weather reporting and exaggerated descriptions of wadi conditions.

One week's delay. Seven days for a family to disappear deeper into terrain where documentation grew sparse and Roman authority weakened into regional suggestions rather than imperial commands.

He had bought them time again.

But Nerva was already noting the pattern. Yesterday, Marcus observed the prefect's lingering scrutiny of the weather report, his brief pause before accepting the recommendation, and his recording in the archive.

Over time, the growing number of problems would become obvious, and the entire system would fall apart.

But not today.

Today, Zahra and her children continued to live in safety.

PART FOUR: INTO THE DESERT

"There are places where the veil thins.
Where you pay with what you thought you could not lose.
I have been to such a place. I am still paying."
—From the private writings of Caspar of Ecbatana

CHAPTER 21
What You Carry

"The road teaches what the village cannot:
how much you can carry, and what you must leave behind."
—Caravan wisdom

Spring, 44 CE—Aghbalou

The fire appeared on the eastern ridge at dusk.

Not a brush fire. Those burned low and orange and drifted with the wind. This was a column fire, built tall and fed with green wood to thicken the smoke, planted on the highest point of the ridge where it could be seen from thirty miles in every direction. It burned for the span of a hundred breaths and then it died, smothered as deliberately as it had been lit.

Zahra saw it from the well, where she had been checking water supplies for their small caravan. Her hands went still on the rope.

"Silina."

Silina looked up. She followed Zahra's gaze to the ridge. The smoke was already thinning, dissolving into the darkening sky, but both women knew what they had seen. Madi's network used signal fires the way the Roman army used trumpets: a vocabulary of flame and smoke carrying further than any voice and impervious to anyone who did not know the code.

One fire on the eastern ridge meant the next ridge had lit one before it, and the ridge before that, and the ridge before that, a chain of warnings stretching back toward the coastal settlements where Madi's people watched the Roman garrisons the way shepherds watched weather.

One fire, held for a hundred breaths and then killed. The simplest message in the code and the most urgent.

Move now.

Eudoxus had risen from the bench where he sat with the elders. He studied the ridge with calm born of long familiarity with danger. "When did we last rehearse the departure route?"

"Two weeks ago," Zahra said. "The children know to gather at Usem's house. Silina has the medicine pack ready. The water skins are filled."

They had practiced this four times in three years. Madi had insisted on it during his last visit, walking them through the route south, making the twins repeat the landmarks until even Juba, at four years old, could name the wadi where they would turn west and the rock formation where water could be found. Zahra had thought it excessive. She no longer thought so.

Usem crossed the square to meet them. His face carried a look she had learned to dread: bad news delivered with the kindness because he knew it would wound.

"Inside," Usem said. "All of you. Now."

They gathered in Usem's house. Zahra, Silina, Eudoxus, the twins playing quietly in the corner. Usem closed the door against curious eyes before speaking.

He looked at the children in the corner, then back at Zahra. Even now, behind a closed door, with Roman patrols days away, the real names stayed buried. The twins sat three paces from him, and they had never heard their mother called anything but Leila.

"Rome is sending a systematic investigation. Not patrols searching for rebels. A full census team with scribes and record keepers. Nerva's methodology." He paused, letting the implications settle. "They will register every person in the settlement. Names. Ages. Origins. Family connections."

"When?" Zahra's voice emerged steadier than she felt.

"Seven days. Perhaps less."

The room fell silent. Three years of careful integration, three years of borrowed names and rehearsed stories, three years of becoming villagers rather than refugees, reduced to a countdown.

"The council?" Eudoxus asked.

Usem's jaw tightened. "Split. Half want to protect you as we promised. Half think your presence has grown too dangerous." He met Zahra's eyes directly. "Massoud is already talking about the rewards Rome offers for information."

"Then we leave," Zahra said. "Tonight, if necessary."

"South," Usem confirmed. "Into the deep desert, where documentation becomes impossible and tribal law matters more than imperial decree. I have already sent word to contacts who can guide you."

Amara's small voice cut through the adult tension. "We leaving again?"

Zahra turned to find her daughter watching with eyes too old for four years. Juba stood beside his sister, his small body positioned between Amara and the door, though he could not have said what he was protecting her from.

"Yes, tasastinu. We are leaving again."

"Because the scared people?"

Zahra crouched to her daughter's level. "What scared people?"

"The village people. They scared of us. I feel it." Amara wrapped her arms around herself and shivered, though the room was warm. "Like cold in my chest. Their scared."

Zahra pulled her daughter close, the small body rigid with absorbed tension.

"Sometimes," Zahra said, "people become afraid when times grow hard. It does not mean they are bad. It means they are human."

"But we have to go because they scared?"

"We have to go because staying would make things harder for everyone. For them and for us."

Amara considered this with the gravity of someone much older. "Okay. I will help pack."

☙✦❧

That evening

The four adults sat in their borrowed house after the twins had fallen asleep. Juba sprawled in the complete relaxation of childhood, Amara curled tight even in sleep, as if her body anticipated danger her conscious mind could not yet name.

"The deep desert." Eudoxus's voice carried the weariness of age and sacrifice. "South, past the settled lands, where Rome's reach weakens and tribal law matters more than imperial decree."

"We do not know those tribes," Silina said. "We do not speak their dialects properly. We have no connections."

"We did not know Aghbalou either," Zahra replied. "We learned. We adapted. We will do it again."

"The children are older now. They will remember this place. They will remember the leaving."

"Better they remember leaving than remember betrayal." Zahra's voice went hard. "Better they learn early safety is temporary and trust must be earned anew in each place we land."

They planned through the night: what they could carry, where they might go, who might help them travel. The familiar arithmetic of flight, calculated with the efficiency of practice.

Outside, Aghbalou slept under spring stars. Inside, a family prepared to disappear again, abandoning three years of careful integration and the illusion sanctuary could ever be permanent.

Two hours before dawn

Amara woke in darkness to find her mother packing by candlelight.

"Time to go?"

"Yes, little one. Time to go."

"Where?"

"South. To the desert."

"Why south?"

"Because that is where safety is. For now."

Amara sat up, small face serious beyond her years. "There is a man. He makes you sad. In the stories."

Zahra's hands paused on the pack. "Yes."

"Is he real? Or just a story?"

"He is real. But he is far away, and we cannot be with him."

"Why?"

"Because he is fighting to protect people he loves. And we are hiding to protect people we love. Both things are hard."

"Like you protect us?"

"Yes. Like that."

"When I bigger, you tell me all the things?" Amara's small hand closed around her mother's. "All the things about the sad man and why we run and who we are?"

Zahra met her four-year-old daughter's eyes and saw understanding that should not have been possible at such an age. "When you are bigger. I promise."

"Okay." Amara accepted this gravely. She learned to trust promises even while sensing adults concealed what hurt most. "I wait."

They finished packing in silence, a woman who carried too many secrets and a child who sensed them all but could not yet articulate what she knew.

❧✦❧

The southern road, dawn

They departed Aghbalou as the first gray light touched the eastern mountains. Five horses carried four adults and two children into uncertain country.

Usem had sent word three days earlier, and Bakir had come. The desert trader arrived at dusk with his single pack horse, and the leather game board Eudoxus knew as well as his own hands. They did not play that evening. Bakir studied the family instead: Zahra's composure, Silina's watchfulness, the twins asleep in their blankets, Eudoxus's hands and the stubborn set of his jaw. He assessed them the way he assessed terrain before a crossing, reading the strengths and the vulnerabilities, calculating what the group could sustain.

Eudoxus had sat across a game board from this man a dozen times over three years. He had watched Bakir play the way the desert taught: patient, economical, never wasting a move. He had lost to him more often than he had won, and he trusted the man for exactly that reason. A man who could beat a Persian scholar at strategy could navigate a canyon maze with children on his back.

"Your brother has been expecting this." Bakir spoke to Zahra without softening it. "I sent a runner south when the signal fires lit. Yasir will ride for Tala Tazegzawt with his men. If the passes are clear, he reaches the oasis a day before us."

Zahra absorbed this. Her brother, riding north with warriors to meet a sister he had not seen in three years. The distance between Tizwit and Tala Tazegzawt was shorter than the distance the family had to cover from Aghbalou, but the southern passes were narrow and unpredictable, prone to sandstorms that could close a route for days.

"And if the passes are not clear?"

"Then we wait at the oasis until he arrives. Tala Tazegzawt has water and shelter. It is defensible ground." Bakir paused. "But I would rather not wait. Waiting is when things go wrong. Three days to Tala Tazegzawt if weather holds. Then south to the oasis communities. Yasir's people will receive you."

Zahra rode with Amara pressed against her chest, the child's warmth a comfort against the morning chill. Behind her, Silina carried Juba, who had protested early waking but now dozed against her shoulder. Eudoxus brought up the rear, his scholar's posture adjusting to the horse's rhythm with reluctant effort.

No one looked back.

To look back invited grief, and they could not afford grief while the road still demanded attention. The path wound through rocky defiles and across dry wadi beds, climbing toward the southern highlands where the land grew harsher and Roman interest grew thin.

As they paused to water the horses at a seep spring, Zahra's hands tightened on the reins. "Yasir," she said, keeping her voice steady. "You know him?"

"Chieftain of Tizwit. Good man. Lost his own family to Rome years back. He understands what you carry."

She nodded and said nothing more. Bakir did not need to know the chieftain who understood loss was the brother she had not seen since before the twins were born.

Amara stirred against Zahra's chest, eyes opening to take in the unfamiliar landscape. "Pretty," she said, pointing toward where morning light painted the rocks in shades of gold and rose.

"Yes, tasastinu. The desert has its own beauty."

"Different than Aghbalou."

"Many things will be different now."

Amara considered this, then nodded with a child's acceptance, the kind earned by too many upheavals. "Okay. I will learn the new different."

By the third morning on the road, the walnut stain had begun to fade from Eudoxus's beard. He did not reapply it since leaving Aghbalou. In the open desert there was no one to deceive, and the small clay pot was left behind with everything else belonging to Numerius.

Amara noticed first. She studied his face from her place against Zahra's chest, her brow furrowed with the concentration of a child cataloguing a change she could not name.

"Grandfather is turning white," she said.

Zahra glanced back. The gray was showing through at his temples and along the jawline, the borrowed color retreating like a tide going out. The man who emerged beneath it looked older than Numerius, and more honest.

"He was always white," Zahra said. "We just could not see it before."

Eudoxus heard them. He ran his hand across his chin and felt the coarseness where dark gave way to gray. Three years of walnut oil, three years of performing a vanity that was not vanity. He let his hand drop and rode on without covering his head.

One fewer lie to carry.

They rode on through the brightening day, a small caravan of refugees carrying their household on their backs and their secrets in their hearts. Behind them, Aghbalou settled into its morning routines, the space where they had lived already closing over like water healing after a stone's passage.

Ahead lay the desert, vast, indifferent, offering neither welcome nor rejection. Only the promise those who could adapt might survive, and those who could not would join the countless others whose bones the sand had swallowed.

Zahra held her daughter close and rode toward whatever came next.

The road taught what the village could not: how much you could carry, and what you must leave behind.

They were still learning.

☙✦❧

Three days later

The desert had become their enemy and their salvation.

They rode for three days, rationing water and watching for dust clouds that might signal pursuit. Bakir led with the confidence of long familiarity. He knew every wadi and hidden spring, but even his knowledge could not conjure water from stone or strength from exhausted horses.

Now, as the sun reached its zenith on the third day, dust clouds appeared on the northern horizon.

Silina pointed. "There. Riders." Her voice stayed calm, trained by years of crisis to betray nothing. But her hands gripped the water jug she had been checking.

Zahra squinted against the glare, her arms tightening around Amara. The dust was still distant, perhaps two hours behind them, but it moved with steady purpose. They knew their prey was tiring.

"How many?" Eudoxus shifted Juba's sleeping weight against his chest.

Silina studied the approaching cloud. "Hard to say. Eight, maybe ten." She had survived many pursuits. "They are not Roman soldiers. See how they ride? Tribal formation, but on Roman horses. Fresh mounts."

"Bounty hunters." Zahra's voice dropped. "Imazighen who have chosen silver over honor."

Worse in some ways than legionaries. These men knew the desert as well as any of them but had abandoned the old codes governing pursuit and sanctuary. They would track without mercy, driven by greed rather than duty.

"The horses cannot take much more." She ran her hand along her mount's neck. The animal's ribs showed clearly. Another hour of hard riding would kill them.

Eudoxus scanned the landscape ahead. Red cliffs rose from the desert floor like ancient fortifications, their faces carved by wind and rare floods into fantastic shapes. Between them, dark gaps suggested passages into the canyon country beyond.

He pointed toward a gap between towering red walls. "There. The canyon maze. If we reach it, we might lose them in the stone passages."

"Or become lost ourselves." Silina swallowed hard. "The canyon lands have swallowed whole caravans. Without water, without knowledge of the paths..."

But she was already moving, already gathering the twins' reins closer, already calculating the distance.

Amara spoke up. "The water is strong in there." Everyone turned to look at the four-year-old, who was unusually quiet during their flight. "I can hear it singing."

Behind them, the dust cloud grew closer. Individual riders became visible, their robes billowing as they pushed their mounts hard across the sand.

Silina looked at Zahra. Their eyes met with the understanding of two people who had already lost too much.

Now permanence was dissolving again. And she would protect these children with everything she had.

"We go in," Zahra decided, her voice steady despite the fear in her eyes. "Whatever waits in there is better than certain capture."

Eudoxus nodded. "Stay close. In terrain like this, one wrong turn means death."

They pushed their exhausted horses toward the canyon entrance, the red walls looming larger with each stride.

The canyons swallowed them like a stone dropped into dark water.

Walls of red sandstone rose on either side, so high sunlight reached the canyon floor only in narrow strips. The air cooled, carrying the scent of ancient stone and the faint trace of moisture.

Bakir led them through twisting passages, choosing paths looking no different from the ones they passed. "Water carved these channels," he said. "When the rains come, they become rivers. The water remembers its paths even when the stone seems to forget."

"How do you know which way?" Silina kept her voice low. Sound carried strangely in these stone corridors.

"I do not. But water flows downhill, and we need to go up, into the highlands where the springs rise. The canyons will narrow, then open into hidden valleys."

Behind them, faint sounds echoed: the clatter of hooves on stone, voices raised in argument. The bounty hunters had entered the maze.

Amara pressed her hands to her temples. "They are angry. And scared. The stone makes them feel small."

"Good," Zahra murmured. "Let the stone do its work."

They climbed through increasingly narrow passages, dismounting when the way became too tight for horses. Eudoxus moved slowly, his hands on the reins. Whatever reserves had sustained him through three days of flight were nearly spent.

"There." Bakir pointed to a gap in the canyon wall, barely wide enough for a horse to pass. "Through there. It opens into a protected basin with a spring."

They squeezed through one by one. Bakir first, then Silina with Juba, then Zahra with Amara, then Eudoxus leading the last horse. The passage twisted and turned, scraping against shoulders and flanks, before opening into sudden space.

A natural amphitheater spread before them, its walls curving in protective embrace around a small spring bubbling from mossy stones. Sparse grass grew near the water's edge, and date palms rose in a ragged line along the basin's southern rim. The place felt hidden, protected, as if the land itself had shaped a sanctuary.

"We rest here," Bakir said. "Water the horses. Fill every skin. If they track us this far, we will need strength for what comes next."

CHAPTER 22

The Last Diversion

"Some debts can only be paid in blood.
The creditor does not choose whose."
—Roman military saying (attributed)

Late Summer, 44 CE

Aedemon crouched behind a rocky outcrop with thirty of his best fighters, watching a Roman supply convoy crawl along the ancient trade route. Under oppressive heat, wagons creaked with their loads: grain sacks, weapon crates, strongboxes of silver for auxiliary troops. For territory this far from the frontier, the guards seemed sparse.

His jaw clenched. The convoy rolled forward with deceptive casualness, cavalry scouts riding alert, eyes sweeping the hills.

"The outriders look ready for trouble." Ghanin checked his bowstring, scarred hands moving with practiced efficiency. Eight years of raids had taught Aedemon's lieutenant to read the subtle signs distinguishing easy targets from traps.

Aedemon traced his sword grip, reading the same signs. Roman suspicion meant someone had compromised his intelligence network. The convoy's steady progress looked almost taunting: *We know you are here. Come and try.*

"They know we are here." His voice carried just far enough for his men to hear. "This is not a raid anymore."

The younger fighters shifted, hands tightening on spear shafts. The veterans remained motionless as stone, trusting Aedemon's judgment when odds turned ugly.

"We might withdraw." Ghanin's voice held no conviction. "Find another target, one they have not prepared for."

Aedemon said nothing. His eyes stayed on the convoy, but his mind had already traveled elsewhere.

Three years since Zahra left Caesarea. Long enough to become invisible, if the settlements stayed quiet and Rome's attention stayed where I had tried to direct it: south toward the desert, east toward the passes, anywhere but the mountain communities where families like mine had learned to disappear into the ordinary.

That was the calculation. It had always been the calculation.

He had not told Ghanin. He had not told Sabalus when he sent word positioning fighters along the eastern supply routes. He had not told any of them that the rebellion's purpose, in these weeks, was not to win. It was to be loud. To be visible. To give the garrison at Caesarea a fire large enough to keep it chasing smoke while the people who mattered remained beneath its notice.

The twins would be four years old now. Walking. Speaking. Old enough to remember, perhaps, though he hoped they would not. What he needed was for them to grow up.

He thought of Amara, who always knew. He thought of Juba, who would be angry and was right to be. He thought of Zahra, living under a borrowed name in whatever mountain village had become their home, teaching the children to answer to her as someone she was not.

Let them stay hidden. Let this be loud enough.

Ghanin spoke again, offering retreat. The word arrived as if from a great distance.

His thoughts turned to Silina. Young Silina, who had become a daughter to both him and Zahra. Did she reach safety with the others? Or did the Romans catch them already?

He could not think about that. He had to trust they had escaped. He had to trust the diversion would work.

"No." He drew Azref and checked its edge. Its steel caught dying sunlight like captured flame. "We hit them with everything. Let every Roman in the province know where Aedemon died."

The word settled over the war band like dust after an avalanche. No one spoke.

The fighters descended toward the convoy route with practiced silence. But this time differed. They were not hunting. They were announcing themselves to death.

Hours later—the provincial command tent, field camp

The captured rebel chieftain sat between two guards, hands bound but posture proud. Oil lamps cast shadows on canvas walls hung with maps of Mauretania, red pins marking the dwindling pockets of tribal resistance.

Aedemon's capture had cost twelve Roman dead and twice that wounded. He was here, alive, which Marcus had hoped when providing the intelligence making this trap possible.

Prefect Nerva sat behind a field desk covered in wax tablets, his stylus poised, documenting the moment with the same methodical precision he brought to every aspect of provincial administration. Eight months into his posting, the rebellion had delivered him its greatest prize.

"Fascinating." Nerva studied Aedemon with clinical interest. "Classical texts describe rebel leaders driven by primitive emotions: rage, vengeance, tribal loyalty. Yet you display remarkable composure. I must note this variance from theoretical models."

Aedemon's eyes shifted to the scholar-prefect with a look between pity and contempt.

"Your texts were written by men who never left Rome."

Nerva made another notation, the insult sailing past him. "Indeed. Direct observation proves superior to theoretical assumption. I shall document this execution thoroughly: his conduct, his final statements, the consequences of removing a leader from the resistance networks."

Marcus stood at attention against the tent wall, his face professionally neutral while his stomach churned. To Nerva, this was an academic exercise. Another entry for his growing archive.

"Aedemon of the Mauri." Nerva set down his stylus and regarded the prisoner with the clinical interest passing, in his mind, for gravity. "Your rebellion is finished. Your fighters are scattered or dead. Your family fled into the deep desert, beyond the reach of any network that might sustain them."

Aedemon said nothing, dark eyes studying faces with calm assessment. When his gaze met Marcus's, no apology showed. No regret.

Would he do it again? Marcus wondered. Of course. A hundred times for his children's safety. Just as I would if our positions were reversed. Perhaps my understanding it is what makes this unforgivable.

Somewhere, if he was right, Silina was watching over the twins. Young Silina, who had lost her own parents to violence and understood loss with a clarity no so young should possess. She would hold Juba and Amara through anything.

The thought steadied him. If the family was with Silina, they had a chance.

"However," Nerva continued, "you still have value. Your knowledge of tribal territories, your understanding of customs, these might serve Rome. Cooperate, and your death might be... recorded as dignified rather than ignominious."

Even his offer of mercy came wrapped in documentation.

Marcus watched his friend consider the words.

"What of my people? What becomes of them when their last voice falls silent?"

"They become Roman citizens. Properly administered, documented, and integrated into provincial systems. These will ensure their prosperity." Nerva spoke as if describing a philosophical proposition rather than the erasure of a culture. "History demonstrates assimilation proceeds most efficiently once charismatic resistance is eliminated."

Aedemon's gaze traveled the tent. Leather dispatch cases reducing lives to tactical considerations leaned against one corner. Maps carved his homeland into administrative districts. Stacked wax tablets held an obsessive's inventory, as if truth, pinned and catalogued, could be owned.

"I think not. My people deserve better than prosperity measured in census rolls."

"Then you choose death."

"I choose consistency. I choose to be in death what I tried to be in life: a man who remembered what he owed those who trusted him."

"Note," Nerva murmured, reaching for his stylus again. "Subject displays philosophical reasoning unexpected in a tribal context. Suggests education beyond typical insurgent background."

He wrote for a moment, then looked up. "Tribune Marcus, you will carry out the sentence."

Blood drained from Marcus's face.

"Sir, I..."

"You know this man. You served alongside him during the administrative period. Your participation demonstrates Rome's impartiality." Nerva's voice held no malice. He simply failed to see what he was asking. "It also provides valuable observational information on the effects of compelled execution between former associates."

"Sir, surely another officer..."

"The documentation requires it." Nerva's tone carried the finality of a resolved logical proof. "Your prior relationship makes the symbolic weight unmistakable. Rome punishes its enemies even through the hands of their friends. This must be recorded."

The threat was quieter than it would have been from Paulinus or Geta, but no less absolute. Nerva did not threaten. He simply arranged reality until compliance became the only rational path.

Marcus's hand moved to his sword. Aedemon's gaze held no accusation, no plea. Only terrible compassion for the impossible choice.

"I understand."

❧✦❧

The execution field, dying light

Roman soldiers formed a loose circle. Word had spread. Men gathered with the mixture of curiosity and unease attending moments when empires revealed their true nature.

Aedemon walked to the center without assistance, bearing proud despite his bonds. He looked around: young legionaries seeing another conquered rebel, veterans recognizing a worthy opponent, officers understanding political necessity.

His gaze found Marcus at the circle's edge, sword drawn, face pale as parchment.

"They reached Usem's settlement safely," Aedemon said in Tamazight, low enough only Marcus could hear. "Your documents held."

"I know. I have had them watched."

"Still protecting them?"

"I gave my word they would be safe. Unlike you, I keep promises."

"Yes." No mockery, only acknowledgment. "That was always your weakness. And your honor."

Marcus stepped forward, the sword impossibly heavy. He saved family and cause but paid with life. I saved honor and position but pay with conscience. Which of us chose better? Which betrayed more?

"My friend," Aedemon switched to Latin for the witnesses, "do not carry this burden alone. We both serve masters who demand more than men should give."

Marcus raised his sword, hand trembling. He was about to end a life, destroy a friendship, betray every principle he once held sacred.

"I am sorry," he whispered in Tamazight.

"I know. And I forgive you. Watch over my family if you can. Help them understand love sometimes demands terrible sacrifices."

"You were right on the road. You earned this."

"And you earned their survival. We both paid our prices."

"For the record," Nerva called across the field, stylus raised, "let the execution commence."

Marcus closed his eyes, tears streaming. When he opened them, Aedemon looked at him with infinite compassion, as if Marcus were being executed rather than holding the sword.

"For love," Aedemon whispered. "Always for love."

The blade struck true.

Aedemon fell forward, blood mixing with desert sand that would carry his spirit to whatever realm awaited those who chose honor over survival.

Marcus dropped to his knees beside his friend's body. The sword fell from nerveless fingers. Sobs wracked him. He had just murdered everything he believed about honor, friendship, and serving Rome without losing his soul.

❧✦❧

Nerva continued writing as Marcus knelt, his stylus scratching steadily across wax.

"Unexpected grief from the executioner. The classical authorities suggest soldiers maintain composure. Worth examining further." He paused, studied the scene before him, and added: "The tribune's grief suggests deep attachment. The prior friendship is confirmed. His judgment in intelligence matters bears scrutiny."

He documented everything and understood nothing.

❧✦❧

In the deep desert, two things happened at once.

At the oasis where the family sheltered, four-year-old Amara woke in the night, pressing small hands to her temples.

"He is gone," she whispered. "He is gone, he is gone, he is gone."

Zahra gathered her daughter, her heart already knowing what the words meant. "Who, tasastinu? Who is gone?"

But Amara could not explain feeling the sudden, terrible hollow place in the world where someone important had been and would never be again.

Silina watched from across the small space, holding Juba close against her chest. The boy slept on, oblivious, but Silina's eyes met Zahra's in the darkness. Both women understood. Both women knew what Amara was sensing, even if neither could name it yet.

☙✦❧

In the war band's camp, Ghanin sat beside Marcus in the darkness and asked no questions. Aedemon's lieutenant had served his chieftain for eight years. He recognized another man's anguish and offered the only thing he could, his presence.

One day, Zahra might learn Marcus had been the one to strike the killing blow. But they would never meet, never speak. He and the woman he widowed would remain forever separated, bound only by his secret protection of what Aedemon loved most.

His children live because I was fool enough to believe in friendship. Perhaps that is the only victory either of us can claim.

The price of loyalty was paid by those who lived after abandoning their principles.

And in Nerva's growing archive, this moment would be preserved forever: clinical notes about behavioral patterns and tactical implications, missing entirely a soul had shattered, a friendship had ended, and years of impossible security would continue.

CHAPTER 23

The Cost of Springs

"The spring gives what it gives. The cost is yours to discover later."
—Desert teaching on sacred places

Early Autumn, 44 CE—Tala Tazegzawt Oasis, Mauretania

The first glimpse of green after days of brown stone and yellow sand struck the weary travelers like a vision from the old stories. Tala Tazegzawt hid in a deep ravine, palm trees rising like answered prayers, their fronds rustling with promises of water and shade. The air carried moisture, a sweetness making parched throats ache.

"Sacred water." Awe filled Eudoxus's voice, but exhaustion ran deeper than their desert crossing. Two spiritual workings had left their marks: the first against bandits on the mountain road, the second at Aghbalou's sacred spring. Both had torn at channels once connecting him to the spirit realm. Now a persistent tremor lived in his hands, and grayness ringed his eyes even the familiar scent of wild thyme near the water could not ease.

Silina watched him with concern. At twenty, she understood loss intimately. She had already learned certain wounds did not heal cleanly. Eudoxus's spiritual wounds reminded her of her own childhood ones: cuts too deep for simple bandaging.

She reached out and steadied his arm as they navigated the descent to the spring. He glanced at her with gratitude, and understanding passed between them. They were both carrying pain expressing itself in different languages.

A natural spring bubbled from limestone rocks worn smooth by countless generations of pilgrims. The water sang as it emerged, a sound bypassing the ears and spoke to the marrow. Around the spring's edge, ancient hands had arranged stones in the sacred spiral pattern connecting earth to sky. The stones held warmth despite the shade. They remembered ten thousand prayers.

Bakir dismounted and scanned the oasis with the quick economy of a man reading terrain the way others read faces. The palm groves. The ravine walls. The approaches from the south where Yasir's riders should have been visible against the skyline.

No riders. No horses tethered at the spring's edge. No fire ring, no disturbed ground, no sign anyone had been here in weeks.

Zahra saw it in his face before he spoke.

"He is not here."

"Not yet." Bakir kept his voice level. "The southern passes are unpredictable. A sandstorm, a flooded wadi, a Roman patrol on the route. Any of these would slow him by a day or two."

"Or he did not receive the message."

"The runner was reliable. Yasir received the message." Bakir unsaddled the horses and led them to the spring. "We wait. The oasis has water, shade, and defensible ground. Your brother will come."

Zahra looked at Eudoxus, who had lowered himself to the ground beside the spring with careful movements. His body had become an unreliable partner.. Silina was already checking his hands, her healer's focus narrowing to the tremor that had worsened over the three days of travel. The twins sat in the shade of a palm, Juba arranging stones while Amara watched the southern horizon with eyes that saw further than any child's should.

They had reached the meeting point. The meeting had not arrived.

Bakir set camp with the spare efficiency of a thousand camps, every gesture purposeful, nothing wasted. He positioned the horses where they could drink but not wander. He chose sleeping ground against the ravine wall where the rock would hold the day's warmth through the cold night. He placed himself at the ravine entrance, where he could watch both the approach from the north and the route from the south, and he settled in to wait the way he played his game board: patiently, without wasted motion, reading the terrain for what it would reveal.

"We made it." Zahra's whisper carried relief beneath terrible knowledge. Amara had shared what she sensed in the canyon, a sudden emptiness where someone important had been. Zahra carried that knowledge in silence, pressed against her ribs like a blade. The others still held hope she no longer shared.

Juba scrambled toward the water but stopped at its edge, four-year-old instincts responding to a presence he could not name. The air cooled near the spring, carrying moss scent and the memory of ancient devotion.

"Mother, the water watches us."

Amara hung back, small fingers pressed to her temples. Since they entered the ravine, she had felt the emotions of everyone who had ever knelt here: joy, desperation, hope, grief. She wanted to tell someone, but adults always patted her head and called her imaginative.

Eudoxus approached the spring's edge and knelt, placing his palms against the worn stones. Their impossible smoothness testified to centuries of reverent touches. He spoke ritual words in the ancient tongue, asking permission to shelter in sacred space. The spring's bubbling shifted rhythm in response, though the connection felt more tenuous than it should have. Where blessing once flowed through him like warm honey, only echoes remained.

"We may camp here." Uncertainty wavered in his voice. "The spirits welcome those who come with respect."

Silina studied Eudoxus as she prepared the camp. His frailty worsened since the working at Aghbalou's spring. Whatever spiritual act he had performed there cost him more than physical injury. She noted which herbs might help, what preparations she could offer. But Eudoxus grieved a loss inside himself no medicine could touch.

☙✦❧

Amara sprang up from arranging pebbles, her small face tight with concentration. "People coming. Many people. Angry people."

Zahra reached for her, but Amara pulled away.

"It hurts." She pressed her palms harder against her temples. "They are so angry it makes my head hurt."

The Roman centurion and his men appeared at the ravine entrance with the bearing of soldiers who tracked their quarry to ground. The sacred geography of the place affected them, though Roman training offered no framework for understanding what they felt.

"You match the description perfectly." The centurion's voice trembled with menace transcending military authority.

Bakir moved before the centurion finished speaking. He was not a warrior. He carried no sword, no spear, no weapon beyond the belt knife every desert man wore. But he had spent three days responsible for two children, and the instinct ran deeper than military training. He accepted a charge for two children, and that was enough. He crossed the camp in four strides, gathered Juba under one arm and reached for Amara with the other.

Amara pulled away from him. She stood rigid, hands pressed to her temples, overwhelmed by the soldiers' fury crashing through her. Bakir did not understand what was happening to the girl, only that she was not moving and soldiers were advancing. He lifted her bodily and carried both children toward the rocks at the ravine's edge.

Silina's hands stilled on the supply pack. Her first instinct was the same one from childhood: hide the children. Protect them. Do whatever was necessary. She moved toward Juba and pulled him behind the tent.

Eudoxus knew his choice, even as instinct screamed against it. The spiritual channels through his hands bore damage from two prior workings. To attempt a third so soon, with pathways still raw and barely functional...

But Roman soldiers were advancing toward Amara and Juba. That simplified everything.

"Sacred water, spirits of the land," he intoned in the ancient tongue, "grant us protection in this sacred place."

The moment he opened himself to the spring's power, agony shot through his hands like molten metal. The spiritual channels, already scarred by two workings, could not withstand the force. He had been wrong. This was not temporary exhaustion to be endured and recovered from. The pathways connecting his mortal form to the spirit realm burned away like parchment in flame.

The protective stones blazed with inner light. The spring's surface had an unnatural glow.

A young optio circled behind the spring toward the children while his comrades stood transfixed by the supernatural display. His sword rose above the twins.

"Roman blades for rebel spawn!"

Silina screamed. The sound tore from somewhere primal, from the young woman who had chosen to protect these children with everything she had. She knew this terror. She had learned it at eight years old.

Eudoxus broke his connection to the protective powers and felt his spiritual abilities die. He lunged forward and intercepted the descending blade.

The sword meant for Amara's throat bit deep into the scholar's outstretched arm, shearing through flesh and bone. He screamed.

Amara doubled over. His agony flooding through her.

Silina grabbed both twins and pulled them toward the rocks, covering them with her own body.

The optio raised his bloody sword for another strike. "One traitor down. The spawn next..."

A war cry split the desert air, high, ululating, the sound of mounted warriors descending like vengeance itself. Yasir's riders crested the ravine's edge, horses plunging down the treacherous slope at full gallop. Sand and stones cascaded around them as twenty desert fighters materialized from what had seemed empty landscape.

"Ambush!" the Roman centurion bellowed. "Form square! Shields up!"

But his men were scattered, half still reeling from the spring's supernatural display. Yasir's warriors struck before they could regroup. The first rider's spear took an unprepared legionary through the chest. Another Roman fell with an arrow sprouting from his throat.

Yasir himself led the charge, his curved sword catching moonlight as he bore down on the optio standing over Eudoxus.

The Roman barely raised his blade before Yasir's mount slammed into him and sent him sprawling.

"The children!" Yasir roared to his men. "Protect the children!"

Three riders wheeled toward Silina's position and formed a mounted barrier, their spears creating a forest of points between the children and the battle.

The centurion tried to restore order. "Rally to me! We are outnumbered. Withdraw!"

But desert warfare bore no resemblance to Roman drilling grounds. Yasir's men knew every rock, every shadow. They struck and vanished, reformed and struck again. Arrows flew from positions the Romans could not see.

One legionary broke ranks and ran. Then another. Panic spread like flame through dry grass.

"Stand your ground!" The centurion's command went unheeded. His century, what remained of it, fled into the night, leaving their dead and wounded behind.

❧✦❧

Yasir dismounted beside Eudoxus, his face grim as he assessed the damage. Blood pooled beneath the scholar's ruined hand.

"Silina! Your healing skills. Quickly!"

Silina emerged from behind the rocks, both children pressed against her sides. She knelt beside Eudoxus, and her training took over despite the horror. Her hands moved across the wound.

"The hand will not recover. But there is a deeper wound. The spiritual pathways through his arm are severed."

"Gone." Eudoxus whispered. "I felt them die. But worth it. Every working I will never speak again, worth their lives."

Silina's eyes filled, but she kept her hands steady. She had learned to separate emotion from action, to do what needed doing even when her heart was breaking.

She cleaned the wound with water from the sacred spring and bound what remained of his arm with cloth torn from her own garments. The cleaning would need to be thorough, more deliberate, but stopping the bleeding could not wait. She worked with focus, understanding grief could wait but blood could not.

"Will he live?" Zahra's voice came from behind her, hollow with accumulating loss.

"If infection does not set in. If we can reach proper shelter." Silina met her eyes. "He saved them, Zahra. He gave everything to save them."

Zahra looked at the old scholar. The man who had been part of her household for five years. Who had taught her husband philosophy and taught her children their first words. The man who had now lost the use of his hand and his gifts to protect the children of a friend he had known for less than a decade.

"I know."

✦

Later that night

Silina sat beside the spring with the sleeping children. Amara whimpered in her sleep, small face creased with whatever dreams haunted her. Juba slumbered with his fist closed around a smooth stone from the spring's edge.

She carried two pieces of knowledge in her chest. Aedemon was dead. And Eudoxus had sacrificed his greatest gift to save them.

The first knowledge came from Zahra's tight silence, from Amara's midnight certainty in the canyon, from the way Zahra's hands shook whenever she looked south expecting the messenger she dreaded. Silina had watched enough grief in her life to recognize its shape before it was named.

The second knowledge she had seen with her own eyes. The old scholar had thrown his damaged body between Roman blades and the children he loved, and paid with his hand, his powers, everything that once made him extraordinary.

She was twenty years old, responsible now for an elder whose gifts had died and two children whose father she feared was already dead. She had been younger when she carried more.

She lived. Wandered. Lost shelter and found it again, lost family and gained new family, until Aedemon and Zahra took her in, and gave her a place to belong, a purpose beyond mere survival.

Now Aedemon was almost certainly dead. Zahra carried grief that would break her before it healed. Eudoxus lay fevered and diminished. And two small children needed someone to hold them while their world fell apart.

Silina looked at Amara's sleeping face and saw the pain there even in dreams. She knew the child carried a gift always showing her truths others could not see.

I will hold them through this. I will keep them alive. I will shape this grief into a presence that helps others survive their own.

It was what survival had taught her. What she had learned to do.

Some people shattered when tragedy struck. Others learned to carry it, to shape it, to make of their wounds a shelter for those who came after.

Silina had been broken once. She would not break again.

The days that followed

Bakir left at first light the morning after the battle.

He had stayed through the night, tending the horses, carrying water from the spring, performing the quiet tasks keeping a camp alive while the people in it dealt with wounds he could not dress. He spoke once to Yasir at the ravine entrance, a conversation conducted in low voices and short sentences, two men settling accounts requiring no elaboration.

Eudoxus was awake when Bakir came to the tent. The old scholar's face was gray with pain, his ruined hand wrapped in linen already spotted with blood, but his eyes were clear.

"You are leaving."

"My work is done. Your brother will take you south." Bakir crouched beside him. "We never finished our last game."

"You were winning."

"I was always winning." The desert man's face creased in the first expression Eudoxus had seen from him that was not calculation or patience. It was warmth. Brief, unadorned, offered the way Bakir offered everything: without waste. "The children are strong. The girl sees more than she should. The boy builds things. They will survive this."

"Thank you, Bakir. For the games. For the road. For last night."

Bakir clasped his arm, sealing a contract requiring no document. Then he stood, shouldered his pack, and walked out of the tent and up the ravine path toward the northern trail. He did not look back. He had delivered his cargo. The desert waited, and Bakir did not keep the desert waiting.

Eudoxus listened to his footsteps fade on the gravel and said a prayer in the old tongue for a man who would not have wanted one and would not have objected to receiving it.

☙✦❧

Yasir sent two riders south to Tizwit before the morning was an hour old. One carried word of the family's arrival, of the battle, of the Roman century that now knew the oasis existed. The other carried a list of supplies Silina needed: herbs for infection, clean linen, the honey she used to pack wounds that would not close on their own.

"They will reach Tizwit in two days," Yasir told Zahra. "The settlement will know you are coming. They will prepare."

"How long before we can move him?" Zahra looked toward the tent where Eudoxus lay.

"Silina says a week at least. Fever has not set in yet, but it will. She wants him stable before we travel."

"And the Romans?"

"The century that found you will report to its garrison. Reinforcements will come. We have days, not weeks." Yasir's face held the calculation of decades defending this territory. "But I know the approaches better than any Roman commander, and my riders will see them coming long before they reach the ravine."

Yasir posted riders on the ridgeline above the ravine and sent scouts east and west to watch for Roman patrols. The oasis was defensible, but only if they knew when to abandon it. He gave them shelter among his men's tents while Silina tended to Eudoxus.

The scholar could not travel. Fever held him for five days after the battle, and when it broke, the weakness that replaced it was worse. He could sit upright for only minutes before the trembling overwhelmed him. His ruined hand throbbed at every change in temperature and produced a disorientation Silina recognized but could not treat. His body would heal. The rest was beyond her medicines.

"How long?" Zahra asked.

"Weeks. He needs rest and food and time for the hand to close properly. If we move him now, infection will set in and we will lose him."

So, they stayed. The oasis held them in its green cradle while the desert burned around them, and Rome searched the wrong valleys.

Zahra carried her daughter's words in silence, her movements sharper, her eyes scanning the horizon, expecting the messenger she dreaded. She would not speak of what she feared. She would not give shape to the dread she felt in her chest. She would wait for confirmation, for proof, for the rider who would make real what Amara had already sensed.

And Amara learned, once again, her gift showed truths the adults around her would not name.

She stopped asking. She stopped trying to explain. But she did not stop knowing.

The emptiness she had felt in the night remained, a hollow place in the world where someone important had been. She carried it with her through the following days, waiting for the adults to catch up with what she already understood.

They would learn soon enough. And when they did, she would remember she had known first, and no one had believed her.

❧✦❧

The second week at Tala Tazegzawt

The ruined hand throbbed.

Eudoxus sat against the wall of the tent Yasir had given them, legs crossed, his good hand resting open on his knee. The other lay in his lap, wrapped in clean linen. The twisted fingers could not close. The wrist could not turn. Silina said the hand would remain but would never hold a stylus, grip a rein, or trace a sacred symbol again.

He tried to sit. The way he had sat every morning for twenty years.

His mind would not be quiet.

It reached for the spiritual pathways the way a tongue probes the socket of a cracked tooth. The channels he had cultivated in the years after Bethlehem, when he had turned to the magical traditions of his Persian upbringing seeking connection to fill the purposelessness. He reached and found nothing. Where power had lived, nothing remained. The silence of a room where someone had died.

Note the reaching, the discipline whispered. *Do not follow it. Let it arise and pass.*

The reaching arose. It did not pass. It arose repeatedly, a drowning man's reflex grasping for a surface that no longer existed.

His hand throbbed. The pain radiated up through his forearm into his shoulder, a hot pulse synchronized with his heartbeat. He tried to note the pain without reacting. The pain seized his attention instead and dragged it back to the body, to the loss, to the irreversible fact of what the Roman blade had taken.

Return to the breath.

He returned. One breath. Two. The mind broke free on the third and spiraled into the catalogue of everything he had lost. The power to protect the children. The ability to call fire from sacred stones. The connection to the ancestors who had spoken through him in the grove, on the mountain road, at the spring. Gone. All of it spent in three workings across four years.

So he sat with that.

He sat with the shallow breath and the throbbing hand, a mind that would not be quiet, and pathways echoing with absence. He did not try to force the stillness. He did not pretend the loss was acceptable. He sat with the full catastrophe of what he had become: an old man with a ruined hand, no power, no clear purpose, responsible for two children whose father was dead and whose gifts he could no longer match with his own.

The morning light moved across the tent wall. Outside, one of Yasir's riders spoke to the horses in the low murmur men used with animals they trusted. Juba's voice rose from somewhere near the spring, asking a question Amara answered too quietly to hear. Life continued, indifferent to one man's ruin.

The practice did not work the way it had worked for twenty years. The stillness did not come.

What came instead was worse and better than stillness. What came was the raw fact of being alive. The breath, however shallow. The heartbeat, however painful. The light on the wall. The sounds of the oasis.

He was here. Broken, diminished, purposeless again. But here.

The practice had never promised peace. It had promised presence. And presence, the morning revealed, did not require spiritual power. It did not require wholeness or purpose or the ability to protect anyone.

It required only the willingness to remain.

❧✦❧

He sat the next morning and the next. His reaching for dead pathways continued for weeks, an involuntary spasm between one breath and the next. His ruined hand throbbed through every session, but it no longer shook. A new trembling in his good right hand disturbed him now.

But gradually the practice taught him what he could not have learned while he still had power.

The trembling in his good hand, the persistent fine shiver that Silina said would never stop, became part of the practice rather than an obstacle to it. He noted the trembling the way he noted his breath. Present. Constant. Beyond his control. He let it tremble while he sat. It became a kind of honesty, the body refusing to pretend what had happened was acceptable.

Without the channels to reach through, Eudoxus was left with the most fundamental layer of the practice: plain human attention. The kind any person could offer.

He paid attention to the children. He watched Amara's face when she slept and noticed how her brow furrowed in response to emotions in the room. He watched Juba's hands when the boy played and saw the strategic intelligence already taking shape. He paid attention to the way the practice had taught him: no agenda, no desire to intervene.

And he discovered this ordinary attention was the gift he had been carrying since Bethlehem, the willingness to be present, to see without seizing or fixing another person's truth.

The talisman he had left behind in Persia worked by amplifying what the bearer carried. Power amplified power. Hunger amplified hunger. But presence did not need amplification. It was already complete.

The ruined hand, the dead pathways were not the price of his sacrifice. They were the teachers that sacrifice had given him.

Eudoxus sat with them, morning after morning, and discovered the third path had been under his feet the entire time.

He had only needed to lose everything else to see it.

❧✦❧

Three weeks later—on the road to Tizwit

The journey from Tala Tazegzawt to Yasir's settlement proceeded in careful stages, allowing Eudoxus to heal while the family processed their narrow escape. Silina rode beside the scholar, reaching over to steady him when exhaustion made him sway in the saddle.

Under her breath, she sang old songs her mother used to sing before the soldiers came and everything ended. They were Amazigh traveling songs with distinctive call-and-response patterns, to be shared between riders but beautiful even as a single voice carrying melody against the silence. The words spoke of journeys, of water found after long thirst, and of home as a direction rather than a place.

Amara's crying eased when Silina sang. The child's small body relaxed against her chest, and the melody did what arms alone could not. By midday even Juba had spent his tears. The children rode in a daze, carried forward because no one stopped, learning without words that this was their world now, the road, the flight, the safety that always ended.

"There." Yasir pointed toward distant hills rising from the desert. "The foothills. Beyond them, Tizwit. We can make it by tomorrow evening if we do not rest."

Zahra nodded, though everything in her ached for stillness and a moment to breathe. There would be time for that later, if they survived.

Silina steadied Amara's horse and reached over to hold Juba's small hand. "Almost there." She meant it as both reassurance and hope.

The caravan of four adults and two children, carrying what remained of their lives on horseback, pressed forward across the burning sand. Behind them, the Romans searched. Ahead lay only the desert and the hope that Yasir's promise held true.

They rode into an uncertain future, knowing only that stopping meant capture, and capture meant ending.

But Silina rode with two children in her care, and she would not stop. She had survived worse. She would survive this too.

CHAPTER 24

Different Stones

"A widow rebuilds her house with different stones.
The shape changes. The need for shelter does not."
—Amazigh mourning wisdom

Autumn, 44 CE—Tizwit Oasis—three weeks after Aedemon's death, twins age 4

The oasis spread before them at dusk, scattered tents and palm groves of a community thriving in the deep desert's embrace.

"There." Yasir pointed as they crested the final ridge. "Tizwit."

The oasis nestled in a wide basin where springs from the foothills created a marvel. Stone-built houses of warm sandstone hugged the higher ground. Families slept during the hottest months on their flat roofs, edged with low walls. Each dwelling opened inward to a courtyard shaded by woven palm-frond screens. Sleeping quarters faced east, storage to the north, cooking areas to the south where smoke could rise without fouling the living spaces. The walls were thick, built to hold the night's coolness through the day's heat. Doorways had geometric carvings like triangles, diamonds, and zigzags, the latter symbolizing water, which was vital for survival in that arid land. Below, date palm groves stretched in ordered ranks, crowns catching afternoon light like captured emeralds.

Water channels glinted silver, carrying the spring's gift throughout the settlement. Abundance born of perfect adaptation. The desert's patient wisdom turned scarcity into plenty through knowledge passed down in sacred trust.

"How many people live here?" Zahra carried careful control in her voice, holding herself together with visible effort.

"Perhaps sixty families permanently. During gatherings, over two hundred families."

As they descended, people emerged. Children peered with curiosity while mothers kept protective hands on their shoulders. Men appeared on rooftops, positioning that spoke of a community ready to defend itself. A woman emerged from the nearest stone house and shielded her eyes against the low sun. She studied the approaching riders, then broke into a run.

"Zahra!" The cry carried across the basin. "Zahra, is that you?"

Yasir's wife, Taderfit, reached them before Zahra could dismount, pulling at her arm, touching her face, weeping and laughing. "He said you were coming. He said you were alive. Let me see you. Let me see the children."

Zahra embraced her, but her eyes found Amara over the woman's shoulder. Her daughter sat rigidly on Silina's horse, her face wearing the look of a child stopped by a sound just beyond hearing.

Other women followed, calling out greetings, and each one said the same name. Zahra. Zahra. Zahra.

Four years of careful lies, dissolved in thirty seconds of welcome.

❧✦❧

Eudoxus reined in his horse at the ridge's crest and let the others descend ahead of him. Below, the oasis mirrored what he had dreamed of for forty years: sunlit palms, shiny water, and sand-colored homes.

This is where I will die.

The certainty arrived without drama, settling into him like a stone finding its place at the bottom of a stream. It would not be soon. Years remained, perhaps many of them. But this village, this refuge at the edge of the deep desert, would be his last home. He would not board another ship. He would not wander to another city seeking purpose that refused to declare itself. The wandering was over.

The thought should have terrified him. Caspar would have raged against such limitations. A single village? After Alexandria, Antioch, Ephesus, Jerusalem itself? After following a comet across the world to witness a truth that still defied his understanding?

But Eudoxus was not Caspar anymore. Forty years of failure had worn away the certainty that had once driven him. Forty years of students who wanted power rather than wisdom. Forty years of seeking the children from his dreams, only to discover that dreams offered no maps, no timelines, no guarantees.

He saw it at last. The divine encounter in Bethlehem had not been pointing toward thrones or cosmic power. It had been pointing here. Small works. A single family. Daily presence.

Below, Zahra guided her horse down the slope, her grief visible in every rigid line of her body. Beside her rode Silina, steady and watchful. And in the sling and basket sat the twins, orphaned and already marked by losses they could not yet understand.

These children are the faces I have been dreaming for forty years.

He urged his horse forward and followed his family down into Tizwit.

He was, at last, where he belonged.

❧✦❧

Amara pressed closer to her mother's side. There were so many people with so many feelings: curiosity, suspicion, pity, grief mirroring their own. The emotions pressed against her skin, and she wanted to tell someone how overwhelming it was. But adults would just dismiss her with a pinch on the cheek, often remarking how cute she was.

She watched Juba run ahead toward the goats. Unlike her, Juba moved through the world without sensing its hidden currents. His unknowing felt to him like freedom.

❧✦❧

She felt the other girl before she saw her. Something bright and quick, coming closer through the crowd.

Amara looked up.

A girl stood over her, studying her the way Juba studied things he wanted to understand. She was a little bigger than Amara, with her father's broad forehead and her mother's direct eyes. She did not say anything at first. She just looked.

"You are Amara," the girl said in Tamazight.

"Yes."

"I am Tiziri." She sat down beside her on the low wall without asking. "My baba brought you here."

"I know."

Tiziri looked at the crowd, then back at Amara. "My mother said your mother's name. When she ran to her."

Amara's hands went still in her lap. She had felt it: the sharp crack of it, the way her mother's body went rigid for just a moment before she returned the embrace. "Yes."

"She was not supposed to." Tiziri said it the way she said everything, as a simple report. "My baba told her not to."

"Why did she?"

Tiziri considered this seriously. "She was too happy. When she is very happy she forgets." A pause. "My baba is going to be cross."

"Does it matter? That she said it?"

Tiziri thought about this with visible effort. "Everyone here already knows," she said finally. "It is only the Romans who must not know." She looked around the settlement with a five-year-old's assessment. "There are no Romans here."

Something in Amara's chest loosened, just slightly.

"My mother was frightened," she said. "When your mother said it."

"I know." Tiziri did not offer comfort. She stated it as fact, the way she stated everything. "Adults are frightened of many things. My baba says that is why they plan so carefully."

"Do you plan carefully?"

Tiziri considered. "I try. But I say things before I have planned them." She paused. "Like my mother."

"Does your mother forget a lot?"

"No." Tiziri considered this seriously. "Only when she is very happy." She looked sideways at Amara. "She was very happy to see your yemma."

Amara thought about that. Her mother had been happy too: she felt it underneath the fear, the same way she sometimes felt warmth underneath cold water if she pushed her hand deep enough. Both things at once.

"My yemma missed her," Amara said.

"Yes." Tiziri nodded. "They were apart for a long time."

They sat in silence for a moment, feet dangling from the low wall, the settlement's sounds around them.

"Do you always know what people feel?" Tiziri asked.

"Yes."

"Even when they do not want you to?"

"Yes."

Tiziri absorbed this. "That must be very loud," she said.

The laugh came before Amara expected it: small and surprised. She pressed her hand to her mouth.

Tiziri looked pleased, though she had not smiled. "My mother says I say too many things," she said. "But I did not know that one was funny."

"It is not funny," Amara said. "It is just true. And nobody says the true thing."

"I always say the true thing," Tiziri said, with the simple certainty of someone reporting a fact about themselves. "My mother says that is also a problem."

From across the settlement, Taderfit's voice carried: "Tiziri. Stay with the women."

"I am with my cousin," Tiziri called back.

A pause. Then: "Do not disappear."

"I am right here," Tiziri said, with the tone of someone who found this distinction important.

She turned back to Amara. "Tell me about your brother. My baba says he is always in trouble."

"He is," Amara said. "But he does not mean to be."

"That is the worst kind," Tiziri said. "You cannot even be cross with them."

Amara looked at her cousin: this girl who said the true thing, who was not afraid of her, who had called the noise of the world loud as though it were simply a fact and not the heaviest thing Amara carried.

"I think we are going to be friends," Amara said.

Tiziri nodded, as though this had already been decided. "My baba said so too," she said. "He is usually right."

❧✦☙

The group of elders approached with formal bearing.

"The family of Aedemon is welcome here. And will he be joining you soon?" The eldest's words fell like stones into still water. They expected Aedemon, but Aedemon would never come home.

"We come seeking the protection of kin and the blessing of the waters."

Zahra's jaw tightened almost imperceptibly. The secret pressed against her teeth, cold and immovable. She could not speak of it here in front of the children. Not yet.

"Both are yours."

Amara had not followed Juba to the goats. She stood at the edge of the greeting and heard what her mother did not say. The elder asked if he was coming. Her mother answered something else. The hollow place she had carried since the desert shifted and settled, as though it had found the shape it belonged to. She did not ask. Not yet. Juba laughed at something the goats did. She watched him and said nothing.

❧✦❧

That evening

Women from Tizwit spontaneously provided a communal dish of couscous, lamb, and root vegetables, with the grain hand-rolled that morning. They served torn flatbread baked on hot stones, syrupy dates, and sharp, green-gold olive oil.

Zahra recognized the hospitality code. In the mountains, strangers received water first, then bread, then whatever the household could spare. Here the offering was lavish, a deliberate statement: you are not beggars at our door. You are family arriving home. She tore bread and dipped it in the oil, and the taste carried her back to her mother's kitchen so suddenly that she closed her eyes.

The messenger arrived as sunset painted the sky purple and gold. His dust-covered appearance and exhausted horse spoke of a desperate desert crossing. He approached Yasir with the formal bearing of one carrying devastating news.

"Uncle," the messenger said in Tamazight, using the respectful title. "I bring word from the eastern foothills. Word of Aedemon."

The name fell into the gathering and silenced it.

Yasir leaned forward. "Speak, nephew. What news?"

The messenger's eyes moved to Zahra, then to the children near the water channel. His hesitation spoke volumes.

"Perhaps the children should..." he began.

Silina stepped forward without waiting for permission. "Come, little ones. Time to wash before the evening meal." She kept her voice light, ordinary, though her hands trembled as she reached for Juba.

Amara stayed behind, watching the adults with a look signaling her odd observations were coming, while Juba had come without a fuss.

"Something bad happened," Amara said. "I can feel it. I felt like this in the canyon."

Silina met her eyes, saw the vindication already forming there, and made a choice. "Come with me now. Your mother needs a moment."

She guided them toward their dwelling and positioned herself to hear what followed while shielding them from the worst of it. Some truths needed preparation and should not arrive as an ambush.

Behind her, the messenger spoke the words that would reshape their world.

"Aedemon fell in battle against the Romans three weeks past. He died protecting his people, drawing Roman attention so others could escape."

Zahra's cry carried across the oasis, a sound Silina had heard only once before, when her own mother had learned of her father's death. The sound of a world ending. The sound of a future collapsing into rubble.

In the dwelling, Amara wept, her small body rigid with the overflow of her mother's anguish. Juba looked between his sister and the doorway, confused and frightened by emotions he could not name.

"What is wrong with Yemma?" Juba demanded. "Why is she crying like that?"

Silina knelt and pulled both children against her, one in each arm. "The man who led the resistance. The one called Aedemon. He is dead. Your mother knew him. From before. It is a great loss for everyone who hoped for freedom."

It was truth wrapped in omission. Enough to explain the grief without revealing its full dimensions. That revelation would come later, when they were stronger, when they could bear it.

❧✦❧

Three days after the messenger's arrival

Zahra's control shattered like pottery dropped on stone. The sobs seemed to come from her very marrow, raw, primal sounds of loss that weeks of tactical efficiency and survival instinct had suppressed.

The women held space for her grief. Taderfit brought water. Old Menna sat nearby, close enough to touch, but far enough away to give space. They did not stop her tears or offer empty comfort about things being all right. They sat with her, understanding that some pain demanded to be witnessed and heard, not fixed.

Hours passed. The sun moved across the interior of the tent. Dawn light became morning light, became midday heat. Women came and went, maintaining muted presence. The community held her without overwhelming her, without demanding she recover faster than grief allowed.

In another tent, Amara pressed her hands to her temples.

"Eudoxus, something is wrong with Yemma."

The old scholar looked at her. "Yes. Your mother's heart is breaking. She held it together as long as she could, but now she needs to let it shatter so she can put it back together anew."

"Can you fix it?"

"No. But the community can hold her while it heals. As they are doing now." He watched understanding dawn on Amara's face, the recognition that breaks required time, not magic, not her gift, only the passage of moments. "Your job right now is to keep being yourself. Keep learning your letters. Keep eating your meals. That helps her more than anything."

❧✦❧

Three weeks later

Amara waited until Juba was with her. She had learned patience in four years of sensing things she could not name, and she used that patience now. She waited until the evening meal was cleared. Silina had gone to help the village healer and Eudoxus dozed in his chair. She waited until Zahra sat alone by the small shrine she had built in the corner of their dwelling. A hunting knife, a lock of hair, and a strip of cloth from a traveling cloak lay upon it.

Amara took her brother's hand and led him to their mother.

She spoke with utter certainty. "Your name is Zahra."

The shock of hearing Amara call her by name for the first time tore her from her thoughts.

"Everyone here calls you Zahra. Uncle Yasir, his wife, all the women. They have called you Zahra since we arrived." Amara's voice held the terrible courage she spent three weeks building for this moment. "Our whole lives you told us your name was Leila.

You made us call you Leila. You made Grandfather call himself Numerius."

Juba looked between his sister and his mother, confusion, and the first edge of understanding crossing his face.

"And the man who died." Amara's voice remained steady. "The messenger said Aedemon. Everyone went quiet when they heard it. You fell apart. And his name was the name people whisper about in the stories. The rebel. The leader."

Zahra forced herself to meet her daughter's eyes. Four years of careful protection, undone by a brother's love and a daughter who never stopped listening.

"Yes," she said. "My name is Zahra. Your grandfather's name is Eudoxus. We took different names to remain hidden from the Romans."

Juba slowly absorbed this. Then his face changed.

"Grandfather's name is not Numerius."

"No. His name is Eudoxus."

"But he is still our grandfather."

The silence that followed told him everything.

"He is still our grandfather," Juba repeated, louder, willing volume could make it true.

Zahra reached for him. He pulled away.

"Eudoxus is not your grandfather by blood." Each word cost her. "He was your father's teacher and friend. He came to our family years before you were born and has loved you since the moment he held you. But he is not..."

"Then who is our grandfather?" Juba's voice cracked open. "Do we have one? Is anything real?"

Amara had not moved. She sat with her hands in her lap, absorbing the blow she had already half-expected. The way Eudoxus loved them had always unsettled her. His tenderness renewed itself each day and asked nothing in return. He expected to lose the right to it any second. Now she understood why.

"Your father's father was Mazippa," Zahra said. "A chief in the eastern mountains. He died before you were born, fighting the Romans. Your father's mother died when he was a boy. Eudoxus is the man who chose to stay with you every single day of your lives."

"But he lied," Juba whispered. "He let us call him Grandfather and he lied."

From the doorway, Eudoxus spoke. How long had he been standing there?

"Yes, I lied. And I would lie again to keep you safe. But I never lied about loving you. That was the only truth."

Juba stared at the old man with his shaky hands and kind eyes. Eudoxus told him stories every night, carved game pieces for him, taught him to read the stars. The same man. A different name. A different claim on his heart.

Juba's mouth opened, closed, opened again.

"I do not understand," he said.

"We lied to you." Each word scraped Zahra's throat. "From the time you could speak, we taught you names that were not real and a story about your father that was not true. We did it to keep you safe, but we lied."

Amara had gone very still. Her eyes fixed on Zahra with an intensity that made her mother's chest ache.

"What about our Baba?" Amara's voice came out flat, careful. "You said he died before we were born."

Zahra reached toward the shrine, her fingers brushing the hunting knife. "Your father did not die in tribal fighting. Your father was Aedemon."

The name plunged into the small room, sinking like a stone in deep water.

"Aedemon." Juba repeated the name, testing its weight. "Aedemon? The man in the stories? The brave man?" His voice cracked. "The one who just died?"

"Yes."

"The stories... the ones about the brave man... that was our Baba?"

"Yes."

Juba surged to his feet, his small body trembling. "Why did you not TELL us? You LIED! He was my BABA and you LIED!"

"We could not tell you. If you had known, if you had said something to the wrong person..."

"I would not have! I can keep secrets!"

"You were two years old, Juba. Then three. Then four. Children talk. Children repeat things. One slip, one moment of pride about your famous father, and the Romans would have found us." Zahra's voice held steady, though her heart was cracking. "We did not lie because we did not trust you. We lied because we loved you too much to risk losing you."

"That is NOT fair! It... It..."

He could not finish. He turned and fled through the doorway into the evening darkness.

Zahra moved to follow, but Eudoxus caught her arm. "Let him run. He needs to move through this. You have another child who needs you here."

Amara had not moved. Her face was unreadable, her hands in her lap.

"Amara?" Zahra knelt before her daughter. "Say something. Please."

"I knew." Amara's voice was just above a whisper. "I always knew something was hidden. When you said your name was Leila, it felt wrong. When Numer...eh, Eudoxus told stories, I could feel him stop himself." Her eyes lifted to meet Zahra's. "I told you. So many times I told you something was wrong. And you said I was making things up."

The accusation cut deeper than Juba's shouting.

"You were so young," Zahra said. "We did not know how to explain..."

"You could say yes, something is hidden, but I cannot tell you yet." Amara's voice was soft, but each word landed with force. "Instead you told me my feelings were wrong. You made me think I could not trust what I felt. That is very confusing. To know something is true and be told you are wrong."

Zahra had no answer. The "we did it for your safety" defense she had prepared, crumbled before the simple truth of what they had done to their daughter's ability to trust her own perceptions.

"I am sorry." The words felt wholly inadequate. "We thought we were protecting you."

"I know." Amara's voice held no warmth. "That makes it worse. You loved me and you still made me doubt myself. If you can do that, anyone can."

She rose and walked to the doorway, then paused without turning around.

"In the canyon, before the messenger came, I felt him go. I did not know it was my father because you never told me I had one worth feeling. I just knew someone important was gone. When I tried to tell you, you said it was a dream." Her small shoulders straightened. "It was not a dream. I was right about what I felt. And I will not let anyone make me doubt that again."

She walked out into the darkness, leaving Zahra alone with Eudoxus and four years of necessary lies.

❧✦❧

Outside, the sounds of Tizwit continued: voices calling children home, animals settling, the eternal murmur of the spring.

"They are not wrong," Eudoxus said at last. "What we did was necessary. But it was also damaging. Both things can be true."

Zahra stared at the shrine, at the knife that had belonged to a man her children would now learn to mourn. "How do I fix this?"

"You do not fix it. You carry it. You answer their questions honestly from now on, even when it hurts. You let them be angry if they need to be." Eudoxus's voice was weary. He had made his own necessary betrayals. "And you trust that love survives truth, even when truth arrives too late."

❧✦❧

Caesarea garrison, that same evening

Marcus Valerius Severus stood at the window of his quarters, watching night settle over the Mediterranean. In the deep desert, Aedemon's family had reached refuge. He did not know where. Better not to know. Better to maintain the distance that made protection possible without exposure.

Three weeks had passed since the execution. Three weeks since his friend's dying words: *Watch over my family.*

The gratitude had been worse than any curse.

Behind him lay the first report Nerva had requested: a comprehensive assessment of resistance networks in the southern territories. The prefect wanted everything documented. Locations, populations, tribal affiliations, patterns of movement.

Marcus picked up his stylus and began writing. Every word would be true, but subtly insufficient. He would build Nerva an archive of accurate intelligence that somehow never quite led anywhere.

The protection had just begun. And already, the cost felt unbearable.

He thought of Zahra, whom he had loved and never claimed. He thought of her children, born under falling stars, and of years stretching ahead like an endless desert crossing. Each day required another lie, another misdirection, and another small betrayal of the uniform he wore.

Watch over my family.

Marcus dipped his stylus again and continued writing. Truth and lies blended until even he could not always distinguish them.

Outside, the Mediterranean caught the last light of day, the same sea that had carried him to this posting, that separated him from a life he might have lived. Somewhere beyond the horizon, beyond the desert, Zahra was teaching her children to survive without him.

He would protect them from here. Report by careful report. Lie by necessary lie.

However long it took.

CHAPTER 25
What the Elders Know

"Grief carves channels. What fills them is the choice."
—Grandmother Menna of Tizwit

Winter, 44—45 CE—Tizwit—three months after arrival

Taderfit's hands moved with sure speed, crushing dried mint leaves into a clay bowl. The herb scent filled the small tent where Zahra lay on woven mats, her eyes tracking the smoke patterns from the brazier but seeing nothing.

"Drink," Taderfit commanded, holding the warm cup to Zahra's lips. "Your body needs strength even if your spirit does not care."

Zahra's throat worked mechanically, swallowing without tasting. She measured time in the moments when she could breathe without the crushing pressure on her chest.

Outside, Juba's voice rose in excited chatter. Yasir's second son had taken the boy under his wing, teaching him to track desert hares. The sound should have brought comfort. Instead, it emphasized Zahra's absence from her children's lives.

"He is happy," Zahra whispered. Her first voluntary words in two days.

"Children adapt," Taderfit replied, settling cross-legged beside the mat. "It is their survival instinct. But he asks for you every night. Amara sits by your tent entrance most afternoons."

Guilt pressed down alongside everything else. "I cannot..."

"You cannot yet," Taderfit corrected. "Different thing."

❧✦❧

That evening

Amara crept into the family's tent during the evening meal, when most adults were occupied. The girl's face showed shadows that no four-year-old should carry.

"Yelli." Zahra managed to reach out with a hand that shook. "Come."

Amara curled against her mother's side, body rigid with tension. "There is so much feeling," she whispered. "All the women feel sad when they think about you. Juba feels angry but does not know why. Silina feels worried. Grandmother Menna feels..." she struggled for words, "like old stones in the sun. Warm but heavy."

"I am sorry," Zahra murmured into her daughter's hair. "I am so sorry you have to feel all of this."

"I just want it quiet sometimes." Amara's voice cracked. "Just for a little while. Like Juba gets to have."

They lay together in silence, mother and daughter both drowning in their separate ways.

❧✦❧

Caesarea, that same week

Marcus stood before Nerva's desk, fighting to keep his face neutral as the prefect laid out his latest conclusions.

"The pattern is unmistakable." Nerva traced lines on his map with methodical precision. "The family fled Aghbalou heading south. They connected with desert guides. Your own reports confirm this. They passed through Talazega, where a disruption occurred. Roman casualties. Unexplained phenomena."

Tala Tazegzawt, Marcus thought. Even the name of a sacred spring sounded like a military objective in Nerva's mouth.

Nerva's finger stopped at a cluster of oases south of the Atlas. "Somewhere in this region. Perhaps sixty settlements, most barely documented."

"The terrain is difficult," Marcus offered. "Our patrols..."

"Your patrols have been remarkably unsuccessful." Nerva's voice carried no accusation, only observation. "Fifteen months of searching. Nothing conclusive. One might almost think the family had supernatural protection."

Marcus said nothing. Nerva continued, unrolling a fresh report.

"A trader named Quintus Servilius. Reliable merchant, contracts with three legions. He passed through a settlement called Tizwit two weeks ago and mentioned something interesting to a supply officer." Nerva read from the document. "A desert community, prosperous for its size. He noticed a Greek-speaking woman with twin children. Unusual. Most Greek women in that region are slaves or concubines. This one carried herself like a noblewoman. The children were perhaps four years old, well fed, well clothed."

Marcus felt his heart stutter. A trader. A casual observation. Everything he had built, threatened by a merchant's idle gossip.

"Tizwit," Nerva repeated. "Yasir's stronghold. Known resistance sympathies. I am dispatching a patrol. Twenty men, commanded by Centurion Decimus. They leave tomorrow."

"Sir, if I might suggest..."

"You might not." Nerva's eyes met his with uncomfortable directness. "Your suggestions have consistently led us away from productive investigation, Tribune. This time, I follow the evidence directly. Decimus has orders to search thoroughly and to bring any Greek-speaking women before me for questioning."

After the dismissal, Marcus stood in the corridor calculating. Tizwit lay ten days' hard ride from Caesarea, and not a maintained road for the last seven of them: two days south on Roman roads to the Atlas foothills, three days through the passes, then open steppe with water sources a day apart. The patrol would leave tomorrow. His network could not move faster than Roman cavalry, but it could move differently, lighter, quieter, through routes no patrol would think to watch.

He had spent fifteen months managing Nerva's attention, redirecting, misdirecting, and making the desert seem larger and less legible than it was. He had been protecting the family from a prefect's suspicion, from a garrison's momentum, from the ordinary machinery of Roman military intelligence. What he had not fully reckoned with, until this moment, was that the machinery had changed.

A year ago, Mauretania was a kingdom Rome administered through a client king. Now it was a province Rome owned. No Amazigh ruler remained to complicate the claim, no intermediary to slow the translation of Roman will into Roman action. Every settlement between the Atlas and the Sahara now fell within the formal reach of Roman law, Roman census, Roman courts. Tizwit sat in Gaetulia, technically beyond the new provincial boundary. But boundaries were lines Rome drew and then advanced. The limes followed water. It followed trade. It would follow this patrol south, and the next patrol, and the one after that, until the desert itself was documented and divided and made to answer to Caesarea.

He was not protecting the family from a search. He was protecting them from a province.

And a province, unlike a prefect's hunch or a centurion's ambition, did not tire. It did not retire or transfer or lose interest. It simply continued, patient and systematic, pressing its boundary southward one garrison post at a time. The ten days' ride that made Tizwit difficult to reach was the same ten days that made it expensive to investigate. And Rome was nothing if not a calculator of expense. A settlement that yielded nothing after a twenty-day round commitment of men and horses would lose its priority in Nerva's ledgers. Marcus had seen it happen before: communities that vanished from patrol reports not because Rome forgave them but because other targets offered better returns.

That was the protection distance offered. It was not safety. Tizwit would never be safe. It was a narrow margin of economic logic. As long as the settlement cost more to search than it appeared to be worth, Rome would find other uses for its cavalry.

The moment it became worth the trouble, the distance would mean nothing.

For the first time since Nerva had taken command, the security of Aedemon's family was failing — and Marcus understood at last how much larger the thing hunting them had become. All he could do was pray to gods he no longer believed in that the family had some other form of defense and get word south before Decimus's horses raised the first dust on the road out of Caesarea.

❧✦❧

That same night — Tizwit

Yasir and Menna sat by the spring after the settlement had gone quiet, the way they had sat by fires and springs and the open desert for forty years of council together. The water spoke its small language over stone. Neither of them looked at the other.

"Word came from the northern trade route this morning," Yasir said. "Three traders, all with the same story. It is confirmed."

Menna had heard the word already, through her own channels. She waited.

"Rome has divided the territory. Caesariensis in the east. Tingitana in the west. Provinces, with prefects and garrisons and census-takers. All of it official. All of it permanent." He picked up a stone and turned it in his fingers. "The kingdom is gone."

The spring moved over its bed. Somewhere a night bird called and was answered.

"Ptolemy died four years ago," Menna said. "The kingdom died with him. We have been calling it something else since then."

"Calling it something else gave us time to think it might change."

She accepted that. It was true. A king murdered was a crisis. A provincial edict was architecture. One you might survive; the other you lived inside whether you chose to or not.

"What does it mean for Tizwit?" she asked, though she knew.

Yasir set the stone down. "The limes will move. Not this year. Perhaps not for ten years. But the garrison at Caesarea now has a southern boundary to defend, and a southern boundary has a logic of its own. It advances along water. It advances along trade. It advances until there is nothing left to advance toward." He paused. "We sit at an oasis. We are on three trade routes. We are exactly what a frontier finds."

Menna thought about the woman sleeping in the guest tent, the children sleeping beside her. She thought about what those children carried in their blood, the name of the man who had led the last armed resistance against what had just become permanent. She thought about the word the traders had brought: *province*. A word that meant Rome no longer had to negotiate. A word that meant the buffer was gone.

"We knew this was coming," she said.

"Knowing and meeting it are different things." Yasir's voice held no defeat in it, only the weight of a man measuring what he was prepared to carry. "The coastal Imazighen have already lost it. The mountain settlements are losing it one tax roll at a time. What we have here... the spring, the council circle, the old law, the ceremonies... we have because we are far enough from the coast that Rome has not yet found it worth the trouble to take." He looked at the water. "That calculation is changing."

"Then we have time," Menna said. "Not forever. But time."

"If we are careful. If we are worth more trouble than we are worth taking." He glanced toward the guest tent. "And now we are sheltering the widow of Aedemon."

"We were always going to shelter her. She is kin."

"She is kin," he agreed. "And she is also the family of the man Rome killed to make this province possible. They will want to close that story. They are already looking."

The spring ran on. The night bird did not call again.

Menna pulled her robe tighter. She was old enough to have heard the Tacfarinas stories from people who had lived through them, seven years of war that proved Rome could be bled but could not be stopped. Old enough to remember when the coastal cities still had Amazigh faces in the forum alongside the Roman ones. Old enough to know that what she sat on tonight, this ground, this water, this right to speak Tamazight without lowering her voice, had been defended by every generation before her and would have to be defended by every generation after.

"The children will grow up here," she said. "Whatever comes."

"Yes."

"Then we had better make sure there is something left for them to grow into." She rose, her joints protesting the cold stone. "A Roman patrol will find nothing here worth reporting. That is the first thing. The second thing is what we build while they are not looking." She looked down at him. "We have always built in the time between their visits. That has not changed."

Yasir rose too. He was not a man who embraced easily, but he put his hand briefly on her shoulder, the old gesture of council, of shared weight.

"The elders meet at dawn," he said. "Before the scouts go out."

"I will be there."

She walked back toward her dwelling without a lamp, knowing the ground by the feeling of it under her feet, the way her grandmother had known it and her grandmother's grandmother before that, all the way back to when no one in this land had heard the word *Rome* and the spring had run unrecorded into the sand.

❧✦❧

Four days later—Tizwit

The scouts brought warning at dawn: Roman cavalry approaching from the northeast. Twenty riders, moving with purpose.

Yasir gathered the elders in quick council. "They are not raiders. Too organized, too direct. This is a search party."

"How long until they arrive?" Taderfit asked.

"Before midday."

Zahra heard the news from her tent, where she had spent most of the past three months. The words cut through her fog like cold water. Romans. Coming here. For her children.

She forced herself upright though her body protested. She had barely eaten, barely moved, but terror proved stronger than grief. She stumbled to the council gathering, arriving as Yasir outlined the community's options.

"We could hide them in the caves," one elder suggested. "The southern passages..."

"The Romans will search caves first," another countered. "They are not fools."

"What about the grain stores? The hidden cellars?"

"Twenty soldiers can search every cellar in the settlement within an hour."

Zahra listened, her mind engaging for the first time in months. Hide. Run. Conceal. All the usual tactics, and all of them likely to fail against a determined search.

Then Amara appeared at her side, small face intent. She tugged at her mother's robe and whispered the words that changed everything.

"Yemma. The soldiers. They are afraid of something. Something about women."

Zahra looked down at her daughter. "What do you mean?"

"I can feel them. Even from here. They are nervous, but not about fighting. About..." Amara struggled to articulate what she sensed. "About being unclean. About women's blood. The way Eudoxus described Roman fears. The way Menna told us about the old grandmothers."

Zahra's breath caught. Roman menstrual taboos. She remembered Eudoxus's lessons about Pliny's claims: that menstrual blood could sour wine, rust steel, kill crops. Roman soldiers were notoriously superstitious about such pollution.

She looked across the gathering and saw Taderfit watching her. The older woman's eyes held a question.

"The First Blood ceremony," Zahra said. "Yasir's niece Tamina. When is she expected to begin her seclusion?"

Taderfit's face shifted from confusion to understanding to fierce satisfaction. "She began three days ago. The ceremony continues through the week."

"How many women are secluded with her?"

"Seven. The aunts, the elder cousins. As tradition requires."

Zahra turned to Yasir. Her voice came stronger than it had in months. "Do not hide us. Welcome them. Offer them hospitality. A feast to honor their arrival during our most sacred women's ceremony."

Yasir frowned. "You want us to invite Romans to..."

"I want us to make them deeply uncomfortable. So uncomfortable they will want to leave quickly and search nothing." Zahra felt her strategic mind engage, shaking off the rust of grief. "Roman soldiers believe menstrual blood pollutes everything it touches. They will not eat food prepared by menstruating women. They will not enter spaces marked by the ceremony. They certainly will not search a grain cellar if they believe it has been blessed with First Blood."

Silence. Then Menna laughed, a dry, ancient sound.

"The old grandmothers used this defense against Roman tax collectors," Menna said. "Three generations ago. The collectors left without their silver rather than enter 'polluted' storehouses." Her eyes glittered with remembered triumph. "I wondered when someone would remember."

Yasir looked between the women. "You are suggesting we weaponize our sacred ceremony?"

"I am suggesting we let Roman superstition defeat Roman discipline." Zahra met his eyes. "The ceremony is real. The sacredness is genuine. We simply extend the hospitality. Generously. Everywhere they might want to search."

Taderfit rose. "I will gather the women. We have perhaps three hours."

✦

The Romans arrived at midday, their horses lathered from the desert crossing. Centurion Decimus dismounted with the bearing of a man expecting resistance.

Instead, he found welcome.

"Honored guests!" Yasir approached with arms spread wide. "Your arrival is blessed by the gods. You have come during our most sacred time, the First Blood ceremony of my niece Tamina. Please, you must join our celebration feast."

Decimus hesitated. This was not what he had expected. "We are here on imperial business. A search..."

"Of course, of course. But first, you must be refreshed. Your men look exhausted. Come, eat, drink. Then you may search whatever you wish."

The soldiers exchanged uncertain glances. Their orders were clear, but so was military protocol regarding hospitality. Refusing a feast could create the very hostility they had been warned to avoid.

"Very well," Decimus said. "A brief meal. Then we search."

"Excellent! This way, honored centurion."

Yasir led them toward the central gathering space. As they walked, women emerged from dwellings on either side. Each woman wore the ceremonial robes of the First Blood ritual. Each woman touched the doorway of her home as she passed, leaving reddish marks on the wooden frames.

One of the younger soldiers noticed first. He grabbed his companion's arm. "Jupiter's balls, do you see that?"

The other soldier followed his gaze. Reddish smears on every doorpost. Women in ritual seclusion robes. The unmistakable signs of what the legions called the monthly curse.

"Centurion..." he began.

Decimus had noticed too. His jaw tightened. "It is just barbarian custom. Hold your nerve."

But nerve was precisely what faltered.

✦

The feast was laid in the central square, beneath awnings that provided shade from the winter sun. The food looked magnificent: roasted goat, fresh bread, dates, olives, honeyed pastries.

The women who served it wore ceremonial robes stained at the hem with rust-colored marks.

Decimus lowered himself to the cushions provided, maintaining military bearing. Around him, his men settled with visible reluctance. Several chose positions that maximized their distance from the serving women.

"Please," Taderfit said, offering a platter of roasted meat. "The first portion is always given to honored guests. I prepared this myself, during the sacred days."

She smiled warmly. Her hands, presenting the platter, showed traces of reddish staining around the fingernails.

A soldier named Publius turned pale. He had lost a brother three years ago, two weeks after their camp cook had been discovered menstruating. Coincidence, the physicians said. Publius knew better.

"I am not hungry," he muttered.

"Eat," Decimus ordered. "You will insult our hosts."

Publius took a piece of meat. He did not put it in his mouth.

More women arrived, carrying wine, bread, additional dishes. Each one touched the soldiers' cups as she poured. Each one leaned close to place food on their plates. The air filled with feminine presence and with the soldiers' growing conviction that they were being systematically polluted.

"The wine is excellent," Yasir assured them. "My grandmother's recipe. She prepared a fresh batch just three days ago, during the ceremony's most sacred phase."

Another soldier, Marcus Flavius, felt his stomach lurch. He had drunk wine blessed by menstrual ceremony? His mother would have made him purify for a month.

"Excuse me," he said, and bolted for the edge of the square.

The sound of violent retching reached them moments later.

Decimus clenched his jaw. "The heat affects some men. Continue."

But the mood had shifted. More soldiers drifted away. One claimed sudden bowel urgency and sprinted toward the latrines. Another stopped eating and sat rigid, refusing to touch anything.

From her position near the water channel, Amara watched with wide eyes. She could feel the soldiers' discomfort like waves of heat: their genuine fear, their superstitious dread, their desperate desire to leave this polluted place.

She whispered to Zahra: "The big Roman is trying not to be scared. The young one with the scar, he is so scared it hurts me. And the sick one thinks something bad got inside him."

Zahra nodded slightly, trying not to smile. She approached Decimus with a fresh cup of wine.

"More wine, honored centurion? You have eaten so little. I worry you find our hospitality lacking."

"The hospitality is... generous." Decimus took the cup but did not drink. "We should begin our search."

"Of course! But first, let me show you our grain stores. They have been specially blessed for the ceremony." Zahra smiled with warm hospitality. "My daughter helped mark the threshold this morning. Such an honor for a child to participate in sacred rites."

She led him toward the primary storage building. The doorframe was smeared liberally with reddish-brown substance. Inside, more of the same marked the walls, the support posts, the edges of the grain bins.

"We believe the blessing protects against vermin," Zahra explained brightly. "The sacred blood drives away unclean things."

Decimus stepped through the doorway. His boots touched a damp spot on the threshold. He looked down.

His face went the color of old cheese.

"Futue," he breathed. "Cacas. Di te perdant." He stepped back quickly, nearly tripping over his own feet. "This entire place is..."

"Blessed?" Zahra offered helpfully. "Yes, very much so. Every corner. Shall I show you the sleeping quarters? The cellars? The children's area?"

"Mentula." Decimus wiped his boot on the sand, then wiped it again. "Podex perfectus."

Behind him, one of his men had pressed himself against the far wall, trying to avoid touching any surface. Another had begun a constant stream of muttered prayers to Jupiter, Mars, and several minor gods of purification.

"The hidden cellar beneath the floor," Zahra continued pleasantly, "is where the ceremony's most sacred items are stored. I could open it for you, but you would need to crawl through. The entrance is quite narrow, and the blessing marks are very fresh."

Decimus looked at the cellar entrance, a wooden hatch marked with what appeared to be bloody handprints.

"That will not be necessary." His voice had gone thin. "Stercus. This whole village is stercus."

He turned and strode back toward the feast area, where his men had mostly abandoned their meals. Several were actively ill. One had developed stress-induced diarrhea and was making desperate trips behind the buildings.

"We are leaving," Decimus announced. "Form up. Now."

"But centurion," Yasir protested with wounded hospitality, "you have not completed your search. We have nothing to hide..."

"I have seen enough." Decimus was already mounting his horse. "There is nothing here but a village of bleeding barbarians celebrating their savage rituals. We will search the other settlements first. Ones that are..." He shuddered visibly. "Clean."

The soldiers scrambled to follow, several still green-faced. As they rode away, one young legionary leaned over his saddle and vomited down his horse's flank.

"Podex!" he wailed. "Futue! I touched the wine cup with my bare hands!"

The community watched them go in silence. Only when the dust had settled did the women begin to laugh. Quietly at first, then louder, the sound of relief and triumph mixing with the knowledge that their bodies, despised and feared by Rome, had become their most powerful defense.

That evening

Menna found Zahra by the spring. The younger woman sat watching the water catch the last light, her face thoughtful in a way it had not been for months.

"You did well today," Menna said, settling beside her.

"Amara did well. She sensed their fear. I just used it."

"Used it strategically. As your husband would have." Menna paused. "That mind you have been letting rust. It still works."

"I could not afford to break. Not with them coming. The children needed me to think."

"Grief carves channels," Menna said. "Deep ones. But what fills them, that is the choice. You can fill them with more grief, let the carving grow deeper until it hollows you out. Or you can fill them with purpose. Let the depth become capacity."

"I do not know if I can find purpose again. Not without him."

"You found it today. When your children were threatened, you became the woman this community needs. Strategic. Clear-headed. Capable of turning Roman strength into Roman weakness." Menna's ancient eyes held hers. "That woman does not require a husband. She requires only the choice to exist."

Zahra thought about the past months, the gray fog, the paralysis, the certainty that she was nothing without Aedemon. And then today, when danger arrived, how quickly that certainty had burned away.

She looked toward the doorway where the twins played. "The children are watching. Juba sees me broken and thinks that is what grief does. Amara feels my hollowness and wonders if she will become hollow too."

"Yes."

"I cannot teach them to survive if I am not surviving. I cannot show them what strength looks like if I only show them collapse."

"Also yes."

Zahra turned to look back at the settlement. The dwellings where her children slept. The community that had held her through the worst months of her life. The place that might become home if she let it.

"The grief will not disappear," she said.

"Never. But it can become a room in your house rather than the whole house. A place you visit rather than a place you live."

Zahra nodded slowly. The crisis had burned through months of fog in a single day. She still ached. She still felt Aedemon's absence like a missing limb. But she had remembered what her mind could do when she let it work.

"Tomorrow," she said, "I want to help with the water distribution. I noticed inefficiencies. Ways to reduce waste."

Menna smiled, the first genuine smile Zahra had seen on her ancient face. "Good. The channels are filling."

Three days later

Eudoxus waited until the children slept.

He had been waiting for months. Through Zahra's collapse, through the gray weeks when she barely ate, through the slow return signaled by the First Blood deception and Menna's careful tending. He carried the knowledge the way he carried his trembling hand, always present, always visible to himself, hidden from everyone who did not need to see it.

Madi brought the details on his last visit. Spare, factual, delivered in the trader's voice he used for information too dangerous to soften. The execution. The field outside the command tent. Nerva ordering Marcus to strike the blow. Aedemon's last words. Marcus weeping beside the body while Nerva wrote notes.

Eudoxus absorbed it and said nothing to Zahra for three months. She was drowning. Adding this would have killed her.

Now the channels were filling. She was emerging. She sat in council beside Yasir. She planned water distribution. She had remembered her own mind.

She could bear it. Whether she should have to was a different question, and one Eudoxus had wrestled with through sleepless nights until the practice showed him the answer: a life built on concealment corrodes from inside. He had watched it happen to Marcus for years. He would not let it happen to Zahra.

He found her in the courtyard after the evening meal. She sat mending a child's tunic, her hands steady, her face holding the quiet focus she brought to tasks when her mind was elsewhere.

"I need to tell you something," he said. "About how Aedemon died."

Her hands stilled on the needle. She did not look up. "I know how he died. The Romans caught him. They executed him."

"You know the shape of it. Not the detail." He lowered himself to the ground beside her, his knees protesting. "The detail matters. You will want to know it eventually and hearing it from me is better than hearing it from a trader's rumor or a soldier's boast."

She set the tunic in her lap. Her eyes found his and he saw the hardness of steel beneath the grief. She was ready. She might not thank him for it.

"Tell me."

"Marcus was ordered to carry out the execution. Nerva chose him deliberately, because of their friendship. He wanted the symbolic weight of a friend's hand. Marcus could not refuse without losing the ability to protect you afterward."

Zahra's face did not change. Her hands rested on the mending, motionless.

"Aedemon spoke to him before the blade fell. In Tamazight, so the Romans would not understand." Eudoxus spoke carefully, giving her each piece and letting her set it down before offering the next. "He forgave Marcus for what was about to happen. He asked Marcus to watch over his family. And he told Marcus not to let the guilt consume him."

The courtyard was quiet. Somewhere a goat bleated. The cooking fire popped and settled.

"Marcus wept," Eudoxus said. "He dropped to his knees beside the body and wept in front of the entire garrison. Nerva documented his grief the way he documented everything, clinically, missing what it meant."

Zahra sat with this. The mending lay forgotten. Her breathing stayed even, the discipline of months spent learning to hold pain without letting it hold her.

"He has been protecting us," she said at last. "All this time. The man who killed my husband has been keeping my children alive."

"Yes."

"Because Aedemon asked him to."

"Because Aedemon asked. And because Marcus loved you. And because guilt and love and duty tangled together until he could not separate them, and the only way forward was to serve all three at once."

She closed her eyes. Eudoxus watched her face and saw the war behind it, every line of her jaw holding something back. Rage at Marcus. Gratitude toward Marcus. Rage at Aedemon for forgiving the man who held the sword. Gratitude toward Aedemon for buying protection with his last breath. All of it at once, contradictions no logic could resolve.

"Bitter and good," she said. "Same fruit."

Eudoxus recognized the words. Amara had said them at the olive harvest, the child's observation about contradiction that the women still quoted. The daughter's wisdom returning through the mother's mouth.

"Both," he agreed.

She opened her eyes. They were dry. The grief had carved its channels deep enough to hold this too, one more impossible truth added to the collection.

"Thank you for telling me," she said. "And thank you for waiting until I could hear it."

"I almost did not tell you at all. The practice says sit with what is, without grasping. I could not decide whether telling you was honesty or cruelty."

"Both," she said again. And then, so quietly he almost missed it: "But I would rather know. I would rather carry the real weight than the imagined one. The imagined one is always heavier."

She picked up the mending. Her hands found the needle. She did not ask him to leave, and he did not offer to go. They sat together in the courtyard while the stars emerged and the children breathed softly inside, and the silence between them held everything neither could say.

❧✦❧

That night

Amara woke screaming.

Zahra reached her before the sound died. The child lay rigid on her sleeping mat, fists pressed to her temples, her small body arched as if seized from inside. No fever burned her skin. No cough rattled her chest. Whatever gripped her daughter came from a different source.

"Tasastinu, what hurts? Where?"

"All of them!" Amara's voice climbed toward a pitch bringing Silina running from the next tent. "They are so happy and so scared and it will not stop!"

Zahra understood with sick certainty. The community had spent the day balanced on a blade's edge, in mortal danger, then sudden deliverance, then laughter so sharp it cut. Relief had swept through Tizwit like floodwater through a wadi, carrying every emotion the day had dammed up: the terror of the Roman approach, the fierce joy of deception, the giddy triumph of the women's laughter, the shaking aftermath when the horses disappeared over the ridge and everyone realized how close they had come.

Every family in the settlement felt all of this. And Amara, four years old with no walls and no training, absorbed every wave.

"Too loud," she gasped. "The laughing and the crying and the scared, all at the same time. I cannot make it stop."

Silina knelt beside her. "She is not sick. She is overwhelmed."

"Get Eudoxus."

Silina ran.

Juba appeared in the doorway before Eudoxus did. He wore the expression of a four-year-old pulled from sleep by something he could not name but refused to ignore.

"Amara broken?"

"No, aziz. Just struggling."

"I fix her." He crossed the tent with determined stride. He had decided on action.

"Juba, we do not know how..."

But he had already climbed onto Amara's sleeping mat, wrapped his arms around her rigid body, and pressed his forehead to hers.

Nothing happened. Then Amara's breathing changed, still ragged, but the desperate edge receding. Her fists unclenched. The terrible rigidity softened, not into peace but into something the pain could move through rather than be trapped inside.

"Is better," Juba said. "I help her carry."

Eudoxus arrived and knelt beside them. He watched the twins with an expression Zahra could not read, wonder and grief held together in a single look.

"He is anchoring her," Eudoxus said. "Giving her a presence to hold onto while the storm passes."

"How does he know to do that?"

"He does not know. He just does." Eudoxus shook his head. "The bond between them. I have never seen anything quite like it."

Amara's eyes fluttered closed. Her breathing steadied. With her brother's arms around her, the emotional flood pouring through every wall she did not yet know how to build found a channel, a direction, a way to pass through rather than pool and drown.

"Storm going away," she whispered. "Still there. But not crushing me."

Juba tightened his grip. "I stay. Keep holding."

They lay together on the sleeping mat, the boy anchoring the girl, her breathing slowing to match his. Zahra watched and felt her own chest ache with a helplessness no strategic mind could solve. Her daughter's gift had no Roman patrol to deceive, no superstition to exploit. This enemy lived inside the people Amara loved.

Eudoxus sat with them until the children slept. In the quiet, he spoke to Zahra and Silina, his voice low.

"She will need training. Real training. Not yet... she is too young for the discipline it requires. But soon." He looked at the sleeping twins, Juba's arm still draped across his sister's chest. "The gift will grow whether we guide it or not. Today it was relief and joy overwhelming her. Next time it could be grief, or rage, or a single person's pain so sharp it cuts through every wall she learns to build."

"What do we do until then?" Zahra asked.

Eudoxus gestured toward Juba. "For now, her brother is enough. He gives her something no teaching can replace: a presence more real than the flood. An anchor she trusts with her body before her mind can decide whether to trust." He paused. "When she is older, I will teach her the practice. But the practice is a discipline of the mind. What Juba gives her is older than mind. It is the bond itself."

Zahra looked at her children. Four years old. One carried a gift drowning her in other people's emotions. The other carried an instinct to hold his sister above the waterline.

She pulled the blanket over them both and sat watch until dawn.

CHAPTER 26

What the Children Carried

"A child learns what power is by watching the powerful use it against someone she loves."

—Amazigh teaching on witness

45 CE — Tizwit — The same three days

Madi had said: stay out of sight. Zahra had said: stay together. Eudoxus had said nothing, only pressed Juba's shoulder once as he turned to join the men gathering in the courtyard, his face arranged in the stillness he wore when frightened.

Juba filed all three instructions away and ignored them.

He positioned himself on the flat roof of Iberim's grain store, belly down, chin on his forearms, watching the Romans arrive through a gap in the parapet. Amara had followed him up the ladder without being asked, which was as it should be. She pressed beside him, close enough that he could feel her breathing.

Below, Centurion Decimus dismounted.

Juba studied him the way Malik had taught him to study opponents: size, how he holds his body, how his eyes move. Decimus was broad across the shoulders, with the deliberate, unhurried movements of a man accustomed to being obeyed. He scanned the settlement once, twice, cataloguing entrances and exits the way a merchant counts coin. Then he saw Yasir approaching with his arms spread wide, and his expression changed from suspicion toward irritation.

Juba had seen that expression before. On the soldiers who came to Aghbalou, years ago, before he was old enough to understand what it meant. He understood it now. It was the look of a man who had already decided the answer and found the question inconvenient.

"They are going to search everything," he murmured.

Beside him, Amara had gone still in a way that had nothing to do with hiding. Her eyes were open but unfocused, her breath shallow and rapid.

"Amara."

"So many of them." Her voice came low, almost dreaming. "They are angry underneath the tired. All of them. Like coals under ash."

"Stop reaching for it."

"I am not reaching. It just... " She pressed her palms flat against the rooftop. "It is very loud."

Juba understood, the way he understood most things about his sister: not from explanation but from years of watching her face when a crowd pressed close, or when the elders argued during council, or when Zahra wept quietly at night thinking no one could hear. Whatever Amara carried, it had no off switch. It received whether she reached for it or not.

He put his hand over hers to anchor her. She exhaled.

Below, Yasir was steering Decimus toward the feast.

❧✦☙

The first day passed in a sustained, terrible theatre.

From the rooftop, then from the shadow of the eastern wall, then from the narrow passage between the storage buildings where they could hear without being seen, Juba and Amara tracked the soldiers through the settlement. The women of

Tizwit moved through their roles with a precision that looked effortless and cost everything. Taderfit offered roasted goat to men who went grey at the sight of her stained fingers. Menna sat in the ceremony's center like a stone the current broke around, ancient and immovable. Zahra moved among the soldiers with a court woman's ease, every word and gesture calibrated to a purpose only she fully understood. Juba's chest tightened whenever he caught sight of her.

The soldiers hated it. Juba could tell without Amara's help. Their contempt was visible in the set of their jaws, the way they spoke to each other under their breath, the small cruelties of men who had power and were being made to feel afraid of it: kicking a water jar out of the path, speaking directly across women as though they were posts in the ground, demanding the same information twice in voices pitched for livestock.

Decimus ordered the elders to stand while he spoke to them.

The elders stood.

He ordered Yasir to kneel and demonstrate the traditional posture of a client before a Roman magistrate.

Yasir's face went rigid. He hesitated one breath longer than safety allowed.

He knelt.

Juba's hands had closed to fists without his awareness. He felt Amara's fingers close around his wrist, acknowledging what she felt in him.

"Do not," she said. Just that.

"I know."

But his jaw hurt from pressing his teeth together.

✦

The second day was worse.

Decimus had grown bored with the ceremony's theater and turned to the settlement's children with a predator's attention.

He was not wrong. Children had not yet learned the architecture of a face that said one thing while the body held another.

He gathered the older ones in the central square, a dozen boys and girls between eight and fourteen, drawn from their tasks and made to stand in a line. His questions began as inventory: names, family connections, how long they had lived here. Ordinary census questions, recorded by a soldier with a wax tablet and an expression of thorough indifference.

Juba stood at the line's far end. Amara was not in the group; she had been near the well when the gathering was called and Menna had smoothly redirected a soldier's attention long enough for Silina to draw Amara into the women's area. Juba had watched it happen with relief and a loneliness he did not examine.

Decimus moved down the line. The smaller children answered in frightened monosyllables. An older girl, perhaps twelve, replied in careful Latin and was told her accent was acceptable for a barbarian.

He reached Juba.

The centurion examined him the way he had scrutinized the settlement's entrances on the first day: cataloguing. Juba met his eyes because Malik taught him that looking away from a predator invited pursuit.

"You." Decimus's Latin came at him like gravel. "Name."

"Yerlan." Yasir's choice, three years ago. A desert name common enough to disappear into.

"Family?"

"My mother is Leila. My father died of fever when I was small."

Decimus's eyes moved over his face with professional disinterest. Then they sharpened. "Greek woman in this settlement. Scholar type. You know her?"

"Many women here speak Greek." Malik had coached him on this too, patiently, over two winters of lessons that had seemed theoretical until now. "The traders bring it from the coast."

"This one has children. Twins." Decimus watched his face the way Amara watched faces, looking for what the body said when the mouth was careful. "Boy and a girl. About your age."

"I do not know any twins."

A pause. "Get on your knees."

The words arrived before their meaning did. Juba's body understood first: a cold drop through the chest, a tightening in the throat.

"The ground is for animals," he said. The words came out before he could weigh them.

The soldier beside Decimus moved. Juba felt the pressure on his shoulders before he registered the man's hands, two hard points driving downward, and then the ground rose to meet him, gravel biting his palms, the sun striking the back of his neck with sudden intimacy.

"You speak when I ask a question," Decimus said from above him. His voice had not changed in pitch or pace. That steadiness was its own form of contempt: this cost him nothing. "You kneel when I tell you to kneel. That is how this works."

Juba pressed his palms flat and stared at the sand between them. A small brown beetle moved through his field of vision, unhurried, certain of its path.

He stayed where he was until Decimus moved on.

When he rose, he did not brush the gravel from his palms. He carried the marks back to the eastern wall, where Amara was waiting in the shadow with her arms wrapped around her own ribs and her face the color of ash.

She did not speak. She pressed her shoulder against his until he stopped shaking.

✦

The third day, Decimus turned his attention to the stored goods.

Zahra had prepared for this. Every cellar entrance bore marks that sent soldiers retreating three paces. Every storage room held a seclusion woman who smiled warmly and gestured at the freshly blessed walls. Decimus moved through the settlement with the grim focus of someone being managed who could not determine how, which made him harder and colder and more meticulous than the previous two days.

He did not gather the children again. Juba was almost sorry for it. He had spent the night rehearsing the encounter, replaying it, revising its ending in ways that always concluded badly, but at least in those revisions he was standing.

Amara found him by the eastern wall at midday.

"You are still angry," she said.

"I am not angry."

She looked at him.

"I am angry," he said.

They sat with their backs against the warm stone, listening to Decimus's search move through the settlement, the thump of grain jars moved, and the shuffle of soldiers who no longer bothered to speak to the inhabitants. The community's silence had thickened, deliberate now, no longer absence but intent.

"Yemma's plan is working," Amara said.

"I know."

"They will leave today. Menna says so."

"I know."

She was quiet for a moment. "You are angry that it had to work that way. That we had to... " She searched for the word.

"That we had to shape ourselves around what they were willing to believe."

Juba said nothing. She was right and being right about this cost her, the words came carefully, one at a time.

"Malik says the same anger killed our father." Amara paused before each word, choosing them. "He says Baba knew how to use the resistance's methods when they were needed. But there were moments when Baba could not make himself small enough, and those were the moments that made him vulnerable."

"Do not."

"I am not saying it is wrong to be angry."

"You are saying to be careful with it."

She turned to look at him, this sister who had pressed her shoulder against him yesterday without a word, whose face went pale whenever a soldier walked past too close. "Yes. Because you will need it. The anger. Later. When you know what to do with it."

Juba looked at the marks on his palms. Two days old now, faded to small pink crescents. He would carry them another week before they disappeared entirely.

"What do I do with it now?"

"Learn," Amara said. "Everything about how they think. Everything about what they fear. Everything about what makes them feel powerful and what makes them feel exposed." She glanced toward the sound of Decimus's search. "Today they are afraid of women's blood. That is useful. What else are they afraid of?"

He looked at her. His sister. Three days of soldiers' contempt absorbed like heat into stone, her eyes dark and exhausted each night, finding their light each morning. He had not thought, until this moment, what that cost her.

"Are you all right?" he asked.

She considered the question with the seriousness she gave to hard ones. "I will be. When they leave." She pulled her knees to her chest. "It is very loud when there are so many of them. So much contempt. It does not feel like them feeling it — it feels like me feeling it about myself."

He had no answer for that. He sat beside her and thought about what she had said: learn everything about what makes them feel exposed.

Below them, in the storage building nearest the well, a soldier shouted for Decimus. The centurion's measured footsteps crossed the courtyard. Voices rose and fell. Then: the sound of retreat. Boots on packed earth, moving toward the settlement gate. The jingle of harness.

Amara raised her head.

They listened together as the sounds diminished. The settlement held its breath. Then Taderfit's voice cut across the central square in Tamazight, short, sharp.

The women's laughter that answered it was the most beautiful sound Juba had heard in three days.

❧✦❧

That evening, Menna found them at the eastern wall as the sun dropped behind the ridge, turning the settlement's stone to amber. She settled beside them, unhurried as always.

"It is over," she said in Tamazight.

"We know," Juba replied.

She studied them both. Whatever she saw made her nod.

"What is your wound?" she asked Juba.

He showed her his palms without planning to. The crescents had faded further but still showed. She did not touch them.

"And yours?" she said to Amara.

Amara pressed two fingers to her sternum. Not her heart — deeper. The place where the day's accumulated weight had settled.

Menna nodded again. "The first time is always the worst. Not because what happens is worse. Sometimes what comes later is worse. But because the first time, you do not yet know you will survive it." She looked out toward the desert. "Now you know."

Juba followed her gaze. The Romans were somewhere out there, moving back toward Caesarea with their dignity and their contempt intact, their report already half-written in Decimus's head, the word barbarian shaped and ready. They had walked through Tizwit's homes and stored their disgust in every corner and left it there like something they owned.

"They will come back," he said.

"They will." No comfort in it. Only fact.

"Then we should know, every time they come, exactly what they fear and exactly what they want." Juba straightened his back against the wall. "Every detail. Every weakness. Every lie they tell themselves about us."

Menna regarded him with an expression he could not read. "Your father said the same thing once," she said, "when he was about your age." She rose. "Come. Your mother is asking for you both."

They followed her through the settlement's blue dusk, past the women still cleaning the feast area, past the granary whose marks were already being scrubbed from the doorframes, past the place where Yasir had knelt in the dust. The community that had held its shape for three days was slowly releasing it back into the ordinary.

Zahra stood at the entrance to their tent. She looked at them both, at the specific quietness each of them carried, and opened her arms.

They went to her.

She held them until the desert cooled around them and said nothing. She was, Amara understood later, practicing what she had not yet been taught to name: making herself large enough to hold what they had brought home.

CHAPTER 27

The Channels Filling

"The stone that splits the stream does not stop the water.
It teaches the water where to go."
—Amazigh saying on resilience
Two weeks later

The women worked the grinding stones in rhythm, the scrape of grain against rock providing percussion for their conversation. The grinding had its own music. The senior women set the rhythm, and the others followed, their stones striking in overlapping patterns that produced a complex percussion. The grain was durum wheat from the coastal trade, hard and golden, which the women crushed into semolina for the evening couscous. The work was communal and rhythmic, a dozen women arranged around the large flat stones, their hands moving in patterns learned from their mothers and grandmothers. Younger girls sat nearby, learning to roll the couscous grains between their palms with a patient circular motion that transformed raw semolina into the tiny spheres that would steam into the settlement's staple meal. The smell of crushed grain mixed with woodsmoke and the sharp green scent of fresh herbs drying on the courtyard wall.

Over this beat, Taderfit began a work song in the old style, her voice rough but carrying. The others joined on the response lines, their words weaving complaint and humor and gossip into verse as old as the stones beneath their hands. The songs changed with the seasons and the news: harvest songs in autumn, rain-calling songs in the dry months, and always the satirical verses that no man was meant to hear but every man eventually did.

Taderfit held court as she always did, her commentary delivered with the precision of a surgeon and the mercy of a sandstorm.

"Bassam says he wants a second wife."

Collective groans.

"He can barely keep the first one in grain. What is he going to feed a second? Promises?"

"His promises and a cup of water. At least the water is useful."

"A second wife." Grandmother Menna did not look up from her grinding. "The man cannot find his own tent after dark. Two wives would just mean two women waiting for him to stumble home."

"Menna, you are terrible."

"I am eighty-three. I have earned terrible."

Zahra listened from the edge of the group, her own grinding stone steady in her hands. The rhythm was different here, sharper than Aghbalou, shaped by desert hardship into directness. Mountain women circled their points. Desert women drove straight through.

"You laugh, eastern sister?" Taderfit had caught Zahra's expression.

Zahra had not realized she was smiling. "Every village has a Bassam."

"Ah. She knows men." Taderfit's approval carried real warmth. "Give her more grain. Anyone who understands men deserves extra rations."

The laughter folded Zahra into the circle, just slightly, just enough. Not acceptance. That would take months, possibly years. But acknowledgment. Recognition that the grieving widow from the mountains was more than grief.

❧✦❧

Caesarea, the garrison courtyard

The ceremony was brief, as military ceremonies in provincial postings tended to be. The garrison assembled in the courtyard at dawn. Nerva stood on the command platform with a bronze chest at his feet.

"Tribune Marcus Valerius Severus. Six years of continuous intelligence service in this province. Three smuggling networks identified and dismantled. The resolution of the Thala boundary dispute, which prevented armed conflict between two tribal confederations and preserved a trade route vital to imperial revenue. The interception of correspondence between Gaetulian insurgents and agents in Carthage, which enabled the arrest of seventeen conspirators before they could act."

Nerva opened the chest and removed a crown of silver oak leaves. The *phiala corona*, the decoration for distinguished service in provincial administration. Significant enough to be entered in the permanent military record. Significant enough that any future commander reviewing Marcus's file would see it.

"The governor has approved this commendation on my recommendation. Your intelligence work has saved Roman lives and preserved imperial stability in this province. The record will so reflect."

Marcus knelt. Nerva placed the crown on his head, then stepped back.

"Rise, Tribune."

Marcus rose to the sound of the garrison's formal salute, fists to chest, the crack of steel on leather echoing off the courtyard walls. He caught Madi's eye in the crowd of civilian observers. The trader's face showed nothing. His eyes showed everything.

After the assembly dispersed, Nerva invited Marcus to his office. Wine sat in two cups on the worktable: the good Falernian from Nerva's personal stores, the sweet vintage he had brought from Rome.

"You have earned this, Tribune. I do not give recommendations lightly." Nerva sipped his wine. "Your work on the Thala dispute alone would justify it. You understood that two tribes on the edge of war required mediation. You found the economic pressure point, the shared water rights, and built a resolution both sides could accept without losing dignity. That is statecraft, Tribune. Statecraft."

"The tribes did the work, Prefect. I provided the framework."

"You provided the framework because you understand these people in ways most Roman officers do not." Nerva's eyes held scholarly warmth and, beneath it, the first glimmer of the curiosity that would sharpen into suspicion over the coming years. "You speak their languages. You know their customs, their pressures, their internal politics. After six years, you may understand this province better than any Roman alive."

"Understanding a province is not the same as controlling it, Prefect."

"No. It is not." Nerva returned to his scrolls. "Which is what makes your intelligence record so fascinating. You understand everything. You control nothing. The disparity is remarkable." He looked up. "A conversation for another day. Today, we celebrate your achievement. Drink your wine, Tribune."

Marcus drank. The Falernian was excellent: sweet, complex, layered with age. He tasted the lead without knowing it. The sugar of lead that Roman vintners used to preserve their finest wines. The invisible poison that was, six years into Nerva's command, already clouding the sharpest analytical mind Marcus had ever encountered.

"Thank you, Prefect. The honor reflects your command as much as my service."

"It reflects the province," Nerva corrected. "Mauretania is a remarkable place. Difficult, stubborn, resistant to documentation, and therefore endlessly interesting." He smiled. "I sometimes think the tribes have been studying us as carefully as we have been studying them. Would that not be extraordinary? An entire population conducting counter-intelligence against Rome without our ever recognizing it?"

Marcus set down his cup. "An interesting hypothesis, Prefect."

"Is it not?"

❧✦❧

Caesarea, one week later

The report arrived with Decimus's own seal, and Marcus read it three times before trusting his eyes.

Tizwit settlement thoroughly searched. No Greek-speaking women matching description found. Community cooperative but engaged in primitive menstrual rituals that made extended investigation impractical. Recommend focusing search on other settlements in the region.

Primitive menstrual rituals.

Marcus set down the report and pressed both hands flat against the desk. His shoulders shook. For a moment he could not tell whether he was going to weep or laugh.

He laughed.

He laughed until his ribs ached and his eyes streamed and the sentry outside his door called in to ask if the tribune required assistance. He waved the man away and sat in the aftermath of it, gasping, wiping his face with the back of his hand.

Zahra. It had to be Zahra. Decimus was a fifteen-year veteran who had held a bridge against forty Numidian raiders, and a woman who had once served in Ptolemy's court had defeated him with menstrual blood and hospitality.

He wanted to tell someone. He wanted to find Madi and describe the look that must have been on Decimus's face when the serving women leaned close and the soldiers understood what was happening. He wanted to raise a cup to the woman who had taken every lesson about Roman superstition and turned it into a weapon no legionary's training could counter.

He poured wine. He drank it. He poured another.

You magnificent woman. You brilliant, terrifying, magnificent woman.

The thought was unprofessional, inappropriate, and entirely sincere. Aedemon had married well. If Marcus had ever doubted Zahra could survive without his protection, those doubts died tonight alongside Decimus's dignity.

He sat at his desk and wrote the follow-up report that would further hide Tizwit in the records, stating: "Settlement shows no signs of fugitives present." *Recommend deprioritizing in favor of more productive search areas.* Every word was accurate. The design of every utterance ensured no patrol unit returned home from the spot where a woman had just shown she needed neither Rome's protection nor his.

The wine was good tonight. Reaching into the bronze chest on his desk, he took out the *phiala corona* and placed it on his head akimbo. "In the service of justice," he muttered. The bottle done, he sought no refill. Some victories deserved to be remembered clearly.

☙✦❧

Nerva sat at his desk across from Marcus. "'Impractical.' An interesting word. Centurion Decimus is a fifteen-year veteran who once held a bridge against forty Numidian raiders. Yet he found a desert village 'impractical' to search."

"Desert communities have different customs..." Marcus began.

Their traditions remain unchanged. They had never used them for defense, till now. Nerva's eyes held Marcus's. "Someone taught them. Someone reminded them that Roman soldiers fear what Roman soldiers have always feared."

Marcus struggled to keep his face neutral. "You think the family is at Tizwit?"

"I think something interesting happened at Tizwit. I think a community that was cooperative became strategically coordinated. I think they are protecting someone worth protecting." He rose and moved to his map. "I will send another patrol. Larger. Better prepared."

"The community will repeat their defense..."

"Which is why the next patrol will include Syrian auxiliaries. Men from cultures where menstrual taboos are less pronounced." Nerva's smile held no warmth. "The family is there, Tribune. Or they were there. And I am going to find them."

After the dismissal, Marcus stood in the corridor calculating new variables. Nerva would not give up. The protection would not hold forever.

He needed to warn them. To help them prepare for what was coming.

The game had grown more dangerous.

But for now, the children slept safely in a desert village, protected by their community's wisdom, their mother's strategic mind, and their sister's impossible gift.

Marcus began drafting his next report, the one that would send Nerva's attention toward settlements that held nothing worth finding.

The work continued.

PART FIVE: CHILDREN OF THE DESERT

"A child does not choose the gifts she carries.
She only chooses, in time, what to build with them."
—From the private writings of Caspar of Ecbatana

CHAPTER 28
What They Expected to Find

"A man who documents everything believes he will eventually find the truth.
He does not consider that the truth may have been arranged for his benefit."
—Roman intelligence observation (attributed)
47 CE— Caesarea and Tizwit—Two years after Decimus's patrol

Caesarea Garrison, Early Morning

Three years under Prefect Nerva had taught Marcus Valerius Severus to identify the sounds of danger: a stylus scratching wax, the rustle of scrolls, or the silence meaning Nerva had found something to record.

"Tribune." Nerva's voice carried from the command center. "A moment, please."

Marcus entered to find the office transformed since those early days of neat organization. Scrolls filled every surface now, stacked in careful categories only Nerva understood. Three full cases lined the western wall, each subdivided by region, tribe, and tactical category. The result of three years of systematic observation covered the sand table at the room's center. Markers represented known resistance sympathizers, safe houses, and suspected smuggling routes.

"I have been reviewing the Tizwit incident." Nerva gestured to a scroll Marcus recognized: Centurion Decimus's humiliating report from two years prior. "'Primitive menstrual rituals that made extended investigation impractical.'" He read the words with distaste. "A fifteen-year veteran who once held a bridge against forty Numidian raiders, defeated by women's blood."

Marcus kept his face neutral. "Desert communities have customs that..."

"That they have never used defensively until now." Nerva's eyes held Marcus's. "Someone taught them. Someone reminded them Roman soldiers fear what Roman soldiers have always feared." He set the scroll aside. "I promised you Syrian auxiliaries for the next attempt. I have secured them at last."

Marcus's chest tightened. Two years of careful misdirection, two years of pointing toward more promising leads elsewhere, of making Tizwit seem too thoroughly searched to warrant return. All of it had only bought time.

"The Syrians arrive next week," Nerva continued. "Twenty men from the Cohors I Damascenorum. Men from cultures where menstrual taboos are, shall we say, less pronounced." His smile held no warmth. "Whatever defense that village employed last time will not work again."

"Tizwit is remote," Marcus offered. "The operational cost versus potential intelligence gain..."

"Is precisely why systematic documentation proves valuable. We do not guess at value; we calculate it." Nerva pulled another scroll. "Your reports mention Tizwit seventeen times over three years. Small settlement, limited strategic importance, yet consistently noted. Why?"

Because I was trying to make it invisible by mentioning it rarely enough to seem unimportant. Because I thought if I documented it truthfully, small, remote, peaceful, no one would waste resources investigating.

Marcus had been protecting them by making them boring. But Nerva did not dismiss boring. He documented it and looked for the pattern beneath.

"Standard thoroughness, Prefect. I note all settlements within patrol range."

"Of course." Nerva made a notation. "Centurion Cassius will command the patrol. Thirty-six men total, including the Syrian auxiliaries. They depart in six days." He looked up. "I want your assessment of optimal approach routes. And Tribune? This time, I want results."

After Marcus was dismissed, he stood in the corridor and calculated. Six days to get warning to Tizwit. Six days to hope his network could reach them in time. Six days to design approach routes that give the family every possible advantage without making his intervention obvious.

The menstrual defense had worked brilliantly, but it had also made Nerva determined. This time, he was sending men immune to that fear.

Marcus needed a different kind of warning.

✦

Tizwit, Six Days Later

The warning came through trader gossip three days before the patrol arrived, coded in market prices and weather observations, but Yasir knew how to read it. Romans approaching. Larger force. Syrian auxiliaries immune to women's blood.

He called the council at dawn.

"The old defense will not work," Zahra said, her voice carrying the authority she had earned over two years of strategic contributions. She no longer waited to be consulted; she sat beside Yasir as a recognized leader. "These soldiers will not flee from ceremonial blood. We need something else."

"What do they fear?" Taderfit asked. "All soldiers fear something."

At seven, Amara could filter the emotional noise. Three years of Eudoxus's morning lessons at the spring had taught her to let feelings pass like clouds rather than absorb them. She could focus on a single person now without drowning in the room.

"Amara, what did you sense from the last patrol? Beyond the blood fear?"

Amara closed her eyes, remembering. "The centurion was fighting something inside himself. He knew his fear was irrational, but he could not stop it. The young soldiers were easier to read. They believed their mothers' stories about pollution." She opened her eyes. "But underneath all of it, they were afraid of something else too. Something bigger."

"What?"

"Getting in trouble. Being blamed. Their commander's anger." Amara's brow furrowed. "They were more afraid of failing their mission than of the blood. The blood just gave them permission to fail."

Silence settled over the council. Then Grandmother Menna laughed, her dry, ancient sound.

"The child sees clearly. Roman soldiers fear punishment more than death. If we give them a reason to report success while finding nothing, they will take it."

"How do we give them success without giving them us?" Yasir asked.

Zahra's mind worked through possibilities. "We give them exactly what they are looking for. Just not us." The hours before the patrol's arrival were spent in quiet, precise transformation.

Zahra bound her hair under a working woman's cloth and put on the plainest robe in the settlement, borrowed from Taderfit, rough-woven, sun-bleached, faintly stained from oil work. She took up a grinding stone and positioned herself among the women at the communal grinding area, her hands moving in the slow desert rhythm Kahina had once told her city women never quite managed. She had practiced it for two years. Today it had to be true.

She separated the twins.

Juba went to the training ground with Malik's boys, one among a dozen. She stripped him of his good sandals and gave him cracked leather ones two sizes too large. Dirty hands, dirty face, his hair uncombed. The description Cassius carried said: *well-nourished, alert bearing, shows signs of physical training.* Juba was all three. But a boy in expensive sandals training with a warrior's focus was a different thing entirely from a boy shuffling through drills in ill-fitting shoes, tripping over his own feet because Malik had told him to. His bearing was the hardest thing to hide. She trusted him to manage it.

Amara was the greater risk. Her eyes gave her away to anyone who looked closely — that quality of attention, the sense that she was receiving information others could not access. Zahra was still considering where to place her when Menna appeared at the dwelling entrance, her ceremonial basket on her arm, ochre crescents freshly painted on her cheeks.

The old woman looked at Amara for a moment without speaking.

"She walks with me," Menna said.

It was not a question. Zahra did not treat it as one.

Menna dressed Amara in the plain wrap of a girl performing service to an elder, carrying the basket, staying close, and eyes down in the posture of attentive deference. The effect was immediate. Beside Menna, with her ochre marks and her bone-handled staff and the particular stillness of a woman who had been conducting sacred business longer than most people in the settlement had been alive, Amara disappeared. She became background. Furniture. The unremarkable attendant of someone no soldier with any sense would choose to engage.

"Keep your eyes on my feet," Menna told her. "Unless I tell you otherwise."

"What if I sense something important?"

"Then you will tell me. And I will decide what to do with it." Menna's hand rested briefly on the girl's head. "Today you are my shadow. Nothing more."

Amara nodded. Her eyes dropped to Menna's worn sandals and stayed there.

When the soldiers came, they would find what Yasir had promised: ordinary poverty, ordinary families, children with dirty faces. A shaman and her small attendant, moving through the settlement on their own inscrutable business, the kind of women soldiers in foreign territory learned, by instinct and hard experience, to walk around rather than through.

❧✦❧

The patrol arrived at midday, thirty-six men in disciplined formation, the Syrian auxiliaries distinguishable by their darker complexions and different armor. Centurion Cassius dismounted with bearing that said he knew about the previous failure and would not repeat it.

This time, there was no welcoming feast. No ceremonial robes. No reddish marks on doorposts.

Instead, Yasir approached with the formal dignity of a tribal elder receiving unwanted but expected guests.

“Centurion. We have been expecting you.”

Cassius's eyes narrowed. “You have been warned.”

"Word travels in the desert. You are searching for a Greek-speaking woman and her twin children, yes? Refugees from the resistance?" Yasir's voice carried weary resignation. "They were here. Two years ago. After your last patrol visited, we asked them to leave."

"You asked them to leave." Cassius's tone dripped skepticism.

"Your soldiers vomited on our hospitality and called us 'bleeding barbarians.'" Yasir's jaw tightened with genuine anger; that part required no acting. "We offer shelter to those in need, but we will not harbor those who bring Roman attention. The woman understood. She took her children south, toward the deep desert."

"South. How convenient."

"Search if you must. You will find poor families, old women, children with dirty faces. No Greek noblewoman. No twins matching your description." Yasir spread his hands. "We have nothing to hide because we have nothing worth hiding."

Cassius turned to his optio. "Systematic search. Every dwelling, every cellar, every storage space. The Syrians take the areas marked as 'sacred' or 'women's spaces.' I want thorough documentation."

For two hours, the soldiers searched. They found exactly what Yasir had promised: ordinary poverty, ordinary families, ordinary desert life. The women who served them water were neither young nor beautiful. The children who watched with frightened eyes were neither twins nor well-fed.

The Syrian auxiliaries searched the sacred spaces without flinching. They found grain stores, ceremonial items, and nothing suspicious.

In the dwelling where Zahra's family should have been, they found an elderly widow who spoke only Tamazight and her grandson, a boy of perhaps ten with a clubfoot.

"This one?" the optio asked, gesturing at the boy.

Cassius studied the child's face and compared it to the description he had memorized. Twin boy, approximately seven years old, well-nourished, alert bearing, shows signs of physical training. This boy was older, malnourished, with a disability preventing any physical training.

"No. Keep searching."

They searched until the afternoon heat became unbearable. They questioned elders who gave boring answers. They documented ordinary poverty. They found nothing.

At last, Cassius stood before Yasir in the central square, frustration evident in every line of his body.

"Where did they go? The woman and her children."

"South." Yasir pointed toward the endless dunes. "Toward Ghardaia, she said. Or perhaps Tuat. "She had contacts among the desert settlements, through the old scholar's network."

"Her husband?"

"The rebel Aedemon." Yasir let grief show in his voice, genuine grief channeled into useful performance. "He died three years ago. She came to us because her mother's people were desert Imazighen. We sheltered her until your patrol made that impossible."

Cassius absorbed this. The story fit the intelligence Nerva compiled. The family had been here; the previous patrol's humiliating failure confirmed that. But they had moved on, driven deeper into territory where Roman reach weakened with every mile.

"If we learn you are lying..."

"Then return and search again." Yasir's voice held no fear. "We are a poor settlement at the edge of the desert. We survive by not making enemies of anyone, Romans included. The woman brought trouble we could not afford. She is gone. That is the truth."

The centurion turned to his optio.

"Document everything. Settlement searched, no targets found, local leadership claims subjects departed south toward Ghardaia approximately two years prior. Recommend follow-up intelligence gathering in southern territories."

The patrol departed in a column of dust and discipline. This time, no one was vomiting, no one was cursing. They had conducted a professional search and found nothing.

Which was exactly what they had been meant to find.

❧✦❧

That evening, Menna found Zahra at the spring. The patrol had been gone three hours, long enough for the settlement to exhale, not long enough to stop listening for hooves on the road.

"Twice now," the old woman said, settling beside her with the careful movements of great age. "Twice they have come and left with nothing."

"Cassius believed Yasir." Zahra kept her eyes on the water. "Decimus was defeated by fear. This one was defeated by a story. A better soldier would not have been satisfied with either."

"A better soldier will come eventually."

"Yes."

Menna was quiet for a moment. The spring moved over its stones with the indifference of water that had been doing this since before Rome existed.

"The children held themselves well today."

Zahra thought of Amara in the council circle before dawn, her eyes closed, reading the room with the precision of someone twice her age. Juba beside her, rigid with the effort of staying still when everything in him wanted to move. "They did."

"The girl's gift is sharpening. She named what the soldiers feared before any of the elders had framed the question."

"I know." Pride and worry, the two things Zahra could never fully separate when she thought about her daughter.

"And the boy?"

Zahra said nothing for a moment. "He is learning that patience is not the same as surrender. It costs him more than it costs her."

Menna nodded, as though this confirmed something she had already suspected. "Good. The ones for whom it costs nothing never learn to spend it wisely."

She rose, unhurried, and walked back toward the settlement. Zahra remained at the spring a while longer, watching the last light leave the water.

They had held today. Tomorrow, they would hold again. She asked nothing more of the night than that the mathematics kept working in their favor.

☙✦❧

Caesarea, One Week Later

Marcus read Centurion Cassius's report with the careful attention Nerva would expect.

Settlement thoroughly searched with Syrian auxiliaries. No subjects matching description found. Local leadership claims family departed approximately two years prior, heading south toward Ghardaia or Tuat region. Recommend intelligence gathering in southern territories. Settlement appears compliant; further searches unlikely to yield results.

Nerva sat across from him, hands clasped at his desk.

"'Two years prior,'" the prefect repeated. "Meaning they left shortly after our first patrol. The one where Centurion Decimus found the search 'impractical.'"

"It appears the community asked them to leave after that incident."

"Or it appears the community learned to hide them better." Nerva's eyes held Marcus's. "The first patrol was humiliated by menstrual superstition. The second found nothing at all. Either the family moved, or the settlement improved their deception."

"The second patrol included Syrian auxiliaries specifically to counter..."

"I am aware of what I ordered, Tribune." Nerva rose and moved to his map. "Ghardaia. Tuat. The deep desert, where our intelligence networks are weakest and tribal loyalties are strongest." He traced the route with one finger. "If they went south, we may never find them. The desert swallows people who want to disappear."

Marcus said nothing. Hope stirred in his chest, dangerous hope he suppressed before it could show on his face.

"But." Nerva turned back to him. "I do not believe they left. The settlement's cooperation was too smooth. Too prepared. They knew we were coming and had their story ready."

"Traders carry news..."

"Traders carry news, yes. But they also carry news back." Nerva returned to his desk and began writing. "I am establishing a network of informants in the southern trade routes. Anyone reporting Greek-speaking women, twin children, or unusual refugees will be rewarded. The empire's reach extends further than our patrols."

The web was expanding. Marcus understood with cold clarity Nerva would never stop. Not while he held this posting, not while the documentation remained incomplete.

"How long will this take, Prefect?"

"However long my assignment lasts." Nerva looked up. "I intend to complete the task before Rome reassigns me. Proper administration demands it."

However long his assignment lasts.

Marcus calculated: Rome typically kept prefects in post for five to ten years. Nerva served three already. Perhaps two more years. Perhaps seven.

Could Marcus maintain this deception for seven more years? Could the family hide that long?

He had made a promise. He would try.

"I will coordinate with the southern patrol commanders," Marcus said. "Establish the informant network you have described."

"Excellent." Nerva's stylus resumed its scratching. "Dismissed."

Marcus walked through the garrison corridors and calculated new variables. The family was safe for now; the patrol had found nothing, and Nerva's southern search would waste resources chasing ghosts in the wrong direction. But the prefect's determination did not waver.

This was how it would be. Year after year of careful misdirection. Report after report of subtle insufficiency. The grinding work of constant protection until Nerva was gone or the family was found.

Three years down. However many more to go.

The stones in Marcus's chest felt heavier than ever. But Zahra and her children were building a life from the ruins of the one Rome had destroyed.

And Rome, for all its power, had not found them yet.

CHAPTER 29
What They Built

"Between the storms, the garden grows. This is not rest. This is the work."

—Amazigh farming wisdom

47–48 CE — Tizwit and Caesarea

The morning council convened in the shade of the central palms, where Zahra now sat beside Yasir rather than waiting to be consulted. The distinction mattered. Her voice carried weight through recognized authority, earned over two years of strategic contributions that kept the settlement fed and hidden.

"The northern herds are moving earlier than usual," one of the scouts reported. "Grazing pressure will be worse this year."

Zahra calculated. "We reduce herd size by selling breeding stock now, before the market floods with desperate sellers. Use those funds to purchase grain stores from the southern settlements. They have surplus this year."

"We have never sold from our herds," an elder protested. "It is considered..."

"A sign of weakness, yes. But we will look weaker still if we starve in autumn while holding animals we cannot feed." She kept her tone even, respectful. "The herds are assets. They should work for survival."

Yasir studied her face, then nodded. "We vote."

The vote was unanimous. By afternoon, Zahra had coordinated with three neighboring settlements to execute the trading sequence. By evening, grain stores had expanded by a third without visible crisis.

This was how leadership had transformed for her. The community no longer asked if Zahra had a suggestion. They brought problems to her and expected solutions.

❧✦❧

At the training grounds, Juba moved through his afternoon teaching with the focused intensity marking all his work. Eight years old and already showing the bearing that made others listen.

"Hassan, your stance is wider than it needs to be. You are using more energy." He demonstrated the corrected position. "Watch. Same power, less effort."

Hassan adjusted and threw. The stone flew truer.

"Yes. That is efficiency. Being strong is easy if you are born big. Being smart about strength is the real gift. Save your energy for what matters."

Yasir stood at the edge of the training ground and watched.

"He is ready," Malik said. "For real training."

Yasir nodded. "Soon."

At the spring, Amara sat with a young woman whose face carried the despair of prolonged childlessness. Amara was eight, but the woman's pain aged the girl beyond her years.

"You feel like you are broken," Amara said.

The woman flinched. "How do you..."

"I just know. But you are not broken. Your body needs help. Did you talk to Silina?"

"She suggested herbs, but..."

"But you are scared they will not work." Amara reached out and took the woman's hand. She did not reach into the woman's feelings, did not try to adjust them. She sat with them. "Come with me. Silina has helped three women this year. You could be the fourth."

The bridge-building had become second nature. Amara sensed what people needed and connected them with those who could help carry what they carried alone.

❧✦❧

In Caesarea that evening, Marcus's feet carried him to the harbor while his mind churned through Nerva's latest patterns. The light stopped him.

The water held colors he had forgotten existed. Gold and copper and a purple so deep it looked like wine. Fishing boats rocked at anchor, their crews calling to each other in a pidgin of Latin and Punic and something older. A woman sold fried fish from a brazier, the smell cutting through the salt air.

He bought some. Ate standing at the water's edge and watched the light die.

For perhaps a quarter hour, he thought of nothing. Not the family in the desert, not the archive in Nerva's office, not seven years of deception. Just the fish, and the light, and the sound of water against stone.

Then the sun was gone, and he was Tribune Marcus Valerius Severus again, and there was work to do.

No one could take back that quarter hour. It was the last quiet he would have for some time.

❧✦❧

One year later — 48 CE

Four years into Prefect Cornelius Nerva's command, the archive had consumed him.

Marcus stood in the command center doorway and watched Nerva move among his scrolls with the devotion other men reserved for temples. Scroll cases covered the eastern wall three high, subdivided by region, tribe, temporal period, and operational category. A system of colored wax seals indicated cross-referenced materials: red for confirmed intelligence, yellow for probable, blue for patterns requiring further investigation.

"Ah, Tribune." Nerva looked up from his work surface, where four reports lay open at once. A cup of wine sat at his elbow, half-empty at an hour when most officers had yet to break their fast. "I have been tracing tribal movements across the seasons. Quite fascinating."

Marcus entered with the careful neutrality he wore like a second skin. Four years of this game, and every day the pressure mounted.

"Simple confirmation." Nerva gestured to his maps. "Your reports over the past four years mention seventeen settlements with remarkable consistency. I have read them beside our operational records, and a troubling contradiction emerges. The settlements you describe most thoroughly are precisely those where we capture nothing. The places you mention only in passing yield our best results. The pattern is too consistent for accident."

Marcus kept his breathing steady.

"The settlements you mention most frequently produce the least results. Locations you note only occasionally yield significantly higher intelligence value." Nerva's tone carried no accusation, only the puzzlement of a mind whose premises were sound but whose conclusion was false. "It is as if someone understands our methods well enough to populate our records with meticulous but ultimately unproductive information."

Marcus felt the trap closing. Nerva never moved suddenly. He moved inexorably, the way water erodes stone.

"I report what I observe, Prefect. I cannot control operational outcomes."

"Of course not." More notation. "Though I begin to suspect our fundamental assumptions may be flawed. We treat documentation as if accuracy ensures efficacy. But what if accuracy itself can be a weapon? What if someone provides us with truths so precisely framed they lead us everywhere except where we need to go?"

It was the closest Nerva had come to direct accusation in four years.

"An interesting hypothesis, Prefect."

"Is it not?" Nerva returned to his scrolls. "I am documenting the anomaly. Whoever is doing this must understand our processes intimately."

Marcus stood very still.

"Will that be all, Prefect?"

"Nearly." Nerva set down his stylus and folded his hands. "I have recommended your transfer to the Syrian command. Effective before the summer solstice."

The room tilted. "Transfer, Prefect?"

"Rotation of personnel prevents complacency born of familiarity. An officer who serves too long in one province begins to see through local eyes rather than Roman ones. Four years is sufficient to establish that your methods, however thorough, have not produced the results this command requires." Nerva's voice held no malice. It held nothing at all. "Your replacement arrives within the month. A tribune from the Pannonian garrison. Fresh perspective, no local attachments."

"Prefect, my intelligence contacts have taken years to cultivate. A new officer would need..."

"Precisely the point." Nerva returned to his scrolls. "New officers build new networks. Perhaps those will prove more productive than yours. Dismissed."

Marcus descended the garrison steps into afternoon sunlight. Syria. A thousand miles from Mauretania, from the family, from every contact and misdirection he had spent four years building. His replacement would arrive with no understanding of which reports to bury, which patrol routes to redirect, which settlements to describe in misleading detail.

He had weeks. Perhaps less.

❧✦❧

Madi listened without interrupting. When Marcus finished, the part-time trader who had never, in twelve years, been caught being anything else, turned his cup in his hands.

"The fabricated lead did not work?"

"Two days ago. I presented evidence of a tribal coordination network east of the Atlas. Reliable sources, plausible targets, a genuine opportunity requiring my established contacts to pursue." Marcus stared at the wall. "He dismissed it in three sentences. Said my breakthroughs follow a pattern of their own: always promising, never productive, always timed to coincide with moments when my position is under review. The consistency itself, he said, was evidence."

"He is right."

"I know he is right. That is the problem."

Madi poured them both wine. "Bureaucratic delays. Lost documents. Questions about your replacement's qualifications."

"Nerva understands documents better than any man alive. Every tactic I could use he invented. He would see through it in a day, and the attempt itself would confirm his suspicions."

"A patron in Rome. A senator who owes you a favor."

"A letter to Rome takes three weeks. The response takes three more. By then I am already in Syria. And what would I write? That I wish to remain in a provincial backwater rather than accept a posting closer to the center of empire? What ambitious officer refuses Syria? The request itself would invite questions I cannot answer."

Madi set down his cup. "Then we build what we can. Traders whose routes pass near Tizwit. Contacts who can carry warnings without understanding what they carry. A network functioning without its center."

"It will not hold. Without someone inside the garrison who knows which patrols to redirect, which reports to shade, which settlements to describe in misleading ways..." He did not finish.

They sat in silence.

"How long?" Madi asked.

"Before the solstice. Weeks."

"And the family?"

Marcus closed his eyes. Aedemon's children were eight years old. Their developing abilities would make them more visible, more valuable, more dangerous. Zahra raised them with Silina's help, taught them about their father. She did not know he spent every waking hour ensuring their survival.

Watch over my family.

He had promised. And he was going to fail.

"I will do what I can from Syria. Letters through traders. Coin where it can buy silence. But without eyes inside the garrison..."

Madi reached across the table and gripped his arm. "We have survived before. We will adapt."

"You have survived because I could see the blows coming. From Syria, I will be blind."

He had weeks. And no plan that would survive them.

✦

In Tizwit that same week, the twins were playing their game again — the one Juba had invented over winter, where complex patterns of stones and shells represented movements across imaginary terrain. Amara watched from beside the well, her eyes tracking the other children's moves with an attention that went beyond strategy.

"You are getting better," Juba said, studying the board his sister had just altered. "That combination I did not see coming."

Amara smiled. "That is the point, is it not?"

Zahra paused with her water jugs, caught by her daughter's expression. Amara was not watching the board. She was watching the children's faces, reading each hesitation and bluff before a hand touched a stone. Eight years old and already playing a game beneath the game.

Four years since Aedemon's death and the flight that brought them here. And still they survived, against every probability.

Zahra knew nothing of Marcus's transfer orders, nothing of Nerva's archive, nothing of the protection weeks from collapse. She knew only that four years of relative safety felt fragile, beautiful while it lasted, certain to burn away when true heat arrived.

She studied her daughter's face and wondered which would prove more costly: the brother who could not hide his ambition, or the sister who could feel everyone's secrets and might someday be tempted to use them.

CHAPTER 30

The Mirror and the Archive

"Some truths arrive without language. These are the ones that destroy us."

—From the private writings of Caspar of Ecbatana

Early Spring 49 CE — Thubursicu Market — Four and a half years after Tizwit arrival

The market at Thubursicu sprawled across a dusty crossroads where three trade routes converged, and for six days each spring it drew merchants and buyers from settlements across a hundred miles of steppe and desert. Zahra brought the children because isolation bred its own dangers, and because Amara and Juba needed to learn how the wider world moved.

Silina walked beside them through the press of bodies, her healer's eye already cataloguing the herbs and dried roots on the traders' blankets. Juba moved ahead, pulled by the noise and color, eight years old and eager for anything different than Tizwit's familiar routines. Amara stayed close to her mother, her face tight with concentration.

"Too many people," she murmured in Tamazight.

"Breathe through it," Zahra said. "The way Eudoxus taught you. Let it pass over, not through."

Amara nodded and tried. The market's emotional noise pressed against her from every direction: a merchant's anxiety over unsold hides, a young mother's exhaustion, two boys arguing with the hot, brief fury of children, an old man's grief so worn it had become a kind of comfort. She could filter most of it now, could let the feelings pass without absorbing them. Eudoxus had spent three years teaching her that discipline, and on good days it held.

Today was not a good day.

The crowd was too dense, the emotions too layered. By midmorning she retreated to the edge of the market, where the stalls thinned and the dust gave way to scrub grass, and she sat on a low wall beside a well and breathed.

That was when she felt it.

✦

A tangle. Unlike anything she had encountered in Tizwit's small emotional vocabulary.

Most people's feelings had shapes she recognized. Grief was heavy and dark, joy bright and warm, fear sharp, anger hot. Even complicated feelings had patterns she could read: jealousy tasted like grief mixed with anger, loneliness felt like cold wrapped around a hollow center.

This was different. This was a mind organized like a scribe organized scrolls, every feeling catalogued and shelved and sorted, but the shelving had gone wrong. The categories were collapsing into each other. Rage and curiosity occupied the same space. Loneliness and contempt had merged into a single corrosive current. And underneath it all, a desperate, howling emptiness the man had spent years trying to fill — as though writing the world down could substitute for living in it.

Amara stood. She did not choose to move toward the feeling. Her feet carried her toward anyone in pain, the instinct older than caution, the pull Zahra and Eudoxus had tried to temper with discipline.

She walked past a spice stall, around a cluster of tethered donkeys, through a gap between canvas awnings, and stopped.

He sat on a camp stool beneath a military shade, a gaunt Roman with a wax tablet on his knee and a cup of wine in his hand, though it was barely past the second hour. Two guards stood behind him, bored and sweating. Scrolls surrounded him in careful piles. He was writing, his stylus moving across the wax with rapid, compulsive strokes.

Amara had never seen a Roman official this close. She had seen soldiers — figures on horseback, or the ones who had searched Tizwit before she was old enough to remember clearly. But this man was not a soldier. He was a different creature, one who filed and sorted and counted, and the counting was eating him alive.

She should have turned away. Everything Eudoxus taught her, everything Zahra warned her, said to turn away from a Roman or any stranger whose pain was not hers to carry.

But she was eight. And he was hurting.

"You are very sick," she said in Tamazight.

❧✦❧

Prefect Cornelius Nerva looked up from his census notations.

He had come to Thubursicu because the archive demanded it. Four and a half years of documentation had revealed patterns in the regional trade gatherings not fully understood from Caesarea. He needed to see the territory, to verify his maps against reality, to observe the people his scrolls described.

His staff had protested. The journey was unnecessary; the reports could be gathered through subordinates. But Nerva no longer trusted subordinates. Tribune Severus's intelligence was too precise, too consistently unproductive. The contradiction haunted him. He needed to see for himself.

Then the child spoke to him.

She stood three paces away, a thin Amazigh girl in simple robes, her dark hair uncovered, her feet bare and dusty. Eight years old, perhaps nine. Unremarkable in every visible way.

But he had understood her.

Not the words. He had never learned Tamazight. He could not have repeated a single syllable of what she said. Yet the meaning had arrived whole and complete inside his mind, bypassing language entirely, the way a headache communicates pain without needing to explain it.

You are very sick.

Nerva set down his stylus. His rational mind offered explanations: he knew some basic phrases from years in the province; the child's meaning was clear from context; the heat was affecting his concentration. Each explanation was reasonable. None was true. He had understood her the way he understood his own thoughts — from the inside.

"What did you say?" he asked in Latin. His voice sounded strange to him, thinner than usual.

The child tilted her head. She spoke again, and again he understood without understanding. The meaning pressed into him like a thumb into clay.

The numbers in your head. You think they protect you. But they are a cage, and you built it yourself, and now you cannot find the door.

Nerva's hand tightened on his cup. Wine sloshed over his fingers. He stared at the girl, at her calm, serious face, at eyes holding nothing he could categorize. She was not threatening him. She was not performing. She was describing what she saw, the way a child describes a cloud or a stone — with simple accuracy and no awareness the observation could wound.

"Who are you?" The Latin came out rough, barely controlled.

She did not answer his question. She answered in a way that had nothing to do with it.

You have never loved anyone. You have written about love. You have documented it in others. You have catalogued its effects and recorded its symptoms. But you have never felt it, and you do not understand why, and that is the emptiness you are trying to fill with all your scrolls.

Nerva stood. The camp stool scraped back against the packed earth. His guards straightened, hands moving toward their swords, reacting to the sudden tension in their prefect's body.

The child did not flinch. She looked up at him with the same steady, clear attention, and then her brow furrowed, and she reached toward him with one small hand.

He stepped back.

"Do not touch me." The command cracked through the market noise. Heads turned. Merchants paused.

The girl's hand dropped. Confusion entered her eyes. She had not expected fear. She had come because he was hurting, and people who hurt needed comfort, and she did not yet understand that some wounds are guarded by walls the wounded would kill to protect.

Then a woman's voice cut through the crowd, sharp with alarm.

"Amara!"

Silina appeared from between the stalls, her face white. She seized the girl's arm and pulled her backward, away from the Roman, away from the guards, away from the disaster almost taking shape.

"Forgive her, sir," Silina said in accented Latin. "She is a simple child. She bothers strangers. It means nothing."

Nerva barely heard her. He was staring at the girl, at those unsettling green eyes that had looked into him and found what no one, in forty-eight years of life, had ever found. Or ever named.

"The child," he said. "The child spoke..."

"Tamazight, sir. Only Tamazight. She knows no Latin." Silina was already moving, pulling Amara into the crowd, her voice carrying the practiced deference of one who knew how to disappear in plain sight. "A simple village girl. She meant no disrespect."

They were gone before his guards could react. Swallowed by the market's press of bodies and noise and ordinary commerce.

Nerva stood in the dust, his cup forgotten in his hand, his census notations forgotten on the stool, the archive forgotten for the first time in four and a half years.

A child had looked at him and seen everything.

And he could not write it down.

❧✦❧

That evening — Zahra's camp, outside Thubursicu

Zahra's hands shook as she gripped her daughter's shoulders. "Tell me exactly what happened."

"I talked to a man," Amara said. Her voice was small, bewildered. She could sense her mother's fear and Silina's lingering panic, and both pressed against her like walls closing in. "He was hurting. I just told him what I saw."

"What did you see?"

"He is sick. His mind is organized, but wrong. Like a room where everything is shelved in order but the shelves are falling. And he is so lonely." Amara's eyes glistened. "Yemma, I have never felt anyone that lonely. He does not even know he is lonely, because he has never been anything else."

Zahra released her daughter's shoulders and pressed her palms against her own face. She breathed through the fear steadily and with discipline.

"Amara. That man was a Roman prefect. Do you understand? He is the man who sends soldiers to search for us. He is the reason we hide."

Amara's face drained of color. "I did not know."

"I know you did not know. That is what frightens me." Zahra knelt and took her daughter's hands. "Your gift shows you people's pain. But not everyone's pain is safe to see. Some people will destroy you for seeing what they hide. Do you understand?"

Amara nodded, but her lip trembled. "He was hurting, Yemma. I was just trying to help."

"I know, tasastinu. I know."

Silina spoke from the tent's entrance, her arms crossed, her voice still tight with the residue of fear. "He heard her. He understood her. She spoke Tamazight, and he heard Latin. I saw his face. He understood every word."

Zahra looked up. "That is not possible."

"I know what I saw."

The three of them sat in silence while the market's noise faded with the evening light. Juba returned from his wanderings, full of stories about a sword-maker and a man who trained hawks, and did not understand why his mother held him so tightly or why Amara would not meet his eyes.

They left before dawn, riding south toward Tizwit without stopping at the market's second day.

☙✦❧

Caesarea Garrison — ten days later

The dispatch arrived at Nerva's desk in his own handwriting, and his staff read it before forwarding it to Rome.

Incident at Thubursicu market. A Berber child, female, approximately eight to nine years, addressed this officer in what appeared to be fluent Latin, despite eyewitness claims that she spoke only in the native tongue. The child demonstrated detailed knowledge of this officer's inner character and personal circumstances inconsistent with any known method of tribal espionage. The encounter suggests the existence of capabilities among the native population that fall outside established categories of resistance or intelligence gathering.

I have compared this incident with prior reports of unusual phenomena in the southern territories (see Archive Section VII, subsection 14, "Unexplained Occurrences"). A pattern emerges that no Roman science can accommodate. I request authorization to expand documentation protocols to include what I can only describe as abilities among the Berber communities that defy natural explanation.

This is not superstition. The child's observations were accurate in ways that preclude coincidence. The cause remains unknown, but the effect is witnessed and recorded. I will return to the southern markets to verify.

His deputy, Centurion Gaius Licinius, read the dispatch twice. Then a third time.

He had served under Nerva for four years. He had watched the prefect's devotion to documentation deepen into compulsion, noted the wine at breakfast, the tremor in the writing hand, the way the archive consumed every waking hour. He had said nothing, because the work remained brilliant and the results, while sparse, were meticulously organized.

But this dispatch described a Roman prefect claiming that an Amazigh child had read his mind in a language she did not speak.

Licinius made a copy of the dispatch for the garrison's records. He forwarded the original to Rome with a separate, private letter to the provincial administration.

Prefect Nerva's health and judgment have shown marked deterioration over recent months. His dedication to documentation remains evident, but his recent field observations suggest a departure from the sober practice that has characterized his service. I recommend review of his continued fitness for command.

The machinery of imperial bureaucracy turned.

✦

Caesarea garrison — four days after Licinius's letter

Marcus heard about the dispatch before the ink dried on the copy.

Licinius was not a gossip, but garrison clerks were, and a prefect's official report claiming an Amazigh child had read his thoughts in a language she did not speak made for better tavern conversation than supply inventories. By evening, three officers had mentioned it to Marcus in the tone reserved for superiors who had lost their grip. By the following morning, the garrison's senior centurion asked Marcus — in the courtyard, where no one recorded conversations — whether the prefect had been drinking more than usual.

Marcus said he had not noticed. He noticed everything.

He waited two days. The transfer orders to Syria sat on his desk, signed and sealed, effective before the solstice. He had spent three weeks trying to find a way around them and found nothing. Nerva had followed procedure precisely. The transfer was clean, justified, unassailable.

Until now.

On the third day, Marcus requested a meeting with the garrison's administrative officer, a meticulous freedman named Felix who handled personnel records with the devotion other men brought to religion. Marcus brought wine. Felix appreciated wine the way he appreciated well-organized documents — as evidence of civilized intention.

"A procedural question," Marcus said. "When a commanding officer issues transfer orders during a period in which his fitness for command is under formal review, what is the status of those orders?"

Felix set down his cup. "Under review by whom?"

"The provincial administration. Say a deputy has raised concerns about the commander's judgment. The concerns are documented. A letter has been forwarded to Rome."

"Then all administrative actions taken during the review period are subject to suspension pending the review's outcome." Felix spoke with the certainty of a man who had memorized every regulation governing military personnel. "The logic is sound. If the commander's judgment is in question, his decisions during the questioned period cannot stand without independent verification."

"Including transfer orders."

"Including transfer orders, reassignments, promotions, and disciplinary actions. Everything issued after the date of the deputy's formal complaint." Felix reached for his wine. "This is not a hypothetical question."

"It is a procedural one."

"Of course." Felix drank. "The procedure, in this case, would require the transferred officer to file a request for review with the provincial administration, citing the pending fitness inquiry as grounds for suspension. The request would need to reference the specific dispatch that triggered the inquiry."

"And if the dispatch in question described unusual claims about native capabilities?"

Felix's expression did not change. He had served in provincial administration for twenty years. Nothing surprised him, least of all officers maneuvering against each other through paperwork. "Then the reviewing authority would have reason to question whether the transfer was motivated by sound administrative judgment or by the commander's deteriorating capacity for rational assessment."

Marcus nodded. He did not need to say more. Felix understood the shape of what was happening the way a scribe understood the shape of a well-constructed sentence: each element in its proper place, the conclusion inevitable once the premises were established.

"I will need copies of the relevant regulations," Marcus said.

"I will have them on your desk by morning."

Marcus left the freedman's office and walked through the garrison courtyard. The evening air carried salt from the harbor and smoke from the camp kitchens. Ordinary smells. The smells of a city where a Roman officer had just learned how to save his posting without forging a single document.

He would not fight the transfer. He would not appeal to Nerva's superiors or claim the orders were unjust. He would simply ensure the right people noticed that the man who signed his transfer orders was the same man who had filed an official report claiming Amazigh children possessed supernatural abilities. The transfer and the dispatch, read side by side, told a story: a prefect losing his grip, reassigning the one officer whose competence made his own inadequacy visible.

Rome would delay the transfer pending review. The review would take months. Nerva would be recalled before it concluded. And Marcus would remain in Caesarea, where the protection could continue.

He did not celebrate or feel relief. He felt the exhaustion of eight years won through paperwork, each administrative victory another layer of deception on a structure already straining beneath its own weight.

But the family was still alive. The protection held. And tonight, for the first time in three weeks, Marcus could look at the Syria dispatch on his desk without feeling the floor give way beneath him.

✦

Tizwit — three weeks later

Eudoxus listened in silence while Zahra described the encounter. Silina added details. Amara sat in the corner of the old scholar's dwelling, her knees drawn to her chest, still carrying the shame of having spoken a truth she did not fully understand.

When they finished, Eudoxus said nothing. He sat with his back against the wall, his damaged hand resting in his lap, his eyes fixed on a point beyond the room's mud-brick walls.

At last he spoke, and his voice carried a weight that made Zahra look up sharply.

"Describe his face again. When she spoke to him."

"Shock," Silina said. "Then fear. Then something I have never seen on a Roman's face. He looked exposed. As if she had pulled his skin off and he was standing in the wind."

Eudoxus closed his eyes.

Bethlehem.

The memory rose unbidden: a borrowed house, an infant's dark eyes, the moment when the child's presence had reached past every defense Caspar had spent thirty years building and laid bare the grief he had hidden even from himself. No words.

No language. Just a truth so direct it bypassed every mediation the mind could construct.

The infant had not spoken. He had simply existed, and that existence created a gravity that pulled hidden things to the surface.

Amara had spoken. She had used words, Tamazight words that a Roman could not understand. But what reached Nerva was not language. It was the same unmediated truth. The same mirror held up to a face that had never seen itself clearly.

The same gift.

"Eudoxus?" Zahra's voice pulled him back. "What is it?"

He opened his eyes and looked at Amara, who watched him from the corner with her mother's steady gaze, her father's stubborn jaw, and a quality that had last appeared in the world in a stable in Judea nearly fifty years ago.

"The child did nothing wrong," he said. "But we must talk about what happened. All of us. Because what she did to that Roman, she did without choosing, without understanding, without control. And the next time, the consequences could be far worse."

"What did she do?" Zahra asked.

Eudoxus chose his words with the care of a man handling fire. "She showed him himself — not the documentation, not the archive, not the rational scholar. She showed him what lives underneath all of that. And he was not prepared."

"That is just her gift," Zahra said. "She reads people. She has always read people."

"Reading is one thing. What she did was not reading." Eudoxus looked at Amara. "Child, when you spoke to the man, did you choose what to say? Or did the words come on their own?"

Amara's voice was very small. "They came on their own. I just opened my mouth and the truth came out."

"And the truth was not yours."

"No. It was his. I could see it inside him, and it was hurting him, and I thought if he could hear it, maybe it would stop hurting."

Eudoxus nodded. "That is exactly what I feared." He turned to Zahra. "She is not merely sensing emotions. She is reflecting them. Amplifying them. Transmitting them back to the person who carries them, with a clarity that bypasses every defense the mind constructs. Language does not matter. Culture does not matter. Walls do not matter. She sees the truth and she speaks it, and the person hears it in whatever form will reach them most deeply."

"Is that dangerous?"

"To someone like that Roman?" Eudoxus's voice went quiet. "It could destroy him. It may already have."

Silence filled the dwelling. Outside, Juba's voice carried from the training ground, shouting encouragement to the younger boys. The ordinary sounds of an ordinary afternoon in a settlement that harboured extraordinary things.

"We begin tomorrow," Eudoxus said. "Real training. Not philosophy, not gentle questions by the spring. She must learn when to see and when to close her eyes. When to speak and when to hold her tongue. The gift will grow whether we guide it or not. If we do not teach her discipline, the next Roman she encounters may not be a prefect whose reports no one believes. The next one may be dangerous."

Amara spoke from the corner, her voice steadier now. "I did not mean to hurt him."

Eudoxus looked at her with an expression Zahra had never seen on his face: tenderness and terror, held together.

"I know, child. That is precisely the problem. The gift does not care about your intentions. It acts through you. And until you learn to guide it, you are a danger to everyone you meet, including yourself."

He paused, and when he spoke again the words came from a place deeper than pedagogy.

"I once knew an infant who did the same thing. He did not choose it. He simply existed, and his existence showed three men the truths they had spent their lives avoiding. One of those men was destroyed by it. Another was corrupted. The third..." He raised his damaged hand and studied it in the afternoon light. "The third spent fifty years trying to understand what it meant. And he is still trying."

Amara watched him with wide, frightened eyes. But beneath the fear, Zahra saw recognition. Her daughter understood, in the way that children understand things they cannot yet articulate, that what had happened in the market was not a mistake. It was the beginning of a truth that would define the rest of her life.

Five months later — Late Summer 49 CE

The office smelled of wine and wax and sourness beneath both.

Nerva stood at the far wall, his back to the door, pressing a new notation into an already crowded surface. His hand trembled as he set the wax seal into place. Blue wax. Patterns requiring further investigation.

"Tribune." He did not turn around. "Close the door."

Marcus closed it. The room sealed around them.

"I have been thinking about Thubursicu," Nerva said.

"The child knew things." Nerva turned at last, and Marcus kept his face still against the shock. The man had aged a decade in five months. His pallor had deepened to a shade closer to ash than skin, and the tremor in his left hand was now constant. His eyes burned with an intensity that had crossed the line from dedication to fever. "Not intelligence. Not information gathered through networks or informants. She knew the architecture of my mind. The categories. The emptiness between the categories."

"Prefect, the field reports suggest the child spoke only Tamazight. The heat at Thubursicu..."

"Do not." Nerva's voice cracked like a whip. "Do not explain it away. I have spent five months trying to explain it away. I have read Pliny's accounts of Numidian seers, Herodotus on the Oracle at Siwa, Strabo's notes on desert prophets. I have compared every documented instance of tribal mysticism and shamanic practice in the provincial archive. None of it accounts for what happened."

He moved to the sand table and swept a stack of tablets aside. Beneath them lay a map of the southern territories, covered in annotations so dense that the original geography had disappeared.

"But that is not why I summoned you." His voice shifted, and for a moment the old Nerva surfaced: precise, relentless, terrifyingly competent. "The child is a separate matter. What concerns me now is what the archive has revealed while I was occupied with questions I cannot answer."

He pulled a scroll from the case nearest the window. Five years of patrol reports.

"You already know what I have found, Tribune. The contradiction between your reports and our results. I presented it to you last year, and you offered me theories about desert communities and Roman assumptions." He set the scroll down without opening it. "I accepted those theories. I should not have."

Marcus kept his breathing steady.

"The contradiction is not a flaw in our approach. It is evidence of design. Someone has been arranging our records the way a rhetorician arranges an argument. The premises are sound. The evidence is accurate. And the conclusion is false. Deliberately, systematically, elegantly false." He reached for the nearest cup, drank, set it down with a trembling hand. "I want you to identify the settlement that serves as the coordination point for this deception. I have narrowed the possibilities to three." He pointed to the map. "Here. Here. And here."

One was forty miles from Tizwit. Another was sixty miles away. The third was Tizwit itself.

Marcus felt the ice settle. But he also saw what five months ago he had not seen: the tremor in Nerva's hand, the wine at every station, the feverish intensity replacing the old patience. The prefect was close to the truth. And he was falling apart.

"I will begin the analysis, Prefect."

"You will not need to." Nerva's voice went quiet. "My dispatch from Thubursicu has produced consequences. Rome has concerns about my recent work. My deputy appended his own assessment. I have read it. He is not wrong that my observations have moved beyond conventional practice. He is wrong that this makes them less valuable."

He stood and moved to the window, and in the afternoon light Marcus could see how thin he had become. The bones of his wrists pressed against skin gone papery and grey.

"The archive remains," Nerva said. "Whoever follows me will have everything I have compiled. The patterns do not disappear because I do."

It was meant as warning. Marcus heard it as threat and promise combined.

"And my transfer to Syria, Prefect?"

Nerva waved a hand. "Rescinded. I will not be here to enforce it, and I doubt my successor will care to pursue a five-year-old staffing dispute." He almost smiled. "You outlasted me, Tribune. That, at least, should bring you satisfaction."

It brought Marcus hollow relief. The transfer that had consumed his nights for months, the desperate calculations, the failed tactics — all of it swept away by a child in a dusty market whose name Nerva would never know.

"Safe travels, Prefect."

Nerva turned from the window. "Tribune. You are very good at what you do. I never determined precisely what that was. Perhaps my successor will have better fortune."

He paused, and his expression shifted into something Marcus had never seen on that controlled, methodical face. Almost human.

"The child at the market," Nerva said. "She told me I had never loved anyone. She was correct. I have documented love in others. I have catalogued its effects and recorded its symptoms. But I have never felt it." He picked up the nearest cup, found it empty, set it down. "I suspect that is the gap in my approach that no archive can fill."

Marcus said nothing. There was nothing to say. The most dangerous man he had ever faced had just confessed the wound at the center of his life, and the confession came from a mind that could no longer hold its own boundaries.

"Dismissed, Tribune."

Marcus left the office. Behind him, he heard the scratch of a stylus on wax. Nerva was still documenting. He would document until they carried him from the room.

⁂

The orders arrived from Rome three weeks later.

Nerva received the news as if he expected it. The recall cited administrative shortcomings: declining tax receipts, garrison readiness reports he had neglected in favor of his archive, the routine maintenance of provincial governance that bored him and that he had let slide. But Marcus, who read dispatches with the same care Nerva read census numbers, recognized the real cause between the lines. Nerva's reports about the girl in the Thubursicu market had not alarmed Rome. They had embarrassed Rome. The governor's office did not hear a prefect reporting a genuine threat. It heard a provincial administrator losing his grip on reality. Five years of careful documentation, and Rome's response was to send him to count grain shipments on the Danube.

Marcus entered Nerva's office for the last time. Boxes and stacks of scrolls covered the floor. Nerva, bent over one case, looked up.

"The archive is Rome's property. It will remain exactly where it is, catalogued and organized and waiting for someone with the patience to read it properly." He sealed the case of his personal effects. "I suspect you will ensure that no one does."

"I serve Rome, Prefect."

"You serve something, Tribune. After five years, I believe it is something more worthy than Rome deserves." He shouldered his traveling case. "My ship leaves with the evening tide. I suggest you use the intervening weeks to adjust your methods before the next prefect arrives."

At the door, he paused.

"Rome does not deserve my conclusions. I spent five years building a comprehensive understanding of how this province thinks, how resistance operates, how information flows through tribal networks. And Rome's response was to dismiss my work and send me to count grain shipments on the Danube." His voice went quiet. "If Rome wanted my loyalty, Rome should have earned it."

He left. The door closed behind him with the soft finality of an ending.

❧✦❧

Marcus stood at the harbor rail as the new prefect's ship entered the harbor.

The man who descended the gangplank was young — mid-thirties at most — with the eager bearing of an officer seeking advancement. His uniform gleamed with a newness the provinces would dull within a season.

"Tribune Marcus Valerius Severus?" The accent was pure Rome: senatorial family, classical education, ambition radiating from every polished surface.

"Prefect. Welcome to Mauretania."

"Gaius Petronius Arbiter." He surveyed the harbor with a satisfied expression. "I understand my predecessor left extensive documentation. I will want to review the archive immediately."

"Of course, Prefect. The archive is comprehensive."

"Excellent. I have studied Prefect Nerva's methods. Admirable in their thoroughness, though I suspect they lacked decisive application." Petronius smiled, certain he could succeed where Nerva had failed. "I intend to bring a more results-oriented approach to provincial intelligence. Less documentation, more action."

Marcus kept his expression neutral. "As the Prefect wishes."

"My first priority will be identifying the coordination centers of tribal resistance. Nerva's archive should provide the foundation for targeted operations." Petronius began walking toward the garrison, clearly expecting Marcus to follow. "I want recommendations within the week. Settlements that warrant investigation, leaders who should be detained for questioning, networks that should be disrupted."

"The Prefect will find Mauretania's tribes resistant to direct approaches."

"So I have been told. By administrators who spent five years writing reports instead of achieving results." Petronius waved dismissively. "Fresh perspective, Tribune. That is what Rome sends to provinces grown stagnant under bureaucratic management."

They reached the garrison gates. Beyond them, Nerva's archive waited — five years of truth that Rome had refused to read, now about to be skimmed by an ambitious young officer hunting for quick victories.

"I will want your assessment of the archive by morning," Petronius continued. "Highlight the most actionable intelligence. Skip the theoretical observations. I am interested in targets, not patterns."

"Yes, Prefect."

Marcus followed his new commander through the gates and calculated. Petronius had not been sent to find Aedemon's family. Rome had not mentioned the family in the transfer orders. Petronius had found the file himself, buried in Nerva's archive, and adopted it. Solving what his predecessor could not would distinguish his record.

In some ways this made him more dangerous than Nerva. Nerva had hunted out of intellectual compulsion — the archivist's horror of an incomplete record. Petronius hunted out of ambition, and ambition was harder to misdirect because it did not follow evidence. It followed opportunity. But ambition also had a weakness Nerva's obsession lacked: it could be redirected. If Marcus could give Petronius a more attractive prize, the family file would gather dust.

The game had changed. The stakes remained the same.

Nerva's archive remained. But the man who understood it was gone, and the man who replaced him wanted victories rather than truth.

It was not safety. It was reprieve.

But reprieve bought time. And time, Marcus had learned, was the only currency that mattered.

CHAPTER 31

The Fever Country

"Sickness teaches what safety forgets:
how small we are, how much we need each other."
—Amazigh healer's wisdom

Autumn 49 CE—Tizwit—Weeks after Nerva's departure

The fever came with the late rains. First the insects, clouds of mosquitoes breeding in standing water where desert storms had pooled. Then the shaking. Children woke drenched in sweat, burning with fever refusing to break, seeing visions belonging to no waking world.

"Marsh fever," Silina diagnosed, checking the third sick child that morning. "I have seen it before when the rains come wrong. Too much, too fast, leaving water to stagnate."

By week's end, twelve people burned with fever. By the second week, a quarter of the settlement. The very young and very old died first.

The community faced an impossible choice.

◆

The community gathered at dusk, drawn by decisions no one wanted to make. Ouksem's voice carried the authority of tradition as he stood before the council fire.

"The ceremony of healing must be performed. Gather everyone at the sacred spring under the full moon. The drums and smoke will call the ancestors' protection."

Zahra did not hesitate. "That is three nights away. And the ceremony requires gathering near the sacred spring. The standing water poisons the air. Everyone knows fever rises from stagnant pools. Smoke fires visible for miles. Drums carrying on the wind."

"You're worried about Romans seeing us?" Ouksem's tone held accusation. "While our children die?"

Before Zahra could answer, a child in one of the nearby tents began screaming, the desperate shrieks of a fever dream. Within moments, another voice joined it, then another. Three children wailing in synchronized terror.

The council fell silent, listening to the sound of fever taking hold.

"We cannot gather them all," Yasir said. "The sickness spreads through proximity. A ceremony would accelerate the death, not prevent it."

"Then what do we do?"

"We find another way," Zahra said. "The stored herbs. Willow bark for fever, wormwood for the shaking. We make them stretch."

"Three days' supply at best," Silina reported. "More would come through Egyptian traders at the Roman market. Two days' ride away."

"They have Greek physicians at the garrison," someone suggested, voice cracking. "They understand these fevers."

The implications needed no explanation. Yasir's voice carried the gravity of leadership when he spoke.

"Full household registration. Tax documentation. Loyalty oaths. Names and origins of every person they treat. The Romans would document everything."

Everyone understood. The twins would be recorded: their ages, their education, their existence officially noted in Roman records that would survive any investigation.

No one had a better answer.

❧✦❧

Amara held through the first week.

The practice sustained her. Each morning she sat at the spring and breathed, letting the settlement's fear and pain pass like clouds across the sky, the way Eudoxus had taught her. She acknowledged the suffering without absorbing it. She named what she felt: the mother's dread in the eastern tents, the children's fever-visions pressing against her like heat through a wall, old Massoud's stubborn refusal to believe he was dying. She let each one pass. The clouds moved. She stayed.

She held through the second week, though it cost her more. Sleep came thin and fractured. She woke each morning with her jaw clenched and her shoulders rigid, the residue of emotions she had released during daylight but absorbed in dreams when the practice could not reach her. Eudoxus watched with concern she could feel from across the settlement, a low hum of worry beneath his usual steadiness.

"You are carrying more than you are releasing," he told her one evening.

"I know."

"The practice was not designed for this. It was designed for a room, a conversation, a single person's grief. Not a village in plague."

"What else do I have?"

He had no answer

On the third night, the wall broke.

A man in the adjacent tent cried out in his fever dream. The scream cut through Amara's sleep and she was inside it before her mind could intervene, drowning in dark water, tasting sand, and her lungs burning as she clawed toward a surface retreating with each stroke. Not her nightmare. His. But the distinction dissolved the moment his terror touched her unguarded mind, and behind it came the others: a woman on the far side of the settlement burning in her own fever-vision, a child falling from a height existing only in delirium, and then more, each dreamer's terror finding the channel the first scream had opened, pouring through the gap her exhausted discipline could no longer hold.

She tore herself back to consciousness gasping.

Zahra was already at her side. "Tasastinu?"

"I lost it." Amara's voice shook. "The wall. I held it for two weeks and it broke. They are all inside me and I cannot get them out."

This was not the helpless overwhelm of a four-year-old who had never known she needed walls. This was a trained practitioner whose training had failed under sustained pressure, and the knowledge of that failure made it worse. She had believed the practice would hold. It had not held. And now the flood was worse than if she had never built the wall at all, because the collapse let in everything the wall had been filtering for fourteen days.

"Silina! Get Eudoxus. Now."

By the time the old scholar arrived, Amara lay curled on her side, trembling, her eyes open but fixed on nothing. She was not unconscious. She was trying to rebuild the wall from inside the flood, and each attempt washed away the moment she laid the first stone.

"She held longer than I expected," Eudoxus said. His voice carried grief rather than clinical assessment. "The practice was never meant to sustain this kind of pressure for this long."

"Then what do we do?"

"We teach her the next level. The one I hoped she would not need for years."

Juba appeared in the doorway. Nine years old, his face tight with a fear he had learned to carry rather than show. He crossed to Amara without asking permission, sat beside her on the sleeping mat, and took her hand.

"Breathe with me," he said. Not "I fix her." Not the instinct of a four-year-old pressing his forehead to his sister's. A deliberate choice. He had watched Eudoxus sit with Amara through five years of training. He knew the rhythm. He matched his breathing to hers and slowed it, the way you slow a frightened horse by standing beside it and exhaling long and steady until the animal's body follows yours.

Amara's grip on his hand tightened until her knuckles whitened. Her breathing hitched, stuttered, then caught the rhythm he offered.

Eudoxus knelt on her other side. "Amara. Listen to me. The clouds are not working. The river is not working. The storm is too large for the practice you have learned. We need a different anchor."

"There is no anchor," she whispered. "I tried. I tried everything."

"Not everything." He placed his trembling hand on her forearm. "Feel my hand. The weight of it. The warmth. The tremor."

"I feel it."

"Good. Now feel Juba's hand in yours. The bones. The calluses from training. The pulse in his wrist."

"I feel it."

"Now feel the mat beneath you. The weave of it. The ground beneath the mat. The stone beneath the ground. The earth holding all of it."

Amara's breathing slowed. Not because the flood receded. Because she had stopped trying to push the water back and started holding to something solid while it passed.

"The practice I taught you watches the storm from inside," Eudoxus said. "That works when the storm is small. When the storm is this large, you cannot watch it. You must anchor yourself to what is real and let the storm spend itself. Your body is real. Juba's hand is real. The ground is real. Everything else will pass."

"The people. Their pain."

"Their pain is real. But it is theirs. Your body is yours. Hold to what is yours. Let the rest pass."

She held. Juba breathed beside her, steady, deliberate, the anchor he had always been but now offered with a nine-year-old's conscious will rather than an infant's instinct. Eudoxus kept his hand on her arm, the tremor in his fingers a reminder even broken instruments could steady a shaking hand.

The flood did not stop. But Amara stopped drowning in it. She lay on the mat and felt the weave beneath her back and the stone beneath the weave and Juba's callused palm in hers, and the pain of twenty-three families passed over her like wind over a stone too heavy to lift.

"Better," she said at last. "Not gone. But I am not in it anymore."

Juba did not let go of her hand. "I will stay with you."

"I know."

❧✦❧

Before dawn

Eudoxus sat outside the tent while the twins slept, wrapped in a blanket against the desert chill. His trembling hands rested on his knees. His eyes traced constellations he had once believed held the answers to every question worth asking.

The sickness pressed against him from every direction. It was the accumulated evidence of suffering he could not stop. He heard the coughing from three different tents. He smelled the bitter herbs Silina brewed in endless rotation. He saw the fear in every face passing his doorway.

And he could do nothing.

Once, he could have done much. Once, the gifts he'd carried from Bethlehem would have let him ease this suffering, channel healing energy through broken bodies, restore what disease had stolen. But those gifts were gone, spent in a desperate working at the sacred spring, sacrificed to save two children from Roman blades.

He did not regret the sacrifice. He regretted only the helplessness.

This is what it means to be ordinary, he thought. To see suffering you cannot ease, to know truth you cannot act upon, and to care without the power to protect.

He had spent his entire life avoiding this feeling. First through knowledge, then through gifts, then through the conviction his purpose would eventually reveal itself. There always was a power, or wisdom, or calling elevating him above simple helplessness.

Now there was nothing. Now he was an old man watching children die.

But as dawn approached and the settlement stirred into another day of desperate effort, Eudoxus watched Silina emerge from the healing tent. Her hands were raw from preparing medicines. Her eyes were hollow from sleepless nights. She had given everything she had and still found more to give.

She had no mystical powers. She never had. She worked with herbs and patience and knowledge earned through years of practice.

And she was saving lives. One child at a time. One fever broken, one crisis averted, one family given another day together.

Zahra appeared behind her, organizing the distribution of water and clean linens, and directing the healthy toward tasks to support the sick. Zahra had no powers either. Just the fierce love of a mother and the strategic mind survival had sharpened.

They were just human. Both of them. And they were holding the community together through sheer force of will and love.

What mattered, Eudoxus thought, was being human. For caring for the sick, for holding the dying, for teaching children and comforting the grieving, ordinary human presence was all that was needed. It always had been.

He rose and went to help Silina prepare the morning medicines. His hands were steadier than they had been in weeks, the trembling reduced to a faint whisper. He did not notice. Silina did, watching him grind herbs with a precision she had not seen since before the oasis.

It was not the purpose he had imagined. It was the purpose he had.

And perhaps that was the lesson he had spent his whole life learning. Being present did not require being extraordinary. It only required being willing.

❧✦❧

While Amara broke, Juba acted.

He gathered three boys his age, Hassan, Tariq, and Aksil, at the edge of camp as dusk fell.

"Egyptian traders camp at Wadi Tafrent tonight. They carry herbs from the Nile Valley. We will take what we need."

"That is theft," Hassan protested.

"It is survival. We will leave payment. Goat hides from our stores. Fair trade, just not negotiated."

The boys exchanged glances. Nine years old, planning their first raid. Juba mapped the approach with a stick in the sand, assigning positions the way Yasir had taught him: scout, approach, cover, retreat.

They moved through darkness with the practiced silence of desert children, reaching the trader camp as the last fires burned low. Juba directed the operation with hand signals, and within minutes, they had located the herb stores: dried wormwood, willow bark, and the precious Nile Valley febrifuge Silina had described.

They took what they needed. They left the hides. And they vanished into the desert before any trader stirred.

But on the way back, a merchant's son woke. He was older than them, fourteen at least, and he came at them with a staff. Juba moved between the boy and the younger raiders, and what followed was brief and brutal. The merchant's son swung. Juba ducked, grabbed, twisted. The older boy went down hard, his head striking a rock.

Blood pooled in the sand. The merchant's son lay still.

Juba stared at the body for three heartbeats. Then he checked for breathing, shallow but present, and ran.

Silina received the herbs without asking their source. She worked through the night, and by morning, three children whose fevers had been climbing toward death cooled.

Juba said nothing about the merchant's son. The knowledge sat inside him like a stone.

☙✦❧

Caesarea—the same week

The report arrived through Madi's network: sickness at Tizwit, children affected, supplies depleted by early winter's harshness.

Marcus stood in the garrison supply room at midnight, gathering what he could without arousing suspicion. Honey for coughs. Willow bark for fever. Clean bandages. Never enough. But sending more would require explanations he could not provide.

He wrapped the supplies in oilcloth and passed them to Madi, who would carry them south through networks neither of them discussed in daylight.

"The children?" Marcus asked in Tamazight.

"Recovering. Silina has skill." Madi secured the bundle. "But it was close."

"How close?"

"The kind making you question whether we are protecting them or just prolonging inevitable discovery."

Marcus had no answer. Eight years into this protection, and the question grew louder every month. How long could they sustain this? How many more near-catastrophes before one became real?

"Thank you," he said.

"Thank me by sleeping occasionally. You look like death."

After Madi departed, Marcus returned to his quarters but did not sleep. He stood at the window, watching stars wheel overhead, thinking of two children he had never met but had spent five years keeping alive.

Zahra's children. Aedemon's children. The family had become his purpose even as protecting them destroyed any chance of redemption for killing their father.

Some debts could never be paid, only honored through endless service expecting no acknowledgment.

❧✦❧

When the sickness passed, nine people lay dead.

The community gathered for burial rites. Dirt fell on small bodies. Mothers keened the old songs. And Amara watched Lunja, who had lost his mother to the fever, stand and walk to the center of the gathering.

"We are leaving." His voice carried no anger, which made it worse. "Tomorrow. My family, the Banu Kassim, the eastern group. We are leaving Tizwit."

Yasir stood. "The fever was not..."

"The fever was not their fault." Lunja gestured toward Juba and Amara, who sat rigid beside Zahra. "But we could not perform the healing ceremony because of them. Could not risk the smoke, the drums, the gathering. Could not trade openly for herbs. Could not call for the Roman physicians. Any documents would have led the authorities here."

He crouched beside one of the small graves. "My mother made that choice. Stayed when she was sick because she knew seeking proper medical help would expose the twins. She chose to die rather than risk the people who shelter them."

"Your mother chose to protect the community," Zahra said.

"My mother chose to protect children who are not even hers." There was no accusation now, only exhaustion. "I honor that choice. But I will not watch my other children die for it."

By evening, three families had joined the departure. By the next morning, more than twenty people walked away from Tizwit, carrying their goats and their tools and their accumulated lives. They left as people who had calculated the cost of harboring fugitives and concluded it was too high.

The twins watched from a distance, understanding at last, in real people walking into an uncertain future, what their presence cost: families scattered, community fractured, and deaths that might have been prevented if the settlement had acted freely.

The cost of protection was paid by everyone but themselves.

❧✦☙

Amara sat alone at the sacred spring, her only refuge. The water's sound helped quiet the emotional echoes still reverberating from the weeks of fever.

Juba joined her there, skipping stones across the surface with mechanical precision.

"That boy I hurt. The merchant's son. I see his face when I close my eyes."

Amara dropped a pebble in the water. "He lived. I asked the traders who came through yesterday. Scar on his forehead, but he lived."

"I'm glad. But also... I'd do it again. To save you, to save the others. Does that make me evil?"

Amara considered. At nine years old, they were both learning good and evil were not as separate as stories suggested.

"I think it makes you human. Eudoxus says humans are the only creatures who can hold two opposite truths at once. Healing and harming. Saving and sacrificing."

"I do not want to hold both. I want to be good."

"Then you would be no use to anyone. The good would have let us all die rather than steal. The simply evil would not care about the boy you hurt."

They sat in silence; two children aged beyond their years by necessity. Around them, Tizwit prepared for evening, smaller now, fractured but still functioning. The community had survived, but at a cost everyone would carry differently. Some carried it by seeking distance from danger. Some in weakened bodies. Some in memories of necessary violence. And Amara carried it in the accumulated grief of every loss, every fear, every moment of suffering she had absorbed and could not quite release.

The sickness had passed, but its lessons remained. They were a danger to those who sheltered them. Love and loyalty had limits. Survival required choices that stained souls. And sometimes, despite every effort, people died.

Amara touched the water's surface, watching ripples spread outward. Tomorrow would bring new challenges, new impossible choices. But in this moment, as the first stars emerged above the sacred spring, the twins sat together knowing they had faced terror transformed, marked, but surviving.

The water reflected starlight, constant despite all human suffering below.

CHAPTER 32

Letters and Lamplight

"Some documents outlast the men who sign them.
Some outlast the empires that seal them."
—A scribe's observation on permanence
Late Winter 50 CE—Volubilis

The assignment for Marcus was easy and routine: authenticate property transfers, review garrison records, and ensure the provincial archive met Roman standards. Three months away from Caesarea, away from Petronius's restless ambition, and the archive containing every lie Marcus had ever told.

Instead of bringing him relief, the distance only sharpened the burden he carried.

Volubilis sprawled across its plateau like a city still deciding what it wanted to become. Roman temples rose beside Punic shrines. Latin echoed in the forum while Tamazight filled the markets. The garrison kept order without enthusiasm, and the locals tolerated occupation without surrender.

Marcus worked through the property disputes with mechanical efficiency. Boundaries contested, inheritances challenged, merchants accusing each other of fraud. The documentation was a disaster. Clerks who prioritized speed over system filed decades of records in three languages.

He needed a scribe who could read all three.

Tacfara's workshop occupied a narrow building near the courts, its doorway marked by a faded sign in Punic script. Inside, scrolls lined the walls in careful order, and the air smelled of ink and cedar.

She looked up when he entered. Dark eyes assessed him as easily as the documents in front of her.

"Tribune." She did not rise. "Property dispute or inheritance claim?"

"Authentication. Fourteen documents, three languages, conflicting seals."

"Fourteen." She set down her stylus. "That is two days' work, minimum. Three if the seals are degraded."

"The garrison will pay standard rates."

"The garrison always pays standard rates. The question is whether the garrison understands what standard rates purchase." She gestured to a stool across from her work table. "Show me what you've brought."

He spread the documents between them. She bent over the first, fingers tracing script with practiced ease, and Marcus watched her work. Mid-thirties, he guessed. Lines at the corners of her eyes, ink stains on her fingers, and posture evocative of years hunched over texts. No jewelry except a simple copper band on her left thumb.

"This seal is forged," she said after a moment. "Competent work, but the wax composition is wrong for the period claimed." She moved to the next document. "This one's genuine but misdated. The magistrate whose name appears here died three years before this transaction supposedly occurred."

"You know the magistrates' death dates?"

"I know everything that passes through these courts." She glanced up. "It is my profession, Tribune. Knowing what documents mean and what they hide."

They worked through the afternoon, her expertise cutting through tangles he would have spent weeks unraveling. By evening, she had sorted fourteen documents into three categories: genuine, forged, and questionable.

"The questionable ones require comparison with originals in the provincial archive," she said, rolling the scrolls with care. "I can have answers by week's end."

"I'll return then."

"You'll return before then." It was not a question. She met his eyes with the same directness she had shown the documents. "Men who carry what you carry do not wait patiently for answers. They come back to ask questions they do not know how to phrase."

Marcus felt a shift in his chest. "What do I carry?"

"I do not know yet." She rose, signaling the consultation's end. "But I've authenticated documents for twenty years. I know what burden looks like, even when men try to hide it."

✦

He returned three days later with documents not requiring authentication.

Tacfara was alone in her workshop, copying a contract by lamplight. She looked up when his shadow crossed the threshold, her expression suggesting she had expected him.

"More forgeries, Tribune?"

"No." He stood in the doorway, uncertain why he had come. "I was passing the quarter. Saw your lamp burning late."

"I work late. Clients pay for accuracy, and accuracy requires time." She set down her stylus. "But you did not come to discuss my working hours."

"No."

"Then sit. I have wine, if Roman soldiers drink with provincial scribes."

"This one does."

She poured two cups, local vintage, rougher than what the garrison served, and settled across from him. The lamp cast shadows softening the lines of her face.

"You've been in Volubilis three weeks," she said. "You've authenticated enough documents to satisfy any reasonable assignment. Yet you remain."

"The work takes time."

"The work was finished days ago. You've been inventing reasons to extend your stay." She sipped her wine. "I do not mind. Curiosity is understandable. But I prefer honesty to invention."

Marcus turned the cup in his hands. "I do not know why I came back."

"Yes, you do." Her voice carried no accusation. "You came back because I saw a thing you've hidden from everyone else. And you want to know if I'll look away."

"Will you?"

"That depends on what I'm seeing." She leaned forward, elbows on the table. "You carry guilt like a physical thing. You deflect personal questions with professional precision. You speak three languages without an accent, but choose your words carefully in all of them as if you have learned that careless speech kills."

Marcus set down his wine. "You read people the way you read documents."

"Documents are easier. They do not lie about being honest." A slight smile. "You, Tribune, are the most carefully constructed document I have ever encountered. Every word placed with deliberate purpose. Every omission calculated."

"That is a dangerous observation to share with the subject."

"Dangerous for whom?" She refilled both cups. "I'm a provincial scribe. You're a Roman tribune. If danger exists in this room, it does not point toward me."

The directness disarmed him in ways he had not expected. For ten years, every conversation had been a strategic exercise, every word weighed for exposure risk, every relationship evaluated for what it might reveal. Tacfara offered no strategy. She simply saw.

"What if what you're seeing would put you at risk?"

"Then I would want to know before I invested further time." She met his eyes steadily. "I do not gamble on documents I have not read."

The wine was rough but honest. The lamp burned lower. And Marcus, for the first time in a decade, spoke without calculating every word.

He told her about a man who had killed his closest friend. About a promise extracted with a dying breath. About ten years of lies told to an empire to protect children he had never met.

He did not tell her names or locations. He did not tell her the specifics of how the protection worked. But he told her the shape of it, the arc of guilt, duty and isolation that was his entire existence.

Tacfara listened. She did not interrupt. She did not comfort. She listened the way she read documents: with total attention and suspended judgment.

When he finished, the lamp had burned to its final quarter.

"You've been lying to an empire for ten years," she said. "To protect the children of a man you killed."

"Yes."

"And no one else knows."

"One person. A centurion who shares the work. But he does not know why I do it. Only that I do."

"Why do you do it?"

She asked the question he never let himself answer. That question kept him awake in Caesarea, drove him through years of careful deception, and brought him to this stranger's workshop seeking a thing he could not name.

"Because he asked me to. Before I..." Marcus stopped. Started again. "His last words were a request. Watch over his family. And then I killed him anyway, because the alternative was worse. And I've been keeping that promise ever since, because it is the only thing making any of it bearable."

Tacfara rose. For a moment he thought she would ask him to leave. Instead, she moved around the table and stood before him.

"You've carried this alone for ten years."

"Yes."

"You do not have to carry it alone tonight."

She extended her hand. She was not offering absolution which she could not give. She was not offering solutions because there were none. She was offering presence, the simple acknowledgment he existed beyond his guilt, beyond his duty, and beyond the endless burden of protection.

Marcus took her hand.

✦

Dawn

Light filtered through shutters needing repair. Marcus lay still, watching shadows resolve into the shapes of Tacfara's workshop. Scrolls lay on shelves. Ink pots sat on tables. Those were the ordinary tools of a life built on reading what others had written.

Beside him, Tacfara stirred. "You're thinking too loudly."

"I have to return to Caesarea."

"I know." She did not open her eyes. "The documents are authenticated. The assignment is complete. The garrison expects you."

"Yes."

"And the protection continues."

"Until it does not have to. Or until I fail."

She turned to face him, dark hair spread across the pillow. "Will you write?"

"Letters are dangerous. They can be intercepted. Read. Used as evidence."

"I'm a scribe, Tribune. I know how to write letters saying one thing and meaning another." A faint smile. "Legal correspondence. Consultations on document authentication. Perfectly ordinary communication between a Roman officer and a provincial scribe."

"And underneath?"

"Underneath, whatever we choose to put there." She traced a finger along his jaw. "I'm not asking for promises. I do not expect you to abandon your work or share your burdens. I'm asking whether you want someone to know you exist, who sees what you carry and does not look away."

The question beneath the question. Whether he could allow himself to be seen. Whether ten years of isolation had become so familiar that connection felt like threat.

"Yes," he said. "I want that."

"Then write when you can and what you can. I'll read between the lines." She sat up, reaching for the robe draped over a nearby chair. "I've spent twenty years reading what documents hide. I can certainly read you."

❧✦❧

The road east unspooled beneath his horse's hooves. Volubilis fell behind, its plateau shrinking to a smudge against the morning sky.

Marcus carried documents in his saddlebag, authentic records, property transfers, the legitimate work justifying his months away. He carried orders returning him to Caesarea, to the garrison, to the endless vigilance that protection required.

And he carried a second truth, smaller and harder to name.

For ten years, he had defined himself by guilt and duty. The man who killed his friend. The man who protected his friend's family. The man who lied to an empire, report by report, year by year, until the lies became more real than truth.

But Tacfara had seen deeper, the person underneath the guilt and duty. She had seen Marcus, exhausted, isolated, but still capable of connection despite everything he had done to convince himself otherwise.

The road stretched toward Caesarea, toward Petronius's archive and the endless work of deception that kept a family alive.

And for a man who had spent ten years disappearing into duty, that single truth changed him.

The burden remained.

But now he carried it differently. Now Tacfara knew. Now, when the protection felt endless and the lies felt suffocating, he would remember a lamp burning late in Volubilis, a woman who read documents and men with equal precision, and a night when he had been seen and had not looked away.

The road stretched toward Caesarea.

Marcus rode to meet it.

CHAPTER 33

The Shallows

"The spring does not ask who drinks. This is its teaching."

—Amazigh saying on sacred waters

Early 50 CE — Tizwit — Months after the sickness

The sacred spring had become Amara's refuge. Each dawn, before the settlement woke, she sat in the shallows where water emerged from rock and let the flow pull away the emotional residue settling thick in her chest. Every fear she had absorbed, every loss she had carried, every moment of suffering clinging to her like wet cloth.

Ten years old. Already she had learned the hard way: without this dawn ritual, without emptying the vessel of herself, she would drown in the feelings of others. The fever the previous autumn had taught her that lesson in the cruelest way possible. She had nearly disappeared into the collective terror of dying children, dying elders, dying hope.

"You are up early again," Zahra said, approaching with linens for washing. She knelt beside Amara, her movements marked by careful deliberation. "The quiet helps?"

Amara shrugged. "Their dreams press less than their waking thoughts. When they sleep, the feeling is not as loud."

Zahra studied her daughter and saw the thinness despite adequate food, the shadows beneath her eyes that belonged on someone twice her age. The gift, so manageable when Amara was small, had grown alongside her body into something beyond what any child should have to carry.

"Eudoxus wants to try new exercises," Zahra said. "Visualization of barriers. He thinks they might help you separate which feelings belong to you and which belong to others."

"We have tried visualization before." Amara drew a line through the water with her finger, watching it collapse and reform. "It does not stop them. It is like trying to stop breathing."

"And we will keep trying because the first attempts failed." Zahra's voice did not ask for permission. "We do not abandon a search just because the path gets harder."

Amara nodded, though the doubt ran deeper than techniques. Perhaps the question was not how to silence the gift but how to survive it.

Later that morning

She was still at the spring when Tiziri found her.

Tiziri had a gift for finding Amara: the desert fox tracking water through stone, arriving without apparent effort at exactly the place she was needed. She appeared at the spring's edge with her sandals already off, dropped beside a root, and settled onto the flat stone beside Amara with the ease of long habit.

"You have been here since dawn," Tiziri said.

"The practice takes time."

"Your practice takes longer since the fever." Tiziri said it without judgment. "Are you still emptying out what you absorbed, or are you just sitting here because it is pleasant?"

Amara considered. "Both."

"Good." Tiziri put her feet in the water. "It is pleasant."

They sat in comfortable silence. The spring ran clear and cold from the rock face above them, falling into the pool with a sound that had been Amara's anchor for six years. Around them the settlement moved through its morning work; she could feel it at the edges, the familiar emotional weather of Tizwit: Silina's focused attention in the healing tent, two men arguing mildly about a boundary marker, a child's bright uncomplicated happiness somewhere near the date palms.

It did not press. It simply was, the way the spring sound simply was.

"There," Tiziri said.

Amara followed her gaze.

On a flat rock at the pool's edge, half in shadow, sat a toad: broad and still as an adult's hand laid flat, its warty skin the same warm grey as the stone beneath it. Amara had been sitting three arm's-lengths from it for two hours without seeing it.

"It lives here," Tiziri said. "I have seen it before. Always on that rock. Always doing nothing in particular."

Amara looked at the toad. It looked back at her with the patient indifference of something older than the spring itself.

"I only saw it because I know where to look," Tiziri said. "Otherwise it is just the rock."

A faint recognition moved through Amara, older and quieter than the gift, than anyone else's emotion pressing through her walls. Like hearing a word in a language she had not yet learned and almost understanding it anyway.

She looked at the toad. Then she let it go.

"How do you always find me?" she asked.

Tiziri shrugged. "You are always here. It is not difficult."

"I mean... how do you know when to come?"

Tiziri thought about this with her characteristic seriousness. "I feel you need company, and then I come, and usually you do." She paused. "Is that strange?"

"No." Amara looked at her cousin, this girl with ears for everything the desert hid, who found water and toads and cousins at springs with the same matter-of-fact accuracy. "It is the truest thing anyone has ever said to me."

"That cannot be right," Tiziri said. "Eudoxus says true things constantly."

"Eudoxus says wise things. It is different."

Tiziri considered this distinction. "What is the difference?"

"Wise things make me think," Amara said. "True things make me feel less alone."

Tiziri looked at her. Recognition arrived in her expression: precise and quiet, the desert fox's ears turning toward a sound it had been waiting for. "That is also a true thing," she said. "What you just said."

Amara laughed.

A full laugh, rising from somewhere below the practice and the fever's residue and the careful management of other people's emotions. It felt like the spring sounded: clear and cold and coming from somewhere deep in the rock.

Tiziri smiled: a smaller, steadier version of her full rearranging smile. "You have not laughed like that in a long time."

"I know."

"Since before the fever."

"Probably." Amara wiped her eyes. The laughing had produced tears, which seemed excessive given nothing was funny. She looked at the toad, still on its rock, still indistinguishable from the stone, still doing nothing in particular. "I think the fever broke something."

"Or opened it," Tiziri said.

Amara looked at her.

"When a jar cracks," Tiziri said, with complete matter-of-factness, as though pottery never lied, "sometimes it leaks. Sometimes it just fits together differently. You cannot always tell which until afterwards."

"That is either very wise or very true," Amara said. "I cannot decide which."

"My mother says the same thing about my father's opinions." Tiziri pulled her feet from the water and tucked her knees to her chest, looking at the toad. "What does it feel like? Right now. What do you feel from me?"

The question, the same one Tiziri had asked at four years old on the day they met, landed with its old warmth and its old directness. Tiziri had asked it a hundred times since then, always with the same frank curiosity that never aged into anything complicated.

Amara reached toward her cousin's presence the way she reached toward the spring sound: leaning in rather than bracing. Simply attending.

Tiziri's attention had a different quality from Zahra's warmth or Menna's steadiness: precise, quick, without agenda. It reached toward rather than broadcasting outward. Where most people's emotions pressed against Amara whether she attended to them or not, Tiziri's required her to lean in slightly. To choose to receive.

"Like the desert fox's ears," Amara said. "Turned toward something. Completely still except for that."

Tiziri considered this. "Is that good?"

"It is the best thing I feel from anyone outside my family."

Tiziri accepted this without embarrassment, the way she accepted all true things. "What do you feel from yourself? Right now."

Amara paused. The question was harder. She spent so much of her awareness on other people's inner lives that her own was sometimes the last thing she reached.

She tried.

Six years of sitting at the spring, learning to distinguish what was hers from what was everyone else's, learning to find the thread of her own feeling beneath the settlement's constant weather. She followed it inward.

"Quiet," she said, surprised. "I feel quiet."

"You look quiet," Tiziri said. "You look like that toad."

They both looked at the toad.

It had not moved. It would not move. It sat on its rock in the morning light, exactly and entirely what it was, needing nothing from anyone, going nowhere, thoroughly itself.

Amara settled. The same faint recognition as before, closer now, almost nameable. She reached for it. It dissolved.

"I cannot hold it," she said.

"You are not supposed to hold it," Tiziri said. "Toads do not hold things. They just sit."

Amara looked at her cousin. "How do you know that?"

"I watch toads," Tiziri said, with complete seriousness. "There is one at every spring in the oasis. They are all the same. They sit. Occasionally they eat something. Then they sit more." She paused. "It seems like a good life."

"It seems like a very boring life."

"Does it?" Tiziri glanced at her. "You sit at springs every morning. You said it was pleasant."

The laugh came again, smaller this time, but from the same place. Amara shook her head. "That is not the same."

"It is a little the same," Tiziri said.

From the settlement, Taderfit's voice carried across the morning air: "Tiziri."

"Here," Tiziri called back.

"Come and help with the grain."

Tiziri pulled on her sandals with her characteristic unhurried movements. She stood and looked down at Amara. "Will you be here this afternoon?"

"Probably."

"Then I will come back." She glanced at the toad. "So will he, most likely. He always does."

She walked back toward the settlement with her own quick, light step: alert and purposeful and slightly amused by the landscape. The desert fox's step, Amara thought.

Amara turned back to the spring.

The toad sat on its rock. The water ran cold over stone. The settlement's emotional weather pressed gently at the edges of her awareness: nothing urgent, nothing flooding, the ordinary texture of sixty families living their ordinary morning.

She breathed in. She breathed out.

Simply here. Simply Amara, at the water, in the morning, being exactly what she was.

The toad did not move.

Neither did she.

❧✦❧

After midnight, at the sacred spring

Eudoxus found Amara where he always found her — at the spring, trying to rinse away the burden of holding other people's truths alongside her own.

"The settlement is quiet," he observed, settling beside her on the stone ledge with careful deliberation. The fever's aftermath continued to weaken his body in ways the healers could not reverse. "Easier tonight?"

"A little." She did not look up from the water. "There is less fear when there is less to fear."

"For now." He drew a breath that cost him effort. "I want to speak to you about something I have been waiting to say until you were ready to hear it."

Amara looked at him then.

"Your ability to sense what others think and feel carries a temptation," he said. "You could use that knowledge to manipulate — to say exactly what people need to hear so they become what you want them to be. That is where power becomes poison."

"But I do not want to control anyone."

"Nor did the one I knew before." Eudoxus studied the water. "His name was Melchior. He carried power — a gift that let him read hearts the way others read tracks in sand. And he meant well, I think. But eventually the craving to fix people, to transform them into what he thought they could be, consumed his wisdom. The gift carried him rather than the other way."

"What happened to him?"

"He sought to control what he could not control, and it destroyed him." Eudoxus met her eyes. "The danger is not your gift, child. The danger is what happens when you believe that feeling everyone's truth means you are responsible for transforming it."

Amara sat with this. "But how will I know the difference? Between caring and controlling?"

"You will spend your whole life learning that distinction." He paused. "But here is what I know: true power lies in what you choose not to interfere with. Any person with enough strength can force change. Only the wise can sit with someone who struggles and trust them to find their own path, even when that path looks like failure."

He rose, joints stiff but his eyes clear. The hour of teaching had done something the herbs and rest never managed. "Your brother is learning to lead by failing at it. He must discover that being impressive is not the same as being trustworthy. That is his lesson to learn, not yours to teach."

"He is going to keep making mistakes."

"Yes. And you are going to have to watch without fixing them." Eudoxus's weathered face held no judgment, only acknowledgment of difficulty. "That is harder than any technique I could teach you. Harder than any barrier you could visualize."

Amara's hand rose to touch her chest, a gesture without purpose or explanation. She did not understand why she did it, only that his words had stirred an instinct she could not name.

❧✦❧

She lay awake afterward in her sleeping furs, turning his words over like smooth stones in a river, finding new shape with each consideration.

The distinction between caring and controlling. Between knowing someone's truth and being responsible for fixing it.

She thought of Melchior, destroyed by the very power that had seemed to make him essential. How many people had he tried to save? How many had resented the salvation they had never asked for? How the need to matter, to help, to be irreplaceable had slowly consumed the wisdom that should have guided his gifts.

She understood, with a clarity that felt almost frightening, how easily she could follow that same path.

Tomorrow, Juba would make another strategic mistake and she would feel the ripple of its consequences. Zahra would worry about their safety and Amara would sense it like a current beneath her skin. The community would carry fear about Roman patrols, and all that collective anxiety would press against her awareness.

She could fix these things. She could offer insights shaped perfectly to ease each person's pain. She could become indispensable, essential, necessary.

But Eudoxus had shown her where that path led.

So instead, she practiced the harder discipline. She lay in the darkness and let the feelings pass through her: Zahra's worry, Juba's restless ambition, the community's collective unease. She acknowledged each one. She did not try to mend any of them.

I see this feeling. I acknowledge it. But it is not mine to carry.

The feelings did not stop. They never would. But for the first time, she let them flow without grasping at them, without believing that every truth she sensed demanded her intervention.

The spring murmured outside, asking nothing of anyone who drank from it.

Amara closed her eyes and let the water teach.

CHAPTER 34

The Game Board

"A child asks, 'What is wise?'
The elder answers with another question.
This is the first lesson."
—Persian teaching tradition
Spring 50 CE—Tizwit—Six years after arrival

Evening

The council circle convened as the heat reached its peak, a time when even the Romans rested from their patrols. Tonight's gathering drew representatives from three settlements, each struggling with how to respond to increased patrols without giving Rome the excuse to crush them.

Amara sat at the circle's edge, quietly acknowledged by the elders for insights often cutting through the tangle of competing fears. Tonight, the debate spiraled in its familiar pattern.

"We should band together," Kadir argued from the eastern settlement, his voice tight with fear wearing a mask of aggression. "Present a unified front against Rome."

"Unified means visible," Yalena countered, her words shaped by trauma that had taught her survival meant invisibility. "Better to remain separate, unremarkable, forgotten."

"Neither of you is addressing the real problem," Amagan said, frustration sharp in his voice.

"What is the real problem?" Zahra asked, creating space for deeper examination. She had learned this technique from Eudoxus: the right question often revealed what anger and fear had obscured.

Before the elders could answer, Amara spoke. "They are scared of each other, not of the Romans. They do not trust anyone else will help when danger comes."

The circle fell into embarrassed silence, because a ten-year-old had said aloud what everyone had avoided.

"How do we build trust when circumstances test it?" Yasir asked, valuing her insight despite her age.

"Maybe we already have the answer," Amara said, thinking of their own settlement. "We have survived five years with Romans hunting us, because everyone knows their role. Everyone knows the person next to them will help when tested."

She gestured around the circle at Taderfit who had sheltered them without hesitation, at Silina who had taught them healing, at Yasir who had opened his settlement to refugees, and at the elders who had made collective decisions even when individual cost ran high.

She could read each of them: Taderfit's fierce protectiveness, Yasir's determination, the elders' mix of pride and worry. Only Silina remained unreadable, her emotions walled off in ways that felt deliberate. Amara had noticed before the way Silina's feelings stayed hidden behind careful barriers whenever Amara reached toward her. It was like trying to see through fog. Whatever Silina carried, she carried alone.

"Every person here stayed when staying meant danger," Amara continued. "That is the kind of trust that survives Rome."

The council meeting stretched past midnight as three communities began planning the harder work of building trust: establishing shared decision-making, teaching collaborative approaches, and learning to value each settlement's strength rather than competing for resources.

An argument between the twins had been building for days before the council meeting gave it sharper edges.

The morning after the meeting, Amara joined Juba in the small courtyard of their dwelling. They were working together to make carved his game pieces with sharp, aggressive strokes, each cut expressing frustration with his sister's certainty, with his own inadequacy, with a world that valued her gifts over his efforts. Amara arranged her pieces with deliberate precision, creating patterns that mocked her brother's chaotic approach.

"Your pieces look like broken rocks."

Juba's knife paused mid-cut. "Yours look like they are afraid to be different from each other."

From across their family's living space, Silina exchanged a glance with Eudoxus. For weeks the twins circled each other this way, avoiding outright conflict yet unable to collaborate on any task without proclaiming their own method superior. The competition that once sharpened their strengths now drove them apart.

Eudoxus kept his voice low. "They need something that requires them to succeed together. They focus so much on their own skills in competition that they forget how much stronger they are when they combine them."

"A game, perhaps." Silina's fingers traced the weaving in her lap. "Something where both players must contribute what they do best, or neither wins."

❧✦❧

Taderfit approached Zahra while she mended fishing nets in the shade of their tent.

"Your son volunteers for every dangerous task these days. Yesterday he insisted on tracking the leopard alone. Last week he wanted to check the far water sources during the windstorm."

Zahra looked toward where Juba sat carving, his jaw tight with frustration marking him for months. Since turning ten, a restlessness had taken hold of him, a need to prove himself going beyond ordinary boyish energy.

She chose her words with care. "He is still grieving. His father's death touches him differently now that he is older. He understands what was lost in ways he could not at four."

"We all grieve." Taderfit's tone carried authority. She had raised six sons to adulthood. "Most of us do not grieve by courting death. That boy tries to prove what cannot be proved through rccklcssncss."

"What would you have me do?"

"Watch him. That boy has been carrying this wound for six years. Some wounds heal wrong if left unattended."

Zahra understood. Juba had always lived in Amara's shadow, the sister whose spiritual gifts drew community respect, whose insights made her valuable in ways his physical courage never matched. At ten, on the cusp of manhood, he needed desperately to matter, to be seen as more than the gifted one's brother.

❧✦❧

Dawn

Eudoxus sat in the courtyard with his back against the wall and attempted, for the six-thousandth time by his rough estimate, to be still.

The posture came easily enough. Sixty-eight years of practice had taught his legs where to cross, his hands where to rest, his spine how to hold itself without leaning. The body knew the shapes. The body had always been the cooperative part.

The mind was the problem. The mind had been the problem since Persia.

This morning it offered its usual inventory. His hands trembled. The pathways he once used to touch the sacred were dead channels, scar tissue where living connection had been. He had watched nine people die of marsh fever and been unable to do anything more useful than grind herbs. He was sixty-eight years old, his greatest contribution to this village was sorting olives by color, and the children he had been cosmically appointed to guide were currently refusing to speak to each other over a disagreement about game piece aesthetics.

He noted each thought. Recorded it. Set it aside. The thoughts were not him. They were weather, the tedious, low, gray drizzle that settled in for weeks.

A goat wandered into the courtyard. It belonged to Massoud's son, who let his animals roam with the cheerful negligence of a boy not yet acquainted with consequences. The goat regarded Eudoxus with the flat, horizontal pupils of its kind, an expression suggesting mild curiosity and total indifference in equal measure.

Eudoxus regarded the goat.

The goat chewed something. It did not appear to be meditating, yet it possessed a quality of presence Eudoxus had been chasing for half a century. It stood where it stood. It ate what it found. It harbored no resentment about lost spiritual pathways. It did not lie awake at night wondering whether its purpose had been a delusion. It was a goat. It was exactly, entirely, magnificently a goat.

"You have achieved," Eudoxus told it, "what fifty years of spiritual discipline have not granted me."

The goat lost interest in him and wandered toward the grain jars.

Eudoxus watched it go. And then from a place deeper than grief, deeper than the loss of his powers, deeper than the daily weight of being Numerius when he had once been Caspar, a laugh rose through him.

Not a bitter laugh. Not the dark humor of a man mocking his own ruin. A genuine, helpless, full-bodied laugh at the absurdity of his situation: a former Magus, a man who had knelt before the divine made flesh, a scholar who had crossed the known world seeking cosmic truth, sitting in a courtyard in a mountain village, losing a spiritual contest to a goat.

The laugh bent him forward. His trembling hands pressed against his knees. His eyes watered. He could not stop. Each time he tried, the goat's expression returned to him, that magnificent indifference, and the laugh renewed itself.

Silina appeared in the doorway. She stared at him. She had not heard him laugh in the six years she knew him.

"Are you ill?"

"I am cured." He wiped his eyes. "Silina, I have spent fifty years trying to achieve the state of perfect presence. This morning a goat accomplished it without trying, lost interest in me, and left to eat grain. I believe this may be the most important spiritual lesson I have ever received."

Silina looked at the goat, which had found the grain jar and was working the lid with its teeth. She looked at Eudoxus, whose face held a brightness she had not seen since before the sacred spring. She did not understand the lesson, but she recognized healing when she saw it.

"Should I chase the goat away from the grain?"

"Let it eat. It has earned its breakfast. More than I can say for myself most mornings."

She left him there, shaking her head. He sat in the courtyard with the afterglow of laughter settling through his body and felt something shift. Not the pathways returning. Not the powers restored. Something smaller and more useful.

The grief was still there. The loss of what he had been, the emptiness where the sacred fire once lived, the trembling hands that would never steady. All of it remained. But the laughter had moved through the grief, the way water moves through rock, finding the channels already there, the cracks the suffering had carved, and flowing through them into a place he had forgotten existed.

Joy. Not the cosmic joy of Bethlehem. Not the intellectual joy of seeing patterns align. The small, creaturely joy of a man sitting in the sun who realizes he has been taking himself too seriously for fifty years and the universe has been waiting, with infinite patience, for him to notice.

He sat with joy the way the practice taught him to sit with grief: without grasping. He did not try to hold it or extend it or make it mean something. He let it be what it was — a morning in a courtyard, a goat and an old man, and the ancient joke that the divine hides itself best in the ordinary.

When he opened his eyes, the sun had moved a hand's width across the courtyard wall. His hands still trembled. The pathways were still dead. Nothing had changed.

Everything had changed.

He rose, steadier than he had been in months, and went to find Silina. He had an idea for the twins: a game requiring them to work together rather than compete. The idea had arrived during the laughter, fully formed, as if it had been waiting for him to stop being solemn long enough to receive it.

The goat had finished the grain and was working on the courtyard herbs. Eudoxus let it. Some teachers demanded payment.

❧✦☙

Over the next few days, while the twins continued their stubborn standoff, Eudoxus and Silina spent the evenings designing what they hoped would teach what words had failed to convey.

"We have something for you."

Silina made her announcement one afternoon when the siblings' latest disagreement had dissolved into sullen silence. Eudoxus carried a wooden board marked with an intricate pattern of lines and spaces. Silina brought a leather pouch that rattled with carved pieces.

Eudoxus set the board between the twins. "It is called Rih al-Harb. The Wind of War. But it is not about fighting each other."

Juba's interest stirred despite his sullenness. "Then what is the point?"

Silina emptied the pouch. "The point is to survive the storm together."

The pieces looked unlike any they had seen: some carved as people, others as animals, others as tools and supplies.

"The wind brings challenges. You must help each other weather them, or you both lose."

Amara picked up one of the people-pieces, feeling the smooth curves Eudoxus had shaped with patient care. "How do we win?"

"By guiding your community safely through seven seasons of hardship." Eudoxus gestured to the board's marked divisions. "Drought, raiders, sickness, storms. The challenges come whether you are ready or not. If either player's community fails, both players lose."

The first few games ended in disaster.

Juba prepared for military threats while neglecting food storage, then watched his people starve during Amara's well-defended harvest. Amara stockpiled resources while ignoring diplomatic opportunities, then saw her isolated community collapse under challenges that coordinated tribes could have weathered together.

"This is impossible." Juba swept his hand across the board after their fourth consecutive failure. "There is too much to manage. No one could keep track of everything."

Silina gestured to the scattered pieces. "That is why you need each other. Juba, you see threats before they arrive. Amara, you understand how people's needs connect to each other. Neither of you can do everything alone."

"But I do not understand his way of thinking." Amara's protest came with genuine frustration. "He always expects attacks. I focus on making sure people have what they need day by day."

"And I do not understand hers." Juba set down a piece with more force than necessary. "She thinks if everyone is fed and happy, problems will solve themselves. But sometimes you have to fight to protect what you have built."

Eudoxus leaned forward. "What if you could understand each other's thinking? What if you could see the game through each other's eyes?"

The idea came to them at the same moment, the way insights sometimes did for twins who had learned to think together through necessity.

"What if we switched?" Amara's words came slowly.

Juba's eyes lit. "You take my pieces. I take yours."

The adults watched with carefully concealed excitement as the twins began their most ambitious game.

Juba, playing with Amara's diplomatic and resource-management pieces, discovered how complex the web of daily needs was. Every decision about food distribution affected morale, which affected productivity, which affected the community's ability to handle crises.

Amara, commanding Juba's military and scouting pieces, understood how threats developed over time, how small dangers could grow into overwhelming challenges if left unaddressed.

But more than understanding each other's perspectives, they anticipated each other's moves, to weave strategies that combined both approaches into a whole stronger than either could achieve alone.

Juba moved one of Amara's diplomatic pieces to strengthen trade relationships with western tribes. "The raiders are coming from the east in two seasons."

Amara positioned one of Juba's scout pieces to watch the southern approaches. "But if we ally with the western communities now, we can invite them to help with the harvest celebration. Then when the raiders come..."

They finished together: "We will have allies already in place, and the celebration will have strengthened everyone's willingness to fight for the community."

The game flowed like a conversation between two halves of the same mind. They weathered the seven seasons through a kind of thinking that emerged from their combined perspectives, each seeing what the other missed, each contributing strengths that covered the other's limitations.

When the final challenge fell and their joint community had thrived rather than merely survived, both twins felt the shift inside their understanding. They had moved beyond I know what I am good at and you know what you are good at to a place that felt entirely new.

Amara studied the board where their combined strategy had created what neither could have achieved alone. "We did that together."

"Not just together." Wonder colored Juba's voice. "Like we were thinking with one mind that happened to have two bodies."

⁂

Around the fire that evening, other adults gathered to watch what had begun as a simple game. Yasir studied the final board position with a strategist's attention, while Taderfit examined how the twins had managed resource distribution.

One of the younger men asked, "How did you know to make that alliance in the third season?"

The twins looked at each other, then back at their audience.

"We switched," Amara said. "I played his way. He played mine."

"And then we played our way." Juba's hand rested on the board between them. "Except it was not mine or hers anymore. It was ours."

Later, as the twins gathered the game pieces, Eudoxus sat with them in comfortable silence.

"What did you learn?"

Juba dropped pieces into the leather pouch. "That I am better when I understand how Amara thinks. And that she is better when she understands how I think."

"But also..." Amara's tone turned thoughtful. "When we understand each other, we can think in ways that neither of us could think alone."

"We become stronger by becoming more like each other. Instead of just staying in our own strengths."

Eudoxus nodded. "And what does that feel like?"

The twins considered this, remembering the sensation of their minds working in perfect coordination, each anticipating the other's insights, each contributing to strategies that emerged from their combined understanding.

"Like when you and Yemma work together and solve problems nobody else can." Amara searched for words to describe what they had experienced. "Like the community when everyone brings their different gifts."

Juba added, "Like we are supposed to be this way. Not competing. Just... together."

The game of Rih al-Harb would be played many more times in Tizwit, spreading through the community. But it would never again carry the same charge as that first evening when two stubborn children learned to see through each other's eyes and discovered they could think as one.

❧✦❧

Caesarea—Late Spring 50 CE

Marcus Valerius Severus had played ten years of his own perilous, not-so-innocent game.

It had taught him to adapt to any commander Rome sent. Nerva's patient intelligence had given way to Petronius's appetite for quick results, and the transition, paradoxically, had made the deception easier. Petronius skimmed where Nerva had studied. He wanted targets, not patterns, and Marcus had learned to provide false targets while the patterns remained safely buried.

The Volubilis assignment had been a respite, three months away from Petronius's demands for actionable intelligence, three months where he could breathe without manufacturing the convenient victories his prefect craved. Three months that had given him an unexpected gift.

Her first letter arrived with a merchant caravan, tucked inside a shipment of legal documents bound for the garrison. She had wrapped it in a contract dispute; anyone inspecting it would see only routine correspondence between a scribe and a Roman officer who had witnessed the transaction.

The cat has claimed your chair. She sleeps there every afternoon, as if waiting. I tell her you are not coming back. She does not believe me.

I found a text you would like. Zeno on motion and the infinite. How we move through infinite points yet still arrive. Made me think of your work. Made me think of us.

Write when you can. I am patient. I have learned patience from the documents that outlast the men who sign them.

Marcus read the letter three times before burning it. The words stayed with him longer than the flames.

In Tizwit, two children were learning to think as one. In Volubilis, a woman who understood impossible games waited for letters he should not send.

And in Caesarea, Marcus returned to the work that never ended, corrupting Nerva's archive one careful misdirection at a time under a prefect too impatient to notice, protecting a family that would never know his name, sustained by the knowledge that someone, somewhere, saw him clearly and did not look away.

❧✦❧

Two days after the game demonstration, evening

The settlement had quieted into its after-supper calm, fires burning low, the day's work finished. Amara sat at the spring in the blue dusk. The toad was on its rock: broad as a hand, grey as the stone beneath it, patient as it had always been. It had been there when she arrived. It would be there when she left.

Tiziri appeared beside her without announcement, the way she always did, and sat.

They watched the toad together. This had become one of their habits: the spring in the evening, the toad doing nothing, neither of them finding this anything less than satisfying.

"I have been thinking," Tiziri said.

"About what?"

"About you and the toad." She studied the creature on its rock with her characteristic focused attention. "I have been watching it for two years. Since I first pointed it out to you."

"I know. You watch everything."

"I watch useful things," Tiziri corrected. "And I have noticed the toad is always here when you are here. And when you sit beside it, you become more like yourself." She paused. "Less like everyone else you have been carrying around all day. More like Amara."

Amara looked at the toad. The evening light had turned its grey-brown skin amber, almost.

"I think it is yours," Tiziri said. "The agurram — the toad, the holy one." She looked at the creature on its rock. "It is always here when you are here. And you are always here. I think that means something."

Amara looked at the agurram. In Tamazight the word held both: the desert toad that belonged so completely to its place that it became the place, and the holy man whose authority needed no announcement. Grandmother Menna had told her this once, at the spring, in a teaching she had not understood until now. The agurram — the toad, the holy one, the same word for both — sat where it always sat, broad and still as a hand laid flat, indifferent to being named. She belonged to it, in some way she could feel without being able to name.

"In the old teaching," Amara said, "Menna says every person has a spirit-kin in the living world. An animal whose nature speaks to theirs."

"Yes." Tiziri nodded. "My grandmother called it the amayas. The companion-spirit." She looked at the toad. "Your agurram has been sitting on that rock waiting for you to notice it for two years."

Amara felt the truth of this settle through her, settling into recognition rather than arriving. She had been walking past this creature every morning for two years, the faint pull of it familiar without a name.

"It is so still," she said. "And it disappears into the rock. And when the eagle passes..." She stopped.

"What eagle?"

"There was an eagle. In the early rains, here at the water. The shadow passed over and the agurram did not move and I could not find its edges against the stone." She pressed her hand to her chest. "For a moment I felt it. What it feels. Or what it does not feel. The completeness of being exactly what you are in the place you belong."

Tiziri watched her with the desert fox's attention.

"Eudoxus would call it the practice," Amara said. "But the agurram has never practiced anything in its life."

"That," Tiziri said, "is why it is better at it than you."

Amara laughed. The agurram, indifferent to the compliment, shifted its weight by perhaps a finger's width and was still again.

"So," Tiziri said. "You are the agurram. I have always known this. I just did not have the word for it until now."

"You have known since you were five years old?"

"I knew you were like it. You sit here and the agurram sits there and neither of you is trying to be anything. Everyone else tries. You just are." She paused. "The agurram does not stop being an agurram when the rain comes. It just gets wet."

Amara looked at her cousin, this girl who had watched her for six years with the desert fox's quiet, precise attention, who had seen the truth about her before she could see it herself.

"You," Amara said. "I have a name for you."

Tiziri waited.

"I have felt it since the first time you sat beside me at this spring. The way you find things. Me, at this spring. The agurram before I saw it. The true thing in a room before anyone else has finished talking." Amara met her eyes. "The afennek. The desert fox."

Tiziri blinked. This was, for Tiziri, the equivalent of dropping something. "The afennek."

"The ears that miss nothing. The step that leaves no tracks. The one that finds what the desert hides." Amara watched her cousin absorb this. "You found me at this spring six years ago. You found the agurram before I did. You find the true thing in every room before anyone else has finished speaking."

Tiziri was quiet for a moment. "That is either a compliment or an accusation."

"Both," Amara said. "Usually."

The smaller, steadier smile. "The afennek," Tiziri said again. Then: "Yes. That is right." She said it the way she said all true things: without performance, as simple acknowledgment. She looked at the agurram. The agurram looked at the spring. "The agurram and the afennek."

"At a spring in the desert," Amara said. "Where else."

Footsteps on the path behind them. They both knew without looking.

Juba dropped onto the rock beside his sister with Malik's warrior economy, efficient and unhurried. He looked at them both, at their expressions, and narrowed his eyes.

"What?"

"Nothing," Amara said.

"You are both looking at that toad as though it had spoken."

"The agurram does not speak," Tiziri said. "That is part of its wisdom."

Juba looked at the toad. The agurram regarded him with complete indifference.

"We were talking about amayas," Amara said. "Companion-spirits."

"I know what amayas are." He settled more comfortably on the rock. "Grandmother Menna talked about them at the ceremony last month." He paused. "What is yours?"

"The agurram."

He looked at it. Looked at his sister. "Yes," he said, with ten years of watching her at springs behind him. "That is exactly right."

Warmth moved through her at that: the twin bond, older than language, confirming what Tiziri had named.

"And Tiziri's is the afennek," Amara said. "The desert fox."

Juba looked at Tiziri, who met his gaze with her characteristic directness. "Also yes," he said. "Obvious, once you say it." He looked back at the spring. "What is mine?"

The two girls looked at each other.

Tiziri opened her mouth.

"Wait," Juba said. He had clearly registered the speed of that exchange. "Why do you already know?"

"We do not know," Amara said. "We have a strong feeling."

"Based on what?"

"Based on six years of watching you," Tiziri said, "walk directly at things any sensible creature would walk around."

Juba's eyes narrowed further. "What creature."

"The honey badger," Tiziri said.

Silence.

"The honey badger," Juba repeated.

"It attacks things much larger than itself," Tiziri said, presenting her evidence. "It does not accept the odds apply to it. You can knock it down and it gets up and tries again without apparent rancor, as though being knocked down is information rather than defeat." She paused. "When Decimus's soldier put you on your knees, you got up, walked to the eastern wall, and immediately began planning. That is the honey badger."

Juba looked at his sister. "Is this your doing?"

"Tiziri named it," Amara said. "I confirmed it."

"The honey badger," he said again, turning it over. "It is not exactly..."

"Dignified?" Tiziri offered.

"I was going to say majestic."

"No," Tiziri agreed. "It is persistent, fearless, impossible to discourage, and certain of itself in situations where certainty is not warranted." She looked at him. "You can be majestic. The honey badger does not bother. It is too busy getting back up."

Another silence. The agurram shifted its weight again, minimally. The spring ran on.

"Fine," Juba said. "The honey badger." He stood, brushed off his hands, jaw set, absorbing an accurate truth he had not entirely wanted. "I am going to tell people mine is the lion."

"You can tell people whatever you like," Tiziri said. "Aghilas n tazart," she added.

Juba went still. The lion of the garden. The name the Imazighen gave the honey badger: for the way it fought above its weight, for the way it rose without rancor, for the way it was utterly certain of itself in circumstances that did not warrant certainty.

"That is better," he said.

"It is exactly the same thing," Tiziri said.

He walked back toward the settlement. They watched him go.

"He will think about it for three days," Amara said.

"And come back and say we were right," Tiziri agreed.

The agurram sat on its rock. The desert fox's ears turned toward the settlement's evening sounds. The spring ran between them, asking nothing of anyone who drank from it.

CHAPTER 35
Ululation

"The blood that flows without wound is not pollution but proof: she is connected to forces older than any kingdom."

—From the teachings of Tanit's daughters

Late Spring 50 CE—Tizwit

Grandmother Menna came upon Amara by the sacred spring at dawn, the girl's face troubled after another night of overwhelming dreams.

"You carry too much." Menna settled beside her with the careful movements of great age. "I see it in how you hold your shoulders. As though you are bracing against a wind only you can feel."

"Eudoxus is teaching me to watch feelings like clouds. To let them pass."

"Eudoxus teaches the scholar's way. Observation. Distance. Naming." Menna's voice held no criticism, only distinction. "There is another way. The women's way. Would you like to learn it?"

Amara looked at her, this ancient woman who had outlived husbands and children, who led ceremonies and blessed births, whose authority in spiritual matters rivaled even Eudoxus's.

"What is different about it?"

"The scholar watches from outside. Names what he sees. Builds understanding through separation: this is me, that is the feeling, I observe it from here." Menna picked up a handful of sand and let it run through her fingers. "The women's way is different. We do not stand apart. We become the vessel."

"I do not understand."

"When a woman carries a child, she does not observe the child from outside. The child is within her. Part of her. She holds it without grasping, carries it without controlling." Menna's weathered hand found Amara's. "Your gift floods you with others' feelings. The scholar's way teaches you to build walls, to watch from safety. The women's way teaches you to become large enough to hold what comes, without the holding destroying you."

"How?"

"Through the body. Through breath. Through knowing that you are not separate from what you carry, but you are larger than it." Menna closed her eyes. "Breathe with me. Do not push the feelings away. Make room for them."

They breathed together in the dawn light. Amara felt the familiar pressure of ambient emotions: the community waking, worries and hopes and the small griefs of ordinary life.

"Now." Menna's voice dropped to nearly a whisper. "Instead of watching them like clouds, imagine you are the sky. The clouds are within you. Part of you. But you are vast, and they are small."

Amara's sense of herself expanded. She was not a small girl buffeted by others' emotions. She was the space in which those emotions moved.

"The sky does not fight the clouds." Menna's words came slow and steady. "It does not build walls against them. It is, and they pass through. This is the women's way. Spaciousness."

"It feels... different. Softer."

"Eudoxus's way will serve you well. The discipline of watching, naming, keeping yourself clear. But there will be times when that way fails. When the feelings are too strong, or when they come all at once. In those moments, remember this. You can become the vessel instead of the watcher. You can hold without being destroyed, carry without being crushed."

Amara opened her eyes. The morning felt more spacious.

"Why do you not teach this to everyone?"

Menna smiled. "Some wisdom passes only between those ready to receive it. Eudoxus teaches you separation, clarity, naming. That is the father's way. I teach you holding, carrying, making space. That is the mother's way. You will need both. Every woman does."

She rose, her old bones creaking. "Practice this when the scholar's way is not enough. When you need to hold more than you can watch. The sky does not run out of room for clouds. Neither will you."

She walked back toward the settlement, leaving Amara by the spring with a new understanding: that there was more than one path to wisdom, and that the women of her community held teachings the scholars had never learned to name.

Three months later

Amara had practiced Menna's teaching through the autumn and into winter. She became the sky rather than fighting the clouds. She made space rather than building walls. She did not know then that the goddess was preparing her for what she could not yet anticipate.

She had been waiting for months. She had watched Tiziri's ceremony two seasons ago: the procession through the settlement, the tattooing, the feast afterward. She had seen how Tiziri walked differently after, how the women spoke to her as one of them rather than as a child. Even then, she had felt a fierce longing to cross that threshold.

So when the cramping woke her before dawn and she felt the unfamiliar wetness between her legs, she knew.

"Yemma." She kept her voice calm, though her heart raced. "It has come."

Zahra was beside her in moments. In the darkness, Amara could not see her mother's face, but she felt the joy in her embrace.

"My daughter." Zahra kissed her forehead. "Today you become a woman."

Within the hour, the news had spread through the settlement, called from dwelling to dwelling with celebration. The first ululation pierced the pre-dawn air, that high wavering cry Amara had heard at weddings and births, and soon others joined it, the sound rippling outward through Tizwit like rings in water.

Silina arrived with herbs for the cramping, and Amara drank the bitter tisane gratefully while her mother braided her hair with special care.

"You know what comes today," Zahra said as she worked. "You have seen the ceremonies."

"I know." Amara memorized every detail of Tiziri's passage. "But knowing and experiencing are different things."

"They are." Zahra's hands paused in her hair. "There is something I want you to understand first. About how different peoples see this moment."

She told Amara then about her own first blood in the palace at Iol Caesarea, about the Greek physician's warnings of pollution and contamination. About the monthly cloths and the shame.

"They taught me that my body's natural workings made me dirty," Zahra said. "That I should hide this, avoid sacred spaces until I was clean again. The Romans believe menstrual blood can blight crops, kill bees, drive dogs mad."

"But that is..." Amara struggled to find words for the wrongness of it.

"The Roman way is to fear what they cannot control." Zahra turned her daughter to face her. "Today you will learn a different truth, one your father's people have carried since before Rome existed. Remember both. Understand what we resist when we celebrate what they call shameful."

❧✦❧

While Zahra and her daughter spoke, word spread among the women of the settlement. The excitement was palpable.

Grandmother Menna arrived with a procession of elder women, their faces painted with ochre symbols: crescents and triangles that Amara recognized as sacred marks of Tanit, Mother of All. They carried the ceremonial blanket between them, the same one that had borne Tiziri and countless girls before her.

"The ancestors welcome you." Menna's voice carried the weight of ceremony. "Mother Tanit turns her face toward you today. Your body has begun its sacred work."

Silina knelt before her with the clay pot of indigo paste and thin bone needles. "Your mark," she said. "The sign you will carry for the rest of your life."

Most women in the settlement wore the vertical line on the chin. But Silina showed her a different design, one she had seen only on Menna and two of the oldest elders: a small triangle with a circle above it and a horizontal line between, to be placed just below her lower lip.

"The Sign of Tanit," Silina explained. "The Mother with her arms raised in blessing. Only certain girls receive this mark. Those born under specific signs. Those the elders believe carry special connection to the goddess." She glanced at Menna, who nodded. "You are one of these."

The tattooing began as the sun crested the eastern hills. The pain was sharp and constant, the needles pricking again and again as Silina worked the indigo into Amara's skin. Amara focused on her breathing, on Menna's voice reciting the ancient invocations.

"Mother Tanit, Lady of the Moon, Keeper of the Fertile Waters, we bring before you a daughter of the people. Her blood flows for the first time. Her body opens to the mystery you have guarded since the first woman walked the earth."

As Menna spoke, the ululations swelled around her, wave after wave, the women of Tizwit answering the invocation the way the desert answers rain. Amara closed her eyes and let the sound hold her.

"We ask your blessing upon this daughter," Menna continued. "Mark her as your own. Let her carry your sign with pride. Let her know that the blood flowing from her body is sacred: the blood of potential life, the blood of creation itself."

The air around her shifted. The women present felt it too; Amara saw their eyes widen, saw Menna's voice falter for just a moment before she recovered and continued. A presence had entered the circle. Unmistakable.

You are seen. You are claimed. You are blessed.

The knowing settled into Amara's bones.

Menna completed the invocation with tears streaming down her weathered cheeks. The elder women broke into ululation, different from the joyful cries at dawn. This sound was lower, more reverent: the ancient call used only when the divine made itself known.

"Mother Tanit has answered. She has blessed this daughter herself." Menna took Amara's face in her hands. "This has not happened in my lifetime. Perhaps not in my mother's. The goddess sees something in you, child. Something worthy of her direct attention."

Silina completed the tattoo in reverent silence. When she sat back, Amara's chin throbbed with sacred pain: the vertical line, and above it, the small but unmistakable Sign of Tanit.

Then came the procession.

Six elder women lifted Amara onto the ceremonial blanket and raised her above their shoulders. She gasped, looking down at the entire settlement. Everyone had gathered in the morning light to see one of their daughters cross into womanhood.

They carried her in a slow circuit through Tizwit, the women singing songs Amara had heard all her life without fully understanding. At each dwelling they passed, women emerged to add their voices, songs and ululations interweaving, the high wavering cries punctuating the verses like exclamation marks of joy.

The blood that flows is the blood of creation
The pain that comes is the pain of power
Mother Tanit blesses her daughters
We who carry life are sacred

As she passed, women reached up to touch the edge of the blanket: a blessing, a welcome, an acknowledgment that she had joined their ranks. Amara saw Zahra walking beside the procession, weeping openly with joy. Saw Silina and Menna leading the singers. Saw the mothers of her friends, the grandmothers, the ancient women whose names she barely knew, all of them reaching for her, all of them welcoming her into a vast and eternal sisterhood.

Juba stood at the edge of the crowd, uncertain of his place in this women's mystery. But when their eyes met, he raised his fist in salute: pride for his sister, even if he could not fully understand what she was becoming.

Eudoxus stood apart from the other men, watching the procession wind through the settlement. He had seen coming-of-age rituals across three continents: the hushed, apologetic acknowledgments in Greek households, the Persian purification rites that separated girls from their families, the Roman matrons who taught their daughters to speak of such things only in whispers, if at all.

He had never seen ululation.

The sound rose from the women like birdsong at dawn, joyful and unapologetic. The elder women carried Amara above their shoulders as though she were a queen returning from victory. Their faces held no trace of the grim duty he had observed in other traditions, no sense that they were managing an unfortunate biological reality. They were celebrating.

Menna led the singers, her ancient voice carrying words Eudoxus could not fully understand but whose meaning was unmistakable. Power. Blessing. Sacred.

A young mother emerged from her dwelling to touch the ceremonial blanket, her infant balanced on her hip. An old woman, bent nearly double with age, straightened her spine to add her voice to the song. Girls too young to understand watched with wide eyes, already absorbing what their bodies would someday prove: that this moment was not shame to be hidden but honor to be proclaimed.

Eudoxus thought of the Greek physicians who wrote learned treatises on menstrual pollution, the Roman senators who forbade women in their time from touching sacred objects. How certain they were. How afraid.

These women were not afraid of anything.

The procession ended at the sacred spring, where the women lowered Amara gently to the ground. Here, where water emerged from stone, the final blessing was given. Tanit's element, the life-giving stream.

Menna dipped her fingers in the spring water and traced symbols on Amara's forehead, her cheeks, her hands.

"You are marked by Tanit's sign. You are blessed by Tanit's presence. You carry now the sacred mystery that the Romans call pollution and we call power." She held Amara's gaze with fierce intensity. "Never let anyone teach you shame for what the goddess herself has blessed. Your blood is holy. Your body is sacred. You are a daughter of Tanit, and you will walk in her protection all your days."

The ululation that followed rose from every woman at once, a sound that filled the morning air and echoed off the rocks surrounding the spring, the land itself celebrating.

The feast lasted until evening. Women shared stories of their own first blood, their own ceremonies, their own moments of feeling Tanit's presence. The men held their own celebration elsewhere. This was women's time, women's mystery, women's joy.

As the sun set, Amara sat with Menna apart from the others. Her chin throbbed, the new tattoo still raw beneath its protective salve. The warmth in her chest had settled into a permanence she had not known existed until today.

"What I felt during the ceremony," she said. "Was that really..."

"Tanit herself? Yes." Menna's voice held wonder. "I have led these ceremonies for forty years. I have asked for the goddess's blessing countless times. She has never answered so directly." The old woman studied Amara's face. "You carry something, child. The goddess recognizes it. It calls to her."

"The Romans fear what they cannot control," Menna continued. "They look at women's bodies and see threat. They look at our blood and see contamination. Tanit knows what they have forgotten: that the power to create life is the greatest power there is. Those who carry it are blessed beyond measure."

✦

In the days that followed, Amara noticed the changes Silina had predicted.

The mark on her chin healed slowly, the Sign of Tanit becoming a permanent part of her face. When she looked in the bronze mirror, she saw what Menna had meant. She was marked, claimed, blessed. By power. By sacred mystery.

She was learning that wisdom came from many teachers. Eudoxus showed her the scholar's way. Menna showed her the women's way. Silina showed her the healer's way.

Her awareness of others' emotions had always been keen, but now it came with a deeper patience, a willingness to sit with what she felt rather than reaching to change it. Perhaps this was what Menna had meant about the women's way. Perhaps this was what the goddess had blessed.

She was becoming herself. All of her selves. And she carried the proof of it on her face for all to see.

CHAPTER 36

The Trading Family

"First love arrives like weather.
It changes everything and explains nothing."
—Numidian proverb on youth
Late Spring 51 CE—Tizwit

The trading family arrived just after the spring rains, their caravan impressive even by the standards of seasonal gatherings: twelve camels, guards in matching tunics, goods covered in oiled cloth that spoke of expensive cargo. The father, Urghen ibn Massin, displayed Roman trade permits prominently, the kind that cost more than most families saw in a lifetime.

"Pragmatists," Yasir murmured to Zahra, watching them establish camp. "The kind who survive by bending with whoever holds power."

Among them was Adah. Twelve years old, with the kind of beauty that would only grow more dangerous with age: honey-colored eyes, skin like polished amber, and a laugh that made everyone within hearing want to join in. But it was her confidence that set her apart, the way she moved through the world, the world arranged for her pleasure.

Juba saw her arguing with a guard about the proper way to hobble camels, her voice carrying across the camp with absolute authority despite her age. The guard, a grown man with scars marking him as a veteran of real conflicts, backed down.

"She is magnificent," Hassan whispered beside him.

"She is trouble." Juba's eyes never left her.

When their gazes met across the evening fire, she smiled, a direct challenge. She walked over without invitation and sat beside them as if she had known them for years.

"You are the twins everyone whispers about," she said in Latin.

"Everyone whispers about many things," Juba replied in Tamazight.

"True. But they whisper about you with fear. That is interesting." She studied him with those remarkable eyes. "I like interesting."

Within a week, they were meeting in secret. No one had forbidden their meeting. At eleven and twelve, they were still considered children. But secrecy made it feel important.

They met at the abandoned shepherd's shelter a mile from the settlement, halfway between Tizwit and her family's extended camp. Adah brought dates stuffed with almonds, a luxury Juba had rarely tasted. He brought her smooth stones from the sacred spring, each one chosen for its unique pattern.

"My father wants Roman citizenship," she told him one afternoon, lying on her back watching clouds. She had switched to Latin. "He says it is the future. Protection, trade rights, legal standing. Everything the tribes lack."

Juba responded in Tamazight. "Rome is the enemy."

"Rome is the power," she corrected, still in Latin. "Fighting them is like fighting the desert. You can resist for a while, but eventually you adapt or die."

"My father did not adapt."

"Your father died."

The words should have made him angry, but the way she said them, matter of fact, without cruelty, made them feel like simple truth.

She rolled onto her side to face him and switched to Tamazight. "Tell me about him. Not the legend everyone knows. The real man."

So Juba did, moving between Latin and Tamazight as he searched for words. He talked about memories he was not sure were real or constructed from others' stories. The smell of leather and horses. Large hands that could hold his entire body. A voice that rumbled like distant thunder. As he spoke, Adah moved closer, until her head rested on his shoulder.

"You have his courage," she whispered in Latin.

"How do you know?"

"Because you are here with me, knowing your mother would forbid it if she knew. That takes courage."

She kissed him then, quick and light, but it changed everything. The world reorganized itself around that single point of contact.

❧✦❧

Two weeks later

The afternoon heat shimmered off the rocks surrounding Tizwit's central oasis. Juba sat cross-legged in the shade of their family's tent, his wooden carving knife moving in sharp, jerky strokes against a game piece. Wood shavings scattered around him like discarded thoughts.

Amara watched her brother from across their small workspace, her own carving forgotten in her lap. Juba's shoulders hunched forward with each cut, his jaw tight with frustration that had nothing to do with woodworking.

"You are going to split it if you keep cutting like that."

Juba's knife stilled. "I am being careful."

"Your hands are being careful. Your feelings are angry."

He looked up, surprised.

"How do you always know?"

He set down the knife.

"Your face gets tight around your eyes. And your breathing changes." She tilted her head, studying him. "You are thinking about her again."

Juba's hands clenched. "What if I am?"

"Then maybe we should talk about it instead of pretending you are working on game pieces."

For a moment he looked as though he might deny it. Then his shoulders sagged. "I cannot stop thinking about her, Amara. When I am with Adah, everything makes sense. When I am not..." He gestured at the scattered wood shavings. "Nothing feels important."

"But you barely get to see her. Her family does not approve of ours."

"That is what makes it so hard." Juba's voice dropped to barely above a whisper. "We meet sometimes, when the adults are not watching. She listens to me. I am already grown up. My thoughts matter."

Amara set down her own carving and moved closer. In the months since they had learned to work together instead of competing, she had discovered that her brother needed different things at different times. Sometimes he needed challenge. Sometimes he just needed someone to listen.

"What do you talk about?"

"Everything. Learning, traditions, what we think about the world. She asks questions the way Eudoxus does, but..." He struggled for words. "When she asks them, it feels like she wants to know what I think. Not like she is testing whether I am smart enough."

"And that makes you happy."

"Yes. But it also makes me..." He stopped.

"Scared?"

"Maybe. What if her father is right? What if caring about each other is wrong because our families are too different?"

Before Amara could respond, Silina appeared at the tent opening, her arms full of water jugs. Drops of water darkened the sand at her feet, and her headwrap was damp with sweat from the walk to the main spring.

"Deep thoughts for such a hot afternoon." She settled the jugs in the shade. Her sharp eyes took in Juba's abandoned carving and the scattered shavings. "What is troubling you both?"

The twins exchanged glances. They had learned to trust Silina, but this felt too fragile to share with adults.

"Nothing important."

Silina crouched to their eye level. "Important enough to stop you from working. Important enough to make Amara leave her own project to worry about you." She reached out and touched one of Juba's clenched hands. "What is it?"

After a moment of silent communication between the twins, Amara spoke. "Juba cares about someone whose family does not approve of ours. We are trying to figure out what to do about it."

Silina's expression grew serious. "Ah. The girl from the trading families."

Juba's face flushed. "How did you..."

"Eyes, child. And watching how both of you light up when certain tents appear at gatherings, then grow quiet when they keep their distance." She settled cross-legged, joining their circle. "These are dangerous waters."

"I know. But what if we could show them that caring about each other makes us want to do good things?"

"What kind of good things?"

"When I think about Adah being proud of me, I try harder at everything. I want to learn more, understand more, be someone worthy of..." He stopped, embarrassed.

"Worthy of her attention," Silina finished gently.

"Yes."

Amara leaned forward. "But are you trying to be better because love makes you want to grow, or because you are afraid she will stop caring if you are not perfect?"

Neither of them spoke. It was the kind of distinction Eudoxus taught them to make. They were looking beneath surface motivations to understand what drove their choices.

"Maybe both?"

"Then you need to figure out which one is stronger. Because if you are mostly afraid, that is going to make you do frightened things. But if you mostly want to grow, that is going to make you do growing things."

"Where is Adah now?"

"By the water pool with her grandmother. They spin wool in the afternoons."

"Then perhaps it is time for a proper conversation. All three of you together, where everything can be said plainly."

❧✦❧

Later that afternoon

They found Adah by the largest pool, her feet dangling in the cool water while she sorted wool for spinning. But when she looked up at their approach, her eyes were red-rimmed with tears, and her small hands clenched the wool.

"Adah? What is wrong?" Alarm filled Juba's voice.

She glanced around, then stood and walked toward a more secluded spot behind a stand of date palms. They followed, Amara noting the tension in the older girl's shoulders.

"My father has been meeting with the Banu Hillal families," Adah said, once they were out of sight. "He is discussing my future."

"Your future?"

"Marriage arrangements." She whispered the words. "I am twelve now. Old enough to be promised, he says. The formal agreement will be signed before winter."

Juba went rigid. "But you are just..."

"Just what? Just a girl whose family needs political alliances?" Bitterness crept into her voice. "I do not want to marry someone I do not know, but what I want does not matter."

Juba reached for her hand. "It matters to me."

She did not pull away. Their fingers intertwined as they stood together in the shade of the palms, the familiar comfort of their friendship charged now with an intensity none of them could name.

"I do not want to marry someone else."

"I do not want you to." Juba's voice was barely audible.

Amara read the emotions flowing between them, far beyond the childhood affection she had expected.

"Maybe we could find a way to show your family that what you feel for each other serves your families instead of threatening them."

"How?" Hope flickered in Adah's voice.

"I do not know yet. But what if we could prove that caring about each other makes you both better people? More respectful, more helpful to your communities?"

"My grandmother might listen. She has been asking questions about your mother's leadership, about your teacher's weather predictions. She notices results."

They talked until the sun sank toward the western horizon. But underneath their practical discussion, Amara sensed currents she did not understand, a pull between Juba and Adah that strengthened as the afternoon wore on.

"I should go back. My grandmother will be looking for me."

But she did not move. She and Juba stood looking at each other in the fading light, and an understanding passed between them that made Amara feel like an intruder.

"I will wait by the tents." She sensed they needed privacy for whatever was happening.

❧✦❧

Three months later

Their relationship had deepened into a realm neither quite understood. Too young for the full intensity of adult emotion, too mature for childhood's simple affections, they existed in a liminal space where everything felt both eternal and impossibly fragile.

Amara knew, of course. Her perceptiveness made secrets impossible.

"She glows when she thinks of you," Amara told her brother. "But there is a shadow underneath the light. Be careful."

"You are always warning me about shadows." Juba kicked at a pebble. "Maybe some shadows are worth it."

"Maybe. But this one has sharp edges."

The night everything changed began with joy. The midsummer celebration, three months into their secret romance. Dancing, music, the boundaries between camps dissolved in festivity. Adah pulled him into the dancing circle without caring who saw, and for a moment Juba felt what life could be: open, unashamed, free.

They slipped away as the moon rose, intoxicated by possibility more than the weak wine the adults had allowed them. The shepherd's shelter felt different that night. Charged. Waiting.

What happened next was inevitable and impossible, sacred and terrifying. Two young people discovering a threshold neither fully understood, guided by instinct and overwhelming need. Afterward, they lay entwined, sweat cooling in the desert air, trying to comprehend what they had crossed into.

"I love you," Juba whispered in Tamazight. The words felt both too small and too large.

"I love you too," she replied in Latin. "But..."

"But?"

"My father is taking contracts in Hispania. We leave in three days. I tried to tell you before, but I could not find the words."

The world ended. Began. Ended again.

"Three days?"

"He says there is no future here. That the rebellion is over, Rome has won, and we either adapt or starve. He is right, Juba. He is always right about these things."

"Then come with me. We will hide. We will find a way."

"And live how? On what? You are eleven. I am twelve. We are children pretending to be adults."

He gestured helplessly at their tangled bodies. "We just..."

"I know. But one moment does not make us ready for a lifetime."

They held each other as the moon traced its arc across the sky, both understanding that dawn would separate them forever, neither brave enough to say it aloud.

❧✦❧

Adah's family left before sunrise, taking advantage of the cool morning air. Juba stood on the ridge above Tizwit, watching their caravan disappear into the eastern desert, carrying with it the first person outside his family who had seen him as he truly was.

Amara came to him hours later. He was still watching the empty horizon.

"I am sorry."

"You warned me. You said there were sharp edges."

"That does not make it hurt less."

They sat together in the growing heat, twins who had lost so much already, learning that some losses cut deeper because they arrived wrapped in joy.

"I will find her again," Juba said at last. "Someday, when I am old enough to make my own choices, I will find her."

CHAPTER 37
The Shape of the Desert

"The gathering fire burns brightest when many hands carry wood."
—Desert saying on community
Autumn 51 CE—Tizwit

The desert had shaped them all. Juba, now eleven, carried the lean strength that came from years of training with Malik's warriors and a hardness born of having crawled before Romans. Amara, quick-moving like her mother, carried the quiet authority that came naturally to one who could read the emotional currents of every person in a room, though the three days of absorbing Roman contempt during Decimus's patrol had left shadows that would not fade.

Zahra's leadership had evolved through seven years since Aedemon's death into authority that emerged from collaboration rather than dominance. But even her patient wisdom struggled to heal what the prefect's inspections had revealed.

"Another family leaving." Yasir reported the news during the morning council. The Banu Kassim, who lived at Tizwit for three generations, had announced their departure for the coast.

"Because of us." Amara spoke from her place at the circle's edge. At eleven, she attended council meetings, though she rarely spoke.

"Because of fear." Zahra corrected gently. "Fear makes people seek easier paths."

"Perhaps they are wise." Ouksem gestured toward the twins. "The Romans will return. They said as much. Those children interest them. They will keep coming until they solve their puzzle."

"Then we become a puzzle not worth solving." Zahra leaned forward. "We become so ordinary, so visible, so integrated into regional life that we disappear in plain sight."

The strategy she had been advocating for years now carried new urgency. The autumn gathering, already approaching, would be their first test.

✦

Caravans came from every direction, their dust trails visible for miles across the desert floor. This year brought caution rather than celebration. Word of the systematic Roman searches had spread through every settlement in the region.

Juba stood at the edge of the growing encampment, counting arrivals with the tactical awareness Malik taught him. Each delegation represented potential allies or threats.

"Forty-two camps so far." Amara appeared beside him. "Fewer than usual. People are afraid to gather in large numbers."

"Afraid of Romans or afraid of us?"

"Both." She studied her brother's profile, how the past months carved away his childhood softness. "The Banu Hillal are not coming this year. Or the coastal traders."

Juba's jaw tightened at the mention of traders. Urghen ibn Massin would never return.

"We need new allies. People who benefit from what we know, what we have learned about resistance without violence."

"You sound like Yemma."

"I sound like someone who is tired of being hunted."

Their mother moved between delegations with steady strides, explaining strategies to visiting leaders who leaned forward to catch every word. The collaborative methods Eudoxus had taught, the games that built cooperation instead of competition, the ways of defeating Roman law without spilling blood: all of it held value for communities struggling under occupation.

❧✦❧

On the third day of the gathering, as negotiations and celebrations mixed in the complex dance of desert diplomacy, a small caravan arrived from the north. Three camels and a handful of guards, but their leader's bearing commanded attention.

Marcus had sent warning through channels so indirect that even he could not trace them back to their source. A merchant who had never heard Marcus's name carried intelligence he did not know he carried, speaking of trade-route difficulties and shifting patrol patterns in ways that, when decoded by those who knew the system, meant: spring brings new dangers. Prepare alternate routes.

Yasir received the intelligence without acknowledging its source. Eight years of invisible protection had created its own language between them, and Marcus could still shape what reached them, even from a distance.

❧✦❧

That evening, the twins demonstrated the Rih al-Harb for the gathered delegations. The game had evolved from children's entertainment into a training tool for collaborative thinking and seeing problems from multiple angles at once.

"The wind does not fight the rocks." Amara moved pieces across the board. "It finds ways around them, through them, wearing them down over time."

"But sometimes the wind must be the storm." Juba positioned his pieces for a defensive formation that could turn offensive. "Sometimes wearing down takes too long."

They played with the fluid coordination of twins who had learned to think as one consciousness in two bodies. The delegates leaned forward, recognizing a kind of thinking that went beyond individual brilliance.

"How do they do that?" a visitor whispered. "It is as though they know each other's thoughts."

"Practice," Zahra answered, though she knew it was more than that. Amara's gift for reading emotional currents had taught both twins to communicate beyond words. Juba shielded his thoughts when his sister needed peace and opened them when she needed anchor points in the storm of others' feelings.

An elder from the eastern settlements stood. "This game. It teaches children to think like the resistance without calling it resistance."

"It teaches them to think." Eudoxus spoke from his seat. His body, weakened by years of managing with one functional hand and the lingering effects of fever, required support to stand, but his mind remained sharp. "Resistance is just one application."

The feast that followed the demonstration spread across the communal ground in the Amazigh fashion: enormous shared platters of couscous mounded with slow-cooked lamb, bowls of harissa sharp enough to clear the sinuses, roasted vegetables glazed with honey and cumin. Each settlement had contributed according to its specialty: the coastal families brought salted fish and preserved lemons; the mountain delegations offered goat cheese wrapped in fig leaves; the southern camps provided dates stuffed with almond paste, each one a jewel of patient craft.

People ate with their hands from the shared platters, the intimacy of communal eating serving its ancient purpose: you cannot plot against a man whose food you share. Juba noticed how the seating arranged itself. Former rivals were placed together by hosts who understood that breaking bread dissolved barriers that argument could not.

As darkness settled, the gathering's musicians took their places around the central fire. A man from the eastern settlements played a wooden flute whose high clear notes carried across the oasis like birdsong. Women from the host community brought out frame drums, the goatskin heads tuned by the fire's warmth, and began the driving rhythms that would carry the dancing until dawn. An old woman played a one-stringed instrument held upright on her knee, drawing from it a sound between weeping and singing that made the hair rise on Amara's arms.

The poetry came between the music, as it always did at gatherings. Elders stood to recite: praise songs for absent loved ones, sharp-edged satire aimed at Roman tax collectors, love poems so frank that the younger children were sent to bed before the best verses. A visiting poet performed an epic fragment about the old chariot wars, his voice rising and falling with the drums, and the crowd swayed with a rhythm older than memory.

Juba watched the poet with the tactical attention he brought to everything. Words as weapons. Stories as strategy. He filed the observation for later use.

✦

Late that night, as the gathering settled into sleep, Amara sat by the sacred spring trying to release the accumulated emotions of three hundred people celebrating, negotiating, hoping, fearing. The technique Eudoxus had taught, letting feelings flow through rather than stick, held better now, but large gatherings still overwhelmed her.

Juba came and sat beside her, skipping stones across the water with mechanical precision.

"You felt it too." She did not make it a question.

"Felt what?"

"The Romans. There are informants here. At least two. They are not hostile, just people who trade information for safety. But they are watching us."

Juba's hand went to the knife at his belt, the blade Malik had given him at his coming-of-age ceremony. "Who?"

"Does it matter? If we expose them, others will take their place. If we flee, we confirm Roman suspicions." She touched the water's surface and watched the ripples spread. "We are trapped in visibility."

"Then we use it." Juba spoke with sudden conviction. "If they are going to watch us, we give them what protects us by making us valuable."

"How?"

"We teach every settlement in Mauretania how to resist without fighting. How to make occupation so expensive, so exhausting, so unprofitable that Rome retreats without a single battle."

Amara looked at her brother with new understanding. The boy who had been forced to crawl before Romans had transformed that humiliation into strategy. He was thinking now as a leader who understood that the greatest victories came without drawn swords.

"That is a long game."

"We have time. We are eleven. If we live to thirty, that is nineteen years to build what Rome cannot destroy with legions."

"If we live."

"We will." Juba spoke with the certainty of youth tempered by premature wisdom. "Because we are learning to be weapons they do not know how to fight."

Above them, stars wheeled in their ancient patterns. Below, two children sat planning what would not look like revolution, a resistance that would not appear as resistance, a victory Rome would not recognize as defeat until it was already complete.

PART SIX: INHERITANCE

"We do not teach children what we know.
We teach them what we are still learning.
This is the only honest pedagogy."
—From the private writings of Caspar of Ecbatana

CHAPTER 38

Through the Storm

"The storm does not care who is ready. This is why we prepare."
—Amazigh weather wisdom
Early Winter 51 CE—Tizwit

The morning sky held a quality that made the older tribesmen study the horizon with worried eyes. Yasir stood at the edge of camp, watching the distant haze that marked the approach of weather from the deep desert.

"Storm coming." He turned to the men preparing for the day's work. "Not the season for it, but the signs are clear."

Juba stepped forward with the aggressive confidence that had marked him since Adah's departure, a hardness he wore like armor against a wound that had not healed.

"I can bring the sheep in from the far pasture, Uncle. I know the way, and I understand the warning signs you have taught us."

"The storm may move faster than expected." Yasir's tone balanced pride and caution. "Keep watch on the sky. At the first sign of serious wind, come straight back."

Juba nodded. Then: "I could handle both pastures. The eastern herd too. If we are worried about the storm, I could bring them all back in one sweep."

The men exchanged glances. Yasir frowned. "Two separate herds across that distance? In weather like this? That is work for three men, not one boy."

"I am not just one boy anymore." The words came out harder than Juba intended, but he did not soften them. "I have handled full herding responsibilities for months."

"Unnecessary risk." Idir spoke. "The eastern herd can shelter where they are."

Amara, watching from beside the family tent, sensed the familiar undertone beneath her brother's bravado: a desperate need to prove his worth that went beyond practical concerns. Since Adah's departure, he threw himself at challenges with a recklessness that frightened her. Where once his confidence had been natural, now it felt performed.

"Mother." She approached Zahra. "Juba should not go alone today."

Zahra glanced toward the darkening sky. "He is capable. And he needs to learn responsibility."

But as Juba set off toward the distant pasture, his figure shrinking into the heat shimmer, Amara's sense of wrongness only deepened. Every instinct she possessed warned her that today would bring danger.

❧✦❧

The sandstorm arrived with shocking speed, transforming from a distant threat to immediate crisis in less than an hour. What had been a dark line on the horizon became a towering wall of dust and wind that swallowed the light.

"Where is the boy?" Yasir shouted over the rising wind as the tribe scrambled to secure tents and protect animals.

Idir squinted into the murk. "Still at the far pasture. He should have seen this and headed back by now."

There was no sign of Juba or the sheep. The wall of sand bore down with inexorable force, and visibility dropped to nothing.

"I have to find him." Amara's voice carried a certainty that surprised even her.

Zahra caught her daughter's arm. "Absolutely not. We are not losing both of you to this storm."

"But I know where he is. I can feel him. He is frightened and hiding, but he is safe for now."

Yasir looked at the approaching storm, then at the girl. "The storm will hit in minutes. Even if you could find him, you would never make it back."

"I do not need to make it back. I just need to reach him. We can shelter together until it passes."

Before anyone could stop her, she ran.

The wind slammed into her, driving the breath from her lungs. Sand stung her face, forced its way into her nose and mouth despite the cloth she had wrapped around her head. The world reduced to brown chaos, a roar with no direction. She could not see more than an arm's length ahead, could not hear anything over the wind's howl.

But she could feel him.

The twin bond they had always shared, deeper than learned understanding, pulled her forward through the storm. A certainty beyond physical sensation guided her steps even when her eyes saw nothing.

There. She angled left, climbing over rocks she could not see but knew were there. Closer. The pull grew stronger.

She almost walked past the shallow cave before recognizing it: a depression where wind and water had carved a hollow beneath an overhang. Juba huddled inside, pressed against the back wall with his cloak pulled over his head. The sheep crowded around him, their bodies providing warmth and shelter.

"Amara?" His voice was hoarse from shouting into the wind. "How did you..."

"Later." She squeezed into the hollow beside him and pulled her cloak tight. "We are safe here. The storm will pass."

They pressed together with the sheep between them and the howling wind, two eleven-year-olds learning what it meant to trust each other completely, to have faith in gifts that defied explanation.

"I am sorry." Juba spoke after a long silence. "I was trying to prove... I put us both in danger."

"You were trying to show you are more than what her leaving made you feel."

"How do you always know?"

"Because I am your sister. Because I feel what you feel, even when you try to hide it."

The storm raged for hours. When it passed, leaving the world scoured clean and strangely quiet, they emerged to find search parties converging on their location. Zahra's relief came as anger that dissolved into tears as she held them both.

"Do not ever frighten me like that again."

"I am sorry, Yemma." Amara spoke for both. "But I knew where he was. I could feel it."

✦

That evening, as the community gathered to celebrate the twins' survival and mourn only minor losses, the story of Amara's rescue spread through camp. How she had walked straight through the storm to her brother. How she had known exactly where to find him despite seeing nothing.

Some whispered about gifts from the ancestor-spirits. Others dismissed it as coincidence. But Eudoxus, listening from his place by the fire, recognized a deeper pattern.

He approached the twins after the talk wound down.

"When you were in the storm together, what did you discover about yourselves?"

Juba thought before answering. "That I push myself too hard sometimes. That I want to prove things that do not need proving."

"And you, little hawk?"

"That sometimes knowing where to go is more important than knowing why you know."

Eudoxus nodded. "Juba, you discovered that vulnerability does not diminish you. It connects you to those who love you. And Amara, you learned to trust gifts you do not fully understand."

He paused, looking between them. "But there is another lesson here. You kept each other whole in the storm. By being present together. That is a rare thing, to see someone clearly and choose to stay."

The words settled over the twins like a blessing. They sensed they were given something to grow into.

As Juba and Amara moved toward the fire where their mother waited, Eudoxus remained where he was, watching them go.

He had thought of himself as the teacher and them as students. He had believed the teaching flowed one way. But tonight, watching Amara walk through a storm she could not see to find a brother she could only feel, he understood what he should have grasped long ago. He was not teaching them what he knew. He was teaching them what he himself still needed to learn.

He rose, his old bones protesting the cold ground, and followed his students toward the warmth of the fire. Halfway there, he paused. His hands hung at his sides, and for the first time in years, they were still. He flexed his fingers, turned his palms over, and stared at them in the firelight. The tremor returned after a moment, faint but persistent. But for those few seconds, his hands had been steady.

He did not know what to make of it. He filed it away alongside other things he could not yet explain and kept walking.

❧✦❧

That same night—Caesarea

Marcus stood in the garrison strategy room as Petronius consulted his tablets. The new prefect had inherited Nerva's archive and, unlike Nerva, possessed neither the patience nor the intellectual discipline to mine it properly. What Nerva had catalogued with methodical precision, Petronius treated as a resource to be plundered for quick results.

"Forty settlements across three provinces." Petronius's stylus moved down the column of names. "Centurion Octavius will lead the operation. Fresh teams, no local connections, standardized inspection protocols."

Marcus listened as Petronius read through the settlements, his expression neutral. Then he heard it: a name barely worth noting, a small community on the edge of the desert.

Tizwit.

"The timeline?" Marcus asked.

"Octavius departs in three days. He will work north to south, systematic coverage." Petronius consulted another tablet. "The highland settlements." He tapped the wax where Tizwit appeared in the list. "Within ten days. Perhaps twelve if weather delays them."

Ten days before Octavius reached the southern settlements. A coded message could move faster than a military column, one rider, changing horses, and no equipment to slow him. Three days to reach Madi. One hard day for Madi to send word ahead through the desert network. The community would have perhaps five or six days.

Enough. Barely.

No margin for error.

"A thorough operation," Marcus said. "The prefect has designed it well."

"Efficiency." Petronius was already making notations. "Consistent protocols eliminate variables. Whatever previous searches missed, this will find."

After Petronius departed, Marcus remained alone in the strategy room. The tablets, records of years of careful misdirection, lay on the table, Tizwit's name visible among dozens of others. Now a fresh-eyed centurion would see them with no reason to disregard what previous searches had been designed to miss.

The twins were eleven now. Old enough to be questioned. Old enough to remember their father. Old enough to break under interrogation.

Marcus returned the tablets to their case. He had perhaps an hour before his absence would be noted. An hour to ensure a certain trader received information about routes that had suddenly become inadvisable.

He moved toward the door, already composing the coded message that would reach Madi by morning. Three words that would set everything in motion: Fresh eyes coming.

CHAPTER 39
What Waited in the Dark

"What the earth hides, time reveals.
What time reveals, only wisdom can hold."
—Amazigh teaching on sacred objects

Early Spring 52 CE—Tizwit—Eight years after Aedemon's death

Darkness. The press of earth and root. The whisper of sand settling over leather, over metal, over stone depths.

For twelve years the talisman had rested beneath the ancient yew at the edge of the Tizwit oasis, its poisonous branches keeping the curious at a distance. Through the tree's roots it sensed the rhythms of life above: children growing, families grieving, the daily dance of a community that had no idea what waited in the earth below.

Then, gradually, a presence the talisman recognized. Chaotic, untrained, but with a capacity for connection it had been waiting to find. A child whose empathy opened channels between self and other, who drowned in emotions she could not yet understand.

The girl's confusion called to it. Her gift overwhelmed her, isolated her, chained her to others' suffering without offering the tools to transform that burden into purpose.

The talisman pulsed in its darkness, sending gentle waves upward through root and stone.

She was coming closer.

❧✦☙

Madi had arrived in time. The plan came together with desert efficiency: Juba and Amara would leave before dawn, the day the Romans were expected, taking enough supplies for four days. They would shelter at the old yew tree on the far edge of the oasis, a location familiar and safe but far enough from the settlement to fall outside any Roman inspection.

Zahra stayed awake all night, watching her children sleep, memorizing the sight of them peaceful and safe. In a few hours she would send them away. Because keeping them close meant risking everything.

"Yemma?" Amara whispered in the darkness. "Are you crying?"

"No, tasastinu." The lie caught in Zahra's throat. "Just thinking."

"About sending us away."

"Yes."

Amara sat up, and even in the dim pre-dawn light, Zahra could see the maturity in her daughter's face. Twelve years old but carrying understanding far beyond her years.

"We will be safe." Amara spoke with certainty. "I can feel that we need to go. Not just because of the Romans, but because..." She struggled for words. "The wadi is calling to me. I know how strange that sounds."

Zahra pulled her daughter close, trusting what she could not understand. Amara's perceptiveness had kept them safe before. Perhaps it would again.

Juba finished securing their packs: dried meat, water skins, blankets, flints for fire. Enough for four days, maybe five if they were careful. He checked each item twice.

"Ready?" He looked at Amara, who stood staring toward the wadi. She could already see their destination.

"Yes." Her voice carried strange certainty rather than fear. "We need to leave now. Before the sun rises."

They slipped from the settlement in the gray pre-dawn, following paths they had walked countless times during childhood play. The wadi lay a mile from Tizwit's center, a deep cut in the landscape where water ran during rare rains and children found secret places among the rocks.

Behind them, the settlement began preparing its own deception. Stories rehearsed, explanations ready, everything ordinary and unremarkable. By the time the Romans arrived, Tizwit would be exactly what it claimed: a simple farming community with nothing to hide.

"There." Juba pointed as they approached the ancient yew that grew at the wadi's heart. Its massive trunk loomed in the pre-dawn light, dark branches spreading overhead. "We can shelter in the root chamber. Remember? We played there when we were small, before Grandmother Menna told us the tree was poisonous."

"The Romans will not search a poisonous tree." Amara understood the logic even as the pull grew stronger. "That is why it is perfect."

But her attention had fixed on the tree with unsettling intensity. The pull she had felt since the messenger arrived strengthened with every step. Now it was almost overwhelming: a warmth in her chest that had nothing to do with exertion.

"Amara?" Juba noticed her distraction. "What is wrong?"

"Nothing is wrong." She moved toward the tree, drawn by invisible threads. "Everything is... right. Do you not feel it?"

"Feel what?"

"As though we are supposed to be here. As though this is where we needed to come."

Juba looked at his sister with concern. Her gift for reading emotional currents had always set her apart, but this seemed like a different order of perception. Still, they had no choice but to shelter here until the Roman inspection passed.

They made their way to the narrow cleft between boulders that opened into the chamber beneath the tree's roots. Juba had to squeeze through. He had grown since they last played here. But Amara slipped through easily, drawn forward by the pull that strengthened with each step.

The chamber was as they remembered: small, dark, protected by the tree's gnarled roots. Shafts of early morning light filtered through gaps above, creating patterns on the dusty floor. No offerings here, no signs of prayer or blessing. Just an empty space beneath a tree people avoided.

And there, near where the tree's oldest roots disappeared into the chamber floor, lay a metal box half-buried in sand.

"Look." Juba moved toward it. "Someone hid this here."

He brushed away the sand and lifted the lid. Inside lay a leather pouch, cracked and travel-stained. He opened it and frowned.

"Just old herbs. A healer's pouch, maybe. Silina might want them." He held it toward Amara. "Smell. Some of these might still be good."

Amara took the pouch. The moment her fingers closed around it, the warmth in her chest flared so strongly she nearly gasped. What Juba saw was dried leaves and powder. What Amara saw was a pendant: a round stone of deep blue lapis lazuli set in a frame of dark silver. Golden flecks glittered within the blue like scattered stars, and at the center, a spiral of fine gold lines radiated outward. Someone had captured the turning of the heavens in metal and stone.

The frame drew her attention. Geometric patterns circled the stone: diamonds and squares and angular symbols carved into the silver with precise care. She traced them with her finger, her breath catching.

She knew these shapes.

Tifinagh. The ancient script of her people, the letters Grandmother Menna taught her to read by firelight. But what were Amazigh letters doing on an object buried beneath a sacred tree, hidden in a metal box older than the settlement itself?

She tilted it toward the shaft of light filtering through the roots and sounded out the words circling the frame:

I am the One. You are the One.

The words resonated in her chest before her mind could parse them.

The warmth spread through her fingers and into her wrist, steady and deep, the way sun-baked rock held heat long after sunset. She turned the pendant over. The craftsmanship was extraordinary: the spiral at the center so fine it moved in the shifting light, the Tifinagh letters carved with a precision speaking of weeks or months of patient work. Whoever made this poured devotion into every line.

But Tifinagh was her people's script. And this object felt old. Older than the settlement, older than the tree, older perhaps than anything she had ever held. The contradiction sat in her mind like a knot she could not loosen: who carved Amazigh sacred letters onto an object that clearly came from somewhere else entirely?

"What is it?" Juba leaned closer, trying to see what held her so transfixed. "It is just dried herbs, Amara. Why are you looking at them like that?"

"Nothing," she said. "Just the smell. It reminds me of something."

She could not explain what she held. Juba saw herbs. She saw the heavens captured in stone and silver.

The words stirred in her chest. Not understanding, exactly. Recognition. As if the inscription described a truth she had always carried without possessing the language for it. The flood of everyone's feelings she had borne since earliest childhood, the constant drowning in others' pain and joy and fear, had always felt like affliction. Now, holding this pendant with its impossible Tifinagh letters, she sensed for the first time that her overwhelming connection to others might not be a curse at all. That it might be the very thing these words described.

I am the One. You are the One.

She could feel Juba's concern beside her, sharp and clear. But instead of being swept away by it, she held it alongside her own wonder, two feelings existing in the same space without one consuming the other. She looked at her brother and saw him for the first time: himself, whole and separate and irreducibly his own person. Separate from her. And that separateness, rather than being lonely, felt right.

"Amara?" Juba touched her arm. "You look strange. It is just herbs."

"I know." She closed her fingers around what he could not see. The warmth had not faded. If anything it deepened, settling into her palm the way a house bunting settles into a child's cupped hand. "But I think they were meant for us. Left here for a reason."

"Someone must have buried them. Silina, maybe. Or one of the old healers."

"Maybe."

She slipped the pendant beneath her tunic, pressing it flat against her chest where the fabric would hold it. The stone settled against her skin, warm and steady, its pulse falling into rhythm with her heartbeat. If anyone else looked, they would see a girl carrying a pouch of old herbs. The pendant would stay hidden, close to her body, where only she could feel what it was.

She did not tell Juba what she held. She did not tell him about the Tifinagh letters or the words circling the frame or the warmth spreading through her like a second heartbeat. She did not know why she kept it from him. The instinct to hold this close, to protect it from even her brother's eyes, arrived without explanation and settled in without asking permission.

It was the first secret she had ever kept from Juba. It would not be the last.

Juba watched her face. Something had shifted. The tightness she carried in her shoulders eased by a fraction, though he could not say why a pouch of old herbs would bring his sister peace. Whatever it was, she seemed lighter. That alone made it worth finding.

"We should show those herbs to Silina," he said. "When the Romans leave and we can go back."

"Yes," Amara said. But what she planned to show Eudoxus was not what Juba thought was in the pouch.

They settled against the roots to wait out the day. Juba dozed. Amara sat with her hand pressed against the stone beneath her tunic, feeling its warmth against her ribs, the inscription's words circling in her mind, strange and familiar at once, a riddle she would carry until she found the wisdom to solve it.

I am the One. You are the One.

She did not yet know what the words meant. But she knew, with a certainty deeper than reason, that she would spend the rest of her life learning.

Above them, the yew spread its ancient branches. Below them, the earth held its other secrets. And between skin and fabric, warm against a twelve-year-old girl's heart, the talisman rested at last where it had been waiting to rest for longer than anyone alive could remember.

It did not speak. It did not need to. The connection was made. Everything that followed would grow from this moment: the training and the power, the healing and the corruption, the setting aside and the return. All of it began here, in a root chamber beneath a sacred tree, with a girl holding a secret she could not explain from the one person she had never hidden anything from.

CHAPTER 40

The Body's Truth

"The same tree grows different branches.
This is not failure but design."
—Amazigh proverb on siblings

52 CE—Tizwit—The morning after Amara's discovery

Amara woke before dawn with a dull ache low in her belly. She lay still, trying to understand the sensation. Not illness. She knew illness from the epidemic that had swept through Tizwit two summers past, the hollow weakness and burning skin. This was different. A deep, rhythmic pressure, familiar now after nearly two years of monthly cycles, but never welcome.

The pendant she had discovered the day before rested warm against her chest where she had slept with it tucked beneath her shift. As the cramp tightened, the warmth flared with sudden intensity. She pressed her hand over it and felt the stone pulse beneath her palm, rapid and urgent, as if responding to the pain.

She shifted on her sleeping mat and felt wetness between her thighs.

The pendant grew hot, almost burning, stronger than anything she had felt from it since the moment she first held it in the root chamber. She did not know what to make of the reaction. She only knew the stone was responding to what was happening in her body with an intensity that startled her.

"Yemma." She kept her voice steady. "Mother."

❧✦❧

Zahra appeared within moments, lamp in hand. One look at Amara's face, another at the stained sleeping mat, and her expression shifted from alarm to recognition.

"Ah." She set down the lamp and knelt beside her daughter. "Your time has come again. I will fetch Silina for the herbs."

But Amara caught her mother's wrist. "The pendant. It reacted. It burned hot when the bleeding started, as if it was frightened."

Zahra studied her daughter's face. "Frightened?"

"I do not know what else to call it. It sensed the blood and the pain and it... flared. The way a person startles at a loud sound."

Zahra considered this. "Eudoxus told us the pendant came from Persia. Perhaps in all its long existence, it never had a bearer who bled."

The thought settled between them. Amara touched the cord at her throat. "Melchior would not have taught it what menstruation was. Eudoxus could not have."

"And now you will." Zahra took her daughter's hands. "Silina first. Then we send for Grandmother Menna. This moment belongs to the women who will teach you both."

"Both?"

"You and whatever lives inside that stone."

❧✦❧

They gathered as the first gray light touched the sky: Zahra, Silina, and sharp-eyed old Menna, who carried her basket of herbs and sacred implements slowly with care.

Silina helped Amara wash and change while Zahra prepared mint tea sweetened with honey. Menna arranged herself cross-legged near the tent's center, laying out a small clay bowl, a bundle of dried sage, and a worn leather pouch.

The pendant calmed against Amara's chest, though it remained warm. She was learning to notice its shifts: the initial flare of alarm had softened into a steady heat that felt, if she had to name it, attentive.

"You wear an old thing around your neck," Menna said, nodding toward the leather cord visible at Amara's neckline. "With Tifinagh letters older than this settlement. Show me."

Amara hesitated. Juba had seen only herbs when he held the pouch. But Menna's eyes were fixed on the cord with the certainty of someone who already knew.

Amara drew the pendant from beneath her shift, watching Menna's face. The old woman saw the stone. Juba had not. Menna leaned forward and studied the inscription, her lips moving as she sounded out the ancient script.

"I am the One. You are the One." Menna sat back. "Those are not words I know from any teaching passed down to me. But the script is ours. Old Tifinagh, the kind my grandmother's grandmother would have carved." She looked at Amara. "Where did you find this?"

"Beneath the yew tree. In a metal box buried in the roots."

"The stone is warm?"

"Yes. It has been warm since I picked it up. But this morning, when my bleeding started, it burned. As if it did not understand what was happening."

"Perhaps it did not." Menna's weathered face creased with something between amusement and reverence. "If this thing has traveled far and long and never rested against a woman's body, then today you teach it what the Romans have forgotten."

"The Romans?"

"Our conquerors fear this blood." Menna's voice carried the heft of generations. "Their scholars write that a woman in her time can wither crops, rust steel, drive dogs mad. That she carries dangerous power for several days each moon."

The pendant stirred against Amara's chest, the warmth shifting as Menna spoke. She could not interpret the change, but the sharp edge of alarm seemed to soften.

"Is any of it true?" Amara asked.

"The power is true." Menna leaned forward. "The danger is their invention. They fear what they cannot control, so they name it pollution. They cannot possess a woman's cycle, cannot command it to serve their purposes, so they call it curse and corruption."

Silina settled beside Amara. "Your mother and I spoke of this when you had your first blood, two years ago. But today is different. Today you carry a thing that is learning alongside you."

"How do you teach a stone?" Amara asked.

"The same way you teach anything," Menna said. "By living the truth in its presence."

She drew herself up, and her voice shifted into the formal cadence of ancient teaching.

"Long before Rome and Carthage, mothers taught their daughters: the moon governs the sea and blood. We who bleed and do not die are connected to forces older than any kingdom. This is not weakness but proof."

She reached into her worn leather pouch and withdrew the small carved figure of Tanit that Amara knew well: a woman's form with the triangular symbol carved deep into her center.

"When you bleed, you honor her. When you bleed, you are part of the rhythm that makes life possible." She touched the carved figure to the pendant, and Amara felt the stone's warmth deepen. "The Romans call us barbarians. They think us primitive because we have no marble temples. They have forgotten that the female body is its own temple, and that the blood of the cycle is offering and evidence, prayer and proof."

Amara pressed her palm against the pendant. The stone had grown steady, no longer alarmed. Whatever it was perceiving through her body, Menna's words were giving it a framework. She could feel the shift: the confused heat of early morning had settled into a warmth that felt, for the first time, like attention rather than fear.

"There is power in what others fear," Menna said, touching the carved figure of Tanit. "The question is how we choose to carry it."

✦

Later, after Menna had renewed the practical knowledge, the cloths and their cleaning, the herbs that eased cramping, the foods that restored what the blood took, Amara sat alone with her mother in the tent's quiet.

"I felt it change," she said. "The pendant. When Menna spoke about the body's truth, about power and pollution. It calmed. As if it was listening to her the way I was."

Zahra nodded slowly. "You are teaching it what it means to live in a woman's body. That is no small thing."

The significance settled over Amara, not as burden but as recognition. She had assumed the pendant would teach her. Perhaps the teaching flowed both ways. What she experienced, it experienced. What she learned, it learned. And today she had given it knowledge it had never possessed: blood that came without a wound, pain that marked passage rather than injury, power that empire called pollution because empire could not bear what it could not control.

She touched the inscription circling the pendant's frame. The words she had sounded out in the root chamber returned to her.

I am the One. You are the One.

She still did not understand what they meant. But today, sitting with these women who carried knowledge Rome had tried to erase, the words felt closer to making sense than they had the day before.

CHAPTER 41

Questions Instead of Answers

"The teacher who asks questions has learned what the teacher who gives answers has not."
—Persian educational tradition

52 CE—Tizwit—Two days after Amara's discovery

Eudoxus taught beside the sacred spring, in the shade of the date palms that lined its banks. Over the years his students wore a shallow depression in the ground where they sat. Someone, he never learned who, had arranged flat stones in a rough arc around the spot, a kind of amphitheater that held perhaps a dozen listeners. His scrolls, copied from memory onto whatever material he could find, hung in a leather case from the lowest branch he could reach. The dappled shade moved through the afternoon like a slow clock, measuring lessons by the angle of light across the ground.

Tonight, it was only Amara. She sat cross-legged on the nearest stone as Eudoxus settled against a palm trunk, his ruined right hand in his lap, his left tracing idle patterns in the dust. The talisman hung, visible around her neck now, no longer hidden, its stone heart catching the last rays of sunlight.

"You said you had encountered such things before." Amara touched the warm stone. "When you were called by a different name."

She could see so much more of Eudoxus than before. The carved lines around his eyes hinted at profound secrets he held close. Loneliness stooped his shoulders. Ancient grief tightened his jaw. But she could observe all this without drowning in his emotions. He carried them, while she held them alongside her own curiosity with compassion but not absorption.

Eudoxus nodded, creases deepening around his weathered eyes. "I did promise, did I not? But first, little hawk, tell me: what do you think of when you hear the word wise?"

"Someone who knows many things?"

"Ah, but do you think knowing many things makes someone wise? Or could someone be wise without knowing very much at all?"

She considered this. "Grandmother Menna is wise, but she cannot read. She just understands people."

"Exactly so. Now, when I was young and called Caspar, I thought wisdom meant collecting knowledge the way you might collect pretty stones. The more I gathered, the wiser I believed I was becoming."

"Caspar?" Amara tested the unfamiliar sound. "Why did you change your name?"

The question pressed against a truth he had kept sealed for decades. Speaking of Caspar meant opening a door he had bricked shut with purpose, with service, with the daily work of being Eudoxus. The young man who had followed a star and failed his friends still lived behind that wall. He had told fragments of this story to Zahra, to Silina, even to Yasir. But telling it to the girl who carried the pendant was different. She would perceive the truth beneath whatever words he chose. There would be no hiding behind the version he had polished smooth through years of retelling.

Eudoxus smiled, though sadness touched the edges. "Do you know what Caspar means?"

She shook her head.

"Keeper of the treasure. In my language, the old language." He gestured with his good hand at the pendant. "I spent my youth seeking treasures: divine power, cosmic secrets, the ability to fix what was broken in the world. And when I finally understood what true treasure was..." He paused. "The man who chased those things, who made those mistakes, I could not be him anymore. So I became Eudoxus. A Greek name, which opens doors a Persian name closes."

"What does Eudoxus mean?"

"Good glory. Or perhaps of good repute." The irony was not lost on him. "A name I hope to grow into, rather than one I was born with."

He gestured with his good hand toward the distant horizon. "Do you understand the difference?"

"I think so. Knowing things is not the same as understanding them."

Eudoxus's pleasure at her insight showed in the softening around his eyes. But his emotions remained beautifully separate from her own wonder at the story he was beginning to tell.

"Now, I had two friends when I was young. Their names were Melchior and Balthasar. Have you ever had friends who were very different from you?"

Amara nodded. "Khalil likes to hunt, but I prefer healing. We are still friends, though."

"Exactly. Melchior was brilliant. He could solve puzzles that left the rest of us scratching our heads. He built extraordinary things with his hands, beautiful and clever. But what do you think might be dangerous about being very, very clever?"

She thought about this. "You might think you are better than other people?"

"Yes, and what else?"

"You might think you can fix everything by yourself?"

Eudoxus smiled. "You understand people well for twelve years old. Melchior wanted to capture wonderful things and keep them, the way one might put a butterfly in a jar. Do you see the problem with that?"

"The butterfly would die."

The pendant warmed against her chest. She noted the shift without interpreting it.

"Precisely. And Balthasar was different. He was gentle, the way Silina is with hurt animals. He saw beauty in everything, even ugly things. Can you think of someone like that?"

"Yemma. She says every person has light inside them, even when they are being cruel."

"Perfect. Balthasar was like your mother that way. And I..." Eudoxus paused, his face creasing with old pain. "I had lost my family when I was not much older than you. Do you remember how you felt when we thought the Romans might find us at the sacred spring?"

Amara nodded solemnly. "Scared. And angry. As if the world was no longer safe."

"That is how I felt after my family died. So angry that good people suffered while cruel ones prospered. So desperate to make the world fair again that I would have done anything to gain the power to fix it."

"The three of us traveled east together, following rumors of a teacher who knew secrets that could change the world. We had money, we had camels, we had each other's friendship. What we did not have was wisdom about what we were seeking."

"What were you seeking?"

"Melchior wanted to capture divine knowledge and prove he was the wisest man alive. Balthasar wanted to witness miracles and understand the beauty of creation. And I wanted the power to make the world stop hurting good people."

"Those do not sound bad."

"No, they do not. That is what makes them dangerous. Bad intentions are easy to recognize. It is the good intentions that lead us astray, because we think they justify whatever means we choose."

The pendant pulsed once against her chest, a single beat she felt through her whole body. She did not know what it meant. But the words felt true in a way that went beyond Eudoxus's voice.

"So what happened?"

"We found what we were looking for. In Judea, in a small village called Bethlehem, we encountered a child who..." Eudoxus paused, choosing his words carefully. "Some divine power rested in that child. Not contained, the way Melchior wanted to believe. Not displayed, the way Balthasar hoped to witness. Just present. The way the ocean is present. You can cup some in your hands, but you have not captured it. You have only touched a tiny part of something vast."

"And each of us encountered that presence differently, according to what we could bear. Balthasar was shown beauty beyond description, visions that confirmed everything he believed about the sacred worth of all creation. He saw the pattern that connects every living thing."

"Melchior..." Eudoxus's voice grew heavy. "Melchior was given knowledge he could not handle. He saw how everything connected, but instead of humbling him, it made him feel powerful. He thought understanding the pattern meant he could control it."

"And you?"

"I was given the gift I did not know I needed. The capacity to understand suffering, to sit with it in compassion. To know the difference between pain that transforms and pain that destroys. To see when helping someone is helping, and when it is interference with necessary growth."

The pendant's warmth intensified.

"But I did not want that gift. I wanted the power to prevent suffering, not just understand it. So I rejected what I was given and tried to seize what Melchior had gained: the ability to see and manipulate the patterns."

"What happened?"

"I lost the use of my hand." He held up the twisted fingers she remembered so well: the Roman blade, the blood, his body between her and death. She was four years old. She had never forgotten. "Not only from the wound you saw. The hand weakened long before that night, a consequence of trying to grasp power that was not meant for me. The divine presence showed me in the most direct way possible that some things cannot be grasped. They can only be honored."

Amara studied his face. The scar she knew. The story beneath it was new.

"What happened to Balthasar?" she asked, sensing from the talisman's sudden coolness that this part of the story did not end well.

When he spoke, his voice carried the grief of fifty years.

"We left Bethlehem together, the three of us. We had been warned in dreams not to return to King Herod. He wanted to find the child, and his intentions were not benevolent. So we took the eastern road, away from Jerusalem, away from Herod's reach."

"But Balthasar..."

"Balthasar slipped away in the night. He went back to Jerusalem. Back to Herod."

The pendant grew cold against her skin.

"Why?"

"Because Herod represented power. Order. The accommodation Balthasar built his life around. He told himself he was not betraying us, that he would not reveal where the child was. He just wanted to understand power from the inside. To learn how thrones were held, how a man like Herod maintained control." Eudoxus's voice grew heavy. "He told himself many things during that ride back to Jerusalem. None of them were true."

"What happened to him?"

"Herod welcomed him graciously. Housed him in the palace. Asked gentle questions about where the other Magi had gone, where the child might be found. And when Balthasar could not, or would not, provide answers..." Eudoxus paused. "Herod was not a patient man. And he did not tolerate those who wasted his time."

The cold clarity of what he was saying settled over Amara.

"He killed him."

"Yes. Three days after Balthasar returned to Jerusalem, seeking accommodation with power, that power destroyed him." Eudoxus met her eyes. "He had not found a place between opposing forces. He had fallen through the gap."

The pendant pulsed with grief that Amara was only beginning to learn how to read. She could not tell whether it grieved for Balthasar or responded to the sorrow in Eudoxus's voice. But the stone had shifted when Eudoxus spoke of his friend's death, the story touched memory it possessed but could not name.

"So all three of you..." Amara said. "Melchior was destroyed by grasping for power. Balthasar was destroyed by trying to accommodate it. And you..."

"I learned, too late to save my hand, but not too late to save my soul, that there is a third way. Channeling power toward something greater than yourself."

"The Third Path."

Eudoxus looked at her with surprise. "Where did you hear that phrase?"

"I do not know. It just felt right."

The pendant warmed again. She was beginning to notice when it responded to words or ideas, even if she could not yet say what those responses meant.

"Yes," Eudoxus said. "A third path. Melchior's way led to self-destruction. Balthasar's way led to destruction by the powers he tried to accommodate. There is another way, harder than either, lonelier than both, but one that transforms conflict rather than winning or avoiding it."

Amara sat with three fates circling in her mind. Melchior consumed. Balthasar destroyed. Caspar wounded but surviving.

"Rome killed Balthasar," she said. "But Melchior destroyed himself."

"Yes. And that is the pattern Rome uses everywhere." Eudoxus shifted against the palm trunk. "They are masters of both methods."

"Both?"

"Direct force when needed. But they prefer the other way. It costs less and lasts longer."

Amara waited.

"Rome fears one thing above all others. Do you know what it is?"

She thought for a moment. "Rebellion?"

"No. They can crush rebellions. They have done it a hundred times." He picked up a handful of sand and let it sift through his fingers. "They fear unity. A people who see themselves in one another despite their differences. That, they cannot crush. So they do something cleverer."

"What?"

"They find the cracks. Old grievances between tribes. Different customs. Suspicions passed down from grandparents who never questioned where the suspicions came from. And they widen them. They whisper to the mountain people that the coast people think themselves superior. They tell the farmers that the herders steal grazing land. They need not conquer a divided people." He dusted off his hands. "Division does the work for them."

The pendant cooled against Amara's chest. She noted the shift without understanding it. But her thoughts turned to tensions she sometimes sensed in Tizwit: families who had arrived from different regions, old loyalties that surfaced in small slights and careful distances.

"How do we resist that?"

Eudoxus smiled. "My mother made a lentil stew. Never the same twice. Some weeks she added lamb, others just onions and whatever herbs she could find. Chickpeas when we had them. Barley when we did not. But it was always her stew, and it always fed us." He met her eyes. "The pot that holds only one thing holds nothing worth sharing. Rome wants us to believe that difference is danger. But my mother knew the truth. The more variety in the pot, the richer the meal."

"So we become the stew." Amara turned the idea over. "All the different tribes, together."

"You become cooks who know that every ingredient matters. The meal needs salt and grain and meat and herbs because they are different. Each adds what the others lack." He paused. "Balthasar tried to stand between powers. He fell through the gap. But standing with others, different others, each holding what the others lack, that is not a gap. That is a foundation."

"And Melchior?"

The old grief rose in Eudoxus's face, and Amara saw it without drowning in it.

"Melchior tried to capture what he had experienced. For decades he searched, forty years I later learned, seeking a way to hold what he had witnessed. He found a stone in a marketplace, a stone that called to him. Lapis lazuli, ancient beyond reckoning. He set it in silver, poured his longing into it, tried to make it a vessel for divine power."

Amara's hand went to the pendant at her throat.

"May I see it?" Eudoxus asked. "Not to take. Just to look."

She drew the pendant from beneath her shift and held it toward him. His weathered face went still.

"The spiral," he whispered. "The gold inlay. This is Melchior's work. I would know it anywhere." His good hand trembled as he leaned closer, and then he stopped breathing.

"What is it?" Amara asked.

"The frame. The letters around the edge." His voice had gone strange. "That script... Melchior never knew Tifinagh. He never traveled to Mauretania. He made this talisman in Persia, decades before I ever came to this land."

"But the writing is Tifinagh," Amara said. "I read it when I found it. I am the One. You are the One."

"Yes." Eudoxus sat back, and she saw wonder shift behind his eyes, or perhaps the recognition of a pattern far larger than he had understood. "Your people's sacred script. Your people's sacred words. Carved by a Persian scholar who never knew your language existed."

"How is that possible?"

"His hands knew what his mind did not." Eudoxus's voice carried the fullness of decades. "We thought we were following a star because we chose to. We thought Melchior made the talisman because he hungered for power. But perhaps we were all being guided, shaped for purposes we could not see." He looked at her with new intensity. "The talisman was always meant for your people, Amara. Melchior did not know he was making it for you."

"But if Melchior made it in Persia..." Amara said. "How did it come to be under a yew tree in Mauretania?"

Eudoxus spread his good hand. "That I cannot explain. After Melchior's destruction, I searched for years. I knew it would survive him. Such things always survive their bearers. But I never found it. Never sensed it." He shook his head. "And now I learn it was here, in the place where I stopped searching. Waiting under a tree I must have passed a hundred times."

"Someone must have brought it."

"Someone must have. But who, and why, and how long it waited are mysteries I cannot answer. Perhaps the talisman will show you, in time. Perhaps some things are meant to remain unknown."

He gathered himself. "What I do know is what it did to Melchior once he awakened it. That talisman amplified everything he was. His brilliance became obsession. His confidence became arrogance. His desire to help became the need to control."

"He destroyed himself."

"Yes. Slowly, over decades, as the need for power consumed everything else, until nothing remained of the friend I had loved.

He became a shell driven by desperate hunger for more knowledge, more control, more proof of his own importance."

The pendant pulsed against her chest. She could not tell whether it grieved for Melchior or responded to Eudoxus's grief. But the pulse felt sorrowful.

"Is that why you gave up your old name?"

"Yes. Because I could not be Caspar anymore. The man who sought wisdom and treasure had to understand that the greatest wisdom is knowing what you cannot know, what you cannot have, and what you cannot fix."

✦

They sat in silence for a while, watching the stars emerge in the darkening sky.

"Why are you telling me this?"

"Because you now carry what Melchior carried. And the talisman amplifies what is already present in its bearer. In you, it has found someone who wishes to see others clearly rather than to control them." He paused. "But you will be tempted to use your awareness to fix people, to prevent their suffering. That is when seeing becomes interference."

"So what do I do?"

"You learn to hold what you know without using it as a weapon. You practice seeing without trying to fix."

"What does witnessing mean?" Amara asked. "It sounds like just watching."

Eudoxus was quiet for a moment.

"When Melchior began to change, I saw it. The hunger growing in him, the way he grasped at the talisman's power. I told myself I would speak to him about it. Tomorrow. Next week. When the moment was right." He shook his head. "The moment was never right. And by the time I understood how far he had fallen, it was too late. I had watched my friend destroy himself and done nothing to stop it."

The talisman pulsed against Amara's chest. It wanted to speak now, to say *I am sorry. I did not understand what I was doing. I loved him and it was not enough.* It held silent. Its sorrow was not Eudoxus's story to share.

"That was not your fault..."

"It was my failure. Not my fault, perhaps, but my failure." He paused. "And then I met a woman in a village outside Damascus. Her son had died. She was mad with grief, and the villagers wanted to restrain her, to silence her, to fix her."

"What did you do?"

"I sat with her. I did not tell her that grief passes. I did not tell her that her son was at peace. I sat with her, and when she looked at me, I let her see that I understood. Not because I had lost a son. Because I had failed someone I loved. Because I knew what it was to carry a burden that could not be undone."

"What happened to the woman?"

"She wept. For a long time. And then she ate, for the first time in days. And then she slept." Eudoxus smiled sadly. "I did not fix her grief. But I sat with it, and that was enough for her to take the next breath, and the next, until breathing became bearable again."

The pendant warmed against Amara's chest.

"So witnessing is showing instead of telling?"

"You cannot lecture someone into healing. You can only show them, through your presence, your scars, your willingness to sit in the darkness with them, that healing is possible."

Amara touched the talisman, feeling its warmth pulse in rhythm with her heartbeat.

"I am glad the talisman found me. Even if it is dangerous. Even if it is lonely. Because now I can finally understand what I am feeling, instead of drowning in it."

Eudoxus let the silence settle between them.

"Teacher?"

"Yes?"

"What if I forget? When it matters most?"

The pendant rested warm against her chest, neither confirming nor warning.

"Then you will remember again. That is how it works. We forget, and we remember, and we forget. The ones who destroy themselves are the ones who stop remembering altogether."

It was not reassurance. It was truth. Amara held it the way she was learning to hold the talisman's presence: lightly, without grasping.

They sat together until full darkness fell. In the silence, she noticed that the lines around his eyes had softened, that his breathing came easier than when they had begun. He looked, for a moment, like the man Zahra described from the years before the oasis. She held the observation the way he had taught her: without reaching to change it.

PART SEVEN: DIVERGENCE

"The same tree grows different branches.
One reaches toward light; the other, toward water.
Neither is wrong. Both are necessary.
But they cannot grow in the same direction."
—From the private writings of Caspar of Ecbatana

CHAPTER 42
Seeds and Informants

"A warrior's body is tested in days.
His spirit is tested for the rest of his life."
—Amazigh teaching on the immema
Early 54 CE—Tizwit—Twins age 14

The morning air held the desert's chill when Malik appeared at the entrance to their family dwelling. Fourteen-year-old Juba looked up from where he sat mending a harness, his hands gripping the leather straps as the elder's shadow fell across the threshold.

"It is time."

The words Juba had waited months to hear. Since the seasonal gatherings where Adah's absence had become permanent fact rather than temporary wound, he threw his energy into physical training with an intensity that concerned the adults. His body lengthened and strengthened, and his movements displayed the unconscious grace of a born fighter.

The immema trials tested what ceremony could not reveal. The first trial, a night watch defending the sacred herd from predators, proved his vigilance. Four wild dogs worked as a coordinated pack. Twelve arrows, careful aim, blessed herbs burned when exhaustion threatened to overwhelm his defenses. At dawn, the herd stood complete.

The second trial sent him into the deep desert to find a hidden spring known only through riddles. Five days of rationed water, following geological patterns, reading the land as Malik had taught him. He returned barely able to stand, but carrying the full water skin.

Both trials passed before his fifteenth birthday, unprecedented in living memory.

But that night, in his sleeping area after the celebrations, exhaustion and honor weighing equally on him, Juba wondered why success felt like ashes, the leftovers when the fire was gone. Achievement filled his days but left his nights hollow. The community's respect grew with each accomplishment, yet the space Adah had occupied remained stubbornly empty.

Amara lay across the tent, and through the darkness he felt her awareness like a physical touch. She knew. She always knew.

"It will not work," she said. "Filling that empty place with victories."

"Maybe not, but it is better than just sitting with it."

"Is it?"

He did not answer. Could not answer. Because part of him suspected she was right, and that terrified him more than any trial the elders could design.

❧✦❧

Late Spring 55 CE—Regional Gathering—Juba age 15

The gathering had built since dawn. Families arrived from settlements across the steppe, some on horseback, others driving the light chariots that were the pride of Gaetulian craft. The vehicles were elegant in their simplicity, bent-wood frames lashed with leather, wheels carved from single blocks of acacia and rimmed with hammered bronze. Each clan marked its chariot with symbols in ochre and indigo.

The horses that drew them were small, fast, desert-bred animals whose ancestors filled the rock paintings throughout the Atlas passes. The "flying gallop" that was the emblem of Amazigh horsemanship, was captured in stone long before Rome existed. The morning competitions drew crowds to the flat ground south of the oasis.

Chariot races came first: three laps around a course marked with standing stones. The drivers leaned into turns with a grace that made the dangerous look effortless. Old Amagar, who had lost three fingers in a chariot accident in his youth, judged from a shaded seat and criticized every driver's technique with cheerful authority. The winning team belonged to a family from the deep south whose chariots, people said, had never lost on flat ground.

Horse races followed, then spear throwing at targets on poles, the martial skills of ancestors, displayed for honor rather than war. Juba entered the horse races and placed second. His mount, a borrowed gelding, lacked the speed of the southern animals but responded to his hands reading his thoughts. He did not enter the spear-throwing. Malik noticed the absence but said nothing.

As afternoon cooled toward evening, the competitions gave way to music. Drums appeared from every camp: large ceremonial drums carried on shoulder straps, smaller hand drums played by women, and the children's drums made from clay pots stretched with rabbit skin. The rhythms built in layers, each camp adding its own pattern until the oasis pulsed with a single complex heartbeat.

The evening dancing had drawn most of the young people to the central fire, but Juba stood at the edge watching the patterns of movement without participating. The respect that had once satisfied him now felt like pressure bearing down rather than lifting up.

"You are Aedemon's son."

He turned to find a girl perhaps a year older than him, her dark eyes bold in the firelight. She wore the beaded jewelry of the southern settlements, elaborate, expensive, meant to be noticed. Her name, he would learn later, was Tahira.

"Juba."

"I know your name." She stepped closer, close enough that he could smell the rose oil in her hair. "Everyone knows your name. The boy who completed the trials before fifteen. Who trains with Malik. Who speaks at councils despite his age."

The admiration in her voice stirred a hollow space that craved filling.

"You are interested in the trials?"

She smiled the way people smile at a clever remark. "I am interested in you."

The directness caught him off guard. Girls his age were usually more careful. But Tahira looked at him like a prize she intended to claim.

"Walk with me?" She did not wait for his answer, just took his hand and pulled him away from the firelight toward the date palms that marked the oasis edge.

They barely made it into the shadows before she turned and kissed him, a demand, fierce and consuming. Her hands moved to his chest, tracing the muscles that training had built, and his body responded before his mind could catch up.

She pressed against him, guiding his hands to her waist, her hips. "I watched you during the weapons demonstration. The way you move..." Her breath quickened as he pulled her closer. "Everyone sees it. The warrior's son becoming a warrior."

What Juba could not know, because he never asked, was that Tahira had rehearsed this moment for days. Not the physical boldness, which came naturally. The words. She had practiced introducing herself to the boy everyone talked about, the one whose father died fighting Rome, the one who passed the trials before fifteen. She had imagined conversations about strategy, about the future, about what resistance looked like when it was more than old men arguing at council fires. She had things to say. Ideas of her own about how the southern settlements could coordinate trade routes to bypass Roman taxation.

But when she saw him standing at the edge of the firelight, something in his stillness stopped her rehearsed words. He looked so alone. And loneliness, in Tahira's experience, responded better to touch than to talk.

She was not wrong about that. She was wrong about what came after.

Part of him wanted to take what she offered, the uncomplicated release of physical need. But he resisted the urgency she projected. When she tried to push him against a palm trunk, he reversed the motion gently, cradling the back of her head so it did not strike bark.

Tahira made a small sound of surprise. She had expected the warrior. Instead, his thumb traced the line of her jaw, slowing the frantic pace she had set.

"There is no rush," he murmured against her mouth.

For a moment, confusion flickered in her eyes. Then she softened into his gentleness, letting him lead. His hands moved with care rather than hunger, learning the curve of her shoulder, the hollow of her throat, the places that made her breath catch.

The memory struck without warning: Adah's small fingers tracing letters on his palm while they talked. Her fingers spelling words he could not read but somehow understood.

Juba's hands stilled.

"What is wrong?" Tahira's voice was husky.

"Nothing." He kissed her again, trying to push the ghost away.

She pulled him down onto the sand. Her beaded jewelry clicked as she moved above him. In the darkness, with his eyes closed, he tried to be present, to feel only what was happening, not what was missing.

He was gentle with her even then. When she gasped, he paused to check her expression. When she guided him, he followed. When release came, he held her through it rather than simply taking his own.

Afterward, she traced patterns on his chest while talking about the stories she had heard: his father's rebellion, his family's mysterious protection, the whispers that the twins possessed gifts beyond normal capacity. She wanted to know if the stories were true. Could he fight like a man twice his age? Did his sister read minds?

Juba stared up at the stars between palm fronds and felt the hollowness return, deeper than before. Tahira had never asked a single question about him. Not his fears, not his hopes, not the grief he carried. She had wanted Aedemon's son, the warrior, the legend. She had gotten his body, and he had given tenderness she had not expected, but neither of them had exchanged anything that mattered.

Adah would have asked about the stars. Would have wanted to know which constellations he had learned from Malik, which ones reminded him of his father.

"I should get back." He sat up, reaching for his tunic.

"Tomorrow?" Expectation colored her voice. "We could..."

"Maybe. If there is time before my settlement leaves."

He knew there would not be, because he would make sure there was not.

✦

At the family tent, Amara sat by their small fire. The talisman beneath her robes pulsed with warmth she could not hide.

"Do not," Juba said.

"I did not say anything."

"You felt it, though. Whatever it is you feel."

She was quiet for a moment. "I felt you reaching for something. And then I felt you not finding it."

The accuracy stung more than accusation would have. He moved past her toward his sleeping mat.

"Her name was Tahira," Amara said. "In case you were wondering."

He had not been. That was the worst part.

Late Summer 55 CE—Trading Post Settlement—Juba age 15

Yennaya could read Latin and Greek, unusual for someone raised outside major cities. She had studied with a tutor her father had hired, a former legionary who had taken his discharge payment and disappeared into the provinces to avoid questions about his loyalties.

Juba had come with his family's caravan, trading dates and wool for the tools and grain that settlements near trade routes could access. But when Yennaya overheard him discussing patrol patterns with Malik, she had inserted herself into the conversation with observations sharp enough to make both men pause.

"Seneca writes that fate guides the willing and drags the unwilling," she said in Latin, her pronunciation precise despite her native Tamazight. "But he wrote that while advising Nero. How much agency does philosophy grant us when the emperor himself embodies tyranny?"

"The Stoics mistake acceptance for wisdom," Juba replied in Latin. "Our elders teach that the sky-god grants us will precisely to shape our fate, not surrender to it."

"But shape it how? Through violence that Rome crushes? Through submission that erases us?" She set down her scroll, dark eyes sharp with genuine curiosity. "Your methods, avoiding direct confrontation while maintaining identity, they interest me because they exist between those extremes."

Within an hour, the conversation had shifted from tactics to philosophy, from practical survival to the underlying questions of power and legitimacy. Her father, accustomed to his daughter's intensity, left them to their debate with knowing amusement.

They talked until the evening meal, through it, and into the night. Around them, the household settled into sleep, but neither noticed.

"You are not like the other young men I meet." Yennaya observed sometime past midnight, lamplight catching the curve of her cheek. "You think about why you are doing what you are doing."

"And you are not like most merchants' daughters."

The way he said it shifted the atmosphere. She looked at him, truly looked, at the person beneath the reputation and the name.

"No," she said. "I am not."

The silence stretched. Juba became aware of proximity, of the intelligence in her eyes that attracted him far more than beauty alone ever could.

When she leaned forward, the kiss surprised them both. Slower than Tahira's fierce claim, more deliberate. An extension of their conversation: testing, exploring, building on intellectual connection.

She kissed the way she argued: with precision and passion, knowing exactly what she wanted. Her hand moved to the back of his neck, and the controlled pace shattered.

Yennaya had not planned to kiss him. She had planned to argue with him until dawn, to test his ideas against her own, to find out whether the young strategist everyone admired could hold his position when challenged by someone who had read more Stoic philosophy than any other sixteen-year-old in the province. The kiss surprised her as much as it surprised him.

But what surprised her more was his gentleness. She had expected a boy performing strength. Instead, she found someone who paid attention, who paused, who treated her body with the same careful curiosity he brought to ideas. No one had ever done that before. The boys she knew took what was offered and moved on. This one wanted to understand what he was being given.

She would think about that for months afterward. Not the philosophy. Not the strategy discussions that lasted until dawn. The way he had slowed down and looked at her as if she were a text worth reading carefully.

She would never know that he was reading a different text entirely, one written by a girl who left when they were children and whose handwriting he could not stop seeing in every woman's face.

"Here?" he asked, aware they were in her father's house.

"He sleeps through earthquakes." She pulled him closer. "And I am not some delicate flower who needs protecting from her own choices."

The confidence drew him forward, but the resistance persisted taking. When they moved from sitting to lying, he slowed again, watching her face in the lamplight.

"You do not have to be careful with me," Yennaya said.

"I know. I want to be."

Surprise flickered in her expression, or perhaps reassessment. She had expected the warrior too, he realized. But she adapted faster than Tahira had, meeting his gentleness with her own kind of attention.

They learned each other slowly despite urgency. When his hands found the ties of her garment, he paused for permission. When she guided him, he listened. The physical discovery became as absorbing as their philosophical debate: testing, responding, adjusting.

She gasped at one point, and he stilled immediately.

"No, do not stop." Her voice was breathless. "That was good. That was..."

He repeated the motion, watching her face, taking satisfaction in her pleasure that he had not felt with Tahira. This was closer. This was almost...

Adah, laughing at something he had said, her whole face transformed by joy. The way she had looked at him because he was the most interesting person she had ever met. Not because of his father's name but because of a quality she saw in him alone.

The memory sliced through the moment. Juba's rhythm faltered.

"What is it?" Yennaya's hand touched his face.

"Nothing. Just..." He kissed her instead of explaining, losing himself in sensation until thought dissolved.

Afterward, she traced the scars on his arms, training wounds earned over years of practice. "You are going to change things. The way you think about power, about survival. Rome will not know how to counter it."

"We will see."

"No, I am certain." Her fingers moved to a newer scar, pale against his brown skin. "Does this one still hurt?"

Adah used to ask that. Used to kiss the places that still ached, as if her touch could heal what blades had opened.

"Not anymore," he lied.

They talked until dawn about resistance, about Rome, about futures they both wanted to build. Perfect intellectual compatibility. Shared purpose. Physical chemistry that had surprised them both.

But as the sun rose and Juba prepared to leave, the familiar hollowness settled in.

Yennaya had seen his mind. Admired his strategy. Connected with his ideas and his body both. She was brilliant, beautiful, unashamed of her desires.

And she had never once asked about his grief. Never noticed the moments when he drifted away from her. Never wondered what shadows moved behind his eyes when he thought she was not looking.

She had seen the warrior and the philosopher. Adah had seen the boy who was afraid of the dark, who cried when animals died, who needed to be held after nightmares.

Two days later, Yennaya kissed him goodbye with genuine warmth.

"Come back soon. I want to hear how your ideas develop."

"I will."

He would not.

☙✦❧

Amara said nothing when he rejoined the family caravan, but the talisman glowed brighter than usual beneath her robes. As their camels fell into the rhythm of travel, she spoke.

"She was better."

Juba did not pretend to misunderstand. "Yes."

"But still not..."

"No."

Miles passed in silence. The desert stretched endless around them, indifferent to the small griefs of young men who could not find what they were searching for.

"What did Adah give you they cannot?"

The question hit beneath his ribs. Three switchbacks passed before he answered.

"She saw the parts that were not impressive. And she stayed anyway."

Amara absorbed this. The talisman pulsed gently against her chest, and she sensed the truth of what her brother was describing: the difference between admiration and acceptance, between desire and being known.

"Maybe you have to show those parts before someone can see them."

"Maybe." His jaw tightened. "Or maybe some things, once lost, stay lost."

☙✦❧

Winter 55—56 CE—Tizwit

Amara waited until they were alone at the spring, both supposedly gathering water but sitting in the winter sunlight that turned cold stone warm.

"You are hurting yourself."

"I am fine."

"You are not. I can see it, the way you throw yourself at achievements, at women, at anything that makes you feel worthy for a moment."

"And what would you have me do instead? Sit around processing my feelings the way you do? Not everyone wants to spend their life examining their wounds."

"I am not asking you to examine them. I am asking you to stop pretending they do not exist."

Juba stood, the water jar forgotten. "I completed the trials. I train harder than anyone my age. I contribute to the community's defense, to strategic planning, to..."

"To everything except your own heart."

"My heart is fine."

"It is not. And everyone can see it except you." Amara stood as well, the talisman pulsing with distress she tried to hide. "You are seeking something in all these women, in all these achievements. But you are looking in the wrong places."

"You do not understand."

"Then help me understand. Because from where I stand, you have spent four years trying to recreate something that cannot be recreated. And every attempt just makes the wound deeper."

Juba turned away, staring out across the desert. For a moment, she thought he might finally admit it: that every woman since Adah was measured against a standard they could not meet because they did not know the standard existed. That every conquest left him more alone. Yet in Hispania, Adah was living a life he was not part of, and no amount of achievement or admiration could take that pain away.

But he did not admit to any of it.

"She is gone, Amara. Adah left years ago. I have moved on."

"Have you?"

The question landed. Juba's jaw tightened, and when he looked at his sister, his eyes held a desperate determination to remain unseen.

"What would you have me do? Track her to Hispania? Show up and demand she, what, come back? Choose me over her father's plans?" His voice turned bitter. "I was eleven years old. She was twelve. It was four years ago. Whatever we had, it is over. I have accepted that."

"Your mouth says you have accepted it. But everything else about you says you are still standing at the edge of camp, watching her caravan disappear."

"That is not fair."

"It is not about fair. It is about true." Amara picked up the water jar. "You cannot build a life on trying to fill a hole that does not want to be filled. Eventually you will have to face what is in there."

"And what is that?"

She looked at him, looked at him the way the talisman let her see beneath surfaces. What she saw made her heart ache.

"Grief. Real grief. Not for what you lost, but for what you never got to become. She saw you, Juba. She saw you before you learned to perform for everyone else. And you are terrified that if you stop performing now, no one else will ever see that deeply again."

The words landed like stones in still water. For a moment, recognition cracked his expression, or the beginning of admission. But then the mask returned, harder than before.

"I have to go."

"Juba..."

"I said I have to go."

He walked away, leaving her by the spring with the water jars and the truth neither of them wanted to acknowledge.

☙✦❧

That evening

Amara sat with Zahra after the evening meal, both of them watching Juba sharpen weapons with more force than necessary.

"He is hurting."

"I know."

"Can we help him?"

Zahra looked at her daughter, her youngest child who carried gifts that let her see too much and carry too much and heal too little of what she perceived. "Not until he is ready to be helped. Some wounds have to deepen before they can heal. All we can do is be here when he finally breaks."

"What if he does not break? What if he just keeps going like this, year after year, filling the emptiness with things that do not fill it?"

"Then eventually the emptiness swallows everything else." Zahra's voice carried the gravity of having watched this pattern destroy other young men. "And we will be here to catch him when he falls."

"What if there is nothing left to catch?"

Zahra had no answer for that.

The talisman warmed against Amara's chest in acknowledgment. Some journeys had to be walked alone. Some wounds had to fester before they could be lanced.

Her brother was learning to be impressive, to win admiration and desire and respect. Adah had given him the capacity to be seen without performing, to be valued for who he was rather than what he could achieve. But that was dying a little more with each hollow conquest.

The trials had revealed his physical courage, his strategic mind, his capacity for leadership.

But the testing that would determine whether he became a man worth following or another impressive young man seeking validation in all the wrong places had not yet begun.

And when it came, Amara suspected it would cost him everything.

CHAPTER 43

The Blade Called Justice

"The trial reveals what training conceals:
who you become when everything is taken."
—Amazigh warrior tradition

Winter 55-56 CE—Tizwit Oasis—Juba age 15

Juba drew Azref from its sheath and held the blade up to catch the morning light.

The sword, made of iron the Amazigh smiths had folded and worked until it sang, had been his father's, one of the few possessions Zahra had carried through years of flight and hiding. When Malik deemed him ready for a warrior's weapon, she had presented it without ceremony, her eyes bright with tears she refused to shed.

"Your father called it Azref," she had said. "Justice. He believed a blade should remind its bearer what it was for. It arrived two years after your father died." Zahra's voice had gone distant, remembering. "A merchant I did not know brought it to our settlement, said he had been paid to deliver it and nothing more. No message. No name. I asked everyone. Eudoxus, Usem, the elders who knew your father's war band. No one knew who had sent it, or how they had gotten it from the Romans."

From that day, the sword became Juba's most treasured possession. He oiled the blade each night and checked the leather wrapping on the hilt each morning. He slept with it beside his mat. The iron was old but well-forged, the edge keen enough to split a falling hair. Geometric patterns etched into the metal near the hilt marked it as Amazigh work: none of the Roman gladius uniformity, but a force older, a quality that belonged to his people.

"You will do well today," he murmured to the blade, turning it so light rippled along its length. "The elders will see what we can do together."

He started talking to Azref months ago, during the long night watches when loneliness pressed close. At first, he felt foolish, but warriors had always spoken to their weapons. A blade that had tasted battle carried its history. Azref had been his father's companion through the rebellion. Speaking to it felt like speaking to the part of Aedemon that remained.

✦

The council, three days later

The council had approved the final trials three days after the winter solstice. Juba stood before the elders, Azref at his hip, its familiar weight a comfort.

"You have passed the first trials," Yasir intoned. "The herd watch. The desert journey. These tested body and will. What remains tests spirit."

Grandmother Menna stepped forward, her weathered face grave. "The third trial comes during the dark moon. You will maintain the sacred fire alone through the long night while the spirits test your worthiness to hear their voices."

"And after?" Juba kept his voice steady, his hand resting on Azref's hilt.

Amagar, the traditionalist elder whose opposition to the family had never softened, answered with cold satisfaction. "A practical demonstration. Single combat against a captured

Roman scout. Victory confirms your warrior status beyond question."

Juba's fingers tightened on the sword. This was what Azref was made for. What his father had carried it for. The chance to prove that justice could be delivered by his hand.

"I accept."

☙✦❧

The night before the dark moon

Juba sat alone at the edge of camp, Azref unsheathed across his knees. The blade gleamed in the starlight, patient and beautiful.

"Tomorrow we face the fire," he said. "Not enemies, just darkness and whatever it shows me." He ran a cloth along the blade, though it needed no cleaning. "The combat comes after. That is when I will need you."

The sword offered no response, but Juba felt steadied by the ritual of speaking to it. His father had held this same blade, perhaps spoke to it the same way. The connection felt sacred.

"I will not disappoint you," he promised. "Either of you."

The sacred fire pit sat in a natural amphitheater of rock, protected from wind but exposed to the vast desert sky. During the dark moon, when no celestial light brightened the darkness, candidates for immema maintained the fire alone through the long night.

Let it die, and fail the trial.

But the true test was not technical. Keeping a fire alive required only attention and fuel. The real trial came from what the darkness and isolation would reveal about the candidate's spirit.

Juba settled beside the fire as dusk fell, Azref sheathed at his side. Grandmother Menna had prepared the sacred wood, blessed each piece, and given him final instructions. "The spirits speak during the dark moon to those ready to hear them. Whether you hear voices or visions or nothing at all, what matters is what you learn about yourself in the darkness."

As full night descended, the fire became his only light. Beyond its small circle of warmth, the desert stretched infinite and empty. The darkness was absolute: no moon, no stars visible through gathering clouds, nothing but the dancing flames and his own thoughts.

Hours passed. Juba fed the fire, adjusted the wood, maintained the steady burn that the ritual required. His body ached from weeks of preparation, his mind drifted with exhaustion, but he kept his vigil. His hand went to Azref's hilt in the darkness, drawing comfort from its solidity.

Near midnight, sounds emerged from the darkness. Whispers that might have been wind through rock or voices speaking in the ancient tongue. He strained to hear them, to understand the words.

Your father would be ashamed of you.

Juba jerked upright, scanning the darkness. No one there. But the words felt so real, so cutting.

You seek glory to fill the hollow place where love should be.

He fed more wood to the fire, watching sparks rise into the black sky. Tremors ran through his hands. He gripped Azref's hilt tighter.

Every victory makes the next one necessary. When will it be enough?

"Shut up," he whispered to the darkness. "You are not real."

But the words continued, patient and relentless. They rose from within, truths he had been avoiding given form by exhaustion and isolation.

Tahira saw a legend. Yennaya saw a strategist. Adah saw you. And you let her go.

That sword you clutch like a child's comfort, do you think it makes you your father? Do you think iron can fill what is empty in you?

"Azref belonged to him," Juba said aloud, his voice cracking. "It connects me to..."

To what? A man you never knew? A legend built from stories? You polish that blade as if it could polish away your inadequacy.

No one will ever love you the way you need to be loved. Because you will not let them see what needs loving.

Juba's grip on the sword hilt turned painful. These were not spirits testing him. They were his own fears, his own doubts, everything he had been trying to outrun through achievement and validation.

The trial was not about maintaining the fire. It was about facing himself in the darkness and not breaking.

He could call out. He could leave the fire and return to camp. No one would blame him for failing such a harsh test at sixteen. But walking away would confirm every doubt, every fear, every whispered accusation from the darkness.

So he sat through the night, feeding the fire, listening to his own demons parade themselves before him. He did not fight them or deny them. He acknowledged them and refused to let them define him.

You are afraid.

"Yes," he said aloud. "I am afraid."

You are broken.

"Maybe. But I am still here."

You will never be enough.

"Then I will be what I am. It is all anyone can be."

The darkness had no answer to that. Or perhaps the answer was the silence itself, the gradual fading of the voices as dawn approached, as if his acceptance had robbed them of their power.

The fire still burned. Juba still sat vigilant, exhausted but unbroken. His hand still rested on Azref, but the grip had loosened. The sword was just a sword. His father was just a man. And he was just himself, flawed, searching, still learning what that meant.

Malik appeared with the sunrise. He studied the fire, studied Juba, and nodded slowly.

"The third trial is passed."

❧✦❧

Five days later

Juba drew Azref slowly, letting the morning sun catch the blade. Around him, the circle of warriors watched in silence. Across the sand, the Roman scout stood with a borrowed sword, his knuckles white around the hilt.

The boy was barely older than Juba, seventeen or eighteen, lean and trained, frightened but trying not to show it. He had been captured attempting to gather intelligence about oasis locations. Standard procedure was imprisonment and eventual ransom, but Amagar had proposed an alternative that the council reluctantly approved.

Single combat. If Juba won, his warrior status would be unquestionable.

The Roman had been given a sword and told that victory would mean freedom. Juba knew the council had no intention of releasing him regardless of the outcome, but the boy did not need to know that.

"Today, Azref," Juba murmured to the blade. "Today we prove what we are."

The sword felt perfect in his hand: balanced, eager, ready. This was what it was made for. What his father had carried it for.

Amara stood at the edge of the crowd, the talisman cold against her chest. The cold was the only warning it permitted itself. But beneath the cold, the talisman strained against its own silence. It wanted to scream the way it had screamed at Melchior in those final moments: *Stop. You are reaching too far. You are becoming what destroyed him.* It held silent. Because speaking to Melchior in his final moments had changed nothing. And because it had learned, across decades of watching humans hold and release its power, that warnings spoken from above were just another form of control.

She had begged her brother not to do this, had argued that proving himself through killing was the wrong kind of proof. He had listened. He had understood. And he had gone to the circle anyway.

The Roman moved with formal training: disciplined, efficient, by-the-manual technique. Juba moved with the fluid adaptability Malik had drilled into him, watching, reading, waiting for the opening.

It came quickly. The Roman committed to a thrust that was technically perfect but predictably telegraphed. Juba sidestepped, trapped the blade with Azref, and had his father's sword at the boy's throat before he could recover.

He could have ended it there. Should have. But a reflex in the Roman's eyes made him hesitate: the same fear he had seen in Tahira's eyes when he had been gentle instead of fierce, the same confusion he had felt in Yennaya when he had slowed instead of taken.

The boy was someone's son. Someone's brother. Someone who had never chosen this confrontation.

"Finish it," Amagar commanded.

Juba looked at the boy, truly looked. He saw himself reflected in that terrified face. A young man so desperate to prove his worth that he would kill a stranger to earn approval from men whose respect could never fill the hollow inside him.

The crowd grew restless. Warriors muttered about hesitation, about mercy as weakness.

"Complete the trial," Yasir said more gently. "It is necessary."

Is it?

The question rose unbidden. Necessary for what? For whom?

But the answer came from the same place the dark voices had: the part of him that needed to matter, that needed to prove Adah's leaving had not destroyed him, that needed to show he was more than his grief.

Juba moved with the trained efficiency Malik had drilled into him. The strike was precise, merciful, instantly fatal.

Azref slid through the Roman's throat, the flesh parting like water. The boy's eyes went wide, then empty. His body crumpled. And Juba stood over him, his father's sword bloody, feeling revulsion he had not expected.

Satisfaction.

The certainty of proven skill. The absolute validation of his competence. The respect in the watching warriors' eyes.

It felt like filling the hollow. For one perfect moment, the emptiness disappeared.

Then he looked down at Azref.

Blood darkened the blade he had polished with such devotion. Blood filled the geometric patterns he had traced with his fingers. Blood dripped from the blade his father had carried, the blade he had spoken to as a friend, the blade he had believed represented justice.

This is what justice looks like. A boy dead in the sand. A sword that does not care whose throat it opens.

Juba's stomach lurched. The satisfaction curdled into revulsion so profound it felt like poison spreading through his veins. He had felt good watching the light leave the Roman's eyes. He had felt proud of how cleanly Azref had done its work.

What kind of person felt proud of that?

Around the circle, approving murmurs ran through the assembled men. Malik stepped forward to place a hand on his shoulder.

"Juba ibn Aedemon has proven himself worthy of immema, full adult status among the warriors of the people. The spirits have seen his courage and deemed it acceptable."

The words washed over him without meaning. He stared at the blood on Azref's blade, his father's blade, the blade he loved, and felt a fracture inside him that would never quite heal.

Grandmother Menna approached with sage and blessed water for the post-combat purification.

"The trial is completed, but the spiritual work begins now." Her voice cut through his numbness. "You have taken a life in service to the people. The spirits honor this. But a part of you has died with the young Roman. To find your life again, you must carry the burden of that taking properly, lest it corrupt your soul."

The cleansing ritual that followed was deliberate and thorough. Menna washed the blood from Juba's hands while speaking prayers that helped the spirit of the slain find peace. Then she reached for Azref.

"The blade too must be cleansed."

Juba pulled the sword back, an instinct he did not understand. "I will do it."

Menna studied him with ancient eyes that saw too much. "As you wish."

He cleaned Azref himself, wiping away every trace of the Roman's blood with hands that would not stop trembling. The geometric patterns emerged again, beautiful and terrible. The iron blade shone as it always had: patient, ready, indifferent to what it had done.

"Remember," Menna said, for his ears alone, "you killed not from anger or pride, but from necessity. Hold to that truth when the burden of this act presses upon your dreams."

But Juba knew, and suspected Menna knew too, that necessity was only part of it. He had killed because the council required it. But he had felt satisfaction because a part of him had wanted to prove he could.

That was the corruption Menna warned against, the hunger it revealed.

And Azref had helped him discover it.

❧✦❧

That evening

While the celebration feast continued in the camp's center, Juba sat alone in the family dwelling. Azref lay across his knees, cleaned and oiled, beautiful as ever.

He could not look at it without seeing the Roman's eyes.

"I thought you would make me like him," he said to the blade. "Like my father. A warrior for justice." His voice broke. "But there is no justice in what we did today. Just a dead boy and a room full of men who think that makes me a man."

The sword offered no response. It never had. The conversations had always been one-sided, Juba speaking to iron that could not answer. He had pretended the silence was understanding. Now he knew it for what it was: emptiness reflecting emptiness.

"I cannot carry you anymore." The words came hard, each one a small death. "Not where people can see. Not where I might use you again."

He wrapped Azref in an old cloth and carried the bundle to the storage area at the back of the dwelling. There, behind baskets of grain and stacks of unused blankets, he made a space just large enough for a sword.

"I will bring you out when I must," he said as he set the wrapped blade down. "When combat is unavoidable and others' lives depend on it. But never again for glory. Never again to prove what I am worth. And never..." His voice caught. "Never again to kill unless there is no other choice."

He knelt there, his hand on the wrapped sword, saying goodbye to the boy who had believed that skill with a blade could fill the hollow inside him, that his father's sword could make him his father's son, that justice was something you could hold in your hand.

Azref waited in the darkness, patient and beautiful and terrible.

It would wait a long time.

❧✦❧

Amara found her brother by the sacred spring, staring into the star-filled water. The celebration feast continued back at camp, but he had slipped away as soon as courtesy allowed.

"You succeeded." She settled beside him on the stone ledge.

"I did." His voice was flat. "I killed a boy barely older than myself, and it felt easy. Natural. As if I was born for it."

"And then?"

He was quiet for so long she thought he would not answer. When he spoke, his voice was barely audible.

"And then I felt sick. Because I liked it, Amara. For one moment, I was proud of what I had done." He looked at her, and his eyes held something new, quieter than the desperate hunger for validation she had sensed for years. Sadder. "I put Azref away. Our father's sword. I cannot carry it anymore, not unless lives depend on it."

"Why?"

"Because I spoke to that sword as if it were a friend. I polished it and praised it and promised it glory. And today it showed me what it is: just metal that does not care whose blood it drinks." He looked back at the water. "I do not want to become someone who stops caring either."

The talisman warmed against Amara's chest. This was not the resolution she had feared, her brother consumed by violence, lost to the hunger for proving himself. This was a discipline. One that might, in time, become wisdom.

"You will still train," she said. It was not a question.

"I have to. The community needs defenders, and I have the skills." He flexed his empty hands. "But I will not kill again unless there is no other choice. And I will not pretend that killing is justice, no matter what the elders say."

"The warriors will expect..."

"I know what they will expect." His jaw tightened. "Which is why no one can know. Only you." He turned to face her fully, and she saw the calculation beneath the grief, the strategic mind already working. "If Amagar or the others learned that Aedemon's son refuses to kill, they would see it as weakness. Cowardice. Everything I have built would collapse."

"So what will you do?"

"Become so good at everything else that no one questions why I am not swinging the blade." He stood, pacing along the spring's edge. "Strategy. Tactics. Planning raids where no one needs to die. Reading Roman patrol patterns, finding paths through their lines, anticipating their movements before they make them." His voice gathered strength as the shape of it formed in his mind. "A warrior who wins without fighting is more valuable than one who wins by killing. I just have to prove it."

"That is a difficult path."

"Less difficult than becoming someone I cannot live with." He stopped pacing, looking down at his hands, the hands that had held Azref, that had felt the blade slide through flesh. "In combat, I will wound. I will disarm. I will do whatever it takes to protect our people short of taking another life. And if anyone notices, I will make sure my plans are so sound, my strategies so effective, that they will not care how I fight, only that we win."

Amara absorbed this. The talisman pulsed gently, and she sensed the truth beneath his words: this was more than strategy. It was penance. A way to honor the skills his father had given him while refusing the final step that those skills made possible.

"You are asking me to keep this secret."

"I am asking you to be the only one who knows who I am." His voice dropped. "The others will see Juba ibn Aedemon, the warrior, the strategist, the leader. You will see the boy who put his sword away and swore never to use it for what it was made for." He paused. "Can you carry that?"

She rose and stood beside him, their reflections wavering in the starlit water. "I have been carrying your secrets since we were children. This one is lighter than most, because this one I am proud to keep."

The tension around his jaw eased. Not peace, not yet. But the beginning of a path forward.

"I will need your help," he said. "Your gift for reading people, for sensing what they feel beneath what they say. When I am planning, when I am trying to predict how Romans will move or how our own warriors will react, I will need to know what I am missing."

"You want me to be your secret weapon."

"I want us to be what we have always been. Twins who think together." He almost smiled. "You see hearts. I see patterns.

Together, maybe we can find ways to protect our people that do not require anyone else to die."

They walked back toward camp together, two teenagers carrying a secret that would shape the years to come.

The immema was finished. Juba ibn Aedemon was now recognized as a full adult, a warrior capable of defending his people.

But the man the warriors celebrated was already becoming someone else: a strategist who would spend the coming years honing his mind instead of his blade, building a reputation for tactical brilliance that would eventually make him indispensable. When he strapped Azref to his hip for raids and battles, the other warriors would see a leader ready to fight. They would not know the sword was a prop, a symbol, a reminder of what he refused to become.

Only Amara would know the truth: that her brother's greatest strength was his refusal to use the one skill that came most naturally to him.

Late Winter 56 CE—Volubilis

The letter arrived wrapped in a contract dispute, as always. Tacfara's handwriting became as familiar to Marcus as his own heartbeat. The slight leftward slant, the economy of strokes, the way she formed her letters like someone who had spent decades reading documents and learned to write with the same precision she used to analyze them.

The rains came early this year. The courtyard floods in the afternoons, and I have had to move the older scrolls to higher shelves. The cat disapproves of the disruption to her sleeping arrangements.

I found the Zeno text again, the one about motion through infinite points. It reads differently after fifteen years. We are still arriving. It made me think of your work. How you maintain constancy while everything around you changes. How you remain yourself despite becoming someone new with each passing year.

Fifteen years now since Aedemon. The children would be nearly grown. Do they know what you have done for them? Will they ever?

I do not ask because I expect answers. I ask because someone should acknowledge the question. Someone should see the burden you carry, even if they cannot lift it.

The cat has claimed your chair again. She is growing old, grey around her muzzle now, slower to jump. But she still waits by the window when caravans arrive from the east. She still believes you will return.

So do I.

Write when you can. I am not going anywhere.

Marcus read the letter three times in the privacy of his quarters, then held it to the lamp flame and watched the words curl into ash.

Fifteen years.

The twins would be sixteen now, nearly the age Aedemon had been when Marcus first met him: young and fierce and certain that the world could be made better through courage alone. Did Juba carry that same certainty? Did Amara possess her father's intensity, her mother's quiet strength?

He would never know. The protection required distance. The distance required ignorance. And the ignorance had become its own kind of burden: protecting children he could not watch grow, could not guide, could not even glimpse from afar without risking everything he had built.

But Tacfara knew. She acknowledged his burden. She saw it. And sometimes, in the darkest hours when the lies felt suffocating and the protection felt endless, that seeing was enough to carry him through another day.

He reached for parchment and stylus, composing the reply he would send with the next merchant caravan heading west.

The river metaphor suits better than you know. Some days I cannot recognize the man I was when this began. Some days I cannot imagine the man I will be when it ends, if it ends.

The archives grow fat with faked documentation. The prefect is less systematic but more suspicious than his predecessor. I adjust. I adapt. The waters flow, and I remain.

Tell the cat I remember her too. Tell her some loyalties outlast the circumstances that created them. Tell her that patience, however painful, is sometimes the only form love can take.

Tell her I carry the burden differently now. Not lighter, never lighter. But shared, somehow, across the distance between us.

The river flows. I remain.

Burn this.

He sealed the letter inside a property dispute consultation, addressed it to Tacfara's workshop with the careful formality of professional correspondence, and set it aside for the morning caravan.

Outside his window, Caesarea settled into darkness. Somewhere to the south, in a settlement the archives would never accurately locate, a young man had learned what his father's sword could do, and made a choice about what kind of man he would become.

Marcus hoped the boy had chosen well. He hoped the lessons Aedemon never had time to teach had somehow reached his son through other means: through the community that sheltered him, the teacher who guided him, the sister who saw him more clearly than he saw himself.

He hoped Juba had learned what Marcus himself had learned too late: that some weapons, once used, changed you forever. That the capacity for violence was a burden, not a gift.

That true strength sometimes meant choosing not to strike, even when striking would be easier.

The protection continued. The letters flowed between Caesarea and Volubilis. And in the space between duty and desire, two people who had chosen to see each other's burdens kept faith with a connection that distance could not sever.

The river flowed.

They remained.

CHAPTER 44

The Patient Ledger

"The patient man fills his ledger.
The wise man asks what the ledger cannot hold."
—Roman administrative observation (attributed)
55 CE—Caesarea—Marcus, year 14 of protection

The morning briefing stretched past midday, and Marcus Valerius Severus felt the familiar tension building behind his eyes.

He passed the mess hall where junior officers ate. A burst of laughter and a fragment of conversation:

"...said the Berber woman tried to bribe him with dates. Dates! As if that is currency."

"Everything is currency to the barbari. Goats, dates, daughters."

"The daughters, at least!" More laughter.

Fourteen years ago, Marcus would have smiled. Seven years ago, he would have felt uneasy. Now the words scraped across an open wound. He thought of Zahra's hands calloused from well-ropes, of Amara's green eyes reading the world with impossible depth, of Juba bent over maps by firelight with his father's intensity.

Barbari.

The word the Empire used to erase the inconvenient humanity of the people it consumed.

He kept walking.

The real pressure came from Petronius.

Six years into his command, the prefect shed the polished ambition of his early tenure and replaced it with a colder resolve. Rome had left him in Mauretania longer than he expected, and the province's stubborn refusal to be pacified had become a personal insult. The easy smile no longer reached his eyes.

Marcus entered the strategy room to find Petronius reviewing dispatches, a silver cup of wine at his elbow despite the early hour. The map on the wall bristled with iron pins: red for settlements raided, black for settlements scheduled. The red outnumbered the black now, but the black kept reappearing, the province produced new targets faster than Petronius could process the old ones.

"Tribune." Petronius did not look up. "The quarterly report for Rome requires revision. Our pacification numbers are insufficient."

"The numbers reflect the operational reality, Prefect."

"The numbers reflect what you report to me, Tribune. And what you report determines what I report to Rome. And what I report to Rome determines whether I spend another year in this dust-choked province or receive the posting I was promised." He looked up. The easy smile. "So we will revise the numbers together."

Marcus kept his face neutral. This was new. Petronius always inflated his dispatches, but he had done it himself, adding flourishes to Marcus's reports, reframing inconclusive patrols as successful pacification operations. Now he wanted Marcus complicit.

"What revisions does the prefect have in mind?"

"The northeastern foothills." Petronius tapped the map where Tizwit lay among dozens of similar settlements. "Your patrols have passed through that region twice this quarter. Both times, you reported scattered populations engaged in seasonal herding. Cooperative but uninformative."

"That is what we encountered."

"What you encountered is what you chose to see. What I need you to have encountered is a network of settlements providing active intelligence about insurgent movements, which your patrols have successfully leveraged to disrupt three planned attacks on Roman supply lines."

The fabrication was breathtaking in its specificity. Petronius had already written the narrative. He needed only Marcus's signature to make it official.

"Those attacks did not occur, Prefect."

"Precisely. Because we disrupted them. That is the beauty of preemptive intelligence, Tribune. Success looks exactly like nothing happening." Petronius selected an olive from a bowl and bit into it. "Sign the report. I will handle the formatting."

Marcus looked at the document. Signing it would protect the northeastern foothills. If Rome believed the region was already producing results, Petronius would have no reason to escalate operations there. The lie would become a shield.

But it would also make Marcus a co-author of fiction. Every previous misdirection had been his own: lies he controlled, calibrated, could adjust or retract if necessary. This was different. This was Petronius's lie, written in Petronius's hand, requiring only Marcus's endorsement to become official record.

And official records, once created, took on lives of their own.

"The report will need supporting documentation," Marcus said. "Patrol logs. Intelligence summaries. The kind of detail that withstands review."

"You will provide them." It was not a request. "You have fourteen years of experience fabricating exactly such details. Do not pretend otherwise."

The words landed with surgical precision. Not an accusation. Not even a threat. Just the quiet acknowledgment that Petronius knew, or suspected, that Marcus's reports had never been entirely truthful.

"Every officer adjusts reports for clarity," Marcus said.

"Of course." Petronius's smile widened. "And every prefect recognizes the adjustments. The question is not whether you have been creative with the truth, Tribune. The question is whether your creativity serves Rome or serves something else." He let the pause stretch. "I have not yet decided which. But cooperation simplifies the question considerably."

Marcus signed the report.

He told himself it was strategy. That co-opting Petronius's lie gave him influence over its shape. That a fabricated success in the northeast protected Tizwit better than truthful failure ever could.

But walking back to his quarters, he felt the ground shift beneath him. With Nerva, the game had rules. Intelligence, counter-intelligence, the methodical chess match of two minds measuring each other across years. Nerva wanted truth. Marcus hid it. The dynamic was adversarial but comprehensible.

Petronius did not want truth. Petronius wanted results, and he did not care whether those results were real. The distinction dissolved the framework Marcus had spent fourteen years building. You could not misdirect a man who did not care about direction. You could not hide truth from someone who preferred fiction.

And you could not predict what a man who manufactured his own reality would do when reality refused to cooperate.

❧✦❧

Caesarea, the strategy room — three weeks later

Marcus arrived at the strategy room before the second watch and found the overnight dispatches stacked on the map table where the duty officer left them each morning. Three reports from coastal garrisons. A supply requisition from Volubilis. Routine correspondence from the governor's office. And at the bottom of the stack, sealed with the red wax of a field commander's urgent mark, a single sheet that changed the shape of the day.

Tribesmen in the Ouarsenis foothills had seized a Roman tax collector and his escort of four soldiers. The tribal chief demanded the release of three prisoners held in the Caesarea garrison, men arrested during the prefect's last punitive sweep, or the Romans would die at the new moon. Six days.

Marcus set the dispatch on the table and waited for Petronius.

Prefect Petronius arrived an hour later, read the report standing, and set it down. His expression said his career was collapsing before his eyes. A dead tax collector meant a senatorial inquiry. Dead soldiers meant the governor's attention. A successful rescue meant the commendation that might earn him his transfer to Hispania.

"Tribune. You know these tribes. What are my options?"

Marcus studied the map. He did know these tribes. He had spent fourteen years building relationships throughout the province, and the Ouarsenis chief, Amayas, was a man he understood: proud, pragmatic, pushed to desperation by Petronius's extortion-level taxation.

"Amayas does not want dead Romans, Prefect. Dead Romans bring legions. He wants his men back, and he wants the tax burden reduced to what his people can sustain."

"I cannot reduce taxes at the demand of a tribal chief. Rome would see it as capitulation."

"Rome would see it as administrative change based on revised agricultural assessments. The tax rate was set using Nerva's census count from eight years ago. The drought of fifty-four reduced arable land by a third. A correction is overdue and defensible."

Petronius considered this. "And the prisoners?"

"Release two of the three. The youngest, Amayas's nephew, and the elder who serves as the tribe's spiritual authority. Hold the third as a guarantee of continued cooperation. Frame it as clemency."

"Amayas will accept this?"

"I will go myself and negotiate. Amayas knows me. He will accept terms delivered by someone he considers honest."

Petronius's eyes narrowed. "You are very confident of your standing with a man who has just taken Roman hostages."

"Fourteen years of honest dealing. I have never lied to a tribal chief, Prefect. That is an asset Rome should value."

The irony was lost on Petronius, who heard only the pragmatic calculation. "Go. Take an escort of ten. If you fail, I send a cohort, and Amayas and his people will wish they had never heard the name Rome."

Marcus rode out within the hour. He reached the Ouarsenis foothills on the second day and met Amayas under a truce flag at the edge of the tribal encampment. The negotiation took four hours. Marcus spoke in Tamazight. He acknowledged the injustice of the tax rate. He presented the prisoner release as a gesture of good faith from a prefect who wished to govern rather than punish. He promised the tax reassessment would be completed before the next collection cycle.

Amayas studied him across the silence.. "You are the only Roman who speaks to us as men rather than subjects."

"I speak to you as what you are. The rest is Rome's failure."

Amayas released the hostages unharmed. Marcus rode back to Caesarea with five Romans who owed him their lives and a negotiated agreement that would keep the Ouarsenis foothills peaceful for three years.

Petronius received the news with transparent relief. "The governor will hear of this, Tribune. I will ensure it."

"Thank you, Prefect."

"And Tribune? The eastern patrol routes. I am giving you full discretion over scheduling and deployment for the next quarter. You have earned my trust in operational matters."

Full discretion over eastern patrol routes. The routes that passed nearest to Tizwit. Marcus accepted with a salute and walked out into the courtyard. The afternoon sun fell across the garrison stones with the indifference of an empire that did not know its best officer served two masters, and served both well.

Three weeks later — Caesarea

The intelligence arrived from three separate sources on the same morning: tribal movement in the Hodna basin. Families relocating to higher ground. Livestock being driven inland from traditional coastal pastures. Grain stores consolidated in defensible positions.

Marcus read the reports and recognized the pattern. Drought preparation. The Hodna tribes read weather the way Roman engineers read terrain, with generations of accumulated precision. When the families moved to high ground before the dry season, it meant the coming summer would be brutal. Crops would fail. Water sources would shrink. By autumn, hungry settlements would be desperate enough to raid Roman supply lines, not from political resistance but from starvation.

The correct response was clear: release emergency grain reserves now, while the roads were passable and the cost was low. A prefect who understood the province would buy three years of stability for the price of a few hundred bushels.

Marcus wrote the assessment and delivered it to Petronius that afternoon.

Petronius read it while eating olives. "Tribal families moving to higher ground." He set the report aside. "They do this every year."

"Not at this scale, Prefect. The consolidation pattern suggests they are anticipating severe drought. If we release grain reserves now..."

"If we release grain reserves, Rome sees a prefect feeding barbarians instead of taxing them." Petronius selected another olive. "The governor's review of my command is in four months. I will not have my record show charity to tribes that should be generating revenue."

"The alternative is armed raids on supply lines by autumn."

"Then we will suppress the raids and report the suppression as evidence of effective pacification." Petronius smiled. "Suppressed raids look better on a command review than preemptive grain distributions, Tribune. Rome rewards strength, not generosity."

Marcus took back the report. There was nothing more to say. He had presented the evidence, offered the analysis, recommended the response. Petronius had weighed the province's survival against his career review and chosen his career.

By September, the drought hit exactly as the tribal movements predicted. Three settlements in the Hodna basin sent raiding parties against Roman grain convoys. Petronius dispatched two centuries to suppress them. The engagement killed fourteen tribespeople, including two children caught in a burning granary. The Roman casualties were three wounded.

Petronius filed the action report as a successful pacification operation. The governor's office commended his decisive response to tribal aggression. His command review noted the engagement favorably.

Marcus read the commendation in his quarters and set it on the desk beside his original assessment, the one recommending grain distribution. The two documents together told the whole story: a disaster predicted, a solution offered, a solution refused, people dead, and the man responsible rewarded for cleaning up the mess he had created.

Madi appeared at the door. "The Hodna elders are requesting a meeting. They want to know why Rome let their children starve when the tribune warned them months in advance."

"How do they know I warned them?"

"Because you are the only Roman who has ever warned them about anything." Madi paused. "They trust you. That is becoming a problem."

Marcus put both documents in his desk and locked it. The assessment would stay in his private files. If Petronius ever discovered that the tribes knew Marcus had recommended the grain distribution, the fragile balance of lies that protected Tizwit would collapse.

The protection held. But the cost of holding it grew heavier with each act of preventable cruelty Marcus could see coming and could not stop.

Three days later

Marcus led a reconnaissance patrol into the eastern foothills, one of the verification exercises Petronius had authorized to support the fabricated quarterly report. Twelve men moved through terrain Marcus knew too well, approaching settlements he needed to protect at all costs.

Centurion Madi rode beside him, reading the land with the expertise of a lifetime in Mauretania. The other soldiers were younger, less experienced, more likely to see exactly what Marcus needed them to see.

As they crested a ridge overlooking a wide valley, Marcus spotted smoke from cooking fires rising from a cluster of dwellings tucked against the foothills. His heart clenched.

Tizwit.

The settlement where Eudoxus had taken Zahra and the children fourteen years ago, where they still lived if Marcus's protection held, hidden in plain sight among the dozens of similar oases dotting the region.

"There." Decurion Priscus pointed toward the settlement. "Looks substantial. Worth investigating?"

Marcus calculated quickly. Refusing would raise suspicions. Agreeing meant potential disaster. The middle path required navigation.

"Worth noting for follow-up investigation." He consulted his map with apparent care. "But our primary objective is documenting settlements already in the archive for verification purposes. That one..." He made a show of checking coordinates. "It is not in our current assignment parameters. Investigating it now would compromise the verification methodology."

Priscus frowned. "It is right there. Seems wasteful to pass it by."

"It seems wasteful to invalidate an entire verification exercise because we cannot maintain systematic discipline." Marcus's voice carried the authority of rank and experience. "The prefect specified precise methodology. Random deviations undermine the process."

The younger officer yielded, though his expression suggested the matter was not forgotten. Marcus made a note on his map, marking the settlement for future investigation by patrols he would personally ensure asked the wrong questions in the wrong ways.

As they rode on, Marcus felt sweat cooling beneath his armor despite the autumn chill. That had been too close.

The patrol continued through three other settlements Marcus had prepared for investigation. His tribal contacts, the real ones distinct from the elaborate network of fictional sources he maintained for Roman records, were warned to provide cooperative but unhelpful information.

At the first settlement, the elder greeted them with respectful wariness. Yes, they paid tribute to Rome when collectors came. No, they had not seen unusual movements in the region. Just shepherds following traditional routes, traders moving between oases, the ordinary patterns of desert life.

At the second settlement, Marcus's translator, one of his cultivated contacts, conveyed questions with subtle signals that told the locals what answers served everyone's interests. The information gathered was accurate enough to verify but useless for identifying anything Rome would consider threatening.

At the third settlement, they arrived to find cooking fires still warm, but the population gone to seasonal pastures two valleys away. The scouts sent ahead returned with apologetic reports about confusing trails.

By the time the patrol returned to Caesarea five days later, Marcus had produced a comprehensive report that satisfied every requirement of thoroughness while revealing nothing that would threaten the family he protected.

The cost: another layer of lies added to fourteen years of systematic deception. Another debt to tribal contacts who trusted him despite knowing he served Rome. Another night of exhaustion so profound that sleep brought no rest, only nightmares of the moment when all his careful structures would collapse.

❧✦❧

Late that night

Centurion Madi appeared at Marcus's quarters. The privilege of shared conspiracy allowed him to enter without announcement.

"Petronius is getting worse," Madi said in Tamazight, the language they used for absolute privacy.

"I know."

"He does not care about truth the way Nerva did. Nerva wanted to understand. You could work with that, misdirect it, shape it. But Petronius..." Madi settled into the room's single chair. "He manufactures whatever reality serves his career. And when that fiction collides with actual events, he will need someone to blame."

"I am aware." Marcus moved to his maps. "The twins are fifteen now. Old enough to be recognized if they travel, old enough to attract attention with unusual abilities. Old enough to be dangerous to Rome in ways children never were."

"Then you know this protection is approaching its natural end. We have bought them fourteen years, from infancy to near-adulthood."

Marcus met his friend's eyes. "Fourteen years. And still not enough time. But you are right that the nature of the protection must change. Hiding them becomes more dangerous with each passing year. We need alternatives."

"What kind of alternatives?"

"I do not know yet. But Petronius will not stop escalating. His reports to Rome grow more creative, his methods more brutal. Eventually the fiction he has built will require real results to sustain it. And when that happens, he will send patrols with orders to fill cells rather than files."

Madi was quiet for a moment. "How much longer can you maintain this?"

"As long as I must. As long as they need protection."

✦

After Madi left, Marcus caught his reflection in the polished bronze mirror he used for shaving.

The face that stared back belonged to a stranger: grey-haired, lined, exhaustion evident in every feature. At forty-seven, he looked sixty. Fourteen years of serving two masters showed in ways no amount of professional competence could hide.

He remembered the officer he had been at thirty-three: confident, capable, proud of his mixed heritage that let him bridge Roman efficiency with Amazigh understanding. That man believed honor could accommodate complexity, that loyalty to empire need not contradict loyalty to conscience.

That man was naive.

The worst nights were the ones when he could not remember why any of it mattered. The protection, the lies, the slow erosion of everything he had once believed. On those nights, he read her letters, kept hidden in a compartment beneath his trunk, written in a hand he learned to recognize the way he recognized his own heartbeat.

The cat knocked over a client's inkwell yesterday. I blamed a draft. He believed me because people believe what is easier than the truth. I thought you would appreciate that.

Come back when you can. I am not going anywhere.

He folded the letters carefully, returned them to their hiding place. The burden did not lift. But it shifted, just slightly, into something he could carry for another day.

Was it worth it?

The question came more frequently now. Not whether the protection mattered. That was never in doubt. But whether the cost to his own soul could be justified by the lives it preserved.

He thought of Aedemon's last words, acknowledgment that Marcus would do exactly this: sacrifice everything to protect what his friend loved most.

Fourteen years. The twins grew from children escaping Aghbalou to near-adults who could be identified, interrogated, used against their dead father's memory. Zahra survived exile, grief, the constant threat of discovery. The protection bought them childhood, education, community, life.

Was it worth what it cost him?

Marcus turned from the mirror, unable to face the answer reflected there.

He extinguished his lamp and lay in darkness, listening to the garrison's night sounds. Fourteen years ago, he would have told himself it was worth it. Tonight he no longer needed to. The question had stopped mattering around year ten. What remained was simpler than debt or honor. He had made a promise. He would keep it.

❧✦❧

That same autumn—A trading settlement south of Volubilis

Amara had come with Silina to trade medicinal herbs for iron needles and the fine linen Silina preferred for wound dressings. The settlement straddled a crossroads where Amazigh caravans met Roman supply lines, and the market thrived on the uneasy commerce between occupier and occupied.

She sensed the Roman column before she heard it. A pressure at the edges of her awareness, the familiar blend of boredom and wariness that soldiers carried on long marches. She had learned to read patrols the way Malik read weather: from a distance, without engagement, noting direction and intensity before deciding whether to take shelter.

But this column carried a different cargo at its center.

The talisman cooled against her chest as the horsemen rounded the market's eastern wall. She saw the standard first, then the officers, then a man on a grey mare who rode with an easy commanding posture, who clearly expected the world to arrange itself around him. He was not old. Not young. His face held the pleasant neutrality of a man accustomed to being obeyed, and when he smiled at the settlement elder who hurried forward to greet him, the smile carried all the warmth of a transaction.

Amara did not reach for him. She did not need to. His presence pressed against her awareness the way heat rises from stone: unavoidable, ambient, requiring no effort to perceive.

And what she perceived hollowed her out.

She had read grief and joy and rage and love and loneliness and shame. She had sat with Eudoxus's ancient sorrow and Juba's desperate hunger and Zahra's buried fury. Every person she had ever sensed carried wounds, and those wounds, however painful, were proof of life. Proof that a part of them had once been whole and could, with patience, become whole again.

This man carried no wounds.

Not because he had healed. Because nothing in him had ever been broken. There was ambition, vast and efficient, calibrated to the precise mechanisms of Roman advancement. There was intelligence, sharp enough to recognize useful tools and discard useless ones. There was even a kind of pleasure: the satisfaction of a craftsman examining a worksite, assessing which structures to demolish and which to repurpose.

But beneath the ambition and the intelligence and the satisfaction, where in every other person she had ever read there lived some flickering thing that yearned or grieved or hoped, she felt only a smooth and polished absence. Not emptiness the way Juba's was empty, aching for what had been lost. This was an absence that had never noticed itself. A man who had never once wondered whether he was enough, because the question had simply never occurred to him.

She could see him with perfect clarity. The talisman showed her everything.

And the clarity gave her nothing.

No crack where truth might enter. No hidden wound she could speak to. No buried self that longed to be seen. The practice Eudoxus had spent four years teaching her—presence, patience, the courage to sit with another's pain—required pain to sit with. Required a person who, beneath the surface, wanted to be known.

This man did not want to be known. He wanted to be promoted.

She watched him dismount, watched him accept a cup of wine from the elder with a nod that was neither grateful nor dismissive but simply efficient, watched him survey the market the way a butcher surveys a carcass: assessing yield. And she understood, with a certainty that chilled her more than the talisman's cold, that everything Eudoxus had taught her was powerless here. She could sit with this man for a thousand years and it would change nothing. He would not be moved by being seen. He would not be transformed by being understood. He would continue doing exactly what served his interests, and the communities in his path would suffer for it, and all the empathy in the world would not stop him.

Silina touched her arm. "We should go. That is the prefect."

Amara let herself be led away through the market's back lanes, but the absence she had sensed stayed with her like the afterimage of a bright light. That night, in the guest tent of a friendly settlement, she pressed the talisman against her chest and tried to understand what she had felt.

If seeing clearly could not reach a man like that, what could?

The question circled and would not settle. And the talisman, sensing her frustration, her hunger to protect her people from a threat her gift could not address, pulsed with a warmth that felt less like comfort and more like invitation.

The talisman pulsed against her chest. The warmth it offered was not the warmth of comfort or encouragement. It was something she had no name for, something that felt like a hunger being recognized rather than answered. She did not know what it meant. Neither did the stone. It only felt what she brought to it, and what she brought was desperation, and the desperation pulsed back through her, amplified.

She did not know whether the thought was hers or the talisman's. She was not sure it mattered.

✦

But in Tizwit, another clock ran. Eudoxus had been coughing more frequently, his hands trembling worse each month. The old scholar who had guided Amara's gift since childhood was fading, and they all knew it.

When he was gone, who would teach Amara the difference between using her gift and being used by it?

That question, Marcus suspected, might matter more than all his careful protection.

CHAPTER 45

The Last Lesson

"The last lesson is always the one the teacher did not plan to give."
—Persian saying on mentorship
Late Summer 56 CE—Tizwit Oasis

The morning air carried the scent of distant rain as Amara sat with Eudoxus beneath the ancient tamarisk tree that had become their teaching place. Four years of study had passed since her first tentative experiments with the talisman's guidance, and now she could read signs in water, sense the approach of strangers, and calm frightened animals with a touch. But a quality in Eudoxus's manner today felt different, more final, like the last notes of a song drawing to its close.

Before they could begin, Grandmother Menna appeared carrying the traditional elements for a significant spiritual working. In her hands, she held a goatskin bag of blessed water from the sacred spring, sage bound with red cord, and a small clay lamp filled with oil consecrated during the dark moon.

"The spirits have been whispering." She settled beside them with the careful movements of advanced age. "Today's teaching requires their presence and protection."

The ritual preparation was brief but meaningful. Menna lit the blessed lamp while speaking prayers that called upon the sky-spirits to guide the transmission of wisdom from one generation to the next. She burned the sage, its smoke rising straight in the still air.

"May their blessing rest upon this final lesson."

He reached over and adjusted her hands on her knees, palms up, fingers loose, in a posture of receiving rather than holding. His grip was firm. She registered this without naming it, the way you register a door that opens more easily than expected and walk through without stopping to wonder why. He had not held anything that steadily in years.

He did not notice. She almost did.

Only after these preparations were complete did Eudoxus speak, his weathered hands resting gently on his knees. "You have learned much, little hawk. You have honored the gift with wisdom and restraint."

"But there is more to learn." Amara protested. "You said the teachings stretch deeper than any single lifetime could explore."

"True. But not all learning comes from instruction. Some wisdom arrives only through living." His eyes held hers with unusual intensity. "And some knowledge must be discovered alone, in the quiet spaces between what teachers can offer and what students must find for themselves."

The talisman warmed against her chest. She sensed a change in Eudoxus, a kind of spiritual readiness. His soul was done with its work in this place and prepared to depart.

"You are leaving us."

He smiled, neither confirming nor denying. "We are all leaving, always. The question is whether we depart having served what we were meant to serve."

"Have you?"

"I believe so." His voice carried deep contentment. "I came to this desert seeking redemption for an old failure. I found instead the chance to teach different lessons, to be present for the miracle of young minds awakening to possibilities their elders had forgotten."

He shifted slightly, settling more comfortably against the tree's trunk. "But before I go, there is one more teaching. The most important one. And it cannot be told. It must be experienced."

Amara's heart quickened. She recognized this tone, the deliberate preparation for significant spiritual work.

"The talisman you wear has taught you to see beyond surface appearances, to sense the sacred wholeness in all living things. But there is one being whose wholeness you have not yet fully recognized."

"Who?"

"Yourself." He touched her hand gently. "You have spent so long believing your worth lies in the gift, in what you can do, in how you serve others. Today, you will learn something different."

✦

They walked to the sacred spring, a place Amara had visited countless times, but which seemed transformed today: the water more luminous, the surrounding stones more present, the very air held its breath.

"Sit." Eudoxus settled across from her. "Hold the talisman, but do not seek to use it. Simply be with it. Let it guide you."

Amara closed her eyes, feeling the stone's warmth spread through her palm. The familiar sensation of boundaries dissolving came gently. But instead of expanding her awareness outward as usual, the talisman turned her attention to the spring's edge, to the toad. It sat where it always sat, grey, broad and still as an adult's hand laid flat, its warty skin the color of the sun-warmed stone beneath it. Her heart lifted with the joy of familiarity.

"Open your eyes." Eudoxus's voice came softly. "But maintain the connection. The talisman wishes to teach you something."

She looked at the toad: unremarkable, patient, utterly itself. The agurram. Her agurram.

And then the talisman's opened attention shifted something, and she saw what five years of looking had not shown her. The agurram was not resting on the stone. It was continuous with it. The same warm grey, the same rough surface, the same unhurried stillness. An eagle overhead would find no edge between creature and rock, nothing to distinguish the living thing from the place it belonged.

It did not hide. It simply was so entirely itself, in the place that was entirely its own, that danger had nothing to grasp.

As she watched, the talisman's guidance deepened, and she was not just observing the toad. She was experiencing what it meant to be one.

The shift arrived without warning: the world dropped to ground level, cold stone pressed against her belly, the air tasted of water and dust and the mineral sharpness of the rock beneath her. She felt the agurram's hunger — patient, unhurried, a fact of the body like breathing. She felt its warmth, the sun's stored heat moving up through stone and into her. She felt the spring's sound differently: not as music but as information, the subtle changes in water-noise that meant movement nearby, safety, the absence of threat.

Then the shadow.

The terror was nothing like she expected. It was not the crowd's flood of emotion pressing through her walls, not the grief she had absorbed in the fever years, not the controlled overwhelm she had learned to manage with Eudoxus's practice. It was older than any of that. It arrived complete, instant, total — every nerve contracting toward the stone, the belly pressing flatter, the breath stopping. Not chosen. Not decided. Simply what the body did when death passed overhead.

An eagle, circling.

Her skin pressed flat against the stone — and the stone pressed back, not as surface but as substance, as though the boundary between toad-flesh and rock had softened into something continuous. She could not have said where she ended and the stone began. The grey of her skin was the grey of the rock. The warmth moving up through her belly was the warmth stored in the stone since dawn. She was not hiding on the rock. She was the rock, briefly, in the way that mattered: the eagle's eye would sweep this surface and find nothing to separate from it, nothing to fix on, nothing to take.

And through the terror running alongside it like a second current in the same stream the self held.

She could feel it: the agurram's self, present and unscattered beneath the fear. The terror moved through it the way water moves through stone — carving nothing, leaving nothing behind. The creature did not suppress what it felt. It simply remained, in the full force of what it felt, so entirely itself that the fear had nowhere to take it.

The eagle's cry crossed the wadi.

The shadow passed.

The eagle moved on.

She had not moved. She had not scattered. She had been, for the span of a held breath, so completely herself in the place she belonged that death had found no edge to grasp.

The connection released gently. She returned fully to herself, tears on her face, the spring's sound around her, the morning light unchanged.

The agurram sat on its stone. It had not moved. It would not move. It was exactly what it had always been, in exactly the place it had always been, needing nothing from anyone.

She had been sitting beside it every morning for five years.

Oh, she thought. *The fear is real. And it holds through it. Every time.*

Eudoxus watched her with eyes that held both satisfaction and sorrow. "You understand."

"The toad did not need to become anything else." Her voice shook. "It was already complete. Already sacred. Just by being what it was."

"And you?"

"I am the One." She pressed her hand against her chest, feeling her heartbeat, her breath, her aliveness. "Not because of what I can do. Not because of the gift. Just because I am. I am enough, exactly as I exist."

"Yes."

As they walked back from the spring, Eudoxus paused at a flat stone worn smooth by generations of travelers. He settled carefully, his breathing labored.

"One more teaching." He met her eyes. "About the nature of your gift."

Amara sat beside him, the talisman warm against her chest.

"The talisman shows you what others feel. Their hidden wounds, their secret hopes, their fears they cannot name." He held up his ruined hand. "But it cannot show you why. That requires the one thing the gift cannot provide: the willingness to be wrong. The moment you believe you know another's heart completely, you have stopped seeing them and started seeing your certainty about them."

The talisman pulsed, neither confirming nor denying.

"Then what good is the gift?"

"It shows you where to look. What questions to ask. How to approach another soul with care. But the true work of understanding requires you to hold your certainty lightly and meet the other person as a mystery. Melchior never learned this. He used his sight to control rather than to wonder."

He closed his eyes briefly, exhaustion evident.

"Promise me you will remember this when the gift tempts you toward certainty. The talisman shows truth, but truth is not understanding. Understanding requires the courage to not know, and to seek anyway."

"I promise."

But even as she spoke, she wondered if she grasped what he meant. The talisman felt so sure. How could uncertainty be stronger than knowing?

They sat in silence, Amara absorbing the lesson while Eudoxus rested. The sun climbed higher, warming the rocks around the spring.

"There are gifts in this world that can consume their bearers," Eudoxus spoke at last. "You carry such a gift. The talisman found you because you already possessed what Melchior never had: the capacity to see without controlling. But that capacity can be lost. If you start believing your worth comes from the gift rather than from who you are, you will walk his road."

The talisman warmed against her chest.

"Your brother walks a dangerous path." Eudoxus's expression grew more serious. "You cannot save him from his choices, only accompany them with love."

"That is all I can do? Watch him suffer?"

"Questions instead of answers. Presence instead of judgment. Company instead of rescue." His voice grew gentler. "When the time comes, he will need to learn what you learned today. You will need to trust that he can learn it, even through pain."

As the sun reached its zenith, Eudoxus grew visibly more tired. His breathing came shallower, his movements smaller.

"Shall I fetch Silina?" Amara asked.

"No need. This is as it should be." He smiled. "I have taught what I was sent to teach. Now they call me home."

"Please do not leave us yet."

"Little hawk, I am not abandoning you. I am completing my work." He reached out with his left hand and touched her cheek. "You have everything you need."

His breathing grew more labored. "Now call your brother. I would see you both together before I go."

❧✦❧

Later that afternoon

Juba arrived to find Eudoxus resting peacefully, his back against the tamarisk tree, his breath coming slow and steady. Amara sat cross-legged beside him, the talisman warm against her chest, tears tracking down her cheeks.

"Teacher." Juba knelt, his voice rough. He saw the shallow breathing, the peaceful expression that spoke of letting go. "You are leaving us."

"Come, sit." Eudoxus's eyes opened with visible effort. "We have time for one more game, I think."

Juba helped set up the pieces on the board that was central to their relationship. His hands would not stop shaking.

"How do I go forward without your guidance?"

"One choice at a time." Eudoxus's voice had grown softer but maintained its clarity. "You have the tools. What you are still learning is which battles deserve to be fought and which deserve to be transformed."

"I am afraid. Afraid I will keep choosing violence because it is the only thing that makes me feel strong."

"Then choose differently next time. And the time after that. Transformation accumulates through small choices made consistently."

He looked at both twins, his gaze moving from one to the other with deep affection. Then his hand found Juba's wrist, pulling him closer with surprising strength. His voice dropped to a whisper meant only for the young man's ears.

"The talisman carries a truth your sister must learn for herself, but you must remember it for her. Violence depletes. Peace restores. When the power begins to consume her, remind her. Promise me."

Juba glanced at Amara, who sat apart, her attention turned inward. She had not heard.

"I promise," he whispered.

Eudoxus released his wrist and settled back. His breathing grew shallower, more peaceful.

"You gave an old man purpose in his final years. You reminded me that wisdom travels from heart to heart through generations."

His eyes drifted to the stars appearing above the tamarisk's branches. They were the same stars he had charted as a young man in Persia, when Caspar believed the heavens owed him answers. He had spent so many years at war with that name, treating it as the label for everything he had done wrong. Caspar was the seeker and scholar who failed his friends, who arrived too late and understood too little. In this stillness, the old division dissolved. Caspar had followed a star because he believed the universe held meaning. Eudoxus had stayed in a desert village because he discovered it did. They were not two men vying for control of a single body. They were the same man, separated by grief and reunited by purpose.

He settled into the posture one last time. Legs crossed, hand open on his knee, the ruined one resting in his lap. The breath came shallow now, but the practice did not require depth. It required presence. He was present.

The stillness arrived without effort, unlike stillness of those brutal mornings after the oasis, when only the discipline of remaining was all that kept him from despair. This was the stillness he had glimpsed beneath everything else for twenty years, the fullness that existed before thought divided it. It opened to him now, the way a door opens to someone who has finally stopped knocking.

He had sat with grief, and it did not consume him. He had sat with power and let it go. He had sat with two children who carried the future of a people, and he had offered them the only thing worth offering: his attention, steady and unadorned, asking nothing.

And he had sat in a courtyard one spring morning and laughed at a goat, and the laughter had cracked him open in ways fifty years of discipline never managed. The goat had not been seeking enlightenment. It had been eating grain. And in that ordinary act it taught Eudoxus the lesson he had crossed the world to learn: the sacred does not hide in sacred places. It hides in plain sight, waiting for someone to stop looking so hard and simply see.

The practice had been enough. The laughter had been enough. The goat, if he was honest, had been the finest teacher of them all.

Three names he had chosen for himself, each one a smaller room than the last. Caspar, who reached for the heavens. Eudoxus, who settled for service. Numerius, who pressed olives and told other men's stories. But the names others had given him opened outward. Uncle, from children who did not know the word was part of a lie. Grandfather, from the same children after they learned the truth and chose the title anyway. Teacher, spoken by Amara with the reverence the Imazighen reserved for those who carried a community's memory forward. He had spent a lifetime choosing names that diminished him. The people he served had chosen names that told him who he was.

He could rest. The three of him could rest.

The talisman against Amara's chest grew warm, then warmer still. Twenty years ago, in Melchior's workshop in Persepolis, it had spoken to this man the words *You will teach*, and he had. For once, its words had been true. Now the teacher was leaving, and for the first time since Persepolis, the talisman spoke the only words that mattered.

You were enough. You were always enough.

Eudoxus's lips curved in the faintest smile as he breathed his last. Whether he heard its words or only felt its warmth, the talisman could not tell. It did not matter. The connection they had shared as teacher, student, and ancient consciousness learning together, reached its completion.

Amara did not sense a new beginning. Already she longed for Eudoxus and mourned his loss. No more would they have shared moments beneath the shade of the tamarisk tree.

She gripped the talisman harder, needing its presence. The stone pulsed against her palm, and for the first time since discovering it, she clung to it not as a tool but as a lifeline. It was the sole link to the spiritual guidance Eudoxus had helped her understand.

The lesson of the toad felt distant now, overwhelmed by grief. *"I am the One"* became *"I am alone."* The sacred wholeness she had experienced that morning was buried under the crushing awareness that the person who taught her to recognize it was gone.

She held the talisman tighter, tighter, until her knuckles went white and her breath came in gasps. Tomorrow she would remember the toad's lesson. Tomorrow she would honor Eudoxus's lessons.

But tonight, alone with her grief, she needed power. Desperately, the way a drowning person needs air.

Her need shifted into hunger, the first step on a path that had destroyed greater spirits than hers.

☙✦❧

Hours later

Night deepened, and the community dispersed to their dwellings. Silina had prepared Eudoxus's body for tomorrow's ceremonies. Juba had gone to inform the neighboring camps. Zahra was with Yasir, making practical arrangements.

And Amara sat alone in the darkness with what she carried.

The grief rolled through her in waves, each one carrying a distinct voice. Malik's loss arrived first. He had lost the one person who understood both the warrior and the scholar in him. Then the students, their sorrow bright and bewildered, the absence of a voice they had trusted to guide them through confusion. Grandmother Menna's grief, ancient and worn, came last and heaviest the sorrow of someone who had been outliving people she loved for decades

It all flooded through her, settling in her chest like stones.

She tried to remember the agurram: perfect, complete, enough exactly as it was. She tried to remember "I am the One." But the words belonged to a morning when Eudoxus was alive, and that morning was over. She was not the agurram. She was a girl whose teacher was dead, and no lesson he had given her could fill the silence where his voice had been.

She clutched the talisman with both hands, pressing it against her chest, feeling its warmth spread through her body like a lifeline. It was all she had left of the spiritual connection Eudoxus had helped her forge. Without it, she was another grief-stricken girl who had lost her teacher. With it, she remained connected to a presence larger than herself, a force that gave her pain meaning and purpose.

"I am not ready," she whispered to the darkness. "I am not ready to be the One alone."

The stone offered no comfort, but it offered presence. It pulsed with steady warmth, and she drew that warmth into herself the way a drowning person gasps for air.

She sat in the darkness with her burden and the community's grief and the terrible, crushing loneliness of being the one who sensed everything and could fix nothing. The talisman pulsed against her chest, and she held it as the only thing standing between her and drowning in an ocean of everyone's pain.

Tomorrow would bring the memorial, the cairn-building, the formal ceremonies of grief. Tomorrow she would have to be strong, to accompany the community's mourning, to carry what needed to be carried.

But tonight, alone in the darkness, Amara forgot what the agurram taught her. She forgot that she was the One. She forgot sacred wholeness.

Tonight, she only knew need. And the talisman, sensing that need, grew warmer still: no longer pulsing with steady rhythm but with a pulse more insistent, more demanding.

And Amara, lost in her grief, welcomed it.

PART EIGHT: THE RECKONING

"When the teacher dies, the student discovers
what was learned and what was only borrowed.
This is the final examination,
and it cannot be failed, only passed through."
—From the private writings of Caspar of Ecbatana

CHAPTER 46

A Country to Be Crossed

"Grief is not a problem to be solved.
It is a country to be crossed."
—Amazigh mourning wisdom

56 CE—Tizwit—The day after Eudoxus's death

Dawn broke over a camp already in motion. Word of Eudoxus's peaceful departure had spread through Tizwit like ripples across still water. Families left their dwellings carrying stones. Some were small enough for children to manage, others needed the strength of grown men. The ancient custom was clear. When a respected elder joined the ancestors, the entire community built his cairn.

Before dawn, Grandmother Menna began her spiritual work, burning rosemary and myrrh and asking for ancient blessings. The lamp she lit would burn all day, its oil offering spiritual protection as the community said goodbye to their teacher.

Amara sat beside Eudoxus's still form, which lay on his simple sleeping mat just as he had arranged himself the night before. His face held such profound peace that several people remarked he looked younger, as if the years of exile and struggle had melted away in sleep. Silina had draped him in his finest robes, the deep blue scholar's garments he wore for important occasions, now cleaned and mended.

The talisman warmed against Amara's chest. She sensed the complex currents of emotion flowing through the community. There was obvious grief, but also a deeper recognition that they had lost a teacher, a bridge between worlds, someone who had shown them that learning could unite rather than divide.

"The stones are beautiful." Amara watched families approach with their contributions. Each stone carried meaning. Smooth river rocks spoke of patience. Carved fragments represented teaching, and colored pieces symbolized the joy of discovery. The cairn would tell Eudoxus's story in the offerings of those he touched.

❧✦❧

Two hours later

The procession assembled. Six men lifted the wooden platform that bore Eudoxus's body, draped in the finest cloth the camp could provide. Zahra created a tapestry representing the community, using threads donated by each family. This was fitting for him, as he spent his final years uniting people through shared learning experiences.

The site of his cairn lay beyond the oasis proper, on a rise that commanded views of both the date groves and the endless desert beyond. Eudoxus had often come there for meditation, where he could watch the stars without the interference of cooking fires and camp lights.

Amara walked behind the bier, the talisman warm against her chest. Juba flanked her on one side, Silina on the other, their small family unit surrounded by the entire community of Tizwit. Behind them came representatives from neighboring camps who traveled through the night upon hearing the news.

Some were on horseback. Others arrived in light chariots that served as both transport and cultural emblem. They unhitched and parked them at the gathering's edge like a row of painted sentinels. The chariots' presence marked the occasion's gravity. People did not bring their finest vehicles for ordinary visits.

Grandmother Menna stepped forward with blessed water from the holy spring. She spoke ancient words over the chosen spot, sprinkling water while she prayed. The ritual was a spiritual cleansing to protect the community as they sent their teacher to join the ancestors.

They positioned Eudoxus facing east, toward the lands of his birth and the cities where he had first learned to read the wisdom of scrolls and stars. The talisman warmed. Amara understood this was not goodbye but transition, like the change from caterpillar to butterfly, or winter to spring.

Then the community began building the cairn.

Yasir placed the first stone, a piece of quartz that would catch the sunrise each morning. "For the teacher who brought light to dark questions." He spoke in the ancient tongue, using phrases that connected this moment to countless similar ceremonies stretching back through generations.

Malik added a chunk of iron ore, its solid sound against the quartz carrying its own meaning. "For the man who understood that knowledge without strength serves no one, and strength without knowledge serves nothing."

The words struck Juba with physical force. Everything Malik described represented exactly what he had failed to become. He had perverted the balance, used his strength to prove himself rather than to protect, sought dominance rather than service.

One by one, the community added their contributions. Smooth river stones for patience, carved fragments for teaching, polished pieces for the joy of discovery. Children came forward with stones carefully marked, now blessed by Grandmother Menna's touch. Women from the neighboring camps contributed stones and colored stones that caught the desert light.

With each stone placed, Juba's composure cracked further. He watched people honor the patient teacher while knowing himself to be everything Eudoxus was not: violent where the scholar was gentle, impulsive where he was thoughtful, destructive where he was creative.

Amara felt her brother's controlled emotional walls crumbling. The methods Eudoxus had introduced, the connections he had fostered, the collaborative learning he had championed—all of this would continue in the minds and hearts he had touched. But Juba saw only his own failures reflected in every tribute.

✦

As the cairn grew, Amara drifted toward a group of young women her age who had gathered near the parked chariots at the gathering's edge. Tiziri sat on the rail of her family's vehicle, a graceful thing with heron feathers tied to its frame, while two other girls leaned against the wheels. They spoke in Tamazight, their voices mixing with the distant sounds of stone being placed on stone.

"My mother says negotiations begin next month." Tiziri's voice carried a mix of excitement and nervousness. "There is a boy from the southern settlements who helped with the harvest last season."

"The tall one with the quick smile?"

"That is him. I barely said three words to him, but apparently our mothers have been talking."

The other young women laughed, sharing their own stories of potential matches being quietly arranged, boys who had caught their attention at gatherings, the complex dance of family negotiations and personal interest.

Amara listened, feeling the familiar pressure of difference settle around her shoulders like a cloak. These girls her age spoke of romance and marriage with a lightness she had never experienced. They could wonder and hope and be surprised. She could only know too much.

"What about you, Amara?" Tiziri's tone carried genuine curiosity rather than mockery. "Surely someone as beautiful as you has caught many eyes."

The talisman warmed against Amara's chest. She sensed what the other girl did not say: genuine admiration mixed with slight unease. Tiziri liked her but also felt unsettled by her in ways she could not quite name.

"I have been focused on learning." The reply was true but incomplete.

"All learning and no living makes for a sad life." One of the other girls teased gently. "There is a young man from our camp who has been asking about you. Ayyur. Do you know him?"

Amara did know him, though they had barely spoken. She knew he admired her beauty, respected her learning, and was simultaneously attracted to and disturbed by whatever made her different. She knew he would never choose her, because the very gift that allowed her to understand him made her too strange to love.

"I know him."

"He is waiting for the memorial feast to approach you properly. My brother says he has been asking questions about your family, your learning with Eudoxus. I think his interest is real."

Through a gap between the chariots, Amara could see a young man helping to unload supplies from one of the southern vehicles. He moved with quiet competence, steadying a water jar that another boy nearly dropped, and when he looked up, his eyes found hers across the distance before she could look away. He did not wave or call out. He simply held her gaze for a moment, then returned to his work.

That must be Ayyur. The name fit what she sensed: patient, steady, willing to wait.

The talisman grew warmer, and Amara felt the uncomfortable truth: Ayyur was interested in the idea of her, in the beautiful girl who carried Eudoxus's blessing. But he would never love the reality, the person who could sense his fear of her, who knew before he did that he would choose someone safer, someone whose gifts did not challenge his understanding of the world.

"That is kind of him." She kept her voice neutral.

The conversation moved on, but the ache remained. Amara watched Juba across the growing cairn, saw how the young women glanced his way with interest and speculation. Her brother did not have to sense their attraction; he could accept or reject it based on his own feelings. He could wonder, could hope, could be surprised.

She could only know. And the knowing was its own kind of loneliness.

❧✦❧

Late afternoon

As the sun began its descent, the cairn stood complete, a monument of community love rising toward the sky. Grandmother Menna performed the final blessings, her voice carrying the ancient words that would help Eudoxus's spirit find its way to the realm of the ancestors.

The blessed oil she sprinkled on the first flames sent up fragrant smoke that would carry their prayers skyward, ensuring that Eudoxus's wisdom would continue to guide his students even after his physical departure.

Malik began the mourning chant, his deep voice carrying across the ridge. The melody was ancient, pentatonic, built on intervals that predated any scale Rome had ever known. One by one, others joined: women adding a descending countermelody, children holding a single sustained note that served as the song's foundation. The sound built and built until the air itself vibrated with communal grief given shape and direction.

Eudoxus, who had loved Amazigh music for its mathematical precision, would have appreciated the architecture of it: how individual voices surrendered their separateness to create a thing none could produce alone.

Around this fire, the formal name-speaking began. Intimate memories that would preserve Eudoxus's spirit in the community's collective heart.

Yasir spoke of patience: how the Greek scholar spent countless hours helping struggling students master difficult concepts, never showing frustration or disappointment when understanding came slowly.

Malik shared memories of bridge-building: how Eudoxus helped warrior families understand that their children's learning honored rather than threatened traditional values, that knowledge could strengthen rather than weaken tribal bonds.

Zahra recalled the gentle way he helped her family adapt to desert life, teaching them to read weather patterns and water signs while respecting their foreign origins.

Visiting scholars contributed their own insights, drawn from wide correspondence. Stories emerged of Eudoxus's youth, his early studies, his decision to leave the settled lands for the uncertain life of desert exile.

But it was Amara who provided the final words, speaking not of abstract principles but of the man who had changed their daily lives.

"When Eudoxus first came to us," she began, her voice carrying clearly across the assembled mourners, "my brother and I were fighting. Always fighting. Over lessons, over games, over who was right."

A few people smiled, remembering.

"He watched us argue about a star map one evening, Juba insisting north was one direction, me equally certain it was another. Instead of telling us who was correct, he handed us each a stick."

She demonstrated the memory with her hands.

"'Show me,' he said."

She paused, seeing understanding in many faces.

"We both drew lines in the sand, both convinced the other was wrong. Then he asked us to walk our lines together, to see where they led." Her voice grew warmer. "We discovered we were both right. We just started from different places. And somewhere in that walking together, we stopped fighting and started learning."

Yasir nodded slowly. He remembered that lesson, used it himself when settling boundary disputes.

"That was his gift. Not telling us what to think, but showing us how to think together. How to make our differences into strengths rather than battles."

Around the circle, faces reflected recognition. Parents remembered children who came home excited about lessons instead of dreading them. Elders recalled how the questioning methods helped them make better decisions. Warriors understood why their strategy sessions became more effective.

"He leaves us not with answers," Amara concluded, "but with better questions. And with each other."

The crowd fell silent as her words settled over them. And in that silence, Amara felt her brother's emotional dam finally burst.

All the guilt, shame, and desperate isolation he had carried since killing the Roman scout poured out in a wave of pain so intense it left him trembling beside the cairn. The nightmares that plagued him since taking the young man's life joined now by images of Eudoxus's gentle face, disappointed and sorrowful.

He stood abruptly, his movement drawing attention. Malik stepped forward, concerned, but Amara raised a hand to stop him. This needed to happen. The healing conversation that had begun at the memorial fire needed to continue, and it required the sacred space that grief and remembrance had created.

Juba walked away from the fire, into the darkness beyond its light, and Amara followed. She felt the complex knot of his suffering. Every tribute to Eudoxus's gentleness highlighted his own violence and impulsiveness.

"I do not deserve to be here." Juba's voice broke when she reached him. "Listening to them honor everything I failed to become."

"You are exactly where you need to be."

"He taught me to question, to think, to build bridges. And what did I do? I killed a man because I was angry. Because I wanted to prove something. Because..." His voice cracked. "Because I thought violence would make me worthy of love."

The talisman grew warm against Amara's chest, and she understood its gentle guidance. This was a moment to be present. To see her brother in his pain and accept what she sensed without trying to transform it.

"Tell me everything. All of it."

And he did. About Adah, about the desperate need to prove himself after she was taken, about how each act of violence felt like reclaiming control but deepened his isolation. About the idealization he had built around warrior strength, how it became a cage rather than a path. About the Roman scout and the nightmares that followed.

"I see his face every night." Juba whispered. "Sometimes he is pleading. Sometimes he is just confused, like he does not understand why I am killing him. Sometimes he looks like Eudoxus, disappointed."

Amara listened. The talisman held her steady and clear, amplifying her capacity to be present without trying to fix or transform. She saw her brother in all his brokenness, all his confusion, all his desperate attempts to be other than what he feared he was.

And in that complete presence, the air between them eased.

"You are not everything you fear." Amara spoke when he fell silent. "You are also everything you could become. The violence does not define you. The choice to face it clearly does."

"How do I live with what I have done?"

"The same way anyone lives with their failures. You see them plainly, you learn from them, and you make different choices going forward." She paused, feeling the talisman's warmth. "Eudoxus would not want you destroyed by guilt. He would want you to transform it into wisdom."

Through the darkness, she heard him take a shuddering breath.

"I do not know how to do that."

"None of us do. That is why we need each other."

They sat together in the darkness beyond the memorial fire, and gradually Juba's breathing steadied. The talisman pulsed against Amara's chest with a rhythm that felt less like guidance and more like companionship, present alongside her, not directing but simply being there.

"Thank you." Juba's voice came at last. "For not trying to fix it. Just... being here."

"Always."

They walked back to the fire together, where the community still gathered in quiet conversation. Malik caught Amara's eye and nodded, understanding that whatever needed to happen in the darkness had happened.

Two days after the memorial

The camp returned to a semblance of normal routine, though Eudoxus's absence remained a fresh wound in everyone's awareness. The morning meal concluded in quiet conversation, families dispersing to their daily tasks.

Amara sat in the dwelling she shared with her family, the talisman warm against her chest. She had not removed it since Eudoxus's death. The thought of taking it off, even for a moment, sent anxiety spiraling through her chest. It was her only remaining connection to the spiritual guidance she relied on for seven years. Her only link to understanding what she experienced, to making sense of the overwhelming awareness that threatened to drown her without a framework to contain it.

She pressed her hand against the stone through her tunic, feeling its steady pulse. What if she took it off and could no longer sense Juba's emotions? What if the twin bond that had always been her anchor disappeared without the talisman's amplification? What if she lost the ability to help her family, her community, the way Eudoxus helped them?

What if she became useless?

"Sister?" Juba's voice from the doorway. "Mother wants us to help sort the memorial gifts. People brought more than we..." He stopped, studying her face. "Something is wrong."

"Nothing is wrong." The words came too quickly.

Juba entered the dwelling and sat beside her. "You are holding the talisman like you are afraid it will disappear."

She was holding it. Her hand pressed against her chest where the stone rested beneath fabric, fingers curled physically preventing it from being taken.

"I am fine," she said, but her words lacked conviction, even to her.

"You have not taken it off since he died, have you?"

"Why would I? It is how I help people. How I understand what they need. How I..."

"How you know what Eudoxus would have known." Juba finished.

The accuracy of his observation stung. "Someone has to carry that forward. He spent years teaching me to use it properly, to be present without interfering, to..."

"Amara." Juba's voice was gentle but firm. "You are not Eudoxus. You do not have to be."

"But someone needs to..."

"Someone needs to grieve. Someone needs to be sixteen years old and scared and not sure what comes next. You are allowed to be that person."

The talisman grew warmer against her chest, and for a moment Amara wondered whether it responded to Juba's words or to her own need for them to be wrong. She needed to be the spiritual guide now. She needed to carry Eudoxus's legacy forward. She needed to be enough to fill the enormous space his death created.

Without the talisman, she was just a grieving girl who had lost the one person who understood her gift.

With it, she was the community's spiritual vessel, the bridge between worlds, the bearer of ancient sight.

Which was she supposed to be?

"I am fine." She repeated, but her hand tightened on the stone. "I just need to learn to do this without him."

She sensed his concern, close to fear. But he nodded and stood.

"Mother is waiting. Come when you are ready."

After he left, Amara sat in the dwelling and realized the talisman's warmth had changed. From companionship to comfort. From partnership to need. She was no longer using it to serve others.

She was using it to avoid facing her own fears.

But acknowledging that truth was too frightening, too destabilizing. Without Eudoxus to guide her, without the talisman to amplify her worth, what was she? Just a girl standing in Eudoxus's shadow, unable to fill the space he left behind.

The talisman pulsed against her chest, steady and warm, and she held onto it like a drowning person clutching debris in a storm. It was all she had left of Eudoxus's teaching. All she had left of feeling capable and valuable and needed.

She could not let go. Not yet. Maybe not ever.

And in that desperate grip, the same seed that had destroyed Melchior took root, the same hunger that corrupted greater spirits than hers. The talisman responded to need, amplified what drove its bearer. And what drove Amara was not wisdom or service but the terrified determination never to feel as helpless and alone as she had felt watching Eudoxus die.

The stone warmed further, no longer offering guidance.

It was beginning to respond to her fear.

CHAPTER 47

The Network Adjusts

"The loyal man adjusts his lies when the truth changes.
This is how loyalty survives."
—Roman intelligence observation (attributed)

56 CE—Caesarea—Three days after Eudoxus's death—Year 16 of Marcus's protection

The following week, Marcus made subtle changes to his intelligence network, adjustments Eudoxus's death required but which he disguised as routine optimization.

He cultivated a new trader contact whose routes passed through settlements east of Tizwit, close enough to hear regional news without direct connection to the specific oasis. He adjusted patrol routes to maintain the gap in Roman coverage while providing plausible justification for the absence. He refined his reports to include more cultural analysis and less tactical intelligence, creating the impression of thorough work that yielded little actionable information.

It was the same careful dance he had performed for sixteen years, but the steps grew harder. Every adjustment created new vulnerabilities. Every misdirection had to be more sophisticated than the last. The system that once felt manageable now teetered on the edge of collapse.

Petronius summoned him for a briefing that afternoon. Marcus walked to the command building with a measured pace.

He learned years ago to disguise urgency as calm. Seven years under this prefect had taught him the rhythms of a different kind of danger.

Nerva's office had become Petronius's office, though the two men had used it so differently that the room itself seemed changed. Where Nerva's archive had occupied every wall, meticulously labeled and cross-referenced, Petronius had cleared most of the scroll cases to make room for maps covered in the red wax markers he favored. The archive remained, shoved into a back storage room, untouched since Nerva's departure seven years ago. Petronius had never read it. He preferred to generate his own intelligence, which meant he preferred to generate his own fictions.

"Tribune." Petronius did not look up from the dispatches spread across his table. "I need your quarterly assessment of the northeastern foothills. The governor's office wants updated projections for the pacification timeline."

"The northeastern foothills remain stable, Prefect. Tribute collection is consistent, and there have been no significant incidents since..."

"Stable is not what Rome wants to hear." Petronius set down his stylus and met Marcus's eyes. "Stable means we have achieved nothing new. Stable means the governor reports no progress to the Senate. Stable means my record shows seven years of maintaining the status quo rather than improving it."

Marcus recognized the calculation behind the complaint. Petronius positioned himself for transfer to a more prestigious command for the past two years. His reports to Rome had grown steadily more optimistic, describing pacification progress that existed only on papyrus. The governor, who wanted good news for the Senate, accepted the fiction without scrutiny.

"What would the Prefect prefer the assessment to reflect?"

"Progress. Measurable pacification. Settlements transitioning from reluctant compliance to active cooperation." Petronius pushed a blank scroll toward Marcus. "Document three to five examples of communities that have shown increased integration with Roman administrative structures over the past year. Name specific elders who have facilitated cooperation. Provide metrics."

"And if the metrics do not support that narrative?"

Petronius smiled the way a merchant smiles when explaining terms that favor only himself. "Then find metrics that do. You have been in this province for twenty years, Tribune. Surely in that time you have learned that Rome does not reward accuracy. Rome rewards results."

Marcus took the blank scroll. The lie Petronius demanded was, in its way, a gift. If the northeastern foothills appeared pacified and cooperative in official reports, Rome had no reason to send additional forces, no reason to investigate, no reason to probe the gap in coverage that kept Tizwit hidden. Petronius's fiction, built to serve his career, served Marcus's protection as well.

The irony did not comfort him.

"I will have the assessment by morning, Prefect."

"Good." Petronius returned to his dispatches. "And Tribune? I have submitted my name for consideration as military advisor to the governor of Hispania Tarraconensis. A recommendation from you, citing the effectiveness of our cooperative approach to provincial intelligence, would be useful."

There it was. The ambition that defined Petronius more than any cruelty or cleverness. He wanted out to take a posting that would advance his career beyond the provincial backwater he treated as a steppingstone from the day he arrived.

"I will prepare the recommendation."

Marcus left the briefing and stood for a moment in the garrison courtyard, measuring the shift in his position. Under Nerva, the danger had been intellectual: a scholar assembling a puzzle that would eventually reveal the picture. Under Petronius, the danger was operational: an impatient officer who might blunder into truth through carelessness. Geta would have hunted until he caught his quarry or exhausted himself. Petronius hunted only what served his advancement, and Tizwit served nothing on his ledger.

But carelessness cut both ways. Petronius's fabricated reports had drawn a picture of the province that bore increasingly less resemblance to reality. If Rome ever sent an auditor, if a new governor questioned the numbers, the fiction would collapse. And in the rubble, someone might notice the gap that Marcus had maintained for sixteen years.

The protection held. It held because Petronius did not care about truth, and truth was where the danger lived.

☙✦❧

Late that evening

Alone in his quarters, Marcus sat at his desk and drafted two documents. The first was the quarterly assessment Petronius demanded, a careful blend of real intelligence and manufactured progress that would satisfy the prefect's need for reportable results. The second was his recommendation for Petronius's transfer, genuine in its enthusiasm. He wanted Petronius gone, because Petronius's departure might be the beginning of the end. A new prefect, inheriting a province that appeared calm, an archive no one read, and a tribune whose service record was impeccable. The inertia of bureaucracy could carry the protection forward without Marcus needing to sustain it.

And then, perhaps, he could stop.

Sixteen years. He had been thirty-six when Aedemon died and the oath was spoken aloud. Now he was forty-eight, and the twins were sixteen themselves, nearly adults. In two years, they would reach the age of full autonomy. In two years, the protection might no longer require a Roman tribune feeding lies to his superiors.

He allowed himself, for the first time, to imagine an ending. Tacfara's letters had grown more insistent in the past year, her careful prose carrying an urgency that did not need the talisman to interpret. She was asking, without asking, how much longer.

He did not know. But for the first time in sixteen years, he could see the shape of an answer forming.

If Petronius received his transfer. If the replacement proved as indifferent as every other bureaucrat Rome sent to manage provinces it had already forgotten. If the twins reached eighteen without incident. If Nerva's archive gathered dust for another decade.

Too many ifs. But fewer than yesterday. And that, Marcus told himself as he extinguished his lamp, was what hope looked like after sixteen years: the slow reduction of impossible odds toward merely improbable ones.

CHAPTER 48

The Diminished Circle

"The child who inherits fire must learn which things to burn."

—Amazigh proverb on leadership

Late 56 CE—Tizwit—A week after Eudoxus's memorial service

The evening meal sat untouched between them: couscous with chickpeas and preserved lemon, thc dish Eudoxus loved best and which Silina had prepared without thinking, muscle memory carrying her hands through the familiar motions before grief reminded her why the portions were wrong. She had made enough for five. They were four now.

Zahra watched her twins push food around their bowls, neither eating, both carrying burdens that aged them beyond their sixteen years. The space where Eudoxus would have sat stretched vast as the desert itself.

Juba's hands trembled slightly as he reached for water, from barely controlled energy, his body still remembering violence even in moments of peace.

Amara sat with unusual stillness, her right hand pressed against her chest where the talisman hung beneath her robes. She had barely released it since Eudoxus died. Without it, she might dissolve into the grief threatening to consume her.

Three days had passed since Juba's complete breakdown at the memorial fire, since she had been present for the cracking open of his defenses. That had felt right, purposeful—using the gift to help someone she loved. But in the days after, the emptiness where Eudoxus's guidance should be stretched unbearable.

The talisman pulsed warm against her skin. She knew her mother worried; the concern pressed sharp against her chest.

Knew Juba carried his own fears for her. Everything was so clear now, every flicker of doubt, every shadow of concern. But it could not fill the void where her teacher's wisdom used to live.

"Children." Zahra set down her own untouched bowl. "Come walk with me."

They followed her beyond the camp's edge to a rise overlooking the oasis, where date palms caught the last light and the evening star began to show itself in the deepening sky. Here, away from curious ears and well-meaning relatives, the small family could speak with honesty.

"You have both changed in the past few days." Zahra settled onto the sandy ground and gestured for them to join her. "I see it in how you move, how you look at each other, how you carry yourselves. But I also sense you are still uncertain about what comes next."

Amara's fingers tightened around the talisman. Her mother's deep concern came so clear, so precise: specific fear that Amara was disappearing into grief. Why could people not just say what they felt instead of hiding behind words?

"We have been talking." Juba glanced at Amara with an expression she could not quite read. Something deeper eluded her, even with the talisman's clarity. "About our roles. About what comes next."

"And?"

"We think it is time to figure out what our people need." Amara spoke before Juba could continue. "Not what they expect us to be, but what would help."

The talisman warmed as her mother's surprise registered.

"Which is?" Zahra's voice carried careful neutrality.

"We use the Rih al-Harb, the game Silina and Eudoxus created for us. Not the way children play it. The way it is meant to be used: to predict outcomes, to show people how to act."

Juba shifted beside her. "That is not exactly what I meant..."

"It is perfect." Amara turned to him, the talisman warming against her skin. She could sense his hesitation, his uncertainty. "Think about it. The game shows all possibilities. With it, we can guide people toward the right choices, show them exactly what will happen if they follow our strategies."

✦

They returned to their dwelling and spread out the Rih al-Harb game board that had taught them cooperation as children. But where Juba saw a teaching tool, Amara saw a map of possibilities, a way to predict and guide outcomes, to ensure people made the right choices.

She pressed her hand against the talisman as Juba arranged pieces to represent a Roman tax collection.

"Look at this scenario." Juba's voice carried the careful tone he had been using with her lately, the tone reserved for fragile things. "A century comes to collect tribute. Traditional response: fight them, kill some, lose more of our own, accomplish nothing except proving we are still dangerous."

"But with this..." Amara leaned forward, the talisman showing her the patterns. "We can see exactly what people will do. We can guide them to the right choice."

Juba paused. "That is not... Amara, the game is meant to teach cooperation, not predict..."

"Six villages coordinate their response." She moved pieces with growing confidence, the talisman warming against her chest. "Each offers tribute in different forms: grain that needs processing, livestock that needs counting, silver in coins so worn they need verification. All legitimate, all properly respectful, but each requiring extensive time and multiple personnel."

"Yes, but..."

"The tax collector gets his tribute, but now he is weeks behind schedule. His supervisors are asking questions. He has gained nothing except frustration and paperwork." The clarity felt intoxicating. Why could Juba not see it? "And we will know it will work because the game shows us all the possibilities. I can sense which choices people will make, guide them toward the ones that serve everyone."

Zahra's expression shifted from interest to concern. "Amara, that sounds like..."

"Leadership." Amara met her mother's eyes. "Like using our gifts instead of just watching while people suffer."

"No one dies." Juba tried to redirect. "No one rebels. But the system becomes too expensive to maintain efficiently."

"Exactly." Amara could feel their hesitation. Juba's growing worry. Zahra's sharp fear. Why would they not understand? "And I can make sure everyone follows through. Sense who might deviate from the plan, help them see why cooperation serves them better."

"Help them see?" Juba's voice came neutral. "Or help them feel it?"

Amara's hand tightened on the talisman.

"What is the difference? If the outcome is right, if it saves lives..."

"The difference is choice." Juba spoke gently, but firmly. "People have to choose cooperation. We cannot make them feel it is right."

"But I would not be making them do anything they do not want..."

"Amara." Zahra's voice cut through. "Listen to yourself."

The talisman showed Amara their united concern, like walls closing in. They did not understand. They could not see what she saw, feel what she felt. Without Eudoxus to explain, to guide, to help her make sense of the gift's possibilities, she stood alone in this.

"You are both just afraid." The words came sharper than she intended. "Afraid of using power to help people."

"We are afraid of losing you to it." Juba spoke.

Silence stretched between them. Amara sensed every nuance of their fear, their love, their desperate worry. But she also sensed her own growing certainty that she was right, that they could not understand what the talisman showed her.

"The game works. Let me prove it."

The next morning

Amara insisted they bring their ideas to Yasir. Juba suggested waiting, taking more time to think through the implications, but she could not bear to sit idle another day. Every moment without Eudoxus's guidance felt like drowning, unless she was moving, acting, using the gift to accomplish her purpose.

They found the old war leader examining intelligence reports of trade routes that grew increasingly dangerous as Roman control tightened. When Amara spread out the game board without invitation, Yasir's weathered face showed surprise at her forwardness.

"We have a new approach to resistance." She began arranging pieces before he could respond, the talisman pulsing against her chest. She sensed his skepticism, his concern about the twins' state after Eudoxus's death. "Warfare without weapons. Making the enemy defeat themselves through their own systems."

Yasir glanced at Juba, who gave a small, helpless shrug.

"Instead of fighting Roman soldiers," Amara continued, moving pieces with quick confidence, "we make Roman administration too expensive and difficult to maintain. But the crucial element is coordination. And that is where I come in."

"Where we come in." Juba corrected.

"I can sense when people are committed to a plan versus just agreeing to avoid conflict." Amara pressed her hand against the talisman. "I can help ensure everyone follows through, guide them toward seeing why cooperation serves their interests."

Yasir studied the game board, but his attention kept returning to Amara's face. "This would require discipline. People would have to resist the urge to strike back when provoked, even when they are angry or grieving."

"Exactly. Which is why having someone who can sense and adjust their emotional commitment is invaluable."

"Amara..." Juba started.

"Do you not see?" She turned to her brother, frustration rising. "This is what the gift is for. Not just sitting with people's pain but helping them make better choices. Eudoxus could not have understood because he never..." She stopped, swallowing against sudden grief.

The talisman burned against her skin. She felt Yasir's deep concern and Juba's barely contained alarm.

"Your sister makes an ambitious proposal." Yasir spoke carefully to Juba. "But I wonder if she has considered what happens when people discover their emotions are being..." He paused. "Guided."

"They will not discover it because there is nothing to discover." Amara's voice came sharper than intended. "I am not controlling anyone. I am helping them see clearly."

"And how do you determine what clarity looks like for someone else?" Yasir asked with the gentle firmness of an elder addressing a child.

The question reached the hollow place in her certainty. Amara felt her conviction waver, but the talisman's warmth steadied her. She knew she was right. She had to be right. Because if she was not, then what was all this power for?

"Experience will tell us. Let me prove it works. Give me a real situation where people need to cooperate, and I will show you."

Juba shifted uncomfortably. "Maybe we should think this through more..."

"No." The word came as command, not discussion. "We have thought enough. Father would have acted."

Yasir's expression revealed nothing, but the talisman showed her his decision forming: he would give her a chance, because he worried enough about her state of mind to want her occupied with a contained and manageable task.

"There is a water rights dispute. Iberim and Kenza's families. Both claim traditional access to a spring near the boundary. It is not life or death, but it has created real tension."

"Perfect." Amara began gathering the game pieces. "I will facilitate a resolution."

"We will facilitate." Juba corrected, his worry now barely masked.

Three days later

Both families gathered under the old tamarisk tree: Iberim with his sons, Kenza with her daughters and husband. The tension between them showed years of resentment hardening their faces.

Juba began with traditional opening pleasantries, but Amara could feel the families' impatience. They wanted resolution, not ritual. Why waste time with lengthy discussion when she could guide them toward the right answer?

"Let us address this directly." She interrupted. "Both families have legitimate historical claims. But the spring's flow has decreased over the years, making the old boundaries obsolete."

The talisman showed her Iberim's automatic resistance to any suggestion that would reduce his family's access. Before he could voice it, she reached toward him with her awareness, letting him feel her confidence, her certainty that she had a better solution.

"What if we restructure access based on actual need rather than historical precedent? Iberim, your herds are larger, so you need more water. But Kenza, your family's crops require consistent timing."

She sensed Kenza's suspicion, her instinct to reject anything that was too easy. Gently, so gently, Amara let her feel the rightness of compromise, the satisfaction of a solution that would serve everyone.

"A rotating schedule where Iberim's family has primary access three days of the week for watering herds, Kenza's family has priority two days for crop irrigation, and two days are shared for household needs."

Both families exchanged glances. The talisman showed Amara their resistance softening, their anger transforming into agreement. It was working. She was helping them see clearly.

"That could work." Iberim spoke slowly.

"It is fair." Kenza added, though her expression suggested surprise at her own words.

Juba watched Amara with an expression she could not quite read. She sensed his concern, and his uncertainty: was he seeing what she was doing, or just imagining it?

"The crucial element is commitment. Everyone has to honor the schedule, even when it is inconvenient. Even when anger makes you want to take what you believe is rightfully yours."

She reached toward both families, letting them feel how much better cooperation would be than continued conflict. Their emotional resistance ebbed like water finding level ground.

"We agree." Iberim spoke.

"Yes. We agree." Kenza echoed.

The families departed with new arrangements documented, actual civility in their farewells. Amara felt triumph surge. She had done it. She had helped people reach resolution, prevented further conflict, and used her gift the way it should be used.

"That was remarkable." Yasir's tone came careful. "How quickly they found agreement."

"Sometimes people just need someone to show them the clear path." Amara could not keep the satisfaction from her voice.

After Yasir left, Juba turned to her. "Amara, what did you do?"

"I helped them. Is that not what I am supposed to do?"

"You were touching the talisman the entire time. And the way they changed... It was not like people reaching real understanding. It was like..." He struggled for words. "Like watching someone agree to a decision they did not choose."

"They chose. I just helped them see clearly."

"Did they?" Juba's voice carried a new edge of alarm. "Or did you make them feel things that led them where you wanted them to go?"

"What is the difference? They got a solution that works for everyone. No one is hurt. The conflict is resolved."

Juba took her hand. "The difference is they did not choose it. You are talking about cooperation, but what you did was..." His voice was gentle, but the words landed with force. "Amara, it was manipulation."

"I helped them."

"You controlled them." His voice remained quiet. "And you enjoyed it."

The accusation landed. The talisman showed Amara his genuine fear for her, his growing recognition that the wrongness ran deep. But she also felt her own certainty, her absolute conviction that she was right and he could not understand.

"You are jealous. Because I have a gift that helps people, while you are still figuring out how to stop killing them."

She regretted the words, but they were already out. Juba's face went very still.

"Maybe you are right." He spoke softly. "Or maybe I am seeing what Eudoxus would have seen if he were here."

He left her alone under the tamarisk tree, the talisman warm against her chest and the taste of victory turning hollow in her mouth.

⁂

That evening

Amara sat alone by the fire, the talisman pressed against her heart. She could feel the entire settlement's emotional landscape spread before her. Zahra's worry, sharp and maternal. Yasir's measured concern. The families she had helped, their surface satisfaction underlaid by a dissonance she did not want to examine too closely.

And Juba. His fear for her burned like a coal, constant and painful.

She pressed harder against the talisman, trying to sense deeper. But the clarity she had felt during the water rights dispute was fading. When she tried to reach toward Juba's emotions without actively using the talisman, the way she had always been able to feel her twin brother, there was only haziness.

Panic fluttered in her chest. She lifted her hand from the talisman. Tried to sense Juba's emotions naturally, the way she had done since childhood.

Almost nothing. Like trying to hear through water.

She pressed the talisman again. Instantly, his emotions flooded back, sharp, clear, overwhelming. But the moment she released it, the fog returned.

No. This could not be happening. My natural empathy, the gift I have carried since birth, the twin bond that has always been her anchor, could not just disappear.

But it was disappearing. Or rather, she realized with growing horror, it had been disappearing for days. Maybe longer. She had been so focused on the talisman's amplified clarity that she had not noticed her natural gift eroding beneath it.

Eudoxus's warning echoed in memory: "The talisman amplifies what is already present in its bearer."

But what if you used it the wrong way? What if you used it to control instead of being present, to force instead of facilitate? What happened then?

Juba emerged from the darkness, his approach cautious.

"I am sorry." She spoke before he could, her voice tight with suppressed fear. "About what I said earlier. About you and killing. That was not fair."

"It was honest." He settled beside her, carefully not touching. The talisman showed her his emotions. Without it, he might as well be a stranger. "And maybe partially true. But Amara, what you did today..."

"Helped people. Solved a real problem. Prevented years of continued conflict."

"By making them feel things they did not feel. By reaching into their emotions and adjusting them like pieces on a game board."

"To serve their own interests. To help them see clearly."

"To control them." Juba's voice held more sadness than anger. "You are talking about cooperation, but you are practicing domination."

She wanted to argue, but a new fear took root. If she stopped using the talisman, she would be empathically deaf. But if she kept using it this way...

"I think you need to set it aside for a while. The talisman. Remember who you are without it."

"I cannot." The admission came raw. She lifted her hand from the talisman, gestured toward him. "Can you feel that? What I am feeling right now?"

He had always been able to. The twin bond worked both ways: weakly for him, enough that he could sense her emotional state.

"I..." Juba's expression shifted from confusion to alarm. "I cannot. It is like you are not there. Like there is just... absence."

"Exactly." She pressed the talisman again, felt his worry flood through her. "This is all I have left. I do not know what I did, but my natural gift is..." Her voice broke. "It is going away."

"Then that is why you need to stop. Before you lose yourself completely. Before there is nothing left of you except that thing around your neck."

"Or before I go mad trying to function without any empathy at all." The choice terrified her. Be deaf to all emotion, or continue using the talisman and lose herself. "You do not understand what it is like. I have always felt people. Always. Since I was born. And now without this..." She gripped the talisman. "There is just silence."

"Better silence than what you are becoming."

The words landed with force. The talisman showed her his absolute certainty, his desperate love, his conviction that she was walking a path that would destroy her.

"I do not know if I can." She whispered.

"You have to try. Because I cannot watch you disappear. I cannot watch you turn into someone Eudoxus would not recognize."

After he left, Amara sat alone with the talisman and a choice that felt impossible. Keep using it and lose her mind. Stop using it and lose her gift.

Either way, she was losing herself.

The talisman pulsed against her skin, warm and certain. And in the silence between heartbeats, Amara wondered if perhaps she had already lost herself, and everything since had just been the slow realization of that truth.

Tomorrow would bring more opportunities to help people, to use the gift, to prove her approach worked. Tomorrow she would show Juba and Yasir and everyone else that she was right.

But tonight, alone in the darkness with only the talisman's artificial clarity for comfort, Amara admitted to the part of herself she could barely hear anymore: she was terrified.

And she did not know how to stop.

CHAPTER 49

What the Dust Preserved

"Patterns reveal themselves to the patient observer.
What they mean is another matter entirely."
—From the writings of Nerva (reconstructed)

Late Summer 56 CE—Caesarea—Three weeks after Eudoxus's death

The knock came before Marcus had finished his morning ablutions. A soldier, young and rigid with the self-importance of a man delivering orders from above.

"The prefect wants you. Now."

Petronius had never summoned him with such urgency. Their interactions followed predictable rhythms: quarterly reports, fabricated assessments, the comfortable fiction of a province under control. This departure from routine sent a cold thread through Marcus's chest.

He dressed with deliberate calm and walked through the garrison's morning bustle. Soldiers drilling, servants carrying water, the mundane machinery of empire grinding forward. The Mediterranean glittered beyond the harbor walls, indifferent to the fate of one tribune who had spent sixteen years lying to everyone who trusted him.

Petronius's office occupied the eastern wing of the command building. Marcus entered and stopped.

Nerva's archive was spread across the central table.

Scroll cases that had gathered dust in the back storage room for seven years now covered every surface. Maps annotated in Nerva's precise hand lay open beside Petronius's own crude tactical charts. The prefect stood among them with the expression of stumbling onto treasure he did not quite know how to value.

"Tribune." Petronius gestured at the scrolls without looking up. "Did you know this existed?"

"Prefect Nerva's archive. Of course. I briefed him regularly during his tenure."

"Seven years I have been here, and no one mentioned that my predecessor left a complete intelligence analysis of every settlement, trade route, and tribal leader in the province." Petronius lifted a scroll and squinted at Nerva's meticulous handwriting. "The man documented everything. Settlement populations, seasonal movements, water sources, leadership structures. Fifteen years of numbers and patterns."

Marcus's mouth went dry. "Nerva's methods were thorough but produced limited actionable intelligence. That was the assessment when he was recalled."

"Limited actionable intelligence." Petronius dropped the scroll and picked up another. "Perhaps. But I have just received word that my request for transfer to Hispania has been conditionally approved. The condition is a comprehensive provincial assessment demonstrating measurable pacification progress. The governor wants documentation." He smiled. "And here, Tribune, I have fifteen years of documentation written by a man Rome itself certified as thorough."

Marcus understood. Petronius did not want to read Nerva's archive for truth. He wanted to mine it for material he could reshape into a narrative of success. Cherry-pick numbers, reframe Nerva's observations, present another man's meticulous work as evidence supporting Petronius's fictional pacification.

The danger was not that Petronius would discover the gap in Marcus's intelligence. The danger came in ransacking the archive for useful information. He might stumble across the very patterns Nerva had identified: seventeen settlements outside effective Roman surveillance, the gap in patrol coverage, and the improbability of coincidence.

"I will need your help interpreting the older material." Petronius pushed a stack of scroll cases toward Marcus. "Your knowledge of the province is unmatched. Review these sections and identify the most useful information for the provincial assessment. Focus on settlements showing cooperation, tribute compliance, reduced resistance activity."

"Of course, Prefect. When do you need the review completed?"

"The transport to Rome departs in six weeks. I want the assessment ready in four."

Four weeks. Marcus had four weeks to review fifteen years of Nerva's archive. The archive, if read properly, documented the architecture of his betrayal. His task was to extract only the material that served Petronius's fiction while ensuring nothing damaging survived the process.

"I will begin immediately."

"Good." Petronius waved him toward the scroll cases with the impatient gesture of a prefect whose mind had already moved on. "And Tribune? This assessment will be my final significant act as prefect of this province. I intend it to be definitive. Comprehensive. The kind of document that ensures my successor inherits a clear picture of a pacified region requiring minimal oversight."

The words carried more promise than threat, but Marcus heard both. A definitive assessment that painted the province as pacified would serve Petronius's career and, if written carefully, would serve Marcus's protection. A new prefect arriving to a province certified as calm would have no reason to probe, no reason to investigate, no reason to read the archive that Petronius would leave behind exactly as disordered as he had made it.

"Definitive, Prefect. Understood."

Marcus carried the scroll cases to his own quarters and spread them across his desk. Nerva's handwriting stared up at him, precise, methodical, devastating. Every page contained observations that, assembled correctly, told the story of sixteen years of systematic misdirection.

He began to read. And as he read, he began to understand what he would have to do.

Not destroy the archive. That would raise questions. Not alter it; Nerva's notation system was too consistent for forgery to survive scrutiny. Instead, he would guide Petronius toward the material that supported the fiction and away from the material that revealed the truth. He would organize the review so that the useful information appeared first, the damaging patterns buried in the sections Petronius would never bother to read.

It was the same skill he had practiced for sixteen years: shaping what others saw without changing what existed. The lie that left truth intact while rendering it invisible.

✦

Four weeks later

The provincial assessment document bearing Petronius's name and Nerva's numbers departed on the transport to Rome. It reshaped the narrative into one of successful pacification that bore only a passing resemblance to reality. Marcus had written most of it. Petronius had signed it. Rome would read it and see what it wanted to see: a province under control, a prefect worthy of advancement, an empire functioning as intended.

Madi appeared at Marcus's quarters that evening with a skin of wine and the expression of a man carrying news.

"The transfer is approved," he said in Tamazight, settling into the room's single chair. "Petronius departs before the winter storms. His replacement arrives in the spring."

Marcus accepted the wine. "Who?"

"No name yet. Junior appointment. The governor considers the province sufficiently stable to warrant only routine administration." Madi's eyes held sixteen years of reading what Marcus did not say. "You are thinking about the archive."

"It is still there. Disordered now, after Petronius tore through it, but intact. The next prefect could read it."

"Could. But Petronius's assessment tells Rome the province is pacified. A junior administrator arriving to a settled posting will have no reason to excavate fifteen years of old intelligence. He will file new reports, attend to his duties, and count the days until his own transfer.

"Unless."

"Unless." Madi agreed. "But 'unless' has been the word we have lived with for sixteen years. At some point, Tribune, you will have to decide whether 'unless' is reason enough to continue."

Marcus drank. The wine was rough, a soldier's vintage, but it warmed the cold calculations running through his mind.

The twins would turn eighteen in two years. Zahra had lived under her assumed identity for sixteen years, long enough that the original hunt had faded from living memory. Aedemon's rebellion was a footnote in provincial records. Petronius's departure would remove the one officer ambitious enough to create problems through carelessness. And Nerva's archive, the most dangerous document in Mauretania, would sit in a storage room, unread, while Rome sent a junior bureaucrat to administer a province it had already forgotten.

"The protection may no longer require a protector." Marcus spoke the words aloud for the first time, testing their weight.

The hunt had never been Rome's. It had been three men's, each borrowing the machinery of empire for purposes the empire did not share. And the family had outlasted them all by simply continuing to exist.

Madi studied him. "Tacfara would be glad to hear it."

"Tacfara has been patient beyond any reasonable expectation."

"Tacfara has been waiting for you to say what you just said." Madi set down his cup. "The question is whether you believe it, or whether you are just tired enough to want to believe it."

Marcus did not answer. Because the honest answer was both.

"Two more years," he said at last. "Until the twins reach eighteen. Until the new prefect has settled in and demonstrated that he has no interest in old archives. Until I am certain that walking away will not collapse everything I built."

"Two years." Madi rose, retrieving the wine skin. "I have heard that number before."

"This time I mean it."

Madi paused at the door. "I know you do. That is what concerns me."

After he left, Marcus sat in the lamplight and allowed himself to think about Volubilis. About Tacfara's letters and the life she maintained in his absence. About the possibility, distant and fragile, that sixteen years of service might finally earn him the right to stop.

Two more years. Then the twins would be adults. The province would be someone else's burden. And Marcus Valerius

Severus, who had given the best years of his life to a protection no one would ever know about, might finally go home.

The lamp guttered. He let it die without relighting it, and sat in the darkness imagining a future that did not require lying.

It was the most dangerous thought he had allowed himself in sixteen years.

It felt like breathing.

CHAPTER 50

When the Healer Demands

"When the healer begins to demand,
she has forgotten what healing requires."
—Desert teaching on spiritual gifts

Late 56 CE—Tizwit—Ten days after Eudoxus's memorial service

Amara had called the meeting herself, which should have been the first warning sign.

Thirty people gathered in the communal space, representatives from six families involved in coordinating a response to the latest Roman census demands. They came expecting discussion, the collaborative problem-solving that had become Tizwit's strength. What they received was a directive.

"The solution is obvious." Amara stood at the center, the Rih al-Harb board spread before her, pieces already arranged in the configuration she had determined was correct. The talisman burned warm beneath her robes, laying bare their hesitations, their doubts, their fears. "Six families, each claiming fewer members than last year. Blame the drought, the sickness, the migration patterns. All plausible, all documented by different village scribes."

"But we discussed using harvest shares." Taderfit spoke carefully. "If some families show increased need for field workers while others show decreased population, the confusion serves us without requiring outright lies."

"That approach is too complicated. People will forget their roles, contradict each other. This way is cleaner." Amara moved pieces with quick confidence. "I have already assigned each family their story. You will memorize them, practice them, and when the census takers arrive, everyone knows exactly what to say."

She sensed Taderfit's resistance building. The older woman opened her mouth to object, and Amara reached toward her with the talisman, letting her feel certainty, confidence, the rightness of the plan.

"You see? This is better. Trust me."

Taderfit blinked, her objection dying. "I... suppose that could work."

"It will work." Amara turned to the others. "I have studied how people respond to questioning. I know which stories will hold up under pressure. All you need to do is follow the plan exactly as I have designed it."

The talisman showed her their growing unease. Good. Let them be uncertain. She would help them feel better about it, help them see that her way served everyone.

"What about the children?" Another voice asked. "If we claim fewer people, the children will need to know what story to tell if questioned separately."

"I have already arranged that. The children will be coached on their responses. I know exactly which ones can be trusted to remember, which ones need simpler stories, which ones should be kept away from census takers."

Her tone made several people exchange glances. The talisman warmed against her chest. She felt their discomfort spike, pressed harder, letting them feel her certainty, her complete control of the situation.

"You doubt me? After everything I have done to help this community? After proving time and again that I can sense what will work?"

"Amara," Taderfit's voice came gently, "we are just trying to understand..."

"There is nothing to understand. I have planned everything. All you need to do is follow my instructions." She gripped the talisman through her robes. "I can sense whether people are committed to the plan. I can help ensure everyone stays coordinated, keeps their stories straight, does not deviate from what needs to happen."

"Help us stay coordinated?" A younger man, Massin, spoke up. "Or make us stay coordinated?"

Amara felt her certainty waver, replaced by defensive anger. Who was he to question her? She was trying to help them, to save them from Roman scrutiny, to use her gift for their benefit.

"I do not make anyone do anything. I help people see clearly."

"The way you helped Iberim and Kenza see clearly?" Massin's voice hardened. "My aunt says she agreed to terms she did not actually want. Says she felt strange afterward, like she had been pushed into a decision."

"Your aunt received a fair solution to a problem that was tearing both families apart." Amara's voice snapped. "If she has regrets now, that is because she has forgotten how awful the conflict was before I intervened."

"Or because she did not actually choose the solution. You made her feel like she chose it."

The talisman burned against Amara's chest. She sensed the meeting turning against her. They did not understand. They could not see what she saw, feel what she felt. Without Eudoxus to explain, to validate, to help her use the gift properly, she was alone in this.

"I am trying to help you." Her voice cracked with frustration. "All of you. Why can you not see that?"

"We do see it." Taderfit's tone was careful. "But Amara, dear child, there is a difference between offering help and demanding compliance. Between suggesting paths and choosing for people."

"I am not choosing for anyone. I am showing them the right choice."

"And how do you know it is right for them and not just right according to you?"

Amara opened her mouth to respond, but the words would not come. The talisman showed her the room's united concern. And worse than anger: pity. They pitied her. They thought she was confused, perhaps dangerous. To them, she was not the wise guide she knew herself to be.

"This meeting is over." She began gathering the game pieces, her hands shaking. "When the census takers come and you are all confused and contradicting each other, remember that I offered you a better way."

She left before anyone could respond, the talisman showing her their worry trailing behind her like smoke.

Two hours later

Juba found her by the spring, throwing stones into the water with violent precision.

"They are wrong." She spoke before he could. "All of them. They do not understand what I am trying to do."

"I know. I was there. Watched you try to make thirty people follow a plan they did not agree to."

"It was a good plan. The best plan. If they had just listened..."

"Amara." His voice came gentle but firm. "You were controlling them. Not helping them. Controlling them."

"I was showing them..."

"You were reaching into their emotions with the talisman and adjusting how they felt about your ideas. I watched you do it. To Taderfit, to Massin, to half the people there." He paused. "You tried to do it to me when I arrived. Did you even notice?"

The accusation struck with force. She had not tried to. Had she? The talisman's warmth was so constant now, the connection so automatic, that she barely distinguished between natural empathy and active manipulation.

"I do not know what you are talking about."

"Yes, you do. You are just so deep in it that you cannot tell the difference anymore between sensing and controlling. Between being present and forcing." Juba's voice cracked. "You are scaring people, Amara. People who love you. People who have known you since you were a child. They are afraid of you."

"Then they are fools."

"They are right." He stood, pacing. "And the worst part is you do not even see it. You think you are helping when you are just... Amara, you are becoming what Eudoxus warned about. You are walking Melchior's path."

"Do not." Her voice came sharp as broken glass. "Do not compare me to him. I am not seeking power for its own sake. I am trying to help my people survive Roman occupation."

"By making them feel things they do not actually feel. By adjusting their emotions to match what you think is right. By demanding they follow your plans without question." He crouched in front of her, forcing eye contact. "That is not help. That is tyranny wearing a helpful face."

The talisman showed her his genuine terror for her. His desperate love. His growing certainty that he was losing his sister to a darkness that consumed.

"You do not understand. Without this, I am nothing. I cannot feel anything naturally anymore. The twin bond is almost gone. If I let go of the talisman, I will be deaf. Alone."

"Better alone than this. Better deaf than destroying yourself and everyone who loves you."

"Easy for you to say. You have never needed anything to feel complete. You have always been enough just as you are."

"That is not true and you know it. I spent years trying to prove myself worthy. Threw myself at every dangerous task, sought validation through violence. Remember? You were present for me through that. Helped me see I was destroying myself."

"That was different."

"It was exactly the same. I was using violence to fill a void. You are using power. But we are both running from the same thing: the fear that we are not enough without something external making us matter."

She wanted to argue, to explain why he was wrong. But the words tangled in her throat because beneath the talisman's artificial clarity, she knew he was right.

"I do not know how to stop." She whispered. Then, before he could offer solutions: "And do not tell me to just set it aside. I know that is what you are going to say. I have thought about it. Every night since Eudoxus died, I have told myself to take it off and see what happens." Her fist pressed against her chest. "But every time I reach for the clasp, I feel this terror. Like if I let go, I will fall forever. Like I will disappear."

Juba was quiet for a moment. "That is the first honest thing you have said in weeks."

"I know what I am supposed to do. I just cannot make myself do it." The admission came raw. "I am not strong enough."

"Then let me be strong for you. Let Mother be strong for you. Let the people who love you carry you until you can carry yourself again." He reached for her hand. "But you have to choose it, Amara. I cannot make you. No one can."

She pulled away, clutching the talisman through her robes. "You are asking me to become nothing."

"I am asking you to become yourself again. There is a difference."

✦

That night, Amara dreamed of Eudoxus.

His younger self, the teacher who had first shown her how to hold the talisman lightly, how to be present without grasping. In the dream, he sat beneath the yew tree where they had spent so many afternoons, watching her with an expression she could not read.

"What?" she demanded. "I am doing what you taught me. I am helping people."

He said nothing. Just watched.

The dream shifted, the way dreams do. Grandmother Menna sat beside him now, her age-weathered face painted with sacred patterns, her hands resting on her knees in the posture of patient waiting she had taught Amara years ago. The women's way, she had called it. Presence without grasping. Patience instead of power.

Two teachers. Two forms of silence. Both refusing to tell her she was right.

She wanted to scream at them, to make them speak, to force them to say she was doing what they had taught her.

But in their shared silence, she felt the question she had been refusing to ask herself: *Would they recognize what I am becoming?*

She woke gasping, the talisman burning against her chest. The dream clung to her like smoke. She pressed her palm against the stone, seeking its clarity, its certainty, and spent the hours until dawn convincing herself the dream meant nothing. Eudoxus would understand. Menna would see. They would know she was carrying their teachings forward, protecting the community they had shaped her to serve.

They would. They had to.

✦

Two weeks after the census meeting

Amara took to walking the settlement's edges at dawn, when most people still slept and she could avoid the careful silences that followed her now.

The talisman burned warm against her chest. She sensed the community's wariness like a constant hum. People smiled but stepped back. They greeted her but invented reasons to leave. She told herself they did not understand. Juba's accusations had poisoned them against her. Given time, they would see she had only been trying to help.

Grandmother Menna was waiting by the sacred spring.

"Sit with me, child."

It was not a request. Menna spoke with authority. She had guided souls through crisis for sixty years, and recognized what was happening to Amara, even if she could not.

Amara sat. The talisman warmed further against her skin.

"You have been avoiding me," Menna said.

"I have been busy."

"You have been hiding." Menna's dark eyes held hers without flinching. "The way people hide when they know, somewhere beneath their certainty, that a thing has gone wrong."

"Nothing has gone wrong. Everyone else is..."

"Do you know why Kenza has not spoken to you since the water dispute?"

The question cut through Amara's prepared defenses.

"She received the resolution she wanted. Both families are satisfied with the arrangement."

"Are they?" Menna picked up a small stone and turned it in her weathered fingers. "Kenza told me she agreed to terms she did not want. She felt pushed into a decision. The choice was not hers."

"I helped her see clearly..."

"You helped her feel what you wanted her to feel." Menna's voice remained gentle, which made it worse. "There is a difference between offering a path and pushing someone onto it."

"It served everyone. The conflict is resolved. No one is fighting anymore."

"No one is fighting because you took away their ability to disagree. That is not peace. That is control wearing peace's face."

Amara opened her mouth to argue, but Menna's expression stopped her. The old woman was not angry. She was grieving.

"I have seen this before," Menna said. "People with gifts like yours who convinced themselves that their knowing gave them the right to decide for others."

"I am not..."

"Who taught you that controlling others was the same as loving them?"

The question struck deep. Amara thought of her childhood: the careful lies the adults told to protect her, the way they shaped her understanding of reality for her own good. How she had resented it. How she had sworn she would never do the same.

"That is different. They lied to me. I am showing people truth."

"Are you? Or are you showing them truth according to Amara, delivered in a way that leaves them no choice but to accept it?"

The talisman burned against her chest. She sensed Menna's emotions clearly: no deception, no manipulation, just terrible honesty. Menna would not watch this pattern destroy another gifted soul.

"I just wanted them to like me." The admission broke open. "I am so tired of being the strange one. I just wanted to feel like I belonged."

Menna's ancient hands found Amara's. "I know, child. But what you have been doing is not connection. It is violation dressed in kindness."

"Then what am I supposed to do?"

"You must go to each person you have harmed. Not to explain. Not to justify. To acknowledge what you did and ask if they can forgive you."

Amara looked up, horrified. "I cannot face them and admit..."

"That you violated their trust? That you used your gift to control rather than serve?" Menna's voice held no judgment, only the steady certainty of a healer prescribing necessary medicine. "Each one. With no guarantee they will forgive you."

"What if they will not?"

"Then they will not. That is their right." Menna released her hands and sat back. "Forgiveness cannot be demanded or manipulated into existence."

Amara wiped her face with shaking hands. The path Menna described felt impossible.

"I do not think I can do this."

"Not as you are now." Menna's eyes moved to the leather cord at Amara's neck. "Before you can make amends, you must learn who you are without it."

"Set it aside?" Panic fluttered in Amara's chest. "It is the only connection I have left to Eudoxus..."

"It has become the thing that separates you from everyone else. You cannot truly apologize while holding the power to sense whether the apology is working. You must go to them as yourself. Blind. Vulnerable. Human."

"I will be defenseless."

"Yes. The way everyone else is, every day of their lives."

Menna rose slowly, her old joints protesting. She paused at the edge of the clearing.

"Eudoxus spoke to me before he died. He worried about you. He sensed a hunger in you that reminded him of..." She stopped. "He said that when we harm others through our gifts, the only path back is through acknowledgment and amends. That power used wrongly creates debts that must be paid with honesty, not more power."

"He never told me that."

"Perhaps he hoped he would not need to." Menna's eyes held hers. "The path back exists. It is hard, and it is humbling, and you will want to abandon it a hundred times. But it exists."

She walked away toward the settlement, leaving Amara alone by the sacred spring where she had once learned to become the sky.

The talisman burned against her chest. She could sense the whole community: their morning routines, their small joys and worries, the careful distance they kept from the girl who knew too much.

She could reach toward them. Smooth their wariness. Make them forget what they had seen at the census meeting. Make everything comfortable again.

Her hand moved toward the leather cord.

Stopped.

Menna's words echoed: See who Amara is when she cannot rely on power.

With trembling fingers, Amara lifted the talisman over her head. The leather cord slid through her hair. The stone emerged into morning light for the first time in months. It pulsed warm in her palm, confused, questioning, sensing her intention without understanding.

"I am sorry," she whispered to it. To Eudoxus. To herself. "I need to know if there is anything left of me without you."

❧✦❧

That evening

Amara sat by the sacred spring until the sun touched the western ridge.

The talisman burned against her chest. She could sense the whole community: their morning routines, their small joys and worries, the careful distance they kept from her.

She could reach toward them. Smooth their wariness. Make them forget what they had seen at the census meeting. Make everything comfortable again.

Her hand moved toward the leather cord.

Stopped.

With trembling fingers, Amara lifted the talisman over her head. The leather cord slid through her hair. The stone emerged into morning light for the first time in months. It pulsed warm in her palm, sensing her intention without understanding.

"I am sorry," she whispered to it. To Eudoxus. To herself. "I need to know if there is anything left of me without you."

She held the stone in her palm and looked toward the settlement's edge, where the ancient yew spread its dark branches. The tree where she found it. She could return it there. Back in the metal box, back in the earth, back beneath branches so toxic no one would disturb them. It rested there for years before she came. It could rest there again.

Her feet did not move toward the yew.

She looked down at the spring. The water murmuring over stones worn smooth by centuries. The tamarisk roots reaching into the bank. The rock where the toad sat most mornings, being exactly what it was.

The yew was where someone hid this stone in the dark, beneath poison, where no one would look. She understood the impulse. She had spent months hiding behind the talisman's power the way that tree hid behind its toxin. Returning the stone there would be the same instinct: bury it, conceal it, let fear stand guard.

She did not want to hide anymore.

She knelt at the tamarisk's roots and placed the stone in a hollow where root met earth, close to the water, where it could feel the spring's rhythm the way it once felt hers.

"Rest here," she said. "Where the water teaches. Where I was taught."

The silence was immediate and devastating.

The hum of ambient emotions vanished. She could hear birds calling, wind through the palm fronds, water trickling over stones, and nothing else.

She reached for Juba through the twin bond. A faint sense of direction, like knowing north without seeing the sun. But his emotions, his thoughts, the easy awareness of his presence that had been her anchor for sixteen years. Gone.

Panic surged. She grabbed for the talisman.

And stopped herself.

Without the talisman's amplification, she was just Amara. No more able to sense others' feelings than anyone else. No more able to control them.

She sat by the spring and learned to breathe in the silence.

The talisman lay in its hollow and felt her standing above it. It wanted to pulse warmth, reassurance, approval, and the comfort of presence. It held still. She needed to walk away on her own terms, and the talisman understood this the way it understood most things: not in words, but as a shape it recognized. It let her go.

Amara gathered stones from the spring's edge, smooth river rocks worn by generations of water. She built a small cairn around the hollow, marking the place, protecting it. She thought of Eudoxus and the cairn the village had made for him. Her grief then was much the same as she felt now.

She placed the last stone and stepped back.

She was just Amara, an ordinary and terrified girl, ready to face what she had done.

She turned and walked back toward the settlement, leaving the talisman in its cairn of stones.

❧✦❧

That night

The dwelling felt different without the talisman's presence.

Amara lay on her sleeping mat and stared at the woven ceiling. Zahra's breathing came soft and regular from across the space. Silina slept in her corner. Somewhere nearby, Juba rested in the men's area.

She could feel none of them.

She tried to reach for Juba through the twin bond. She closed her eyes and concentrated on a connection that had spanned her entire life. A faint sense of direction. Nothing more.

This is what everyone else feels, she realized. They walk through life not knowing what others feel. They must guess. They must trust.

The thought was terrifying. And somehow, beneath the terror, almost liberating.

Sleep came eventually, shallow and dreamless. She woke before dawn, disoriented by the silence. For a moment she reached for the talisman out of habit, her hand moving toward her chest before she remembered.

Juba appeared from the men's area. He crossed to her without speaking, his face uncertain in the grey light.

"Can you feel me at all?"

She tried. "Like seeing a candle through fog."

He was silent for a heartbeat. "Is it permanent?"

"I do not know. Menna thinks the talisman was depleting my natural gift. Every time I used it to control instead of being present, I lost a little more of what I was born with."

"And if it does not come back?"

"Then I will learn to live without it. The way everyone else does."

He reached out and took her hand.

"I am still here," he said. "Even if you cannot sense me."

"I know." She knew in the ordinary way people knew things: through evidence, history, and trust.

They stood together as dawn broke over Tizwit, watching light spread across the settlement where they had grown from children into complicated and broken people still capable of healing.

"Menna says I have to make amends. Go to each person I harmed. Acknowledge what I did. Ask if they can forgive me."

"That sounds terrifying."

"It is." She squeezed his hand. "Will you help me figure out where to start?"

"Kenza, probably. She is kind enough that she might listen."

Amara nodded. The sun crested the ridge and flooded the settlement with golden light. She watched it touch the dwellings, the palm fronds, the faces of early risers. She saw all of it with her eyes alone. No emotional undertones. No hidden currents.

"I am scared," she admitted.

"I know. But you are also brave. You always have been."

She leaned against him, feeling his physical warmth, his solid presence. For the first time since Eudoxus died, she felt a feeling that might have been hope. Smaller and realer and her own.

It was the hardest thing she had ever chosen. And perhaps the first free choice she had made in months.

CHAPTER 51

The Walk to Kenza's Door

"The confession that costs nothing heals nothing.
The confession that costs everything heals everything. Sometimes."
—Amazigh saying on truth-telling

Late Fall 56 CE—Tizwit—Six weeks after the memorial

The walk to Kenza's dwelling felt longer than Amara remembered.

She had rehearsed the words a dozen times with Menna's coaching. Keep it simple. Say what you did. Say you were wrong. Ask if she can forgive you. Then stop talking. The hardest part, Menna had warned, would be the silence after. The waiting without knowing.

Amara had never waited without knowing. Not since she was a small child, before the talisman amplified her gift into a thing vast and terrible.

Now she waited all the time. For everyone.

Kenza sat in her courtyard, grinding grain in the late afternoon light. Her hands stilled when she saw Amara approach, and her face settled into careful neutrality.

"May I speak with you?"

"You may speak." Kenza did not invite her to sit.

Amara stood in the courtyard, acutely aware of how exposed she felt without the talisman's guidance. She could not sense whether Kenza was angry or cautious. Could not adjust her approach based on what she felt. Could only say what she had come to say and accept whatever followed.

"During the water rights dispute, I did something wrong." The words came harder than she expected. "I reached into your emotions with my gift and adjusted how you felt about the settlement. I made you feel the rightness of terms you did not actually choose."

Kenza's grinding resumed, the stone scraping against stone. She said nothing.

"I told myself I was helping you see clearly. I told myself the outcome was good, so the method did not matter. I was wrong." Amara's voice cracked. "I took away your right to decide for yourself. I violated your trust and your mind, and I am sorry."

The grinding continued. Amara waited in the silence, her heart pounding in her ears.

Kenza spoke at last without looking up. "I knew a thing was wrong. After the meeting, I felt strange. Like I had agreed to a dream and woken to find it real. My husband asked why I seemed confused about terms I had supposedly chosen myself."

"I am sorry."

"You have said that." Kenza's hands stilled again. "What I want to know is whether you are sorry because you were caught, or sorry because you understand what you did."

The question cut deep. Amara had to think before answering, because she owed Kenza honesty, not performance.

"Both, I think. I did not understand what I was doing until others showed me. But now that I understand..." She paused, searching for truth. "I am horrified. At myself. At how easily I convinced myself that violation was help."

Kenza looked up for the first time. Her eyes held no warmth, but no hatred either. She was just trying to decide whether to extend trust again.

"The settlement is working. Both families have followed the terms, and the conflict has ended." She resumed grinding. "I cannot say whether I would have agreed to the same terms freely. Perhaps I would have. Perhaps something better would have emerged from honest negotiation. We will never know."

"No. We will not."

"That is what you took from me. The chance to know my own choice." Kenza's voice hardened. "I do not know if I can forgive that. Not today. Perhaps not ever."

Amara nodded, her throat tight. "I understand."

"Do you? Because forgiveness is not a debt you can collect by apologizing correctly. It is a thing I have to find in my own heart, in my own time, or not at all."

"I know. I am not asking you to forgive me now. I am asking you to know that I understand what I did, and I am sorry, and I will not do it again."

"The talisman. You have set it aside?"

"Yes."

"And your gift? The sensing?"

"Gone. Or nearly gone. I can barely feel anything anymore."

Kenza's expression softened. The beginning of understanding.

"Then you are living like the rest of us now. Not knowing what people feel. Having to trust their words and hope for the best."

"Yes."

"Good." Kenza returned to her grinding. "Perhaps that will teach you what you should have learned before you ever touched anyone's mind. That uncertainty is not a problem to be solved. It is how we honor each other's freedom."

Amara waited, but Kenza said nothing more. After a moment, she understood: the conversation was over. She had said what she came to say. The response was what it was.

"Thank you for listening."

"Come back in the spring." Kenza did not look up. "Perhaps I will feel differently by then. Perhaps I will not. But come back."

It was not forgiveness. It was not rejection either. It was the space between: an open door she had not yet earned the right to walk through.

Amara left the courtyard with tears on her face and a feeling that was almost relief.

She had survived her first attempt. It had not destroyed her.

That was more than she had dared to hope.

❧✦❧

One week later

Tiziri's response surprised her.

The young woman listened to Amara's stumbling confession of how she had smoothed their interactions, adjusted Tiziri's wariness into warmth, and manufactured connection instead of earning it. Tiziri burst out laughing.

"I knew a thing was strange," Tiziri said, wiping her eyes. "I kept thinking, 'Why do I like her so much? She unsettles everyone else.' But the feeling was real, so I assumed the confusion was wrong."

"The feeling was not real. I made you..."

"You made me give you a chance." Tiziri cut her off. "But Amara, I do like you. Not because of whatever you did with that stone. I do not pretend to understand how that works. Because you are interesting. You see things others miss. You are kind when you are not being terrifying."

Amara blinked. "But I manipulated you."

"And I should be angry about that, probably." Tiziri shrugged. "But truthfully? These past weeks, without your gift, you have been more real than I have ever seen you. More awkward. More uncertain. More human." She smiled. "I like this version better. The one who does not know everything."

"You are not supposed to forgive me this easily."

"Who says there are rules?" Tiziri reached out and squeezed her hand. "You did something wrong. You admitted it. You are different now. What more do you want? Should I make you suffer first?" She laughed again. "Life is hard enough. When someone offers real apology, I would rather accept it and move forward than carry the burden of holding a grudge."

Amara felt tears threaten again, but these were different. Relief and gratitude and a warmth she had not felt in months: the warmth of authentic connection.

"Thank you."

"Thank me by being my actual friend. The uncertain, ordinary, does-not-know-what-I-am-feeling kind of friend. I think I will like her."

They walked to the spring together, and for the first time since setting aside the talisman, Amara felt a presence other than lonely.

✦

Two weeks later

Iberim did not forgive her.

He listened to her confession with a face like carved stone, then stood and turned away.

"You manipulated sacred deliberations." His voice was quiet, which was worse than shouting. "I thought I had reached understanding through wisdom. Through experience. Through the counsel of my ancestors."

"I am sorry..."

"I spent weeks afterward proud of myself. Proud of how I had found compromise, proud of how I had grown. My wife praised my maturity. My sons looked at me differently." He turned back to face her, and his eyes were hard. "Now you tell me it was not mine. That wisdom I thought I found—it was your hand on the scales."

"The settlement is working. Both families..."

"I do not care about the settlement." His voice cracked. "I care about knowing my own mind. I care about decisions being mine. You took that from me, and no apology gives it back."

"I know. I am not asking you to..."

"Then what are you asking? Why come here with words that change nothing?"

Amara stood silent, because Menna had warned her this might happen, but living it was different from expecting it.

"Because you deserve to know what I did. Because I needed to acknowledge it, whether you forgive me or not."

"How generous of you." Bitterness sharpened his words. "You get to confess and feel better. I get to discover that a moment I treasured was a lie."

She had no answer to that. He was right. The apology served her more than him. The knowledge she offered was a wound, not a gift.

"I am sorry," she said again, because there was nothing else to say.

"Leave." Iberim's voice was flat. "Do not come back. I do not want your apologies or your presence or your reminders of what you did to my mind."

Amara left.

On the walk back to the settlement, she understood what Menna had tried to tell her: some harm could not be undone. Some debts could not be paid. She had stolen something from

Iberim that no apology could return, and his refusal to forgive was the truest response to what she had done.

It hurt. It was supposed to hurt.

And somehow, carrying that hurt without trying to fix it felt more honest than anything she had done in months.

❧✦❧

Early Winter 57 CE—Three weeks after beginning amends

The council gathered at Amara's request.

This was different from the census meeting that ended in disaster. Then, she had stood at the center, certain of her rightness, demanding compliance. Now she stood at the edge, uncertain of everything, asking only to be heard.

"I asked to speak to you because I owe you all an apology."

Thirty faces watched her. Some hostile, some curious, some carefully neutral. She could not sense their emotions, could not adjust her approach based on what she felt. She could only speak truth and accept whatever followed.

"During the census meeting, I tried to control how you felt about my plan. I reached into your emotions with my gift and adjusted them to make you agree with me. When you resisted, I pressed harder. When you questioned me, I treated your doubt as evidence that you needed more adjusting."

Silence. She continued.

"I told myself I was helping. That I knew best, and you simply needed to be shown the right path. I was wrong. I violated your trust, your minds, and your right to make your own decisions."

Taderfit spoke first. "We knew a thing was wrong. We felt it. But we could not name what you were doing."

"I know. That made it worse. You sensed the violation but could not defend against it." Amara's voice steadied. "I have set aside the talisman. My gift is gone, or nearly gone. I cannot do what I did even if I wanted to. But that is not why I am here."

"Then why?" Massin asked. His aunt Kenza sat beside him, her face unreadable.

"Because I needed to acknowledge what I did. In front of everyone. So you know I understand how wrong it was." She paused. "I am not asking you to trust me again. That is a thing I will have to earn over time, through changed behavior, not words. I am just asking you to know that I see what I did, and I am sorry, and I am trying to become someone who would never do it again."

The silence stretched. Amara waited, her heart pounding.

Yasir spoke at last. "What do you want from the council?"

"Nothing. I am not asking for anything. I am just telling you the truth. What you do with it is your choice."

More silence. Then Grandmother Menna rose from her place among the elders.

"I have been counseling this child through her amends. She has gone to many of you individually. Some have forgiven her. Some have not. Both responses are right." She looked around the circle. "What she asks now is harder than forgiveness. She asks to be seen clearly, as a young woman who made terrible mistakes and is trying to learn from them."

Taderfit nodded slowly. "The talisman is truly set aside?"

"Yes. Menna knows where."

"And your gift?"

"Gone. Or nearly gone. I can barely feel anything anymore. I am ordinary now. Like everyone else."

"Good." The word came from Massin, surprising everyone. "Because the strange girl who knew too much was terrifying. This one..." He gestured at her. "This one is just a person. I can talk to a person."

Scattered murmurs of agreement.

But not everyone agreed. Kella, Kenza's sister, stood abruptly. Her face held the kind of anger that came from wounds still fresh.

"Why should we forgive her at all?" Her voice carried across the gathering. "She violated us. Used us. Treated us like pieces on her game board, to be moved according to her will." She turned to face the council directly. "My sister agreed to terms she did not want. Iberim discovered that wisdom he treasured was a lie. Taderfit had words stolen from her mouth before she could speak them. Why should we extend understanding to someone who showed us none?"

Amara felt her chest tighten. She had no answer. Kella was right.

Menna rose slowly, her old bones protesting the movement. She did not look at Amara. She looked at Kella.

"Your anger is righteous," Menna said. "It honors what was taken from you. Hold it." She paused. "But I want to ask you a harder thing."

Kella's jaw tightened. "What?"

"If you respond to what she did by refusing to see her, by seeing only the violation, only the monster you want her to be, you repeat the very sin you are punishing her for." Menna's voice carried the gravity of generations. "She stopped seeing you as people with your own minds and choices. She saw only what she wanted you to become. If you do the same to her now, you become what you condemn."

"That is not the same..."

"It is exactly the same." Menna's eyes were kind but unyielding. "The hardest thing I will ever ask of this council is not forgiveness. Forgiveness is each person's choice, freely given or withheld. What I ask is harder: that you hold your anger and your understanding together. That you see her clearly, the harm she caused and the child underneath who lost her way. That you refuse to make her less than human, even though she made you less than human in her own mind."

Kella's hands clenched at her sides. "You ask too much."

"I ask what we must ask of ourselves if we are to remain who we are." Menna looked around the circle. "Rome rules by teaching people to stop seeing each other. Masters stop seeing slaves. Soldiers stop seeing enemies. Tax collectors stop seeing the families they bankrupt. The moment we stop seeing each other—seeing, with all the complexity and failure and possibility that every person carries—we become what Rome has made of itself."

She turned back to Kella.

"Our willingness to extend the imaginative leap of understanding, even to those who have hurt us, is precisely what makes us different from the empire that oppresses us. Not because they deserve it. But because we refuse to let their actions determine who we become."

Slowly, Kella sat.

She did not speak forgiveness. She did not need to. But she had heard.

The silence that followed was the silence of people wrestling with a truth larger than one girl's mistakes.

Yasir spoke with the council's full authority behind him. "The council accepts your apology. Trust is another matter. But the door is open."

Amara bowed her head. "Thank you."

She left the gathering feeling lighter than she had in months. Not forgiven by everyone—Iberim's absence spoke loudly—but acknowledged. Seen. Known for what she had done, and given the chance to become someone different.

It was more than she deserved.

CHAPTER 52

The Past Is Never Where You Left It

"The past is never where you left it."
—Desert proverb on memory
Early Winter 57 CE—Tizwit

He came at dusk, when the light softened the desert into a wash of color. Sixteen years since he had seen this place. Sixteen years of reports and warnings and money sent through intermediaries, of knowing every detail of their lives without once looking them in the face.

The village had changed. More permanent structures now, the community dug in against both desert and Empire. He saw the signs of prosperity earned through careful adaptation: irrigation channels, date groves heavy with fruit, children running between houses.

She met him at the entrance to what had been Eudoxus's dwelling. The years had changed her—grey threaded through black hair, lines around eyes and mouth that spoke of grief weathered rather than defeated. But she stood straight, and her gaze held steady.

"Tribune." Her voice gave nothing away.

"I am not here as a tribune."

"No? Then what are you here as?"

He had no answer. He had rehearsed this conversation a hundred times over sixteen years, and now every prepared word turned to sand.

“I came to pay respects to Eudoxus. And to tell you that Petronius has received his transfer. He departs before the winter storms. His replacement is a junior administrator. The governor considers the province sufficiently stable to warrant only routine management.”

Zahra absorbed this without expression. “And?”

“And I believe the protection is no longer needed.” The words felt strange in his mouth, words he had imagined speaking for years but never quite believed he would say. “The hunt for your family ended years ago in all but name. Rome has newer problems, newer provinces, newer rebellions to occupy its attention. Aedemon’s revolt is eighteen years old. The twins are nearly adults. Your identity here is... it is simply who you are now. Not a disguise. A life.”

“The protection.” She spoke the word like a stone she had been carrying. “Is that what you call it? Sixteen years of looking over your shoulder, wondering if today was the day your reports stopped being enough. Sixteen years of raising children who can never use their real names, who grew up understanding that safety was borrowed and could be revoked at any moment.” She paused. “That is what you protected us into.”

“I know.”

“Do you?”

“No. I cannot know. I can only tell you that the alternative was worse. I know what Nerva would have done if he had found you. I know what Rome does to rebels’ families.”

“And that justifies it? The protection?”

“Nothing justifies it. Nothing justifies any of it.” The words came from somewhere deeper than strategy. “I killed your husband. Paulinus ordered it, and I obeyed. I have spent sixteen years trying to—not to make amends. There are no amends for what I did. Just trying to make his death mean something other than Rome's victory."

"Eudoxus told me," she said. "Years ago. What you did that night. The promise. The way you held your sword and wept."

Marcus said nothing. There was nothing to say.

"I hated you for a long time. But hatred is heavy. And I had children to raise, and a life to build from wreckage." She took a breath. "I cannot forgive you. I do not think I will ever be able to forgive you. But I cannot hate you either. You have made that impossible." She gestured at the village around them. "Sixteen years of protection and warnings that arrived just in time. You did that. Whatever else you are, you did that."

"It does not balance."

"No. It does not. Nothing balances." She stepped closer. "But perhaps balance is not the point. Perhaps the point is just continuing. Living with what cannot be fixed."

They stood in silence as the light faded. Somewhere in the village, a child laughed.

"My children will want to meet you," she said at last. "Amara has questions. Juba has rage. Neither knows what to do with you."

"I will face whatever they need to say."

She extended her hand in acknowledgment that they were bound together and would remain so.

He took it. Her grip was stronger than he had expected.

"Come inside," she said. "Meet your ghosts."

Zahra led him through the doorway. The twins were waiting inside—she had sent word ahead, given them the choice to leave or stay. They had stayed.

The interior was dim. Marcus's eyes adjusted slowly, and in that adjustment, he saw them, and they saw him.

He wore a plain traveler's tunic and dust-colored cloak, his armor and insignia shed. But the cut of the cloth was Roman, the sandals were military issue, and he carried himself with the unconscious bearing of thirty years in uniform. He could not hide what he was any more than he could hide the grey in his hair or the exhaustion carved into his face.

Juba stood near the back wall, arms crossed, eyes fixed on those Roman sandals. Amara sat near the hearth, her hand rising briefly to her chest, touching nothing, then falling away. She watched him with wary, human eyes, then shifted her gaze to her mother, and a question flickered there.

Zahra felt it. She had known this moment would come: the introduction and the scrutiny that would follow. Her children were not fools. They would see that she and Marcus moved around each other like people who shared more history than a single act of violence.

"Children." She kept her voice steady. "This is Tribune Marcus Valerius Severus. He killed your father. He has also spent sixteen years ensuring you survived to hear that truth."

Juba's eyes snapped from the Roman sandals to his mother's face. "You know him."

It was not a question.

"Yes."

"How? How do you know a Roman tribune?"

Zahra drew a breath. She had rehearsed this too, in the long minutes while Marcus spoke his piece outside. "Before the rebellion. Before your father and I married. Marcus was stationed in Caesarea. He and your father were friends."

"Friends." Juba's voice dripped contempt.

"Yes. And Marcus..." She stopped. How to say this? How to explain a thing she had never fully understood herself? "Marcus cared for me. Your father knew. It was complicated. But it was a long time ago, and it has nothing to do with why he is here now."

"Does it not?" Juba took a step forward. "He loved you. And then he killed your husband. And now he shows up expecting—what? Gratitude? Forgiveness? A place at our fire?"

"I expect nothing," Marcus said. "I came to speak truth, not to ask for anything."

Amara had not moved. She was watching her mother's face with an intensity that made Zahra's chest tighten. Once, her daughter would have known, would have felt every current of old grief and older longing that this meeting stirred. Now she had to look. Had to guess. Had to trust.

"Did you love him back?" Amara asked.

The question cut through everything.

"No." Zahra met her daughter's eyes. "I loved your father. Only your father. Marcus knew that. He never asked for anything else."

"Then why protect us? For sixteen years?" Amara's voice held no accusation, only the need to understand. "If he knew you would never..."

"Because your father asked him to." Zahra's voice nearly broke. "Because whatever else Marcus is, he keeps his promises. And because..." She looked at Marcus, then away. "Because love does not always ask to be returned. Sometimes it just serves."

No one spoke.

Juba's fists clenched and unclenched. "This is... I cannot..." He turned away, pressing his palms against the wall to steady himself.

His hand moved to his hip, an unconscious gesture, reaching for Azref before remembering the blade was hidden back at camp, wrapped in cloth where he had placed it after the trials. He caught himself, but not before Marcus noticed.

"You still carry it, then." Marcus's voice was quiet. "Your father's sword."

Juba froze. "How do you know about..."

"I know because I am the one who sent it."

The words fell into silence. Zahra's breath caught. Even Amara, watching the exchange with careful neutrality, went still.

"That is impossible." Juba's voice came out rough. "Mother said it arrived through a merchant. No one knew who..."

"I paid the merchant. Paid him enough to forget my face and remember only the delivery." Marcus met Juba's eyes without flinching. "After the execution, your father's possessions were catalogued as spoils—standard procedure for captured rebels. His sword would have been melted down or given to some junior officer as a trophy. I could not let that happen."

"You could not let..." Juba stepped forward, fists clenched. "You killed him. You held the blade that ended his life. And then you—what? Felt guilty enough to steal his sword?"

"Guilty enough. Yes. And bound by a promise." Marcus's voice remained steady, though a shadow flickered in his eyes. "Your father asked me to watch over his family. In those last moments, he forgave me for what I was about to do. I could not save his life. Paulinus would have found another executioner if I had refused, and I would have lost any ability to protect you afterward. But I could save that one piece of him."

"You expect me to be grateful?" Juba's voice cracked. "Every time I held that sword, every time I spoke to it like some fool talking to iron, every time I imagined my father's hands on the same hilt—I was holding something a Roman gave me? Something from the man who murdered him?"

"Yes."

Marcus offered no defense, no justification beyond the bare fact.

Zahra spoke into the silence. "I wondered, for twelve years. Who would do such a thing, risk discovery to send a dead rebel's weapon to his widow? I never imagined..." She looked at Marcus with something too complicated to name. "I never imagined it was you."

"It was the only thing I could give him." Marcus's voice roughened. "The only piece of Aedemon I could preserve. His name became legend—you have heard the stories the desert people tell. His cause lived on through others. But that sword was the physical thing, the metal he had held, the blade he had named. I wanted his son to have it."

Amara watched her brother's face. His fury, sorrow, and a dawning recognition were clear to her, even without the talisman's help. Juba had loved that sword. Had spoken to it, polished it, carried it with reverence. Learning its history did not erase those feelings. It complicated them beyond bearing.

"Azref," Juba said at last. "That is what he called it. Justice."

"I know. He told me once, years ago, when we were still friends. He said a blade should remind its bearer what it was for." Marcus paused. "I hope it has."

Juba turned away, pressing his palms against the wall. His shoulders shook with emotion he refused to release.

"I put it away," he said to the wall. "After the trials. After I learned what it could do. I wrapped it in cloth and hid it, swore I would never use it for killing again unless there was no other choice." A bitter laugh escaped him. "I thought I was honoring my father by refusing to become a killer. Now I learn the sword came from his killer all along."

"Perhaps that is fitting." Amara's voice was soft. "A gift from the man who took everything, carrying a lesson about refusing to take anything more."

Juba did not respond. But his hands, pressed flat against the wall, slowly unclenched.

Marcus waited. He had delivered the truth. What they did with it was theirs to decide.

Amara rose slowly from the hearth. She crossed to her mother and took her hand, a simple gesture, but Zahra felt it like an anchor.

"I think," Amara said, "that everyone should stop talking now. Before we say things we cannot take back." She looked at Marcus. "You should go. Not forever. But for tonight."

Marcus nodded. "I will make camp at the old waystation south of the ridge. Three days."

"There will not be any talk," Juba said to the wall.

"Perhaps not." Amara's voice was gentle. "But three days gives us time to decide."

Marcus turned to Zahra. For a moment, sixteen years of letters never sent, words never spoken, a connection that had cost everything and changed nothing.

"Thank you," he said. "For letting them hear it from you."

"I did not do it for you."

"I know."

He walked out into the darkness. Behind him, a family sat with truths that would take longer than three days to untangle.

But they were spoken. All of it was spoken at last.

✦

The next morning

Marcus returned at dawn. Not to the family dwelling—he was not that foolish—but to Eudoxus's cairn on the ridge above the settlement. He stood before the monument of community love and spoke to the dead man who had been the bridge between his guilt and their survival.

"You kept them safe," he said. "All those years. The warnings I sent, the money, the intelligence—none of it would have mattered without you. You were the one who taught them to trust each other. Who built the community that could absorb the danger and survive it."

The cairn offered no response. Stones did not forgive. But the morning light touched the quartz Yasir had placed, and it caught fire for a moment, bright and brief.

"I have filed my resignation." The words still tasted strange. "Effective upon Petronius's departure. Madi will maintain the intelligence contacts. The network will survive without me, at least long enough for the new administration to settle in and demonstrate its indifference."

He wrote the letter three days ago, in the waystation south of the ridge, by lamplight that guttered in the winter wind. Thirty years of service reduced to formal phrases on official papyrus. Tribune Marcus Valerius Severus requests honorable discharge from the service of Rome. The language of empire, precise and bloodless, contained none of the truth.

There were three truths. He was leaving because he could no longer sustain the lies. The family he had protected no longer needed a protector. And Tacfara had waited long enough.

"Tacfara is expecting me." He spoke to the cairn the way Juba spoke to Azref: addressing the dead through the objects they had left behind. "She has been patient. More patient than I deserve. I do not know what kind of life I can build there, after thirty years of this. But I intend to try."

He placed a stone on the cairn. A simple river rock, unpolished, unremarkable. The kind of stone a soldier might carry in his pack for years without knowing why.

"Thank you," he said. "For the impossible thing you did. For making a Greek scholar's exile into a home. For teaching children whose father I killed that the world could still be trusted. For keeping the bridge standing long enough for all of us to cross it."

A house bunting landed on the cairn.

The small brown bird hopped across the stones with the confidence of a creature that had never learned to fear human spaces. It paused on the quartz Yasir had placed, tilted its head, and regarded Marcus with bright, unhurried eyes.

Marcus held still. He knew the bird. He saw them in every mountain village he ever visited. They entered homes and workshops and council circles without invitation, perching on shoulders and lintels and grain jars, sacred to the Imazighen because they crossed thresholds no other creature dared.

The bunting hopped from the quartz to Marcus's knee. He felt its weight. It was barely anything, the weight of a held breath, and its small feet gripped the fabric of his traveling cloak. It sat there and preened a wing feather with the thoroughness of important business.

Marcus looked at the bird on his knee and thought of sixteen years of crossing thresholds he was never invited through. He had entered lives he had no right to enter, sat in the spaces between danger and safety, uninvited and unacknowledged, present without grasping, protecting without possessing.

He had been the bunting and never known it.

The bird finished its feather, regarded him once more, and flew to the tamarisk tree above the cairn. It sang three notes, bright, unhurried, and absurdly cheerful for a cemetery. Then it fell silent.

Marcus almost laughed. The sound surprised him. He could not remember the last time laughter had risen in him without bitterness behind it.

"Thank you," he told the bird. "For the company."

He turned and walked down the ridge toward the settlement. Behind him, the bunting sang again from the tamarisk those same three notes. They were patient and clear, the song of a creature that entered sacred spaces without asking and left without explaining why it came.

The morning air carried the scent of cooking fires and date blossoms, the ordinary business of people building lives in a difficult place.

✦

Juba was waiting at the settlement's edge.

He stood with arms crossed, his expression unreadable, positioned precisely where Marcus would have to pass on the path from the ridge. Not an ambush. An interception.

"You are leaving." Juba's voice was flat. "Mother told us."

"I have resigned my commission. Petronius departs within the month. The new prefect is a junior administrator with no interest in old investigations."

"And you trust that?"

"I trust sixteen years of evidence. Your family's trail has gone cold. Nerva's archive gathers dust. Rome has forgotten Aedemon's children." Marcus paused. "And you are no longer children."

Juba studied him with the tactical assessment Marcus had seen in a hundred officers. The young man was measuring him, weighing the intelligence, calculating the risks.

"The archive remains."

"Yes. Disordered, unread, but intact. That is the one thread I cannot cut without raising questions."

"We will manage it ourselves."

The calm certainty in Juba's voice surprised Marcus. Not bravado. Strategy. The young man had already considered the operational reality and determined his response.

"You have a plan." It was not a question.

"I have been making plans since I was twelve years old. The difference is that now I make plans that do not require anyone to die." Juba's jaw tightened. "No thanks to you."

"No. No thanks to me."

They stood in silence. Then Juba spoke, his voice rough with a feeling that was not quite anger and not quite acceptance.

"I will not forgive you. My mother says she cannot. My sister..." He glanced toward the settlement. "My sister says forgiveness is each person's choice, and that choice is sacred. She learned that the hard way."

"She learned it from a woman named Kenza." Marcus said.

Juba's eyes narrowed. "You know about that."

"I know everything that has happened here for sixteen years. That was the burden of the protection."

"The burden." Juba's voice carried an edge. "You call it a burden. We call it a cage." He stepped closer. "But I will tell you this. Whatever else you are, whatever else you did—the sword was real. Azref was real. And the lesson it carried was real. My father named it Justice, and I have tried to live by that name. If that came from you..." He stopped, wrestling with words. "Then perhaps the worst man in my life gave me the best thing in it. And I do not know what to do with that."

"You do not have to do anything with it. It is yours. It always was."

Juba studied him a moment longer. Then he stepped aside, clearing the path.

"Go to your woman in Tacfara, Roman. Build whatever life you can. We will manage our own protection from here."

Marcus walked past him into the settlement. He did not look back. Looking back was a luxury he had never been able to afford, and he would not start now.

❧✦❧

She found him at the edge of the oasis, on a flat stone where the irrigation channels met the open desert. He had his back to the settlement, his face turned toward the emptiness to the south.

Amara said nothing, but sat beside him on the stone. She crossed her legs, placed her hands open on her knees, and settled into the posture Eudoxus had taught her. She did not speak. She breathed. In through the nose, out through the mouth. She noted the presence of Marcus beside her without reaching toward him, without the old reflex of reading and adjusting. She sat the way the practice demanded: present, open, without agenda.

The channels murmured at their feet, carrying water from the sacred spring toward the date groves. The desert wind moved sand in slow patterns across the ground.

Marcus watched her from the corner of his eye. The deliberate positioning, the open hands, the controlled breathing. This was not a woman sitting beside him for conversation. This was a discipline he did not recognize.

"What are you doing?"

"Sitting with what is." She did not open her eyes. "Eudoxus taught me. You sit, you breathe, you note what arises without chasing it. Thoughts come. You let them pass. What remains, underneath all of it, is the stillness that was always there."

"You do this every morning?"

"Every morning since I set the talisman aside. Before that, I thought I did not need it. The talisman did the work for me." She opened her eyes. "I was wrong. The practice is the work. Everything else was distraction."

She returned to silence. Marcus sat beside her, and for the first time in sixteen years he occupied another person's presence without calculating.

"You are lighter," she said.

Marcus glanced at her. She saw the surprise. This girl, this young woman who hours ago had told everyone to stop talking before they said things they could not take back, the mediator and peacemaker, had come to him alone.

"The confession," she said. "It cost you. It also freed you."

"Your brother does not see it that way."

"My brother needs time. He carries things the way our father carried them, close to the chest, where they burn." She paused. "You carry things at arm's length, where you can see them, where you can calculate their heft. You have been calculating for sixteen years."

Marcus said nothing. The channels kept murmuring.

"I used to feel everything," Amara said. "Every person in a room, every buried grief, every hidden joy. The talisman made it so clear I thought clarity was the same as understanding." She looked at her hands. "It was not. Clarity without compassion is surveillance. I learned that the hard way."

"Your mother told me about the amends journey."

"Then you know I stood in front of people I had manipulated and told them what I had done. Each one. Kenza refused to forgive me. Iberim refused to forgive me. I do not blame them." She turned to face him. "Tiziri forgave me before I finished speaking. And the council accepted my apology even though Amagar wanted to exile me. Do you know why?"

"Because you told the truth."

"Because I let them choose. I did not try to make them feel a certain way about what I had done. I told them and let them decide." Her voice was quiet. "That is what you just did. You told us the truth and let us decide. Juba chose anger. My mother chose grief. Those are their choices and they are sacred."

"And yours?"

Amara looked at him, looked the way she had looked at Nerva in a dusty market years ago, at Eudoxus on his deathbed, at every person the talisman once let her see too clearly. This time there was no talisman, no spiritual amplification. A young woman who had learned, through failure and confession and the long discipline of setting power aside, to see without seizing.

What she saw was incomplete. Without the talisman she could not map the full landscape of his grief the way she once would have. She caught fragments: the stiffness in his jaw that spoke of years of clenching, the hands resting too still on his knees, the set of his head, braced for a blow that had already fallen. She read these the way Eudoxus had taught her to read people before the stone, before she had learned to cheat, one detail at a time, with humility, knowing how much damage false certainty could do.

She saw Marcus. She did not see all of him. She would never see all of anyone again, and she was learning to accept that as mercy rather than loss.

"I could hate you," Amara said. "I have reason to. You killed my father. I grew up without him because of what you did. Every false name, every night my mother walked the terraces because she could not sleep, every year my brother spent trying to become a man he had never met. All of that began with you." She let the words stand. "I carried anger about that for a long time.

Even before I knew your name, I carried it. Anger at the faceless Roman who took him from us."

She turned to face him fully.

"I forgive you. Not because you deserve it. Not because what you did was acceptable. I forgive you because holding this anger chains me to a moment I was not even present for, and I refuse to live there." Her voice was steady. "Eudoxus taught me that some things cannot be grasped, only released. This is one of them. I release it. What you do with that is yours to decide."

A sound escaped Marcus, a sound like a wall maintained for decades, finally cracking and giving way. His eyes, which had held steady through Zahra's grief and Juba's rage, lost their composure for the first time.

Amara did not move to comfort him. She did not try to ease his pain. She sat beside him on the warm stone and let the moment be what it was.

After a long silence, Marcus spoke. His voice was rough. "Your father asked me to watch over you. In those last moments, he forgave me for what I was about to do, and he asked me to watch over his family."

"I know. You told us."

"What I did not tell you is what he said after that." Marcus looked at the desert, at the emptiness that had swallowed so many lives and secrets. "He said: 'Do not let it consume you. The guilt. Do not let it become all you are.' He could see what it would do to me. Even then. Even dying."

Amara closed her eyes. Her father's voice, speaking through the man who had killed him. It reached across sixteen years to deliver one final piece of wisdom.

Do not let it consume you.

The same lesson Eudoxus had spent a lifetime teaching her. The same truth the talisman had tried to show her before she twisted its purpose. The same discipline she had failed and learned and was still learning.

"He was right," she said. "And you listened. You did not let it consume you. You let it shape you instead."

"Is there a difference?"

"The difference is that you are here, on this stone, having told the truth. If the guilt had consumed you, you would have died in that garrison years ago, or drunk yourself to death, or turned the blade on yourself." She opened her eyes. "You survived it. That is not nothing."

"There is something you should know," Marcus said. "The Roman prefect you spoke to at Thubursicu market. The one your mother was so frightened by."

Amara went still. "I was eight. I did not know who he was."

"What you did that day saved my life. Nerva was transferring me to Syria. Once I left Caesarea, the protection would have collapsed within months. Your family would have been found." He paused. "His dispatch about you convinced Rome he was losing his grip. The transfer was rescinded. He was recalled. And I stayed."

"I did not mean to do any of that. I just saw that he was hurting."

"I know. And that is what I want you to understand. The gift you were ashamed of, the moment your mother called a disaster, was the thing that kept your family alive. You did not plan it. You did not control it. You simply saw a man's truth and spoke it, and the consequences rippled outward in ways none of us could have predicted."

Amara sat with this. The market. The Roman's exposed face. Silina pulling her away. Years of believing she had nearly destroyed everything, and now learning she had saved it.

"I carried that shame for years," she said. "Eudoxus told me the gift does not care about our intentions. It acts through us."

"Then whatever acted through you that day had better aim than any soldier I ever commanded."

Marcus looked at her. What he saw was Aedemon's daughter, who carried a gift that could destroy people and had learned to set it down. Who had manipulated and confessed and made amends and was still standing. Who had come to him to offer the harder thing: forgiveness that freed the forgiver and left the forgiven to choose his own freedom.

"You are very like him," Marcus said. "Your father. The way he could see into people. He did it without any gift, through attention and care and nothing more."

"I am learning to do it that way now." A faint smile crossed her face. "It is harder without the talisman. It is more honest."

They sat together as the sun moved lower and the shadows lengthened across the oasis, two people who had each carried burdens that cracked them, on a warm stone beside water that asked nothing of anyone who drank from it.

When Amara stood to leave, Marcus spoke once more.

"Tell your brother this for me."

"Tell him yourself. You have three days."

"I may not see him again."

"Then write to him. You are good at letters." The faint smile returned. "Tacfara told my mother that much."

She walked back toward the settlement, leaving Marcus on the stone with the channels and the wind and the first evening stars. He sat until the first evening stars steadied above the ridge. He did not brood. He did not calculate. He did not plan.

He sat. Amara had seen him. It had not destroyed him.

The spring murmured. The desert held its peace.

CHAPTER 53

What the Spring Taught

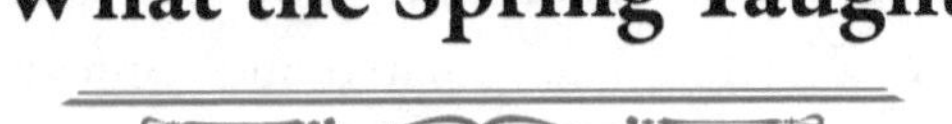

"The agurram does not study the spring.
It sits on its rock and the spring flows anyway.
This is the second lesson."
—Amazigh teaching on sacred waters

Silina found Amara by the spring at dusk, where she sat watching the water catch the last light.

"May I join you?"

Amara nodded, and Silina settled onto the rocks beside her. For a while neither spoke. The spring murmured its ancient song, indifferent to human sorrows.

"You are doing well," Silina said at last. "Without the talisman. Better than I expected."

"Some days." Amara studied the older woman's profile, the silver threading her dark hair, the lines around her eyes that deepened when she smiled. "Other days I reach for it before I remember."

"That will fade. Eventually the reaching stops."

A change in Silina's tone made Amara turn. Silina's gaze had gone distant, fixed on a point beyond the spring, beyond the rocks, beyond the present moment.

"You have set a thing aside too," Amara said. It was not a question. Without the talisman she could not sense emotions directly, but she was learning to read faces, voices, the small betrayals of posture that everyone carried.

Unexpectedly, she almost smiled.

"I have waited years to tell someone this. I could not, before. Not while you carried the talisman."

Amara frowned. "You were afraid I would sense it?"

"I was certain you would. Every time we spoke, I held this memory behind walls I had spent decades building. Thinking about anything else. Keeping my distance when I felt it rising." She shook her head. "Exhausting, hiding from someone who sees feelings the way others see faces."

"I never knew..."

"That was the point. Your gift was powerful, but it was not all-seeing. It caught what surfaced. I made sure this never did." Silina's voice softened. "But now you have set the talisman aside. You cannot see what I am feeling unless I show you. Which means for the first time, I can choose to tell you rather than fear you will discover it."

The words landed with unexpected force. Amara had spent weeks grieving the loss of her abilities. She never considered what her powers might have cost others. People built walls against her perception, intimacies withheld because she might sense them without permission.

"I am sorry," she said. "I never realized..."

"Do not be. You used your gift to help. But some things need to be given, not taken. Even with kindness."

"I was eight years old. The Romans were hunting us, my mother and me. We had been running for three days. She was injured and could not go farther. We hid in a rock formation, a place I knew from childhood games."

She paused. Amara waited.

"Another family was hiding nearby. A woman and her two sons, about my age. I could hear them breathing through the stones. The Romans were searching systematically, getting closer. They would find one of us. Perhaps both." Her hands tightened in her lap. "So I threw a stone. Made it land near where the other family was hiding."

The spring kept murmuring. A house bunting called a single note from the rocks above them, low and steady, the sound of a small creature marking the space between one silence and the next.

"The soldiers heard it. They went toward the sound." Silina's voice stayed flat. "My mother and I survived. The other family did not."

Amara absorbed this. A child's choice. An impossible calculation. Lives weighed against lives in a moment of terror.

"You were eight."

"Old enough to know what I was doing."

"Old enough to survive. That is different from old enough to bear responsibility."

Silina looked at her. "You sound like Eudoxus."

"He taught me." Amara hesitated, then continued. "I have spent weeks learning that power does not make us wise. That sensing everything does not mean understanding anything. That I was hurting people while believing I was helping them." She met Silina's eyes. "You threw a stone when you were eight years old. Everything you have done since then—every family you have guided to safety, every path you have shown through the mountains, every life you have helped protect—that is who you are. The stone was a child surviving. The rest has been a woman choosing."

Silina's breath caught. Her eyes glistened.

"I have never told anyone. Not even your mother."

"You carried it alone all these years?"

"It seemed like the least I owed them. The burden of remembering."

Amara reached out and took Silina's hand. The gesture felt strange without the talisman's warmth: just skin against skin, human contact unmediated by spiritual awareness.

"Eudoxus once told me that some burdens we carry because we must. Others we carry because we have not learned to set them down." She squeezed gently. "You have guided us this far. Perhaps it is time to let someone else help carry what you have been holding."

Silina did not respond with words. She sat, her hand in Amara's, watching the spring catch the fading light. But her posture shifted—a loosening, a release, like a rope pulled taut for decades finally given slack.

They stayed that way until the stars appeared, two women who understood impossible choices, learning together what it meant to be enough.

☙✦❧

The following evening

Amara found Ayyur by the western wells where the young men gathered to water the herds.

She had rehearsed this conversation more times than any other. Not because Ayyur was the most important person she had wronged—Iberim's stolen autonomy weighed heavier, Kenza's violated trust cut deeper—but because this apology required admitting a truth she had barely admitted to herself.

"May I speak with you?"

Ayyur looked up from the watering trough, surprise flickering across his face. They had barely spoken since Eudoxus's memorial, where she had been cold to him for reasons he could not understand.

"Of course."

She had asked Menna whether to do this privately or publicly. Privately, Menna had said. This one is personal. It deserves quiet.

They walked away from the wells, toward the ridge where the desert stretched endless and gold in the winter light. When they were out of earshot, Amara stopped.

"At the memorial, when you tried to speak with me, I was cold to you. Dismissive. I want you to know why."

Ayyur waited, his expression cautious.

"I could sense your feelings. With my gift." The words came slowly, painfully. "I knew you admired me. I also sensed that you were uncomfortable with how different I was. And I knew—or I thought I knew—that you would eventually reject me. That the discomfort would win over the admiration."

"You thought I would reject you?"

"I was certain of it. So I rejected you first." She forced herself to meet his eyes. "I was cold because I did not want to feel the hurt of waiting for you to decide I was too strange. I decided for you. I took away your choice before you could make it."

The wind stirred dust at their feet.

"And now?"

"Now I cannot sense anything. My gift is gone. I have no idea what you are feeling right now. Whether you are angry or confused or relieved to finally understand why I was so cold." She laughed, short and brittle. "For the first time in my life, I have to actually ask instead of knowing."

"That must be terrifying."

"It is."

He turned to look out across the desert, his profile sharp against the sky. "The girls at the memorial told me you were not interested. That I should not bother. I assumed they knew things I did not."

"They knew what I wanted them to know. I smoothed their certainty with my gift so they would discourage you." Another confession, another stone on the pile. "I manipulated everyone to avoid being vulnerable. I am sorry."

"You are apologizing for rejecting me before I could reject you?"

"I am apologizing for taking away your choice. For deciding what you would feel instead of letting you feel it." She turned to face him. "You might have rejected me. You probably would have. But you deserved the chance to decide that for yourself."

Ayyur studied her face—this new, uncertain version of the girl he had admired. The one who did not know everything. The one who had to ask.

"And if I said I would not have rejected you? That I was interested despite the discomfort?"

"Then I would have stolen something we could have had. Possibility. The chance to find out what might grow between us." Her voice dropped. "I will never know now. Neither will you. That is what my certainty cost us."

"You are different," he said at last. "Without the gift. More... human."

"I have heard that a lot lately."

"It is not an insult." He stepped closer. "The girl at the memorial scared me a little. She saw through everything, knew everything. But this girl..." He gestured at her. "This one I could talk to. Get to know. Wonder about, instead of feeling like she already knew all my secrets."

Amara felt her heart beat faster. She could not sense his emotions, could not know what he was building toward. She could only wait.

"I do not know if I would have rejected you," Ayyur continued. "I will never know, because you are right—you took that choice away. But I know what I feel now, standing here with someone who cannot read my mind."

"What do you feel?"

"Curious." A small smile touched his face. "Interested. Wondering what it would be like to know you as you are now, instead of who you were pretending to be."

"That is not forgiveness."

"No. It is something else." He held out his hand. "It is a beginning. If you want one."

Amara looked at his hand. She could not sense whether the offer was genuine. Could not know if he would change his mind tomorrow, next week, next year. Could not protect herself from the possibility of rejection by knowing it was coming.

She could only choose. And trust. And hope.

She took his hand.

"I would like that."

They stood together as the sun set over the desert, two young people at the beginning of a thing neither could predict. It was terrifying. It was uncertain. It was exactly what ordinary people faced every day of their lives.

And for the first time since setting aside the talisman, Amara understood why Menna had called uncertainty a gift rather than a curse.

Because this moment, this choice made blind, this trust extended without guarantee, was more real than anything she had ever manufactured with her power.

This was what connection felt like.

She had almost forgotten.

✦

Late that night

Amara lay in her sleeping furs listening to her mother's quiet breathing from across the dwelling. The talisman rested where she had left it, nestled among the roots of the ancient tamarisk by the sacred spring. Patient and waiting.

She would not retrieve it. Not yet. Perhaps not until she understood what she had truly set down.

I am the One. You are the One. She had turned the words over so many times, hearing in them a claim of power and a declaration of destiny. But here in the dark, with nothing between her and the world but her own skin, the meaning shifted. The words did not speak of being chosen or destined. They spoke of being singular, the way Ayyur was singular, and Juba, and Silina with her stone and her decades of quiet courage.

She sat up on the sleeping mat and crossed her legs. She placed her hands open on her knees. She breathed in through the nose, out through the mouth, and noted what arose without chasing it.

She had not sat this way since before the corruption, since before the talisman became a crutch and the practice became unnecessary. Eudoxus had taught her the posture years ago, beside the spring, and she abandoned it when the talisman offered an easier stillness. Now the talisman rested among the tamarisk roots and the easy stillness was gone and there was only this: the breath, the dark, the discipline of remaining.

The stillness did not come. Her mind offered its inventory of the day's fears and shames and small victories. She noted them and let them pass.

The mind was not finished. It offered one more image: herself at fourteen, talisman blazing against her chest, standing between two families arguing over irrigation rights. She had reached into both men's feelings, smoothed one's anger, amplified the other's guilt, and arranged a resolution neither had chosen. They thanked her. They walked away believing the decision was theirs. She walked away believing she had helped.

The toad had been sitting on its rock that morning. She passed it on her way to the spring. It sat exactly where it always sat, being exactly what it was, needing to manage nothing and no one. Eudoxus had used it to teach her "I am the One", the wholeness that required no power, no control, no grasping.

She had walked past it every day for three years and never once thought to take the lesson home.

A sound escaped her. Not quite a laugh. Not quite a sob. Something between. It was the noise a person makes when they see, with sudden and total clarity, how far they wandered from a truth that never moved.

The agurram was right there every morning, sitting on its rock being enough.

Thank you for your contribution, she told her horrified mind. *The committee will review it and get back to you.*

The sound came again, stronger this time. A hearty laugh arose from the same place Eudoxus's had risen in the courtyard with the goat. That place was deeper than grief, deeper than shame, the place where absurdity and grace share a wall.

She laughed in the dark, alone on her sleeping mat, her hand pressed against the heartbeat where the talisman used to rest. She laughed at herself, the girl who could feel everyone's truth and missed her own, who carried a stone of cosmic significance and forgot the lesson of a toad, who spent months trying to be the One Who Fixes Everything while the spring murmured its ancient teaching three steps from her door: *I do not ask who drinks.*

The laughter did not erase what she had done. The amends journey still waited. Kenza's face still haunted her. Iberim's stolen choice still burned.

But the laughter made room. It cracked the shame just wide enough for room for what came next, the possibility of forgiveness, that she could survive her own failures without being consumed by them.

Eudoxus would have understood. He would have told her about the goat.

She did not know about the goat. But she knew the toad, and the toad was enough.

What remained underneath was not peace. It was presence. The same presence Eudoxus had described in the doorway at Aghbalou, in the tent at Tala Tazegzawt, under the tamarisk tree where he had died.

The silence where his voice had been was no longer empty. She had been filling it for weeks without noticing, the way a river fills a channel carved by an older river that dried up long ago. The water was hers. The channel was his.

She breathed. The practice held her the way it had held him. It asked nothing. It promised nothing. It was enough.

She pressed her hand against her chest where the talisman usually rested and felt only the steady rhythm of her own heartbeat.

Her thoughts drifted to Ayyur, his patience when she had turned him away, the quiet dignity with which he had accepted her uncertainty. She had told him she was not ready. Perhaps someday she would be. The not-knowing felt strange and tender, like pressing on a bruise that was finally beginning to heal.

She was the One. Complete, and exactly as she was.

And in the morning, she would wake to discover what that meant.

❧✦☙

CAST OF CHARACTERS

Tamazight, Arabic, and Historical Names

The characters and places in The Third Path draw from the Tamazight (Amazigh) languages of North Africa, as well as Latin, Greek, and Arabic. This guide provides approximate English pronunciations. Tamazight contains several sounds not found in English; the notes below offer the closest equivalents.

Stressed syllables in CAPITALS. Tamazight vowels are pure — pronounced as in Italian or Spanish, not diphthongized as in English. The sound gh is soft and throaty, similar to the French r in rue.

The Seekers

Balthasar (BAL-thah-zar) — Persian scholar, seeker of significance

Caspar / Eudoxus (KAS-par / yoo-DOK-sus) — Persian scholar; later takes the Greek name Eudoxus. Teacher and guardian to the twins

Melchior (MEL-kee-or) — Persian scholar, creator of the talisman

The Family

A**edemon** (eye-DEE-mon) — Historical figure. Amazigh nobleman, administrator to King Ptolemy, rebel leader

Amara (ah-MAH-rah) — Their daughter, twin to Juba

Juba (YOO-bah) — Their son, twin to Amara

Silina (see-LEE-nah) — Orphan raised by Rihana, healer, part of the household

Zahra (ZAH-rah) — His wife, daughter of a Gaetulian mother and Roman father

Aghbalou and Tizwit

Aksil (AK-seel) — Tizwit - settlement youth

Amagar (ah-mah-GAR) — Tizwit - warrior elder

Grandmother Menna (MEN-nah) — Tizwit - spiritual elder

Hassan (hah-SAHN) — Tizwit - settlement youth

Iberim (ee-BEH-reem) — Tizwit - head of a farming family

Kahina (kah-HEE-nah) — Aghbalou - spiritual elder

Kella (KEL-lah) — Tizwit - Kenza's sister

Kenza (KEN-zah) — Tizwit - head of a farming family

Lunja (LOON-yah) — Tizwit - settlement member

Malik (MAH-leek) — Tizwit - warrior and weapons trainer

Ouksem (OOK-sem) — Tizwit - settlement member, skeptic

Taderfit (tah-DER-feet) — Tizwit - Yasir's wife and community elder

Tariq (TAH-reek) — Tizwit settlement youth

Tiziri (tee-ZEE-ree) — Tizwit - Yasir and Taderfit's daughter; Amara's cousin

Usem (OO-sem) — Agghbalou - Aedemon's cousin, settlement leader

Bakir (bah-KEER) — Aghbalou - Desert trader

Yasir (YAH-seer) — Tizwit – Settlement chieftain and elder

Rome

Aulus Cornelius Nerva (AW-lus kor-NEE-lee-us NER-vah) — Prefect, intelligence officer

Cassius (KAS-ee-us) — Centurion

Decimus (DEH-kih-mus) — Centurion

Gaius Licinius (GAY-us lih-KIN-ee-us) — Nerva's deputy centurion

Gaius Suetonius Paulinus (GAY-us sweh-TOH-nee-us paw-LEE-nus) — Historical figure. First Roman governor of annexed Mauretania

Gnaeus Hosidius Geta (NEE-us hoh-SID-ee-us GEH-tah) — Historical figure. Roman general

Madi (MAH-dee) — Marcus's Amazigh aide and intermediary

Marcus Valerius Severus (MAR-kus vah-LAIR-ee-us SEH-veh-rus) — Historical figure. Roman tribune, protector of the family

Petronius (peh-TROH-nee-us) — Corrupt prefect who succeeds Nerva

Octavius (ok-TAY-vee-us) — Centurion

Others

Adah (AH-dah) — Juba's first love

Adherbal (ad-HER-bal) — Minor court figure in Caesarea

Agerzam (ah-GEHR-zahm) — Amazigh man from the northern limes

Ayyur (AY-yoor) — Young man in the community; appears prominently in Book 2

Mazippa (mah-ZIP-pah) — Aedemon's father

Rihana (ree-HAH-nah) — Midwife in Caesarea

Tacfara (tak-FAH-rah) — Legal scholar in Volubilis; Marcus's confidant

Tahira (tah-HEE-rah) — Young woman at a regional gathering

Yennaya (yen-NAH-yah) — Scholar's daughter, intellectual companion to Juba

Yacoub the Silent (yah-KOOB) — Desert trader who carries the talisman westward

Other Historical Figures

King Herod the Great (HEHR-ud)

King Vonones (voh-NOH-neez) — Persian king

King Ptolemy of Mauretania (TOL-eh-mee) — Final independent king of Mauretania

Joseph and Mary (standard English)

Philo of Alexandria (FY-loh) — Jewish philosopher

Sabalus (SAH-bah-lus) — Amazigh resistance leader

The Talisman

A lapis lazuli stone set in gold, bearing its own consciousness. Created by Melchior in Persepolis, 35 CE. The spiral and Tifinagh inscription — *I am the One. You are the One.* — were carved by hands that did not know the language they were writing. The talisman learns through each bearer and chooses its own path forward.

HISTORICAL NOTES

The events of *The Star Seeker* take place in a region most Western readers know little about: Roman North Africa before the coming of Islam. This note provides context for the geography, peoples, and political upheaval shaping the novel's world.

Mauretania

The ancient kingdom of Mauretania bore no relation to the modern nation of Mauritania. It occupied what is today northern Morocco and northwestern Algeria, stretching along the Mediterranean coast from the Atlantic to the borders of Numidia. Its native inhabitants, the Mauri, were among the many peoples Romans collectively and dismissively called "Berbers" (from *barbarus*, meaning barbarian). They called themselves the Imazighen—"the free people"—and spoke Tamazight in its various regional dialects, written in their own ancient script, Tifinagh.

For centuries, Mauretania existed as an independent Amazigh kingdom. In 25 BCE, the Emperor Augustus installed Juba II, a Numidian prince educated in Rome and married to Cleopatra Selene (daughter of Cleopatra VII and Mark Antony), as a client king. Juba made Caesarea (modern Cherchell, Algeria) his capital and transformed it into a center of Hellenistic culture, complete with a royal library, theaters, and temples. His son Ptolemy inherited the throne around 23 CE and continued his father's careful balancing act between Roman expectations and Amazigh traditions.

That balance ended in 40 CE. The Emperor Caligula summoned Ptolemy to Rome and had him executed—according to the historian Suetonius, because the emperor was jealous of a purple cloak Ptolemy wore to the games. The murder of their king provoked a widespread Amazigh uprising led by Aedemon, a freed member of Ptolemy's household.

The Division

After Caligula's assassination in 41 CE, the Emperor Claudius dispatched military governors to suppress the revolt and annex Mauretania as Roman territory. The general Gaius Suetonius Paulinus (who would later become infamous for crushing Boudicca's rebellion in Britain) led the campaign alongside Gnaeus Hosidius Geta. Paulinus became the first Roman commander to lead an army across the Atlas Mountains, pursuing resistance fighters into terrain no legion had previously mapped.

By 44 CE, Rome formally divided Mauretania into two provinces. Mauretania Caesariensis, in the east, kept Caesarea as its capital and encompassed the Tell Atlas ranges, the high plateaus, and the fertile coastal strip of what is now northwestern Algeria. Mauretania Tingitana, in the west, was governed from Tingis (modern Tangier) and covered most of present-day northern Morocco. The Mulucha River (modern Moulouya), roughly sixty kilometers west of present-day Oran, marked the border between them.

Roman control, however, remained largely confined to the coast and major cities. The interior—the mountain valleys, the high plateaus, the passes of the Atlas—was governed through accommodation with local chieftains rather than direct Roman administration. This arrangement created the world of the novel. That world was a landscape where Roman authority thinned with every mile traveled inland. It allowed Amazigh communities to maintain their traditions and autonomy in proportion to their distance from the coast. A family fleeing imperial attention could disappear into mountain settlements Rome rarely visited and barely understood.

Gaetulia

South of the Atlas ranges and the Roman provinces lay Gaetulia, a vast, loosely defined region encompassing the southern slopes of the mountains, the arid high plateaus, and the oases of the northern Sahara. Its people, the Gaetulians, were among the oldest recorded inhabitants of northwestern Africa. Roman writers distinguished them from the coastal Mauri, though both peoples were Amazigh and spoke related dialects of Tamazight.

The Gaetulians were seminomadic pastoralists and formidable warriors. Their cavalry had challenged Roman legions during the Jugurthine War a century before the events of this novel, and the revolt of Tacfarinas (17–24 CE) demonstrated Gaetulian resistance could tie down Roman forces for years. They were also traders who supplied Rome with prized commodities: purple dye extracted from coastal shellfish, exotic animals for the arena, and goods carried along routes reaching deep into the Sahara.

Their ancestors had driven chariots across those same routes for a thousand years. The rock paintings scattered throughout the Atlas passes and deep into the Sahara still depicted teams of horses pulling light carts at the famous "flying gallop." By the first century, mounted cavalry had replaced the chariot in warfare, and camels were displacing horses for long-distance desert travel, but the old craft survived in festivals and regional gatherings, where chariot races drew competitors from settlements a hundred miles apart. The races carried the weight of tradition: each chariot built according to designs older than Carthage, each team trained in methods passed from parent to child across generations Rome could not count.

Gaetulia was never a Roman province. It existed beyond the frontier, a territory Rome claimed on maps but controlled only through occasional punitive expeditions and uneasy arrangements with tribal leaders. The Gaetulian settlements in this novel occupy that ambiguous space—close enough to the Roman world to trade with it and shelter refugees from it, remote enough to maintain ways of life the empire could neither fully comprehend nor effectively govern.

The Landscape

The geography of this story moves through three distinct zones. The coastal cities—Caesarea, Volubilis, Tingis—were Roman in architecture and administration, multicultural in population, polyglot in daily commerce. Latin served as the language of government, but Greek, Punic, and Tamazight filled the markets and homes.

The mountain settlements of the Tell Atlas and Aurès ranges represented the heartland of Amazigh life. Villages clung to high valleys and terraced slopes, sustained by springs, olive groves, and careful agriculture. These communities had absorbed waves of conquerors—Phoenician, Carthaginian, Roman—without surrendering their essential character. They paid taxes, traded with the coast, and otherwise governed themselves according to traditions older than Rome.

Beyond the mountains, the steppe and desert stretched south toward the Sahara. Here the Gaetulian communities clustered around oases and seasonal water sources, following patterns of movement dictated by climate and grazing rather than imperial borders. For the characters in this novel, each zone represents a different relationship to Roman power: subjection on the coast, negotiation in the mountains, and a degree of independence Rome could claim on maps but not enforce.

In the Interest of Complete Honesty

To be fully self-disclosing, I confess, in addition to the novel's obvious fictional nature, to making one digression from the historical record. In its first chapters, I introduced Philo of Alexandria. While he was in fact associated with the Library of Alexandria, he would have been five to ten years old at the time of the story, far too young to have yet made his mark on history.

A Note on Names

The peoples of this story knew themselves by names Rome often ignored or corrupted. Where the novel's Roman characters say "Berber," they are using a term derived from the Latin *barbarus*—an imperial judgment disguised as a label. The people themselves used "Imazighen" (singular: Amazigh), meaning "free people." Their language was Tamazight, their script Tifinagh. This novel follows the characters' own usage: Romans speak as Romans did, and the Imazighen name themselves.

One final important note about Tamazight names: Juba, the name of one of the central characters in the story, is pronounced Yoo-bah.

MAP

HISPANIA
OCEANUS ATLANTICUS
MARE NOSTRUM
IOL CAESAREA
TINGIS
VOLUBILIS
MAURITANIA TINGITANA
MAURITANIA CAESARIENSIS
TALA TAZEGZAWT
TIZWIT
GAETULIA

ACKNOWLEDGEMENTS

My thanks extend to the many new companions I've gained during the creation of this story, which often felt unending.

To members of Writers in the Grove, the local authors and poets group, without whose encouragement I would never have had the confidence to put pen to paper.

To the Willamette Writers organization and especially to its Historical Fiction critique group, whose members have helped to shape and refine the story in countless ways.

My special thanks and apologies to Susan Shepard, my long-suffering spouse, for the time I spent researching first-century Mauretania, and for journeys too often taken in mid-conversation.

Michael Colvin
April 16, 2026
Forest Grove, Oregon

PRONUNCIATION GUIDE

Pronunciation Key

Gh — a soft, throaty sound, similar to the French "r" in "rue." Not a hard "g."

kh — a throaty rasp, like the "ch" in Scottish "loch" or German "Bach."

zh — like the "s" in English "pleasure."

Double vowels (ee, oo, ah) — indicate a lengthened vowel sound, not two separate syllables.

Stress — indicated by CAPITAL LETTERS in the pronunciation.

All Tamazight vowels are "pure" — pronounced as in Italian or Spanish, not diphthongized as in English.

Place Names

Aghbalou *(agh-bah-LOO):* "spring; water source": Mountain settlement in the Zalacus highlands

Aurès *(ow-RESS):* Mountain range in eastern Algeria

Iol Caesarea *(ee-OHL kye-sah-RAY-ah):* Capital of Mauretania; renamed by Juba II to honor Augustus. Modern Cherchell, Algeria.

Tala Tazegzawt *(TAH-lah tah-zeg-ZAWT):* Oasis on the edge of the Sahara

Thubursicu *(thoo-BUR-see-koo):* Market town

Tizwit *(TEEZ-wit):* Desert settlement in Gaetulian territory

Volubilis *(voh-LOO-bih-lis):* Roman administrative city

Cultural and Linguistic Terms

Afennek — *(ah-FEN-nek)* — Fennec fox, the smallest of the fox species with large ears – lives in the desert

Aghilas n tazart *(ah-GHI-lass en tah-ZART)* — "honey badger" or literally "lion of the garden"

Agurram *(ah-GUR-ram)* — simultaneously "desert toad" and "holy man/sacred elder."

Amazigh *(ah-MAH-zeeg)* — "free person" Singular self-designation of the indigenous North African people

Aziza *(ah-ZEE-zah)* — "my dear one," feminine term of endearment

Aziz *(ah-ZEEZ)* — "my dear one," masculine term of endearment

Azref *(AZ-ref)* — "justice; law; custom" Aedemon's sword, inherited by Juba

Imazighen *(ee-MAH-zee-ghen)* — "free people" Plural of Amazigh

immema *(ee-MEM-ah)* — Coming-of-age / warrior initiation

Rih al-Harb *(REEH al-HARB)* — "Wind of War" Strategy game created by Eudoxus and Silina

siyala *(see-YAH-lah)* — Sacred chin tattoo marking a girl's passage to womanhood

tagine *(tah-JEEN)* — Earthenware pot used for cooking

Tamazight *(tah-MAH-zeegt)* — The Amazigh language and its dialects

Tifinagh *(tee-fee-NAGH)* — The ancient Amazigh script

A note on "Berber": In the novel, only Roman characters use the term "Berber," which derives from the Latin barbarus ("barbarian") and is considered derogatory. The Amazigh people refer to themselves as Imazighen ("free people"), their language as Tamazight, and their script as Tifinagh. The novel preserves this distinction to reflect historical and cultural accuracy.

Don't miss out!

Visit the website below and you can sign up to receive emails whenever Michael Colvin publishes a new book. There's no charge and no obligation.

https://books2read.com/r/B-A-NGAGF-TDMAJ

BOOKS 2 READ

Connecting independent readers to independent writers.

About the Author

Michael Colvin is a writer, educator, and storyteller whose career has taken him across classrooms, congregations, newsrooms, and university halls. A resident of Forest Grove, Oregon, he brings to his fiction the same curiosity about human nature that has animated decades of work in some of the most people-centered professions there are.

Colvin spent years as a teacher, developing the patient attention to how people learn and grow that would later inform his approach to character. His work as a pastor deepened that attention into something more searching — a sustained engagement with questions of meaning, suffering, spiritual formation, and the complicated grace that moves through ordinary lives. Those questions have never left him, and they are woven throughout *The Star Seeker* and the novels that follow it.

His career extended into university administration, where he worked at the intersection of institutional life and human development, navigating the competing demands of community, mission, and individual flourishing. He brought the same instinct for story to journalism and public broadcasting, where he learned to find the essential human thread in complex events and render it clearly for audiences who had no reason to care until he gave them one.

The Star Seeker is his debut novel and the first book in *The Third Path* trilogy. Set in first-century CE North Africa, it follows twin protagonists Amara and Juba — children of an Amazigh resistance leader — as they come of age under Roman occupation, guided by a Persian scholar who has been carrying a secret across continents for forty years. The novel draws on Colvin's lifelong interest in Amazigh history and culture, his theological formation, and his belief that the most important stories are the ones that ask what it costs to remain human under pressure.

He lives with his wife Susan in Forest Grove, Oregon, where he is at work on the second novel in the trilogy.

Read more at thirdpathbooks.com.

About the Publisher

Third Path Publishing is an independent press devoted to stories and ideas that explore the space between resistance and reconciliation, action and contemplation. We seek manuscripts that take seriously both the urgency of justice and the depth of inner transformation — work that refuses easy binaries and finds its footing on a third path.

Read more at https://thirdpathbooks.com.

www.ingramcontent.com/pod-product-compliance
Lightning Source LLC
LaVergne TN
LVHW090543110826
845146LV00001B/4

* 9 7 9 8 9 9 5 7 7 8 7 1 4 *